KU-068-407

**Jenny Colgan** is the author of ten bestselling novels, most recently *The Good, the Bad and the Dumped*, which is also published by Sphere. She is married with three children and lives in London and France.

For more information about Jenny and her books, visit her website at www.jennycolgan.com

*Praise for Jenny Colgan*

'She is very, very funny' *Express*

'A delicious comedy' *Red*

'Witty and clever' *Heat*

'Fast-paced, funny, poignant and well observed' *Daily Mail*

'Hugely entertaining and very funny' *Cosmopolitan*

'A funny, clever page-turner' *Closer*

'A quirky tale of love, work and the meaning of life'
*Company*

'A smart, witty love story' *Observer*

'A Colgan novel is like listening to your best pal, souped up on vino, spilling the latest gossip – entertaining, dramatic and frequently hilarious' *Daily Record*

'An entertaining read' *Sunday Express*

'The perfect summer sunbather, easy to read, packed with gags and truths' *Irish News*

*Also by Jenny Colgan*

Amanda's Wedding
Talking to Addison
Looking for Andrew McCarthy
Working Wonders
Do You Remember the First Time?
Where Have All the Boys Gone?
Diamonds Are a Girl's Best Friend
The Good, the Bad and the Dumped

# JENNY COLGAN OMNIBUS

## West End Girls

## Operation Sunshine

sphere

SPHERE

This omnibus edition first published in Great Britain in 2010 by Sphere
Reprinted 2011

Copyright © Jenny Colgan 2010

Previously published separately:
*West End Girls* first published in Great Britain in 2006 by Time Warner Books
Paperback edition published in 2007 by Sphere
Reprinted 2007 (twice), 2008, 2009
Copyright © Jenny Colgan 2006
*Operation Sunshine* first published in Great Britain in 2007 by Sphere
Paperback edition published in 2008 by Sphere
Reprinted 2008 (three times), 2009
Copyright © Jenny Colgan 2007

The moral right of the author has been asserted.

*All characters and events in this publication, other than those
clearly in the public domain, are fictitious and any resemblance
to real persons, living or dead, is purely coincidental.*

All rights reserved.
No part of this publication may be reproduced, stored in a
retrieval system, or transmitted, in any form or by any means, without
the prior permission in writing of the publisher, nor be otherwise circulated
in any form of binding or cover other than that in which it is published
and without a similar condition including this condition being
imposed on the subsequent purchaser.

A CIP catalogue record for this book
is available from the British Library.

ISBN 978-0-7515-4446-6

Typeset in Caslon by M Rules
Printed and bound in Great Britain by
Clays Ltd, St Ives plc

Sphere
An imprint of
Little, Brown Book Group
100 Victoria Embankment
London EC4Y 0DY

An Hachette UK Company
www.hachette.co.uk

www.littlebrown.co.uk

# WEST END
# GIRLS

In memory of my beloved papa,
who taught me how to swear

# Acknowledgements

Thanks to Ali Gunn of Gunn Media, Jo Dickinson, Ursula Mackenzie, Tamsin Barrack, Louise Davies, Kerry Chapple and all the reps at Little, Brown.

Tally Gardiner, Lynne Drew, Rachel Hore and Deborah Schneider; Debra Sweeney for saving my copywriting bacon; Chris Manby for plotting help; Joaquim Caetano, whose English is *much* better than George's, and the Board, by far the most fun office I've ever worked in.

Special thanks to Marina and Galina, without whom – no book; Andrew Mueller, Roni Dutta, Theo Burrow and Roseline Beaton for friendship and emergency babysitting; my family; and all my love to Mr and Baby B.

# Chapter One

Lizzie squinted at the old LED alarm clock she'd had since she was at school. 03:39. She had to get up in three and a half hours, which was a slightly comforting thought in itself – that was *ages* away, so that wasn't why she'd woken with a start.

There was a stumbling noise. Lizzie's heart stopped. Someone was in the room. Someone was definitely there. It was a burglar. A murdering, raping burglar. There were loads of them round here, everyone knew it. God, if only she kept a gun under her bed. She had never seen, touched or learned how to work a real gun, and disagreed with them in principle, but . . . she wanted a gun, goddamn it!

'Oh, *tittin'* hell,' came a familiar voice.

Penny. Lizzie's longing for a gun lasted for a couple of seconds longer than it ought to have done.

In drunkenness, Lizzie noticed, and at 3.39 in the morning, Penny's Essex accent rang out even stronger than usual.

'What the *effin' eff* was that?'

Lizzie sat upright and turned on the bedside light, from which Penny recoiled, hissing crossly.

'*That* is my shoe,' said Lizzie, trying not to shout and so wake their mother down the hall, although the walls were so thin she could hear her snoring from here.

'What's it doing in my bloody room?' Penny squinted. 'And what are you doing in my bloody bed?'

For a second, Lizzie double-checked just in case it *was* Penny's room. 'This is my room, you idiot.'

Penny looked dumbfounded. 'I know my own bloody room.'

'You'd think.'

Penny looked around her. 'Oh. Bugger it.'

Lizzie sat up. 'It doesn't matter,' she said. 'I'm awake now.'

This room had belonged to both of them when they'd had to share and their mother had had Sarcastic Alex, the lodger. When he'd moved out Penny had taken the smaller room, claiming it didn't matter, she'd be moving out practically any day to get married and live in London and only occasionally come to visit them in a really big car. Well, that was six years ago now, and it was the last unselfish act on her part Lizzie could remember.

'How was it?' said Lizzie, passing Penny her water glass. She could feel the waistband of her pyjamas dig in as she did so. Oh, God. She wasn't going up another size, she absolutely wasn't, 16 was bad enough, 18, no way.

'What time is it?' said Penny, ignoring her question.

'It's an inbetween-y kind of time: between a good night out and a really, really bad one. So?'

Penny took a long gulp of water, then shrugged. 'Hmm.'

'Terrible?'

'Hmm.'

'Did he lavish you with compliments and jewels?'

'Hmm,' said Penny, squinting at the water glass. 'You know, I'm beginning to wonder if this lavishing-with-jewels-type really exists.'

'My God,' said Lizzie. 'You can't stop searching now. That'd be like a nun renouncing Jesus on her deathbed.'

'Shut up,' said Penny.

There was a break in the snoring from down the hall.

'You shut up,' said Lizzie. 'And go to bed.'

Penny sighed theatrically. 'We *did* go to Gordon Ramsay's restaurant. He wasn't there though.'

'That's good. That's very good. I'm very pleased for you. I thought restaurants shut at twelve, but we'll just draw a veil over that.'

'And he spent the entire time complaining about the cost of his divorce. And the chateaubriand, as it happens.'

'I don't know what that is,' said Lizzie.

'Never mind, darling,' said Penny patronisingly.

Don't think about the gun, thought Lizzie. 'What is it then?'

Penny sniffed.

'So? What have you been doing? Taking cocktails at the Ritz? Dancing under umbrellas in the rain? Ice skating in Central Park?'

'Night bus.'

Lizzie winced in sympathy. 'Who'd you get?'

'One bung-eye, three general lunatics and one wanker.'

'Only one wanker on a night bus? That sounds amazing. There's usually hordes of them putting traffic cones on their heads.'

'No, just one literal wanker. One man having a wank. There were thirty-five with traffic cones on their heads.'

3

Lizzie tutted.

'And I had to change at Seven Sisters.'

'Seven Sisters is far too *dangerous* for girls! What kind of man is he?'

'*Not* one who sends a nice girl home in a cab.'

'What about a slightly sluttish girl?'

'Shut up.'

'Get out of my bedroom then.'

Penny heaved a big sigh. 'Oh, it's *so* boring.'

'Going to the Ritz for cocktails and out to fancy dinner. Well, it does sound boring. Mum and I watched *Property Ladder* and ate potato waffles.'

'I had to hear about his terrible divorce and how that witch kept the house and how he's terrified of gold-diggers getting hold of what's left of his money and did I mind getting my half of the bill.'

Lizzie flinched. This was not something, she knew from previous vicarious evenings, that could be tolerated. Although Penny's minimum-wage waitress job was supposedly supplemented by tips, in reality her attitude, and the fact that a lot of men tried to ask her out, failed and got aggressive, made the tip-giving side of things fairly erratic.

'Oh, my God! What did you do?'

Penny glanced in the mirror above the cheap dresser crammed in the corner of the tiny room. Despite the hour, Lizzie noticed, she still looked wonderful – her make-up had dribbled down under her eyes, but she looked sexy and a bit dangerous, not like Lizzie would: fat and a bit dirty.

'Legged it out the bathroom window.'

'You *didn't*.'

'No, of course I didn't, you idiot.' She paused. 'I told him I'd forgotten my purse.'

'That's all right then.'

'I'd have legged it out the bathroom window *next* though.'

Penny rubbed her pretty face blearily. 'Anyway it went a bit downhill after that.'

Lizzie tried to smile sympathetically – she was going to have to listen anyway – but this wasn't exactly the first time she'd been woken up in the early hours. Penny was a cad-magnet, but, as she pointed out (none too kindly), she was the only one with a hope in hell of getting them out of this shithole.

'Go to bed,' said Lizzie.

'I mean, I didn't know the bloody brandy was a hundred quid a glass, did I?'

'No,' said Lizzie calmly.

'I'm not the one saying, "Hey, how's about a brandy?" whilst eyeing up my fishnets.' She glanced down. There was a huge ladder up the left leg. 'Shit. Shit, shit, shit.'

'Say it's punk.'

'"How's about a brandy? Chilled? You know, my ex-wife was really chilly in bed. Makes a man feel, you know . . . so lonely."'

'Lonely and poor.'

'Poor my arse,' said Penny dramatically. 'My three ninety-nine ripped tights cause me a lot more pain than spending bloody six hundred pounds on bloody brandy does him.'

'*Six hundred pounds*,' said Lizzie. How on earth could people do something like that? Lizzie lived as she ate: hand to mouth.

'Should have read the menu, the dick, instead of yelping "Two glasses of your finest brandy" over and over again. No wonder the waiter was smiling.'

'Did he tip?'

'Did he fuck. They were still screaming at each other when I ran out of the door.'

'Finish the water,' said Lizzie. It might not get Penny to work on time, but it might get her to work.

Penny took a long slug. 'Ah,' she said. 'Like finest brandy on my lips.'

'You're a bad, bad girl,' said Lizzie. 'Go to bed or I'm telling Mum.'

Six hundred pounds kept running through Lizzie's head the next morning as she made her way to the bus stop. Six hundred pounds. That was unbelievable. Who could, did, spend money like that? Even by accident. Penny was still in bed; she didn't start her job, as Brandford's most glamorous and also grumpiest waitress, until later.

Non-identical twins can have a head start on the knowledge, usually learned by children through a procession of tedious and time-consuming upsets, that life isn't always fair.

'Twins? *Really?*'

That was one of Lizzie's earliest memories; people disbelieving their mother as to their provenance. Along with, 'Look at the size of you!' and, Lizzie's personal favourite, 'So, is Lizzie *terribly* clever, then?'

Being dressed alike only made matters worse, so they both started having tantrums about it from as early an age as possible. After all, it wasn't Lizzie's fault that she stayed short and plump while Penny shot up. It might have been her fault that whilst Penny made sure her dolls were immaculately dressed for their tea party, Lizzie scoffed all the scones. And whilst Penny smiled politely and learned to simper at adults from an early age, in case they had a spare pound coin in their pockets, Lizzie preferred to stay in the background before anyone had the chance to say, 'Good eater, are we?'

'They're so different, aren't they?' their mother's friends

would say, smiling meanly in a very unconvincing fashion.

'Out! Out! Out!' Lizzie would say to herself quietly in the kitchen. 'Goodbye visitors, time to go!' And once they'd gone, her mum would come in and give her a special hug and a biscuit, just for her plain little daughter.

And here the twins still were, twenty-seven years old and in the same tiny council house in Parkend Close, Brandford. Lizzie sometimes felt as if there should be a bus to take them off to real life, but if there ever was she knew she'd miss it, staying indoors and reading *TV Quick*.

Maybe the bus *had* come, she thought occasionally, as she spent yet another Friday night sharing a big box of Celebrations with her work friend Grainne and her mother in front of *Easties*, whilst Penny was off, weighed down by lipgloss, in borderline dangerous nightclubs, chatting up prosperous idiots who left their expensive shirts untucked and reeked of Hugo Boss. Maybe their dad had caught it instead.

Penny woke at eleven, screwed up her eyes and groaned. OK. Another day, another minimum wage. That stupid bloody man from last night. She thought for a second and realised she could only just remember his name, and that it would probably be gone in a couple of days. Excellent.

She blinked in the cheap bathroom mirror. The whole place needed grouting, it was incredibly dingy. But their mother worked far too hard, Lizzie inexplicably was refusing to do it by herself, and Penny had paid a lot of money for these nails so she couldn't be expected to under the circumstances. They seemed to have reached something of an impasse.

She threw on her Tesco ultra-skinny jeans and diamanté top, and got to work on her make-up. OK, she was only going to work, but you didn't know who you were going to meet on the way, and by the time she'd changed into her uniform she'd look so awful anyway she'd be lucky to get a second glance from anyone half decent.

Penny rarely dwelled on her genetic luck, seeing it mostly as a means to an end, and preferring instead to wonder if she should get her boobs done and whether it really was worth applying for one of those loans she saw on television. So far, Lizzie's shocked expression had just about held her off, but if she had bigger knockers she'd definitely pull a better class of bloke, and would be able to pay it back anyway. But even in her work uniform she stood out. Pale hair – when she didn't go overboard with the highlighter, which she usually did – glowed over a small, heart-shaped face with a high forehead and full lips. Her eyes were long, like a cat's, which she made even longer with liberal amounts of eyeliner in daily changing shades, and she had the figure that only comes to someone who had spent too much time watching what really went on at a deep-fat fryer.

Lizzie accused her occasionally of anorexia, but it was pretty much sour grapes. Penny knew she had to be thin – preferably with big knockers – and didn't think about food terribly often, unlike Lizzie, who turned to the biscuit barrel in times of joy, sadness, stress, tiredness, boredom and random television.

Penny hated Brandford. She hated its estates, its graffiti. The underpass, the horrid cheap corner shops with plastic mop buckets, and cheap sweets being guzzled by fat grubby babies. She hated the stoved-in cars, the fact that practically her entire class had got pregnant at sixteen. She didn't feel like she was made for this. Was it so wrong to want more? Really? Just a nice car? Clothes that didn't come from a supermarket? So, school hadn't worked out so well. It was a shit school. There was nothing wrong with liking nice things, was there? Even – Penny bit her lip as she applied the white layer of her mascara – someone to fall in love with one day, though she'd never have admitted that to Lizzie in a million years. Lizzie was such a drip when it came to romance, and everything else. She'd seen *Dirty Dancing* nine million times, snottering into her extra-large popcorn all the while. Penny and her friends had scoffed. Penny's favourite film was *Pretty Woman*, closely followed by *The Thomas Crown Affair*.

Penny took the bus – God, she hated the bus – out to the junction of the motorway where the big shops were, at the entrance to London and the M11. In the vast fields of hyper-markets and massive, elongated versions of ordinary high street shops, there were mega-restaurants, huge places seating hundreds for birthday parties, hen nights, reunions and kiddies' parties. Penny's was called the All-American New York Diner. There was a bucking bronco at the back, where girls would get on and shimmy their bosoms, and men would pretend they were having a laugh whilst taking it all incredibly seriously; the food was entirely brown and came in huge portions, and the cocktails were gigantic and sticky.

Penny hated it, but it had one major advantage: everyone went there eventually. Whether a works' night out, or a divorcing couple meeting for a child handover, all sorts of people ended up prodding uselessly at the Death By Chocolate with triple-brownie fudge ice cream and chocolate sauce supreme. And she could spot them a mile away; they'd look slightly perturbed about walking in, wouldn't know what to do with the sparklers in their drink, ask if she had fizzy water or salad ('There's our bacon-bit surprise, sir,' she would say insouciantly), and she'd check out their shoes, or their watch, then play the comely wench a bit more. There weren't many well-off single men in Brandford – one or two footballers in nearby Saffron Walden, but the competition for them tended to be intense and exhausting – but serving four hundred covers a night very often yielded results, as well as occasionally spectacular tips, which made Lizzie green, particularly as she had an indoor job, in an office and everything.

'I'm off,' shouted Penny, heading for the door. Her mother was at home again today. She'd been having horrible problems with her varicose veins – standing up doling out big scoops of cabbage, and nowadays chicken twizzlers, to ungrateful schoolchildren for nearly thirty years had pretty much done for her legs. Making it through to Friday tended to be a bit on the tricky side.

'Penny?' shouted her mother as Penny slunk past the sitting-room door. Fat and florid, she lay with her feet higher than her head, and an enormous flask of tea – made by Lizzie – by her side. 'Where were you last night?'

'Why?' said Penny sulkily. For goodness' sake, she was twenty-seven, not fourteen. 'I went to Paris to visit Kylie Minogue.'

'Well, could you let me know when you're going to be so late? I worry about you, you know.'

'Well, you should stop, I pay housekeeping, don't I?'

'Not very bloody much,' said her mother. 'Wouldn't keep a mouse in cheese.'

Penny rolled her eyes. 'I'm running my own life, OK?'

'Just a bit of consideration, darling. That's all I ask for.'

Penny heaved a sigh. She and her mother had been having this argument for ten years. 'What are you watching?'

'The 1979 RSC *Macbeth*,' said her mum. 'Ian McKellen and Judi Dench. One of the best ever.'

'Right. God, that crap is so boring. Do you want me to bring you back some salad?'

Her mother's face brightened. 'Oh, go on then, sweetheart. And what about some potato wedges? And some of the fried chicken?'

'Mum! It's horrible! I've told you where it's from! It's not even all real chicken! And the doctor told you to lose weight.'

'I know,' said her mother, looking slightly ashamed. 'But it tastes so good.'

Penny tutted, and left the house.

Lizzie marched into work in an even worse mood than usual for a wet Thursday morning.

Stamp importing wasn't quite what she'd had in mind when, after a school career of almost total mediocrity spent entirely in the shadow of her misbehaving sibling, she'd landed a proper office job in Brandford – and she hadn't planned to be there for ten years either, but it was undemanding as jobs go – processing stamp orders from overseas. She'd made a friend, Grainne, who controlled reception and the import desk.

Grainne's hobbies were cats and crisps. It was an undemanding friendship. But it was nice, for once, not to be the shy one, especially when she'd been the one with a boyfriend for a change too. Felix had been tall and slim and handsome, and Lizzie couldn't believe her luck when she pulled him at an awful party Penny had dragged her to one night. It had taken her six months to realise he was actually as dumb as a stone box full of rocks. Lizzie had thought he was just amenable. His constant mumbled 'Whatever you like' to films, TV and sex had eventually grown tiring, even for Lizzie, for whom the novelty of a real live boyfriend was something that took a while to wear off. And she missed having something to talk to Grainne about; now they were back to pussies and Pringles.

*

'Nice evening?' said Grainne as she walked in.

'Uh, yeah.'

'Why haven't you washed your hair? Were you out with a new man?' Grainne lived in fear of Lizzie getting a boyfriend and leaving her.

Lizzie slung her bag in the corner of her desk. It had taken her ages to get back to sleep again when Penny had bowled off to bed, and she felt fuzzy and out of focus.

'No,' said Lizzie. 'How's your cat? Bought her any new outfits?'

'Miss Friss is fine, thanks,' said Grainne. 'And she likes getting herself dressed up, don't you, sweetie?' She was addressing this to one of the photos.

'Are you sure it isn't a bit cruel to put animals in hats?'

'Oh, I think they're adorable,' said Grainne. 'And Miss Friss loves her little bonnet. She told me.'

The reception phone rang.

'That's her now,' said Lizzie. 'All the mice are laughing at her and she wants to know what to do.' On seeing Grainne's face she immediately regretted it.

'Actually, it's Mr Boakle,' said Grainne. 'He wants to see you.'

Lizzie flinched. Why was the boss asking to see her? She had a horror of getting into trouble; she'd spent so much time trailing after Penny into the headteacher's office. 'You've got to look after your sister.' She could hear her mother's voice again. 'We're all she's got.'

Lizzie sidled into the back office, which was dark, chilly and piled up with files of colourful stamp samples from around the world.

Mr Boakle looked at her. 'Ah. Yes. Ah, Lizzie, isn't it?'

Given that she'd worked there for ten years, maybe it would have been nice if he occasionally remembered her name. No matter. She blushed anyway. Lizzie hated her tendency to blush, especially at times like this when really someone else should be embarrassed, surely.

'Take a seat. You may have noticed that it's been pretty quiet around here recently.'

'Uh.' Actually, it always seemed quiet, but now she thought about it, yes, for the past few months Grainne really had been spending a lot of time knitting Miss Friss a Santa Claws outfit.

'People just aren't using too many stamps any more,' said Mr Boakle sadly. 'So they don't collect them, see. There's some new invention – can't quite figure it out myself – called EU mail.'

'EU mail?'

'Yes, you know. Something to do with joining the Common Market, probably.'

'You mean email,' Lizzie ventured. 'The thing that's been around for years.'

'Something like that. Anyway, whatever the bloody thing is called, it's cutting down on people writing letters something terrible. Sounds like a dreadful thing.'

'How it works is, you type in a letter then you send it for free and the other person receives it instantaneously. For free,' said Lizzie.

Mr Boakle paused. '*Really?* That sounds fantastic.'

'It is,' said Lizzie.

'Hmm,' said Mr Boakle. 'Hmm. That's not good at all. Do you get many letters?'

'Do council tax summonses count?'

'Those damned franking machines,' said Mr Boakle, his face going red. 'Worst invention ever.'

'Until email,' said Lizzie meekly.

'Well. Anyway, that doesn't matter because frankly the

world of post has gone to hell in a hand basket and as a result I've got to lose a member of staff.'

Lizzie suddenly had a horrible vision of herself in a dinner ladies' uniform and closed her eyes tightly to get rid of it. She couldn't lose this job. Please no.

'Oh, please,' she said. She'd always thought being quiet and dependable, they wouldn't mind her staying there . . . but now. What would she do? Well, she hadn't thought that far ahead. But she couldn't do what Penny did, shouting at drunks and hollering across hen parties asking who'd ordered the double portion of ribs. But without any qualifications . . .

'Elizabeth,' said Mr Boakle. Briefly, Lizzie felt like she was in *The Apprentice* and wondered if he was going to point a big finger at her like Alan Sugar did, and growl, 'You're FIRED!' like a big grizzly bear, but he didn't.

'I'm going to have to let you go. I'm really, really sorry.'

'But . . . but . . . '

'You're young,' said Mr Boakle. 'There's a big wide world out there. You should go and see some of it.'

'And how would I pay for that?' said Lizzie, feeling a huge lump in her throat.

Back in Brandford, their mother groaned a little and lifted up her legs again. They really were killing her. Oh well. She thought about her girls. She worried about them so much, she really did. Penny was out and about all over the place, never stopping, never eating a proper meal, and she didn't even want to think about the kind of people she was hanging out with. Penny reminded her so much of Stephen it wasn't funny. She was her father's daughter all right.

And Lizzie was quite the opposite, seemed entirely happy to spend the evening with her old mum, eating choccy and catching up on the soaps. That didn't seem right either. She'd wanted so much . . . well, wanting didn't help anything, did it? It felt like such a long time ago, before she'd had them, when she'd met Stephen and everything had felt exciting and full of promise, and she'd been a young girl about town. He'd been so handsome and different to the boys she'd known at school. She'd grown up in Brandford, and headed to London as soon as she could, finding a job in Chelsea Girl, sharing a tiny, freezing flat in Bermondsey with four other girls. She'd loved it. They'd all shared clothes and spent all their money going up to town and having a laugh. She'd even had dreams of taking up acting. Best time of her life.

And Stephen. He'd swept her off her feet without a second thought. And she'd fallen for it too, completely. Upmarket boy like him, bit of Essex trash like her. Why had she thought it could work? But she'd thought it would be fine, that love would pull them through.

She remembered, after five whirlwind months, the mixture of terror and excitement she'd felt on finding herself in the pudding club. Her mother would have a fit. But he'd do the right thing – Stephen Willis was a proper, well-brought-up boy, not like the drunken wife beaters from round her area. She hadn't known it was bab*ies* then, not till the doctor said he thought he heard two heartbeats.

In a pub in Chelsea, on a really lovely sunny autumn day, round the corner from his mum's cluttered flat, he'd had a port and lemon (she was paying), and she'd had a Bacardi and lime (they weren't so hot on not drinking during pregnancy in those days), and she'd broken the news. He'd just stared into his glass.

'Darling,' he'd said. 'You daft cow. You stupid cow. That's no good, is it?'

And his handsome face – Penny looked just like him – had twisted up into a mean look, and his eyes had turned cold on her, just like that.

She'd managed, of course. Well, she'd had to. Oh, the neighbours had been awful; that Eilish Berry, thinking she was better than them, taking herself off to London, and back less than a year later with a bun in the oven. Two buns, actually. Her mother had been furious to begin with, and softened, inevitably, when the babies came. They'd got their own council house and they'd all been there ever since, even though the estate just got worse and worse. She'd liked working at the school when the girls were little, she could walk there with them and home again at night and be off at holiday times. Until they got to about ten, of course, when Penny disowned her completely through embarrassment, which she didn't seem to have shaken off now, seventeen years later. Eilish sighed.

She hadn't seen Stephen much after that; he'd practically disappeared off the radar altogether. His mother, though, had tried – sent her some money and some ludicrously impractical knitted outfits, itchy and full of buttons. She'd taken the girls over there a few times when they were small, but Stephen's mother's place was a terrible mess, a huge old apartment in Chelsea which she'd filled with junk since his father had died. Mrs Willis was a bit like one of these shutins, with piles of newspapers all over the place. It wasn't hygienic, and it took four hours to get there and back and the girls screamed so hard that, after a while, they just stopped and got on with their own lives. She'd watched the girls. It wasn't as if having no dad was particularly unusual in their part of the world. He'd visited for a while, every now and again, turning up with toys. Whenever he left, Lizzie would sit by the doorway for the next two days in case he came back. Penny would bite everyone in their nursery. She didn't think they'd remember; they were three when he stopped.

Then they'd seemed all right, until they'd hit their teens. Lizzie had gained puppy fat she couldn't grow out of. She never mentioned it, just gradually became more and more introverted till now, in her twenties, she barely went out at all. There'd been hardly any boyfriends – that last chap was a plank of wood – but she seemed happy to sit at home and watch life pass her by.

Penny on the other hand turned wild. She couldn't get out the house fast enough, up to all sorts of trouble. She'd done her best, thought Eilish. She'd tried to get Lizzie to be more sociable, whilst at the same time keep Penny in check. Forcing them together only made Lizzie more painfully shy and Penny more outrageous than ever, but she was glad they were still together.

'Look out for Penny,' she said to Lizzie all the time, till Lizzie worried sick. 'She's not sensible like you. She could do something stupid in a heartbeat.'

And she would have told Penny to look after Lizzie too, if Penny would listen to her, or stop for just a second. But she didn't.

Probably for the best their dad never appeared again. But she still had her lovely girls.

'Oi! You! Wanker!' Penny was shouting at the back of a departing fat man, part of a group of blowhard salesmen who'd come in for lunch to celebrate some bonus, then acted like they were city millionaires, ordering ridiculous cocktails and not drinking them, making her run around, asking if they could order 'off menu', to which Penny had retorted that they'd cook one of their heads if they could fit it in the

17

deep-fat fryer. They'd guffawed lustily and asked her if this was one of those American theme bars where the women wore bikinis, and she'd said no, it was one of those American theme bars where everyone tipped 20 per cent. Whereupon they'd got up to go, leaving a catastrophe of thrown food, knocked-over glasses and ripped-up paper napkins, and they'd left her . . . a pound.

She held it up in the air.

The fat man turned round. He had grease from his surf and turf platter spattered all down his Crazy Frog tie.

'What?' he said.

She held the pound coin out to him.

'You left this behind.'

His Neanderthal brow furrowed in incomprehension.

'That's for you, darlin',' he said.

'You'd have got more if you'd have given us a quick flash,' said a weaselly-faced man next to him. He looked at his watch. 'There's still time!'

'Why don't you take it,' said Penny, advancing and handing it to the fat man. 'Buy yourself a magnifying glass so you can see your own dick one of these days.'

Eilish was falling asleep. She got so tired these days. The phone rang, starkly, shaking her out of her dream. Her television programme had finished, and some house show was on. Eilish loved house shows. She would pretend she was the one who had to choose between the townhouse, the modern bungalow, the apartment in the stately home. Very rarely were the customers offered two-up two-downs on a council estate.

The phone rang again and, grunting a little as she moved her legs, she leaned over to pick it up, listening in silence, until finally, 'Oh my God,' she said. 'Oh my God.'

*

Lizzie looked at the phone. Mum. How was she going to tell her she'd been let go? Just shucked off, not needed. After all the work . . .

'How's Mr Boakle?' said Grainne.

'Sorry,' said Lizzie, making her mind up. 'I have to take this call.'

She sank to her desk, steeling herself not to cry. But her mother didn't even ask her how she was, just poured it all out in a rush. After asking her to slow down and repeat herself several times, Lizzie just blew her ratty fringe out of her eyes, and pushed back her chair from the desk.

'Oh my God,' she said.


Penny was staring at Ravi, who was staring at the floor.

'You can't talk to customers like that!' Ravi was saying. He was about sixteen years old, and on a management training scheme which somehow made him her boss even though he hadn't started shaving yet. Disciplining people obviously made him unbelievably unhappy.

'OK,' she said. 'I won't do it again. But they were disgusting losers.'

'They were *customers*, Penny,' said Ravi.

'I know, I know,' said Penny. 'Most of our customers are disgusting losers, right, what can you do . . .'

'No,' said Ravi miserably. 'I mean, it says in the handbook . . .'

The handbook was a huge colour-coordinated folder which laid out every single piece of information required to run the All-American New York Diner, including how many umbrellas per pina colada (2), how many napkins per rib rack (7) and how strong a word you could use against a customer before you were in serious trouble (meanie). Penny could get round Ravi, but nobody could get round the handbook. She sighed. Her phone rang, again.

'Oh, answer it,' said Ravi, trying to put off the inevitable. Why hadn't he gone in for musical theatre like he'd always dreamed of? He could be living in the real New York by now. He stared out of the window, looking at the 1500-space car park and the way the clouds looked like they were touching the top of the grey corrugated-iron Bowl-o-rama.

'Mum?' said Penny. 'What is it?' She listened intently.

And, finally, 'Oh my God!'

She ripped off her employee badge, which said, 'Hi. My name is Penny and I want y'all to have a nice day now, d'you hear?', threw it on the floor and stamped on it.

'Ravi,' she said. 'You are a nice man. And not a very big one. So, it's going to be a bit painful to do what I'm about to suggest next. But I really do insist that you take this' – she lifted up the heavy handbook – 'and turn to the colour-coded section where it explains *exactly* how to get it up your arse.'

# Chapter Two

The three of them crammed into the small front room at Parkend Close. This in itself was unusual. Penny was always just passing through.

'So, explain again slowly,' said Penny. Lizzie had come in with a tray holding three cups of tea, the strongest thing they had in the house, and a new packet of chocolate digestives.

'Your gran . . . not Nana, but your dad's mum. Well, she's not well. She's had to go into a home.'

'What's wrong with her?' said Penny impatiently.

'I don't know,' said their mum. 'Just old. Not dementia, just an "episode" they think.'

'You mean, crazy,' said Penny with a shudder. 'Remember you used to take us there. Brr. There were tins of dog food everywhere.'

'And she didn't even have a dog,' said Lizzie and Penny at the same time.

'Yes, well, she's not crazy,' said their mum, 'just a bit mixed up, that's all.'

'There were cobwebs. And spiders,' continued Lizzie, suddenly sounding exactly like her six-year-old self.

'But she wants to—' Penny shook her head. It didn't feel quite real.

'She wants you to move in there, yes,' said their mum. 'According to the nurse, she thinks somebody's going to nick her fifty years' worth of back copies of the *Radio Times*.'

'But why us?' said Lizzie.

'You,' said their mum. 'Not me, of course, oh no. But you two apparently are the only family she's got left, or at any rate the only family she kept mentioning to the nurses.'

'But we don't know her,' said Penny.

'Well, blame your useless bloody vanishing dad for that, love.' Their mother reconsidered. 'And it's my fault, too. She did want to see you, but it was always such a long way in, and you two hated going so much, and she never offered to help pay the fares, or buy you anything. She lives in that big place in Chelsea and she never helped us out at all. I think she gave it all to your dad. I expect that flat's all that's left.'

'Big place in Chelsea,' breathed Penny, as if saying, 'the magical land of Oz'. 'We're moving to Chelsea.'

'For a bit,' said their mum. 'Just till she gets well enough to go home.'

'But she's really old and mad and stuff,' argued Penny. 'I mean, she's not likely to be—'

'Penny!' said their mother sharply. 'Have a little decorum for once.'

'I don't see why I should,' said Penny. 'She owes us, doesn't she? We haven't had so much as a Christmas card from her for over twenty years, and as for . . . '

'Did she . . . I mean, doesn't she know where Dad is?'

asked Lizzie timidly. Although their mother almost never talked about their dad, saying only it had been short, occasionally sweet and that she'd been delighted with the results, i.e. them, she had never quite got over her childhood fantasy that it might all have been a mistake; that he might have been hit on the head by a brick and suffered terrible amnesia, and didn't even know he had twins.

Her mother shrugged. 'Well, obviously not. Good for nothing.' Her face clouded briefly. 'And his mother obviously thinks she owes you for that. So, I think you should take advantage of your good fortune.'

'Deffo!' said Penny, her eyes shining. 'Oh God. I'm going to live up West.'

She tried on a ridiculous accent. 'Haylo! My name is Penelope Berry and I live in Chelsea. I have a terribly rich luff-er end I only shop at Christian Dior.' She clapped her hands in glee. 'Oh God. At last. I knew something good was going to happen. I just knew it.'

'Well, an old lady is in a home,' said their mother.

'Yeah. But an evil one, though,' said Penny. 'Honestly, until you tell me that she really encouraged *Stephen*' – Penny always referred to their father as Stephen, never as Dad – 'to even phone us once, ever, I'm having real trouble dredging up the sympathy.'

'I'm not sure about living in London,' said Lizzie. 'I need to find a new job, and it's really dangerous and expensive and busy and I don't know anyone . . .'

'But that's what makes it *great*,' said Penny. 'Honestly, you're such an old maid.'

'Shut up.'

'OK. Don't. Fine. I'm perfectly happy to move into a huge Chelsea apartment for free on my own. See you at my Chelsea registry office wedding, suckers.'

'Stop it, you two,' said their mum. 'Lizzie, pet. You know, it really is time you thought about getting a place of your own. And now you've lost that job . . . it's a great opportunity for you, darling. You don't want life to pass you by.'

'I don't mind,' said Lizzie.

Their mother smiled. 'Well, maybe I do. Just, you know, try not to get knocked up with twins in two months or anything.'

Lizzie had a month's salary in hand, and Penny had raided the tips jar on her way out, so together they would have enough to afford a taxi to take them into town.

'And I'm never coming back,' said Penny. 'Well, only in a gigantic big car. Not a limo, you can get those for twenty quid an hour down at Rumours. A Rolls-Royce or something. It can come and get me in my wedding dress on my way to Westminster Abbey.'

'Who are you marrying?' said Lizzie. 'Prince William?'

'Or I'll have found some fabulous job. PA to a celebrity or something. And they'll pay me masses of money.'

Lizzie stared out of their little bedroom window. Four ten-year-olds were jumping on top of a burned-out car.

'I'm not sure I'd know what to do if I had any money.'

It was true, she mused, staring at the grey paint factory under the grey sky. She and Grainne had talked it over a lot, what they'd do if they won the lottery. For a start, she'd *have* to lose the weight. And, she thought, I'd get a horrid stick-thin personal trainer with an aggressive Australian accent who'd shout harshly at me in the park and act absolutely stunned when she found out how many Pot Noodle I get through in a week, and talk about how, once you're used to it, mung beans and broccoli are actually nicer than cake and hot buttered toast. Or it'd be some perfectly proportioned bloke with a wide-boy smile, and I'll end up getting a terrible crush on him because he's being a cheeky charming chappie and I won't realise that's how he speaks to all his 'ladies' because it helps them to stay motivated, and he'll have to kindly explain this to me after I've been fantasising madly about him for weeks and have convinced myself he's falling for my inner beauty. Then he'll be really kind and explain that actually he's seeing this Australian personal trainer girl whom he really thinks is the one.

'Don't be stupid,' said Penny, interrupting her reverie. 'You could buy something you've always wanted.'

'A horse, maybe,' said Lizzie, throwing her cheap market knickers into a holdall.

'What would you do with a horse?' said Penny. 'Eat sugar cubes together?'

'Well, maybe,' said Lizzie, making a face at Penny's narrow back. '*Maybe* we'd have a special bond nobody else could understand, and no one else could tame him and he'd have beautiful black hair and . . . '

'Ah, see what you've done?' said Penny. 'You've confused a horse with Colin Farrell again, haven't you?'

Lizzie sighed and went back to throwing knickers in a pile. It was all right for Penny. She was good-looking and everyone liked paying attention to her. It wasn't quite as much fun when you were trailing along behind carrying the bags.

Their mother had been acting strange all week. Lizzie had tried to believe it was because she was sad they were leaving, but she seemed happy and excited.

'Well,' Lizzie said finally, just as the taxi was drawing up outside the house on Sunday morning. It was a proper black cab and everything; Penny knew lots of the neighbours would be coming out to see the 'little twins' head off to London, and wanted to do it in style. 'I guess we're off.'

'Oh, it's only London,' said their mother. 'I'll see you all the time.'

'We're moving away from home!' said Lizzie.

'Yeah,' said Penny. 'That's how it works in *EastEnders*, isn't it? They go up West and they're never heard from again.'

'And it's a good thing for you,' said their mum. She leaned over and gave Lizzie a big hug.

'What are you going to do, then, Ma?' said Penny. She didn't really like being enveloped in her mother's big beefy arms.

'Well, get a couple of lodgers in, won't I?' said their mum. 'I've had some good news too. The school's going to give me early retirement.'

'Oh, that's brill,' said Lizzie. 'So you really will be able to put your feet up!'

'Oh, I don't think so,' said their mum. 'I've got a bit put away, after all these years. I was keeping it for you two, when you moved out to find your own feet, but you won't be needing that now, so . . . '

'So what?'

'So I'm going.'

'Where?'

'Bingo?' said Penny.

'To the RADA, of course!' said their mother. Her face suddenly creased into a big smile.

'To the what now?' Lizzie had no idea what she was talking about.

'To the RADA, of course! I hope they've kept my place.'

'Have you suddenly caught whatever Gran has?' said Penny.

'No, no, no,' said their mother. 'I've got a place at the RADA. The Royal Academy of Dramatic Arts. I'm going to be an actress, darlings.'

'How can that be?' said Penny.

'Well,' said their mother patiently, 'I auditioned and I got in. It's really difficult.'

'Yes, I know that . . . when?'

'Uh, let me see . . . how old are you two now?'

'Twenty-seven.'

'Must have been twenty-eight years ago, then,' said their mum. 'Fell pregnant with you guys, couldn't take up my place. They said they'd defer it for me, though.'

The children were silent.

'For twenty-eight years?' asked Penny finally. 'You think they'd keep your deferred place for twenty-eight years?'

'I don't see why not,' said their mother huffily. 'It's my place.'

Lizzie put her suitcase down and headed towards her mother. 'Why did you never tell us?' she said.

'I didn't want you to feel sorry for me for missing all my opportunities by having children and ruining my life.'

'We wouldn't have thought we'd ruined your life,' said Lizzie. 'Oh. Oh, did we ruin your life?'

There was a long pause.

'Uh, no, of course not!' said their mum finally. 'But, you know, I am a dinner lady. Usually though I pretend I'm really heavily into method acting and playing a part in which someone is required to work as a dinner lady for thirty years.'

'That sounds like the kind of movie I'd like to see,' said Penny.

'Then she becomes embroiled in a conspiracy to defraud school funds and is the only one who can solve the crime.'

The twins nodded.

'And she has to have a torrid affair with one of the children's fathers who turns out to be a spy. Only he's working for the other side.' Their mother had started to go slightly pink.

'Oh, Mum,' said Lizzie, giving her another hug. 'That's fantastic! That's brilliant! It's so great!' The taxi honked noisily outside.

'And we really have to go,' said Penny.

'Course you do,' said their mum. 'See you at my first West End opening!'

'And I thought it was only Stephen's side of the family who were completely crazy,' said Penny, hoisting up her suitcase and leaving through the yellow-panelled front door.

# Chapter Three

Neither of the girls spoke much on the way in to London. Penny was too excited. Lizzie was upset at leaving home, even though she was twenty-seven and thus it was patently ridiculous to feel that way. She wished her mother had come with them. Coming in to London from the east the sun bounced off Canary Wharf, and even Lizzie felt a jump in her heart.

The cabbie muttered something about the congestion charge as they came down in through the city, past the Gherkin and the large white buildings of the Stock Exchange. Of course they'd been here a million times, up in town to shop or, very occasionally for Lizzie, to go out, but now . . .

'In for a holiday, are youse?' asked the cabbie.

'No,' said Penny, in what almost sounded like a drawl. 'We live here.'

Lizzie suppressed a smile, and tried to stop looking at the meter. They were arriving in style, that was all. And it was stylish. Lizzie felt her heart leap. And their mother too! RADA! What if she became one of those famous old lady actresses? They couldn't keep casting Judi Dench for ever, could they?

They whizzed round past Big Ben and along the Embankment. Chelsea Bridge was pink and looked as if it was made of spun sugar, little lights popping along its length. The cabbie turned right and they were in Chelsea proper, heading down the King's Road. Tantalisingly, every street off it was filled with little pink and blue cottages, or large mansions, or big glass-covered apartment blocks. Neither of the twins could remember anything about the flat from the outside, except that it had seemed big to them when they were little, and dark and dusty. Both felt a definite thrill of anticipation.

'I suppose it will look really small to us now,' said Lizzie.

'What, smaller than the shoebox rooms we have now?' said Penny. 'That'll be interesting, given that I can touch all four walls at once.'

'What if there's only one bedroom?'

'She brought Stephen up there, didn't she?'

The cab slowed, and turned left, as the twins stared out of the window.

Redmond Street connected the King's Road to the river. It was lined on both sides with high white-stuccoed houses, like a long wedding cake. There weren't ordinary street lights – covered in graffiti and dog crap and with the lights blown out – like the girls were used to; instead, elaborately carved lamp posts held up little clusters of bulbs. Black polished railings lined the small front gardens, all immaculate, behind which were painted and polished huge heavy doors in dark green, black, navy and red.

The cabbie stopped outside their gran's flat. This door was navy blue, with a black knocker, and a large round brass doorknob inexplicably placed in the middle. The girls got out and stood, simply staring.

'OK, loves,' he said, and named the price for their journey, which made Lizzie want to be physically sick. Penny, however, handed it over blithely, adding a fat tip on top.

'Come on,' she said, at Lizzie's aghast expression after he'd driven away. 'It's the high life now. You've got to fake it to make it.'

'Fake it to make it . . . all the way to debtor's prison,' said Lizzie crossly, picking up the bag with the broken strap. 'You do remember we're both unemployed.'

'Yeah, yeah,' said Penny, looking round the perfect street. It looked as if the cast of *Mary Poppins* might hop out and start dancing at any moment.

At last. She was where she belonged. She pulled out the heavy keys that had arrived for them, and fitted one into a large old lock. She pushed the door open tentatively.

Inside there was a large hallway with parquet flooring and a staircase with an elaborate balustrade and pale rose-covered carpet; Lizzie wondered how it was ever kept clean. To the right of the door was a shelf with neat piles of interesting-looking mail, and a huge mirror with a gold frame. A little white door indicated the first flat, but they went on up to the second floor.

On the landing, two flights up, it was a little darker, with only one window at the end of the hallway letting in light, along with a small electric candelabra set above another large gilt-edged mirror. Penny, fumbling with the keys, opened the door.

'Ready?' she said.

'Mmm,' said Lizzie.

'One . . . two . . . three . . . ' Penny attempted to flamboyantly throw open the door. But she failed immediately when it scraped and jammed.

'OK,' said Penny, she put her shoulder to it and shoved again. 'Three . . . '

And this time, with a grind and a twisting of paper, they were in.

The girls stood there, stunned, looking around.

'Well,' said Penny eventually, 'you can't say it's not big.'

'No,' said Lizzie. They had stepped directly into the main sitting room. It was vast, opening out on their right to a huge bay window. On the left, over by the windows at the back, was a kitchen. Straight ahead – although it seemed miles away – was a fireplace, and beyond that, a passageway with three doors leading off it.

Every single bit of surface, every single possible spot, was completely and utterly obscured by junk. The entire room inside was grey, despite the brightness of the day outside. The windows were utterly encrusted with grime. There was a table, placed in the bay, with five or six chairs around it, all mismatched and looking mostly broken, with legs and bits of wood on the floor. Everywhere else there was rubbish of the most spectacular fashion. There were broken children's toys; huge piles of dusty, ancient magazines; odd bits of knitting and macramé; a whole crate full of empty medicine bottles; boxes full of who-knows-what; piles of dresses and skirts; trolleys full of bric-a-brac of every description. Books, old dusty hardbacks giving off a terribly musty smell, were untidily scattered over every available surface and piles of newspapers lined the corridor leading off the back of the room.

The kitchen was full of plates, chipped and mismatched, more than one person could use in a lifetime. Hundreds of pots were chaotically stacked up, along with at least a hundred washed-out milk bottles. Lizzie breathed a huge sigh of relief when she noticed that someone had cleaned out the fridge and left the door open. She didn't think she could have managed that.

'So,' said Penny after a time. 'We're not supposed to move anything, right?'

'Right.'

'Fuck that. I'm off to choose a bedroom.'

And she started to pick her way across the rubbish.

The two bedrooms proved just as bad even though they were a wonderful size, with near perfect views if you squinted through the murk of the filthy panes, over the rooftops and Mary Poppins chimney pots of Chelsea. They were piled high with old shoes, and each had three wardrobes. The bathroom, with its old-fashioned claw-foot bath, was full of old perfume bottles and an odd collection of wooden-handled toothbrushes.

'You have to say,' said Penny, 'she's a site-specific crazy old bat.'

Lizzie was too overcome to speak. She wondered how long the old lady had sat here, surrounded in rubbish, all alone. How they'd found her . . . and who. Despite realising it wasn't her fault – she didn't exactly owe this woman much – her eyes cast over a huge box of old photographs, and she felt sad, culpable and guilty.

Lizzie knew her mum didn't think she could remember their dad, but she could. He used to bring sweets and he was incredibly handsome. Penny used to shriek all the time. Lizzie used to think that was why he didn't come back, and practised being quiet. If they hadn't been twins . . . if she hadn't been so dumpy and useless, maybe they'd all still have been a family and they'd have been coming to Chelsea for years.

'Right,' said Penny, 'let's dump our stuff in this shithole and head out.'

'You are joking?' said Lizzie. 'Nobody is going anywhere until . . . ' and she handed Penny a pair of rubber gloves.

'Oh for God's sake.'

'House and jobs first. Fun later,' said Lizzie. 'Please, Penny. Please, let's not fall out quite yet.'

Penny rolled her eyes.

'Plus, we've spent all the money on the cab,' said Lizzie. 'Plus, what if you want to get up for the toilet in the middle of the night and fall over and get smothered and die?'

Penny pouted.

By the end of the day, it looked a little better, but not much. You could make toast in the kitchen without immediately contracting salmonella, and even risk a bath, but Lizzie was conscious of her grandmother's strict orders not to move anything, and even if she wanted to, where would it go? Every square inch of the property was already stuffed full. She didn't know, it might even be valuable, though she doubted it very much, looking at the empty milk bottles. She'd done most of the scrubbing and Penny had sat around grumbling about it, but now, as they sat down with their Pot Noodle in front of the ancient television, she wondered if it had even been worth it.

'Ah. Pot Noodle in front of the TV,' said Penny, casting a glance out of the window. 'This is almost as good as being at home.'

'You go out if you want,' said Lizzie. 'I'm tired.'

Penny wobbled a bit. 'I will,' she said. 'I'll go out there. Take it by storm. And all that.'

'Yes,' said Lizzie.

'Maybe a job first.'

Lizzie nodded, a little surprised, but not much. Penny might have a veneer of hardness, but underneath there was a bit of mush only her twin got to see. Which was why, she thought glumly, she'd had to stick by her for so bloody long.

'But then,' said Penny, 'hold us back.'

'Get up, get up!' shouted Penny the next morning, forcing her way into Lizzie's room. Four filing cabinets filled with leaves were piled in front of Lizzie's window. Lizzie had woken up a lot in the night, dreaming she was being buried alive. But now, as she woke, she realised where she was, and her heart leapt.

'It's a Chelsea morning! And we're going on a job hunt!'

'Aren't we lovely privileged ladies living in Chelsea?' said Lizzie, sleepily rolling over. 'I don't have to go on a job hunt. I'm going out in my four-by-four to buy expensive belts and luxury wallpaper.'

'No you're not,' said Penny. 'You're pulling yourself together and you're going to put food on the table.'

'You don't eat food,' said Lizzie. 'And we don't have a table. We have six tea chests stuffed with identical copies of the 1967 Cheltenham telephone directory.'

'That's detail,' said Penny. 'We're here now, and we're getting out there. We are going to find jobs and then meet men. Who will buy us Range Rovers and think our penchant for luxurious soft furnishings is simply hilarious.'

'Why don't you just walk up and down the King's Road in a negligee winking suggestively?'

'Tried it. Up!'

'What kind of job am I going to find anyway?'

'Some crazy stamp-collecting one? I don't know. It's a new world out there.'

'It's a scary world in here. What's for breakfast?'

'Water,' said Penny. 'But when we start making some money we'll get a juicer and juice up fresh fruits and vegetables in the morning and have them with sunflower seeds and grass and things.'

'Water?' said Lizzie. 'Are you sure? Is there nothing else?'

Penny rubbed the corner of her mouth. 'Well . . . '

'Are those *crumbs*?' said Lizzie. 'What have you got? You're holding out on me! Stop it!'

Penny shrugged. 'Well, maybe . . . '

Lizzie leapt out of bed and into the kitchen.

'Jaffa Cakes!'

'And they're not even own brand,' said Penny.

'Nothing like a good breakfast to set you up for a busy day,' said Lizzie, munching happily.

'But we're going to get that juicer,' said Penny with a warning glint in her eye.

'Yeah,' said Lizzie sadly. 'You maybe. I think I'll stick to a biscuit-based morning.'

'OK,' said Penny. 'Clothes next! What are you going to wear?'

Lizzie's face turned down. 'Well, I was thinking of black . . . with a further helping of black.'

Penny nodded thoughtfully. 'Well, maybe you could think of it as artfully chic.'

'The trousers have an elasticated waistband.'

'Don't eat any more Jaffa Cakes then.'

'I won't,' said Lizzie.

'Good.'

'I've finished them.'

'Oh. They were meant to last us until teatime.'

'Do you think the smashing orangey bit counts as one of my five portions of fruit and veg?'

Ignoring her, Penny picked her way through the mess. 'I'm going to wear my Dolce and Gabbana top.'

'It's so obviously fake,' said Lizzie. 'You totally so obviously picked it up in Wellings market.'

'It's not,' said Penny. She picked up the corset thing from her suitcase and slipped it on over her vest.

'Penny, it says "Dolce e Banana" on the front.'

'Oh, who'd notice that?'

'Only anyone leaning over to get a look at your tits, which as you stick them out all the time means absolutely everyone.'

Penny sniffed. 'We'll just see, shall we?'

'See what?'

'Who gets a job the fastest.'

'What do you mean?'

'Have a little competition, shall we?'

'No,' said Lizzie. 'We don't need a competition. You'll get a job the fastest. You've got blonde hair and perky tits and you smile nicely and look like you might conceivably be up for it. I wear elasticated trousers. Can we not have a competition, please?'

'You know, all you have to do is just drop a few pounds and you'd be really attractive, Elizabeth,' said Penny, looking serious.

'Oh, and could we definitely not have the "all you have to do is drop a few pounds" conversation,' said Lizzie. 'It's not as much fun for me as you seem to think, given how often you bring it up.'

Penny stuck out her bottom lip. 'Well. We're in a borough with no unemployment whatsoever and a definite need for what us Essex girls do best.'

'Drink Bacardi Breezers?' said Lizzie.

'No.'

'Go to Lakeside?'

'No.'

'Do the shitty jobs nobody else wants to do?'

'No . . . uh, yes. Yup, that's us.'

Chelsea looked shinier in the morning. Lizzie wondered if the people here just spat out their chewing gum less than people in Brandford. But then she saw the massive street-cleaning machine purring up and down. So everyone who lived here just got more good things even though they had more to start with. That didn't seem fair.

But it was so lovely. It was early and clear and bright and the pavements were being polished. What was it Penny had said? 'Remember: we're looking for posh jobs in nice places where we meet nice men and you don't have to get salad-bar bits in your hair.'

She crossed the King's Road, shivering slightly at the sight of the smart clothes shops. She certainly wasn't going to start in there; if she was too scared to shop in them, she certainly wasn't going to put herself through the humiliation of asking for a job there. Plus she feared that, for example, part of the interview might be having to get herself into an outfit they stocked, then all the other staff would come out and have a good laugh at her and she'd break the zip and be unable to get out of it and she'd end up three hundred quid down.

No, not the clothes shops.

Pondering whether to spend her last few pounds on a coffee so she had something to cling to as she pounded the streets, she wandered up past the rows of perfect, huge, white-stuccoed buildings – just like hers, she thought happily – interspersed with red mansion blocks. She wondered who lived in these; how there were so many rich people all living so close to one another. What did they all do? They couldn't all be rock stars and bankers, could they? Maybe they could.

Out of a large building with pillars on either side of the huge front door came a young family with a baby in a pushchair. The baby was snortling contentedly, and the couple, her with a lovely figure and long blonde hair, him looking successful and well dressed, were laughing together at some little joke. Lizzie looked at them and found her teeth grinding slightly. She told herself they must be really unhappy underneath, or really nasty and were laughing horribly because they'd just ritually disembowled the underpaid foreign help. The idea that you could be rich, attractive, live here and be happy . . . Well, Lizzie thought, she lived here now. She could be like that too. She was skint, chubby, squatting, jobless and single, but apart from that they shared a postcode so they were the same really.

The little family got into a beautiful shiny black car just as it started to rain. Probably on their way to the divorce lawyers, thought Lizzie, as she trudged on, getting wet.

The Fulham Road was next up. It was full of rare book shops; incredibly expensive florists with about three carefully selected perfect blossoms on display; furniture showrooms that looked like they'd just been flown over from Versailles and old-fashioned pubs quietly being scrubbed down, with beer being brought in and the doors and windows thrown open to get some fresh air. Lizzie wondered about a bar job. She could be the friendly, busty heart-of-gold barmaid cheerily serving foaming pints of frothy ale to the local squire's son . . .

Hmm. One of the bar staff threw a bowlful of soapy water out across the pavement, just missing her legs. She skipped out the way, and shot him a dirty look before she could help herself. Whoops. Maybe not apply there, then.

Right, no clothes shop, no street cleaning, no bar work . . . this was getting ridiculous. Either they were going to starve to death or she was going to have to go in and ask someone about a job. The next shop she saw . . .

The next shop was a smart-looking antiques shop. Nothing in the window had a price on it. She pushed on the door, before noticing there was a little bell she had to press before she could get in. Quickly she pressed it before she could change her mind.

After an age, an old man wearing a bow tie came to the door.

'How can I help you?' he said, looking at her somewhat distrustfully.

'I was going to buy your entire shop but now I see your unpleasant face I've decided against it,' Lizzie wanted to say, but restrained herself.

'Uh, hello there.' She took out her CV nervously. 'My name's Elizabeth Berry and I'm particularly interested in working in the field of antiques. So if you have a vacancy . . . '

The man squinted at her.

'Vacancy? What do you mean, if I die or something?'

'No,' said Lizzie slowly, 'I mean, if you need an assistant or something.'

The man looked behind him into the empty shop.

'Well, I suppose we could do with someone to manage the enormous queues in the mornings.'

'There you go, then,' said Lizzie. 'And I'm sure you'd need someone at lunchtime?'

The man sighed. 'OK. What's your opinion of that piece there?'

He pointed to an old earthenware vase. It looked like the

kind of thing you could pick up at a furniture shop for about
a tenner, and was entirely featureless.

'It's a vase,' said Lizzie. 'Uh, and . . . very suitable for all
sorts of places in the home. Indoors, outdoors . . .'

'Well, well, well, it's a classical historian,' said the old man.
'Sorry, could you get off my step? I need to dust it for the
hordes that come down here straight after queuing all night
at Ikea. Oh, and it's Abyssinian and worth thirty thousand
pounds.'

'That's exactly what I was going to say next,' said Lizzie,
but it was too late. She trudged across the road to the pub.
The man who'd sent the water along the pavement was still
out there, looking at her.

'So, you're really an antiques dealer but you want to work
in a pub?' he said when she approached him, CV in hand.

'No, I just want to work generally.'

'Sorry, love,' he said. 'We're looking for people who really
love pubs, you know, love the customers and all that.'

Lizzie tried to think of a pub she'd been in where the bar
staff had really loved her, but failed. She tried to smile, realising as she did so that a) she seemed to be taking quite a lot
of shit she didn't really deserve, and b) she would never be
able to go in that pub, or possibly any pub in the street ever
again as long as she lived, and headed further up the road.

Everywhere it was the same. Skinny girls working in art
galleries looked at her blankly and indicated that they
thought she was trying to physically throw them on to the
streets so she could have their jobs. Shop managers sniffed
and, mentioning high interest rates and credit card debt, said
they weren't hiring staff, which made Lizzie shuffle uncomfortably. Specialist shops wanted to know if she was specially
qualified, which seemed a bit unfair. There weren't any
stamp shops, she'd checked, and anyway, she didn't want to

go back to that. And why did everyone have to be so *rude*? She only wanted a job, not ten pence for a cup of tea. She'd now been sneered at by girls who looked twelve, pinched-nosed women in Chanel suits with foreign accents, fat men wearing waistcoats and polka-dot ties and bar and restaurant staff from every country in the *entire world*. What had happened to low unemployment?

Now she was getting too wet to be anywhere near presentable enough to go job hunting. Chelsea, soaking now, with shiny red postboxes and shiny red pensioners, no longer looked as if it was about to provide a backdrop to an Austin Powers spectacular. It looked hostile and hard and closed up. And she was hungry. Extremely hungry. Feeling in her purse she found a two-pound coin at the bottom. Right, that was it. Thank goodness she hadn't had that coffee. She was going to find something to eat and . . . reappraise her options.

She slunk into a little café on the corner, painted bright yellow on the outside, with cheerful hanging baskets. Inside it was dark and cosy, with wooden walls and tiles on the floor. Food was hung all around; large sausages and cooked meats from the ceiling, fresh fruit on the counter and sweet-smelling herbs over the doorway. It all looked rather nice. Lizzie swallowed manfully and sat down, glancing around for a menu. What if it was one of these really expensive places that Penny went to with dubious men, places that charged a tenner for a piece of asparagus floating in olive oil?

'Yes. What you want?' shouted the man behind the counter. Lizzie winced. She didn't know what she wanted, but she'd quite like it to cost less than four pounds fifty.

'Uh . . . have you got a menu?' she said quietly.

'What's that?'

Oh, for goodness' sake. It was entirely reasonable to go into a café and ask for a menu. He was just pretending not to understand her because her face didn't fit round this stupid part of the world, and didn't everyone like to make her know it.

All the frustration of the morning – of being rejected and looked down on by every Tom, Dick and Harry in the entire damn postcode – welled up in her suddenly, and she felt her face redden as she stood up.

'Nothing,' she said. 'Don't bloody bother yourself. I'm fine, obviously. I'll just go outside and lick the bloody McDonald's boxes in the gutter, shall I? In fact, maybe I should look for a job there. After all it wouldn't matter if I was all covered in grease and shit, would it? And I'd hate for anyone around here to *trouble* themselves.'

She grabbed her handbag and headed for the door, shaking with humiliation and fury. The rain hadn't let up in the slightest.

'What? Hang on,' shouted the man, but Lizzie pushed at the door. Of course, it was a pull door. As she stood there, fuming, she grabbed it again just as a great big hand came out and stopped it.

'Sorry. What is this babbling about? Are you OK?'

Lizzie turned round. 'I came in to eat and you were incredibly rude to me and everyone has spent the entire morning being incredibly rude to me and I'm just sick of it, OK? You can all take your Chelsea attitude and stick it up your arse.'

'Wait, what . . . '

The man stood back. He was dark and round, and Lizzie saw now his hands were covered in water and one was holding a huge, angry-looking langoustine. He also had a concerned look on his face.

'Sorry . . . you came in and I have fish brains on my hands, I miss you. Bad fish brains, no?' He smiled at her apologetically.

43

'We have no people today. Well, only me, as you can see.'

His accent was difficult to place. She looked round.

'Well, you're not exactly busy, are you?'

'You are very grumpy lady. Eleven o'clock is not the big time lunch rush.'

He wiped his hands on a tea towel that was hanging out of the tie of the apron enclosing his capacious belly. 'OK. You want lunch or you want to have big temper fit once again?'

Lizzie attempted a half smile. 'Well, I don't know, do I? That's why I need to see a menu.'

'I do not have a menu.'

'You're too exclusive and smart to have a menu?'

'I make whatever is good and fresh on the day. You do not like the sound of that?'

'How much is it?' said Lizzie.

The man looked her up and down, taking in her cheap shoes and elasticated waistband.

'You are the first customer of the day and guinea pig, so you get a discount.'

'How much of a discount?'

The man screwed up his face.

'I can do you some lunch for . . . two pounds. That's my absolute low price of the day for angry wet girls.'

'Hurrah,' said Lizzie, then remembering herself, said, 'Uh, that sounds nice. Thank you.'

She sat down again as the fat bloke went to work behind his counter, chopping and stirring things up. She found herself watching him, engrossed in his work. Although short, he was large all over; his hairy forearms were like the hams hanging over his head, his stomach was massive; even his features were big. Mediterranean she would have thought, but his eyes weren't black but a heavily fringed blue.

'You want something to drink?' came the voice.

'Tap water, please,' she replied.

The man smiled to himself then brought her a small glass filled with something light and golden and fizzy and delicious.

'Here,' he said. 'On me. As I am such a terrible host. And you have had such a terrible morning.'

Lizzie accepted, feeling slightly giddy. Well, her day may have started horribly, but now a large stranger was giving her drinks and it was only eleven-thirty in the morning.

'That's delicious,' she said.

'Prosecco. Better than champagne,' said the man.

'Oh, yes,' said Lizzie. 'Champagne gets terribly boring as the morning drink of choice.'

The man laughed. 'So why are you so sad, wet girl?'

'I wasn't miserable, I'm job hunting. Do you have any jobs free? No, you're looking for someone with ten to fifty years café management experience, I do understand.'

'Hmm,' said the man. 'Job hunting is difficult. What's your speciality?'

'Stamp collecting.'

'This is a popular job in England?'

'Not as much as you'd think.'

'Why are you looking in Chelsea? The people don't collect stamps here. They work in American banks and make their tiny dogs wear clothes.'

'I know,' said Lizzie. 'But we just moved here . . .'

'We?' said the man. Lizzie's heart jumped. Oh, my goodness, was he hitting on her? Why would he ask if she was a 'we'? Hang on, she thought, was she going to be some kind of unbelievably easy lay for a dodgy waiter type? But on the other hand, she thought with some remorse, her life was so barren these days a dodgy waiter type marked a blinding improvement in her love life. Boy, was that depressing.

'Me and my sister,' she explained. 'We're looking after my gran's flat.'

'That sounds nice,' he said.

'It does, doesn't it?' said Lizzie. 'It *sounds* nice.'

'But it is not?'

'Well, it's tricky getting started. It's not the friendliest of areas.'

The man nodded. 'Well, let me say hello. I'm Georges.'

'Hello, Georges. I'm Lizzie.'

'What do you think, Lizzie?'

He placed a plate in front of her with sizzling hot langoustine on a bed of linguine with olives, chillies and little red roasted tomatoes that burst their flavours onto her tongue.

'Oh, my goodness!' exclaimed Lizzie, trying it before it had even had a chance to cool down. 'This is absolutely delicious.'

'You like, huh?' Georges said. 'I like a woman who enjoys her food.'

Lizzie swallowed abruptly. 'Are you saying I'm fat?'

'I'm saying nothing, very grumpy girl!' said Georges, looking offended. 'I'm saying you look like you're enjoying the food I cooked for you!'

'I am,' said Lizzie.

'Now me, I am very fat,' said Georges, but he didn't sound too sad about it. In fact he sounded quite jolly.

'No you're not,' said Lizzie, who had a lifetime's experience of telling Penny she didn't look fat and was therefore convincing under all circumstances.

'But yes, of course I am, can't you see this?' he said, extending his large wobbly belly. 'What is this, then? Am I having a baby?'

'It would eat very well if it was a baby,' said Lizzie, wiping up the last of her sauce with bread. 'That was amazing.'

The man smiled. 'I'm glad you liked it. And now . . . I must get back.'

The clock on the wall struck twelve, and almost immediately people started coming through the door. Georges greeted them cheerily, many by name, and started dishing up great tongsful of pasta into polystyrene boxes. A small chap appeared behind him and started dashing about at a hundred miles per hour, dishing up teas and sandwiches and filtering through as many people as possible as they yelled out requests and grabbed their white paper bags. It was engrossing to watch and, having nothing better to do, Lizzie sat and enjoyed the atmosphere. Steam rose and mingled to form condensation that ran down the inside of the windows, making the place feel even cosier and protected from the damp and hostile world outside. Slender blonde girls ordered salads, or the langoustine without the pasta; local workmen just asked for 'Whatever, Georgie'; businessmen signalled what they wanted without looking up from their telephones. Occasionally, Georges would glance over at Lizzie and give her a wink, and she'd try not to smile and feel all pleased.

Suddenly the view from the window was totally blocked, and the entire sky went dark. Lizzie leaned over to see what on earth it was. It turned out to be a huge holiday coach, too wide for the road, the type prone to knocking off cyclists whilst a sleep-deprived driver on the left-hand side tries to decipher a Hungarian road map from 1964. It appeared wedged on the pavement of the narrow street.

Everyone looked round as a small bus driver walked through the door.

'Ah, I have a coach here,' he said, looking almost apologetic, 'they're all very hungry . . . do you think you could do some takeaway for them?'

Georges looked round at his already bustling café.

'I'm not sure,' he said. 'I'm very busy . . . how many?'

'Sixty?' said the man. Georges looked disappointed. 'Oh. Then I don't think . . . '

Lizzie leapt up so fast she nearly knocked the table over. Here was her chance! She could help! OK, it wasn't stamps but surely she could dish stuff up – she'd watched Georges for nearly twenty minutes now and it certainly looked easy. She could show how useful she could be, then she could work here, and Georges seemed nice and . . .

Oh. She had indeed knocked the table over. A large glass sugar pourer smashed onto the floor into a thousand shards. Lots of ladies yelped and lifted their elegant ankles out of the way of the smashed glass.

Both Georges and the bus driver turned their heads towards her, Georges with a flash of irritation.

'Uh, sorry,' said Lizzie.

'It's all right,' said Georges. 'Benoit!'

The younger boy dashed over with a dustpan and brush.

'We're too busy,' said Georges to the bus driver. 'I'm sorry. It's impossible.'

'What if I help?' said Lizzie desperately.

Georges's smile was strained.

'You would probably help best by not standing up.'

'I could help!' said Lizzie indignantly, 'I'll pass things out and you can take the money.'

'But when you drop things on the floor I'm afraid I lose money,' said Georges.

'Well, I won't do that,' said Lizzie. 'I promise. And if you turn down this coach party, you'll lose a lot of money.'

Georges sighed. 'Can you heat things up and make sandwiches?'

'Do you lick the back of them and stick them in a book?'

He pointed her towards the back of the shop.

'Put an apron on. And wash your hands. Benoit will show you what to do.'

For the next two hours Lizzie cut bread, dunked pasta, wrapped things (not terribly well), got drinks out of the fridge, ran up and down to the tiny cellar for more tomatoes, and was generally run ragged. As soon as she'd finished one thing there were plates and pots to wash in the tiny sink out the back. Georges shouted instructions overhead and handled the money, Benoit flitted to and fro like an extremely helpful mouse and Lizzie kept her head down and got on with things. It was exhausting but slightly exhilarating too, the way it never stopped.

By two-thirty the rush had begun to die down and Lizzie finished washing up the last big pot. Exhausted, she took a cloth to wipe the surfaces with and headed back into the café.

Georges was standing behind the counter with a big smile on his face.

'We are done! We have sold everything in the shop! We even used that catering margarine.' He frowned. 'Which I said I would never, ever use. Ah, well.'

Benoit dashed around picking up every coffee cup he could find.

'Benoit! Coffee for the lady, please,' shouted Georges. Then he straightened up and looked at Lizzie properly. Lizzie smiled hopefully at him, but his face, briefly, looked concerned.

Lizzie knew exactly why. Her carefully applied job-hunting make-up of that morning was, she could feel now, halfway down her face. She wiped under one eye and it was black with melted mascara. Her hair, which had taken ages to tame into submission with Penny's ridiculous straighteners, was now bouncing around her head like a crunchy straw helmet. Beads of sweat prickled on her upper lip and she remembered she hadn't got round to bleaching her moustache . . . oh, fucking hell. This is why she hated going out.

Lizzie wiped her forehead with the back of her hand. 'I must look terrible,' she said.

'Not at all,' said Georges. 'You look . . . you look like you've been working very hard.'

With a mouse-like squeak Benoit delivered a tiny cup of dark espresso. It didn't taste like the Nescafé Lizzie was used to but she sipped it nonetheless, feeling enervated.

'So, uh . . . ' said Georges, looking at her from the table where he was sitting. He looked a little nervous and shy, for the first time.

'Yes?'

'I wondered if maybe you'd like to . . . '

Ridiculously, her heart suddenly thumped in her chest. Was he going to ask her out? Maybe he'd think she was an amazing woman with nice child-bearing hips who didn't mind a bit of hard work, i.e. exactly the opposite of everyone else he'd meet around here.

' . . . take a job here.'

Oh, of course. A job. Exactly what she was after, of course.

'Oh, now I realise,' said Georges, noticing her slightly disappointed-looking face. 'You are looking for places that can more fully satisfy your stamp-sorting requirements.'

'Doing stuff like I did today?' she said.

'Yes,' said Georges. 'Apart from knocking over the sugar thing. Benoit wants to leave. He is aiming to become a rugby international.'

Lizzie glanced at Benoit, who couldn't have weighed more than eight stone soaking wet. He gave her the thumbs up.

'OK,' said Lizzie, nodding slowly. 'OK.'

It was only as she was leaving the café that she caught sight of herself in the glass door and realised she hadn't calmed down her hair or reapplied her lipstick. She was amazed Georges had given her the job at all in her customer-frightening state. But it wasn't as if he was looking at her like that, of course. Men didn't, on the whole.

Penny knew she looked good the moment she stepped out of the house, a good hour or so after Lizzie. She was wearing her red PVC raincoat and her high boots which put a strut in her stride. She jangled the big key – oh, the bliss of having a big key – so that anyone walking past would know this was hers, her house, her part of the world, and be outrageously jealous.

Penny hated working. She remembered a documentary she'd seen once about It girls. How they spent their mornings getting waxed and manicured and going to the gym, had lunch, then spent their afternoons shopping and their evenings going to the millions of parties they'd been invited to. So they had the time to look much better than everyone else, plus they'd meet lots of people at parties, therefore they had a much better chance of meeting a bloke who'd like to keep them living like that. It seemed entirely unfair, but a completely perfect arrangement.

She looked down the King's Road. No more waitressing. It hadn't gotten her anywhere in all the years she'd been doing it. And no shops. She'd hate working in a shop too, all that folding and turning up on time. What did that leave for someone without much of a CV and no qualifications?

Wandering in no particular direction, Penny fell into Barnes Street. Even smarter and more exclusive than the rest, it was lined with trees shading small exquisite shops

51

selling art and furniture. It was a beautiful scene. Or rather, it would have been except that outside one of the galleries there was something of a commotion. Penny liked commotions, and slowed down.

A beautiful, extremely tall and slender blonde girl in a fawn skirt and opaque tights was yelling.

'He pinched my arse,' she shouted, in a very loud clipped voice.

'Maud, Maud, Maud,' came a grizzled-sounding voice. 'He was demonstrating Giotto's interpretation of the beauty of the female form.'

'He pinged my thong!'

'Oh, come on, he's not that bad. He's ninety anyway. What was he going to do after that, ask you to take him to the toilet?'

'Right, that's it. I'm off. And you'll be hearing from Daddy.'

The girl stalked off down the street like a disgruntled giraffe. The man looked around vaguely, as if trying to pretend he'd just come out to take the air. Penny thought about it for two seconds, then sashayed forward.

'That sounds uptight.'

The man eyed her suspiciously.

'What, not liking getting your knickers pinged? Bit early for trade, isn't it, love?'

Penny puffed up her chest. 'Ex*cuse* me?'

The man looked at her more carefully.

'Oh, sorry, I've got the wrong glasses on. Or something.'

Penny looked at him. He wasn't wearing glasses. 'I am looking for a job though.'

'Really,' said the man, retreating into his shop.

'Yes.' Penny followed him. 'What did Maud do?'

'She sat in here and looked pretty.'

Looking round, Penny realised she was in an art gallery, or, she supposed, shop. She'd never been in one before. It looked warm, dry and quiet. She liked it already. The owner himself was a long, skinny, cadaverous-looking chap, with sunken eyes and cheekbones. He was wearing a three-piece suit in a Rupert Bear check.

'I could do that.'

The man looked at her again. 'Hmm,' he said.

'What?'

'Oh, no, you are very pretty. I wonder . . . a girl like you.'

'What do you mean?'

'I mean, you wouldn't mind a bit of, uh. Well, some of our clients, they're a bit old-fashioned in their ways, and . . .'

'They'll want to pinch my arse.'

The man waggled his head. 'Not hard or anything.'

'It's OK,' said Penny. She was used to it. A huge number of men she met in her life tried to pinch her arse, including her PE teacher. 'I wouldn't mind.'

'You know,' said the man, 'sit on that chair there.'

She sat behind the desk.

'You just might work,' he said. 'All the girls down here are exactly the same. Boring-looking really. Whereas you . . .'

'Great,' said Penny. 'Can I start today?'

'I think,' said the man, 'we should have a little lunch to get acquainted. I'm a great believer in the art of lunch. Gordon Ramsay?'

'Not there again,' said Penny, shivering.

The man raised his eyebrows approvingly.


'So, I will see you at eight tomorrow?' Georges was saying. He reached out and pulled open the door for her.

'Yup!' said Lizzie. 'Bye, Benoit! Good luck!'

'Eep,' said Benoit.

As she emerged she nearly bumped into a tall blonde girl who was with a tall man. They were both laughing hysterically.

'Excuse *me*,' said Lizzie.

'Whoops!' said the blonde tipsily, just at the instant Lizzie realised it was Penny.

'What the hell are you doing?'

Penny whizzed round.

'Darling! It's so good to see you! This is my twin,' she said to her companion, in a strange accent that sounded like Tara Palmer-Tomkinson wrestling with a mouthful of chewing gum.

The tall, thin man looked Lizzie, then Georges, who stood in the doorway behind her, up and down.

'How charming,' said the man. 'Which one?'

'Oh, Sloan,' squealed Penny, 'you are awful.'

'This is my twin, Penny,' said Lizzie to Georges. 'And "Sloan". They're both awful, apparently.'

'I see,' said Georges, wiping his hand on his apron and holding it out. Penny affected to ignore it.

'Darling, I have to tell you. I've got the most wonderful job! In Sloan's art gallery! The first place I tried! Isn't that utterly fabulous! We had to go to lunch to celebrate.'

'Well, it's not every day an angel from heaven drops in to improve your life,' said Sloan elaborately.

Georges sniffed loudly.

'She's so unbelievably foxy,' said Sloan. 'She'll attract all the old codgers with cash. She flashes that grin and that little arse and we'll be quids in.'

'That sounds like a great job,' said Lizzie.

'Oh, I know it's difficult for you, darling. Maybe Sloan knows of some more openings . . . '

There was a silence during which Sloan examined the

particularly intricate pocket watch he had tucked into the breast pocket of his Rupert Bear yellow-checked waistcoat.

'I've got a job too,' said Lizzie finally.

'Congratulations! Oh, you should have called me; you could have come celebrating with us! Where is it? Ooh, please can it be somewhere hip where we can get into after hours. Or a private club! That'd be great, now I'm going to be moving in the art world.'

'Actually, it's here,' said Lizzie, indicating the little café behind her. 'Great, eh? You can come and have your lunch and . . . things.'

'Oh my God, carb central!' said Sloan. 'Imagine.'

Lizzie decided the safest thing to do with Sloan would be to ignore him.

'And this is my new boss, Georges.'

Georges went to put his hand out, then decided against it.

'Hello,' he said.

'Hello, Georgie Porgie,' said Penny, giggling drunkenly. 'Is this a pie shop?'

Lizzie's face was truly flaming now. She looked apologetically at Georges, who appeared to be politely biting his lip.

'Uh, I'll see you tomorrow,' she said.

'Mmm,' said Georges. Lizzie scarpered before he could reconsider the job offer.

'Right. Cocktails,' said Sloan. 'It's after three. Let's go to the Collection.'

'I don't know what that means,' said Penny, 'but I'm up for it anyway.'

'I think I'll just go home,' said Lizzie, and she turned back down the Fulham Road, as Penny waltzed up it.

*'Owwwwoww.'* Penny was roaming the flat like a very slim bear with a very sore head. *'Owoowwowow.'* She'd had such a

good day, she didn't deserve this. She was going to be a proper Chelsea girl, she was on the way up, and she was sure Chelsea girls didn't get nasty headaches as a result of over-doing the celebrations with new boss, Sloan.

'Drinking in the afternoon?' said Lizzie. 'How classy of you. Is that what people in Chelsea do now?'

'Shut up,' said Penny, gulping back an Alka-Seltzer. She'd got back about four and immediately fallen asleep for two hours.

'This is either going to work or make me really sick. Kill or cure.' She paused for five seconds. 'Excellent. It's down.'

'So you got a new job and immediately went and got pissed up with your boss? Are you sure that's wise?'

'Are you joking? Sloan is incredibly influential in the London art world. It's going to be fabulous for me.'

'How do you know that? Have you been keeping up with the art world, or did he tell you? And what kind of name is Sloan anyway?'

'A joke one,' said Penny seriously. 'I asked him. All posh people have joke names. Maybe I should get one.'

'What about Pissed-face?'

'Oh God, this place is depressing.' Penny looked around her, her gaze settling on the pile of Victorian photographs Lizzie had tidied out of her room and put up on a shelf. 'Every single person in these photographs is dead, dead, dead. Dead, dead, dead, dead buried and gone. Dead. Doesn't that depress you?'

'Well, when you put it like that . . . '

'And that noise.'

From the apartment below was coming the deep bass of Duran Duran being played extremely loudly.

'It's doing my head in,' said Penny. 'I think I'm going to go and talk to them.'

'Don't,' said Lizzie. 'It's been a long day. Have you ever been confronted with an angry Duran Duran fan? I'm telling you, it's not pretty. They slap you with bleached denim and spray Sun In in your eyes.'

'I don't care,' said Penny. 'My head is spinning, and I've got to go to work tomorrow.'

'With someone whose head will also be spinning,' argued Lizzie, 'and don't forget, it's only seven-thirty in the evening. You can hardly accuse them of keeping antisocial hours.'

Penny rolled her eyes. 'Well, anyway, I want to meet our neighbours. They might . . . be nice.'

'They might be minted, you mean,' said Lizzie. 'You were never very interested in meeting our neighbours in Parkend Close.'

'That's because I could hear them screaming, "Wayne! You're a fucking wanker that slept with Shelley-Marie" all night, every night, and I think I knew them about as well as I needed to.'

'Do you remember when Shelley-Marie turned up?'

'Do I? "I'm going to cut you, Wayne, cut you with this knife."'

They were both silent for a moment.

Penny shivered. 'And now I'm working in a Chelsea art gallery and I'm making lots of nice new West End friends. Fantastic.'

'Do you think telling our neighbours to turn the music down is the best way to make new friends?'

Penny shrugged. 'You never know. There might be a nice man down there.'

'Listening to maximum-volume Duran Duran?'

'Maybe he's a wild boy,' said Penny, heading out and slamming the door.

\*

Forty minutes later, Lizzie was getting slightly worried. Maybe there was a New Romantic psycho downstairs, locked up listening to 'Fade to Grey' and planning terrible tortures and murders. Oh no! She left her bedroom, where she'd been looking at the clothes she'd brought with her. They were almost uniformly black, with a couple of cheap suits she used to wear in the office. They wouldn't be much use now, if she was going to get covered in grease every day. She really needed to wash her hair too, but was scared of that big bath. If she slipped in it she might never get out again.

Suddenly, she noticed Penny had left her mobile on the only bit of work surface not covered in antique cups and saucers. Oh, crap. She couldn't even phone her to see if she was all right. By now, she had undoubtedly been tied up with leg warmers and dumped in a cupboard.

Carefully she crept into the hallway. It smelled of polish and fresh flowers, and much nicer than their flat.

She went downstairs and listened outside the door. The music was still going as loudly as ever. Maybe she should go and get a weapon. No, that was just stupid. Nothing was wrong with her sister. But just in case, kick in the crotch. The crotch.

She knocked on the door. 'Hello?'

Nothing.

'Hello?'

No one. Taking a deep breath, she reached for the door-knob. It turned in her hand.

'Hello?'

She pushed the door harder and, slowly, it started to open.

Lizzie stood in the doorway and stared. The huge sitting room was spread out in front of her, an exact replica of upstairs. But this room was completely different; it was clear and white, and the huge windows were shiny clean, letting the evening light pour in.

Two red sofas, deep and luxuriant, sat either side of the white wooden fireplace. Red-and-white striped chairs provided extra seating. On the other side of the room, near the spotless stainless-steel kitchen, was a large circular table with a large bowl of green apples sitting on it. Large abstract canvases hung on the wall. Lizzie realised immediately it was how she'd like her flat to be, if she ever had a choice in the matter.

'Uh, hello, yeah?' came a drawling voice.

Sitting on the sofas, as she took in more than just the furniture, were three skinny creatures. Two of them were blonde, including, she noticed, Penny, who was not, in fact, being held hostage in an eighties fan's torture cellar after all. The other was dark and dusky, absolutely gorgeous in the manner of those who get off with married footballers.

'Uhh . . . I'm from upstairs,' stuttered Lizzie, finding, annoyingly, that she was intimidated just because she was standing in front of such good-looking people.

'This is obviously our night for having the neighbours drop in,' said the brunette with a sleepy look.

'I think having the neighbours drop in is a bit common,' said the blonde, who had a pinched face and ridiculously long pin legs. 'A bit *EastEnders*.'

'Shut up, Minty,' said the brunette. She made an enquiring face.

'Oh,' said Penny from the sofa, looking up at Lizzie for the first time, as if surprised to see her there. 'Yah.'

'*Yah?*'

'This is my . . . my sister.'

The brunette gave a slight smile. 'Oh, you didn't mention her.'

There was an uncomfortable silence.

'Penny was just telling us she works for an art gallery?' said the brunette, who was obviously the only one with manners more advanced than that of a stick insect.

'That's right,' said Lizzie. 'She sells crayons.'

The girls didn't even smile.

'I'm Lizzie,' said Lizzie, conscious that she hadn't changed out of her stained top. If she tried to sit down on their beautiful sofa they'd probably shoo her off.

There was a momentary pause before the girls raised themselves from their exquisite longeurs to respond.

'I'm Brooke,' said the brunette. Araminta was the pinched-faced blonde who didn't seem the slightest bit interested in suggesting Lizzie call her 'Minty'. Penny looked a little bit uncomfortable and moved up from the sofa. Lizzie noticed they were all drinking white wine but hadn't offered her any.

'Well, I've got to go,' said Penny. 'Busy schedule.' She cleared her throat when they looked at her expectantly, and Penny thought of the newspapers she pored over, where celebrities were always getting into trouble for throwing punches at the paparazzi. 'Boujis?' she ventured.

'Who goes there these days?' said the one called Minty. 'It's common.'

Penny bristled. 'Really? I saw Prince William there last week.'

'We'll see you there,' said Minty.

Penny nodded.


'You're going *where* tonight?' said Lizzie as she trailed her sister upstairs.

'I don't know, do I? I've read about it. The kind of place these nobs go and there's photographers outside. It'll be in Yellow Pages.'

'So you're definitely going out?'

'Yes!' said Penny. 'I've always wanted to go to these places. So I'm going to, and you're coming too.'

'Are you sure they're real places and not something you just made up?'

'Yes.'

'We don't have any money.'

'We'll share a Vimto.'

'How're we going to get in?'

'I'm going to hide you behind my breasts. Would you shut up with these really stupid questions?'

'But we've got work tomorrow.'

'Yes, and for ever, if I don't pull Prince William.'

Lizzie sat down on one of the broken chairs back in their own apartment. It creaked ominously. 'But I don't want to.'

'Don't be daft, Lizzie.'

Lizzie hung her head. 'Why don't you go with your real friends, rather than drag me along everywhere?'

Penny snorted. 'I don't think Kelly Anne and Dwaneesa would really fit in with Brooke and Minty, do you?'

'Oh, I don't know,' said Lizzie. 'They're all horrible. Just Kelly Anne and Dwaneesa are probably more inclined towards actual physical violence.'

'It was just that one time,' said Penny in a bored tone.

'That one time,' said Lizzie. 'That one and sole time I had my first period and they flushed my head down the bogs.' Lizzie could never quite get over her resentment at having to hang out with Penny all the time, and the misery it had caused her.

'Well, that's all over and in the past and ages ago and they're not like that any more.' Penny had never understood why Lizzie bothered trailing after her at school; it wasn't like they let her join in. Penny'd never made the connection between Lizzie's calming influence and the fact that she was the only one of her group not to be expelled.

'Dwaneesa's got an ASBO!'

'That policeman was racist.'

'She threw a fox at his head!'

'Just get dressed,' said Penny.

'No!'

'Get dressed.'

'No.'

'OK, well, come in that dirty thing that makes you look retarded.'

'I'm not going.'

'Please.'

'No.'

'Please.'

'No.'

Penny pouted when it became obvious this wasn't going to work.

'But we're celebrating,' she said. 'We both found jobs on our first day out. And we live in Chelsea! And it's our duty to have fun and get to know the beautiful people and get our pictures in the back pages of *OK!*'

'You never recognise anyone in the back pages of *OK!*'

'That's not the point, is it? I want to be someone people go, "Who's that cow and why on earth is she always in the back pages of *OK!*?"'

'And that's your life ambition, is it?'

'Well, yeah. Followed by "Royal Wedding Special Edition".'

'Well, a fondness for old bags does run in that family.'

'Fuck off! And get changed.'

'No!'

Penny came up to Lizzie. 'You know,' she said sincerely,

'this is all I've ever wanted. Just a chance. Just a chance to change our lives and try and do a bit better for ourselves. It's all I've ever wanted. For both of us. To have more than Mum ever got. To have our chance . . . '

'By going out to some overpriced nightclub?'

'It's our new life,' said Penny. 'It will be so good for us. Us, together, striving to make a new way of . . . '

'OK, OK, make it stop!' said Lizzie. Why was she so weak? But someone had to look out for Penny, otherwise who knew what she'd do? 'I'll come. For half an hour. Then I'm going to bed, I'm cream crackered.'

'Don't say cream crackered,' said Penny.

'I'll stop saying cream crackered, when you *start* saying thank you,' muttered Lizzie, stomping off to her own room to find her trusty mascara.

Lizzie realised, staring disconsolately at her wardrobe for the second time that day, that she had no idea what Georges was going to pay her. She tried to think of some kind of innovative mathematical formula that would allow her to earn a magnificent salary selling sandwiches and spaghetti in a box, but she couldn't figure it out.

So it looked like she'd be sticking to TK Maxx and George at Asda for a while yet. There probably wasn't a TK Maxx in Chelsea, she reflected.

Oh, well, what was it Trinny and Susannah always said? V-shapes to show off those big bosoms and generous waist. And wide hips and big bottom. She wondered what it would be like to buy something that wasn't an act of disguise.

Next door she could hear doors and cupboards noisily being thrown open, with loud music being played. The wine seemed to have perked Penny up considerably, which was worrying and encouraging all at once.

'OK!' she shouted eventually, and Lizzie went out – in her black V-neck top – to see what was up. She gasped. 'You're not.'

'What?' said Penny. 'Are you going to say, "You're not going out dressed like that"?'

Lizzie knew Penny desperately wanted her to say it. Lizzie flashed back to all the occasions of this in their lives, from high heels worn to school when she was eight, to the boob tube fiasco of the Year 7 Christmas party. Penny had a history of wearing things that made her look like she was walking out the house with the distinct intention of getting pregnant. Why did Penny always make her feel so old?

'Are you sure the girls here dress the same as you do down at Coasters?'

'What?' said Penny innocently. 'They're worse here. You should see the girls who go to these places. They wear artillery belts over their nips and nothing else at all.'

'And that's the kind of girl you'd like to be?'

'It's just a bit of fun!'

'Slutty, slutty, slutty fun,' said Lizzie.

Penny was wearing a transparent black shirt – that had been designed to be worn over a vest – without the vest – and a see-through bra. Her nipples were obvious from almost every angle. She'd teamed it with a denim mini and pink cowboy boots.

'Penny, it's illegal to walk about the streets showing your nipples.'

Penny rolled her eyes. 'Well, I've got something for that, haven't I? Look. I found it in one of the cupboards.'

She threw a fur stole around her shoulders.

'Oh my God,' said Lizzie, genuinely shocked. 'You can't wear that!'

'Why not?'

'Well, one, it's not yours, and two, it's not anybody's, it belongs to an animal.'

'An extremely old animal,' said Penny. 'Smell it, it smells like the Second World War.'

# Chapter Four

There were more than a few raised eyebrows on the bus but whilst Lizzie felt mortified, Penny didn't seem in the slightest bit concerned; she was more worried that the girls downstairs would see them leaving to catch a bus. Not quite knowing the protocol with guest lists etc., they'd decided to arrive at Boujis super early and sit and nurse a drink in the corner.

Even so, there was an early queue forming outside the club, the place Penny had chosen on the basis that according to the 3am girls it was a dead cert if you wanted to pull an ex-member of a boy band or a third-division footballer.

There were one or two boys, nervously tugging at their Ted Baker shirts, but overwhelmingly the queue was formed of girls; and girls who made Penny's outfit look like a shelf-stacking uniform in Tehran. Tall girls, model-types shouting loudly and cavorting around up the front, nervous fat girls, freshly bronzed, wearing the latest glittery halterneck from Morgan with their striped hair piled high on their heads; black girls and white girls in tiny little strips of dresses; girls from out of town that appeared to be wearing every piece of jewellery they owned simultaneously and more blue and green eye make-up than Lizzie had seen since secondary school.

Everything was tanned, squeezed, plumped and primped to its very limits. Hairspray and heavy musky perfumes hung in the chilly night air like a dark velvet curtain. Across the road a small bank of photographers with huge lenses and heavy overcoats were limbering up for the evening in case they got lucky with a Page Three girl flashing her norks or a rap star out on the lash. It wasn't that different from Brandford after all – just, Lizzie suspected, a lot more expensive.

Lizzie realised she felt terribly nervous for some reason, almost as if she was about to be judged. Then she remembered that she *was* about to be judged, by some clipboard Nazi on the door who was going to bar her entry on the grounds that she'd kept her lipliner to the inside edge of her lips.

'Are you sure about this?' she moaned. She didn't usually go to nightclubs. She went to pubs with Grainne, where they sat and ate a lot of dry roasted peanuts and prawn cocktail crisps. When they'd finished eating from their crisp bags, they'd fold them up into perfectly neat triangles and place them tidily in the ashtray.

In fact, she only went to nightclubs proper for their bloody birthday because Penny would insist on a night out with the girls. They usually went to Coasters in Walthamstow because Penny knew the barman and they'd get free drinks. Lizzie supposed they weren't exactly free because Penny would repay the bar staff by flashing them and dancing wildly on the tables of the 'VIP' section, which had never seen anyone more famous than the roofer out of East 17, and was bookable by anyone who didn't mind buying a bottle of horribly overpriced and revolting Jampagne ('It's just like champagne,' the owner Billy was always saying, 'except it comes from Japan'). Lizzie would sit in the dark and look after people's coats for ages then suddenly get pissed very quickly and jump up and dance her head off and the next day everyone would say, 'Oh, Lizzie, you were totally outrageous,' and she'd want to disappear into a big hole and die.

She didn't want to be outrageous. She'd just like to move as easily through the world as other people seemed to, without blushing and feeling as if her hips were too wide for the available space.

Lizzie heaved a big sigh.

'Just stand behind me,' ordered Penny, and she sashayed into the shorter queue. This was patently the queue to be in, with fewer bridge-and-tunnel style ASOS knock-offs and a lower BMI.

At the front was a scary-looking but beautiful dark-haired woman with a severe expression and a large clipboard, which she was hugging to her chest. She looked extremely grumpy, except for when a young actress Lizzie recognised from *Coronation Street*, together with someone else from *Hollyoaks* (Lizzie made a mental note to watch less television now she lived in Chelsea) flounced up to the front, wearing between them about three diamanté studs and some fringing.

'Hello, darlings!' said the scary woman, and the flashbulbs started going off. A little whisper of excitement went through the other queue, the one that didn't think it was on the guest list. After all, *Coronation Street* already, and it wasn't even half past ten!

'Have a few voddies on us!' shouted one of the photographers, 'and we'll see you later. Falling over, hopefully.' There was a nasty snigger, but the girls beamed big white smiles and waved chirpily.

The dark-haired woman was growing ever closer. Lizzie felt her heart in her mouth like she was being sent to see the headteacher. This was ridiculous. Penny's earrings twitched as she approached the podium. The woman barely glanced up.

'Minty de Lougis,' she announced, in her very best 'I'm not from Essex' voice.

'Oh yes, of course, that's here,' she said. 'Minty! How's Brooke?'

Penny jumped back into the shadowy doorway and turned her head away in a bored fashion so that all that could be seen was her long blonde hair.

'Yah, fine,' she said.

'Wait a minute,' said the woman, as the bouncer was pulling across the red velvet rope. 'You're not— Krystanza!' she exclaimed suddenly, as, to their right, the most ridiculous thing Lizzie had ever seen got out of a stretch Hummer.

It had long skinny legs coloured Easyjet-orange and balanced on a pair of six-inch heels made of perspex and feathers, wore a tiny miniskirt made of denim and lace and, juddering above this, floated the most absurd pair of balloon breasts imaginable. Two huge footballs were stapled to a chest above a tiny waist. They were so plump and bouncy on the top you could let kittens use them as trampolines. Barely held in with a tiny piece of stretchy pink tiger-skin fabric, they cast their own shadows over the waiting crowds, who drew back oohing. It was like the spaceships landing in

*Independence Day.* Above the robo-bosoms, which were at neck height, was a vast mane of blonde hair that looked to be made of several types of synthetic fibre, crowning a shiny mahogany face swimming in at least half a kilo of lipgloss. The apparition batted her eyelids.

'What is that?' said Lizzie, standing stock-still before Penny grabbed her by the elbow and pushed her through the double doors while everyone's attention was still diverted by the huge top-heavy apparition who was clunking past the bouncers; a horde of voices yelling 'Pull your top down, love' and flashbulbs popping behind her. 'And who are you? Did you just pass yourself off as our downstairs neighbour?'

'Well, I knew she'd be on the list.'

'How?'

'She seems like the kind of person who'd be on the list. And I nicked her surname from the post. Right, let's go.'

'OK, Sherlock Holmes,' said Lizzie. Behind them came gasps as Krystanza tottered carefully down the lit-up stairs.

'Is that a man in drag or what?'

'No,' said Penny, glancing behind her. 'That's Krystanza. I think she's fantastic. For a dirty old slapper, of course. She's slept with four premiership footballers and most of her record company.'

'Oh, yeah,' said Lizzie. 'I just didn't think she'd look so . . . weird up close.'

Penny looked around. 'Now, where were we?'

The club was already jam-packed full, and people in the room – it was much smaller than Lizzie had been expecting – looked up expectantly as they descended the staircase, only to look down again dejectedly when they realised that the new arrivals did not play for a football team or star in Hollywood movies.

There were girls draped everywhere, up against pillars, over the bar, here and there huddled in small groups around men, who were laughing and smiling indulgently as the women fluttered and twittered over cocktails. On the dance floor were girls with fabulous figures grooving with one another and showing off their moves which were, to Lizzie's unpractised eye, bordering on the obscene.

'Are they lesbians?' she asked.

'No, they just pretend to be to get the blokes to notice them,' said Penny.

'That's moral. What are we going to do for drinks?'

Penny tried to look like she knew what she was doing but she didn't really.

'Uh, well, I think we just hang around looking decorative.'

Lizzie swallowed. 'Look, I brought twenty quid. It's all I've got, but we should at least get a couple of drinks if we're going to be here.'

'I thought there'd be more men around,' said Penny. 'This looks more like a—'

'Bordello?' said Lizzie.

'No. No.' Penny looked around. 'It's nice really.'

A huge girl with a massive Afro elbowed them out the way to get to Krystanza, whereupon she started showering her with kisses.

Finally they compromised; Lizzie bought one cocktail (she'd asked for beer, but they didn't serve it – it was champagne cocktails or nothing), which used up almost all of her twenty quid, which almost made her weep but didn't – and they found a tiny space by the toilets where they crouched, sipping it morosely. Every so often Penny would announce she was going to do something – get up, dance, introduce herself to some people – and Lizzie would nod encouragingly, then Penny would hear the squeals and giggles of everyone greeting each other like old friends and yelling with glee and change her mind.

'Actually this place is really past it,' she announced after an hour. 'You can tell. It's shit really.'

'Isn't that Will Smith?' said Lizzie, who as she hadn't been asked to do anything embarrassing yet was actually having not that bad a time. It didn't hurt that, for once, Penny was feeling just as uncomfortable and out of it as she was.

'No,' said Penny without turning round.

By one in the morning Lizzie was wondering if they'd mind terribly letting her have a little lie down in the cloakroom.

'Well, hello, you lovely ladies,' said the DJ. Everyone yelled. Lizzie had been trying to work out if DJ 'lovely ladies' was being ironic or not but she didn't think he was. It was obviously cool now to behave like you were about to put a Bros record on.

'I'm about to put a Bros record on,' said the DJ. The crowd screamed. Obviously not as young as they were trying to look then.

'But first, there's a special prize . . . for tonight only . . . a bottle of champagne . . . '

Penny's ears pricked up.

' . . . for the first girl to get them out and have a bit of a dance on the table.'

A roar went up from the few men stationed around the room, most of whom looked disconcertingly seedy.

Lizzie closed her eyes. No. No, no, no, no, no. Please. Just call the night a bit rubbish then they could go home. Just hop on the bus and chalk it up to experience, and they could relaunch the central London experience again tomorrow. Please. When she opened them, Penny had gone.

The first, familiar bars of 'When Will I Be Famous' had

72

started up. To Lizzie's utter amazement, several other girls were already tearing at their thin bikini straps.

'Help me with these goddamn buttons,' hissed Penny from a few feet away, striding towards the centre of the floor.

'No!'

Penny took a panicky look round. Already a petite Tara Reid lookalike had nearly finished wrangling two big plastic melons out of her cerise Barbie top.

'Bollocks to it,' said Penny finally, pulling off the rest of the buttons which scattered on the floor. 'Grab my bra, Liz!'

Lizzie tried to crouch down behind the nearest table as Penny tugged at the elastic. Mission accomplished, Penny hauled herself, in a most ungainly fashion, onto the nearest table, knocking over someone else's glass in the process.

'Oh, for fuck's sake,' came a female voice that was purest Essex. The man also sitting at the table, however, whom Lizzie recognised from her peeping vantage point as having once, many years ago, appeared in a soap opera was clearly delighted.

'Up you get, love,' he shouted, proffering a hairy arm.

Red-faced and slightly out of breath, Penny finally succeeded in getting rid of the bra and threw it straight at Lizzie. It landed on her head.

'Hold on to it,' she hollered and began swaying gymnastically, if not necessarily rhythmically. The people around started to clap half-heartedly. To Penny's horror, though, there were at least four other girls dotted around the club, also with their tits out. And they undoubtedly outshone Penny in the mammaries department, as they universally had the exact same breasts, jutting out of their emaciated ribcages at a ninety-degree angle, like they'd been swallowing apples whole.

'And it's a dead heat in the Zeppelin race!' chortled the

DJ as if he was being incredibly witty. 'So, girls, I guess it's up to you to dance your way to that bottle of champers!'

Immediately, Penny sprang into action. Lizzie wanted to cover her face with her hands. It was so . . . undignified. Was that the right word for writhing about half naked in front of washed-up TV stars for a bottle of bubbly? Actually, undignified didn't really cover it.

Penny had stepped up her game quite considerably and was shimmying up and down like she'd made an unexpected stop on her way to Stringfellows. The television actor was completely mesmerised. The girl whose glass Penny had knocked over was making loud sighing and tutting noises and mouthing 'slut' to her friends, but Penny was oblivious. That champagne was going to be won. She stuck out her little bottom and swivelled her rump down to the table top.

'Ooh,' said the DJ. 'Looks like there's a girl there that really, really wants it. So I think we're going to have to declare a winner . . . And, I know you'll find this hard to believe, chaps, but I think those might even be real!'

There was another loud holler. Penny raised her arms in the air and shimmied in triumph.

'Come on down then, hot stuff.'

The other girls slunk off their tables looking slightly shamefaced as Penny put out her hand for the actor to take it as if she were stepping down from a carriage. She demurely put her hands over her bosoms and picked her way towards the DJ station. The DJ was a ridiculous white man in his mid-thirties with long blonde dreadlocks falling over his shoulders, wearing a pair of dungarees with nothing underneath them. He beckoned Penny over, gyrating in what he evidently thought was a pretty sexy manner.

Just as Penny – revelling in the attention – nearly made it, there was a distinct 'whoo' from the crowd as Krystanza strode off the dance floor and stood directly between Penny and the DJ.

'Excuse *me*,' said Penny, but the DJ had already turned the music up.

Slowly, desultorily, Krystanza lifted her arms above her head and brought them down behind her back. Winking one eye, that was drooping slightly from the weight of eye-shadow on it, she ran her tongue over her lips. The men in the club were on their feet.

Carefully, she unhooked the eye of her bra top. Lizzie screwed her eyes up, in case one of Krystanza's mega bosoms sprang out and hit her in the face.

Indeed, they popped out with an almost audible plopping, bouncing noise, as if they were full of jelly. The entire club went silent in awe. Like two enormous flying plum pud-dings they seemed to defy the laws of physics. The nipples alone were larger than Penny's perfectly nice pert pair. It was impossible not to stare at them. Lizzie tried but absolutely could not discern the attraction for a man of getting stuck between two things bigger than his head.

Krystanza was now fondling her two footballs with the same lazy uninterested air.

'And it looks like we have a new winner, ladies and gen-tlemen,' announced the DJ. Krystanza extended an arm and grabbed the champagne.

'Oh no you don't!' shouted Penny suddenly, seeing all her efforts (and buttons) going in vain. 'Give me that! It's mine!'

She launched herself at Krystanza in a feral leap, finger-nails pointing outwards.

Krystanza merely turned round, ensuring Penny bounced off her huge mammaries without leaving a mark.

'Rrr!' yelled Penny, ploughing in for another go.

'Fight! Fight! Fight!' shouted the crowd delightedly.

Penny managed to get hold of some of the girl's hair, but it came out without causing her any noticeable discomfort whatsoever.

'Urgh!' shouted Penny. 'What is this? Did you shave it off a starving Russian prostitute, you skank?'

The DJ, whilst clearly enjoying the scene, realised something would have to be done as Krystanza turned round, slowly, like a ship.

'How dare you talk to me like that?' she said poisonously. 'Do you want a scrap? You'll get one.'

'Fantastic,' said Penny. 'Have you seen *Million Dollar Baby*?' And she started bouncing up and down like a boxer.

Lizzie hid further down behind the chair, until she was practically kneeling on the floor, burying her face into her knees. From behind her fingers she noticed Brooke and Minty enter, wearing white jeans and glittery little tops.

'*Nobody* touches my hair, you bitch,' Krystanza was screaming.

'You want a piece of me?' Penny was screaming back. 'Do you? Give me my champagne, bitch.'

Lizzie saw Brooke and Minty break into broad smiles as they saw Penny in the middle of the floor. Clearly their new friend was going to prove excellent entertainment.

'Go, Penny!' shouted Brooke. Penny pushed her arm out again, grabbing another handful of Krystanza's hair in the process. Krystanza went wild and ran for Penny, looking exactly like Miss Piggy, whomping her on the chin with her crystal-studded handbag.

Lizzie rushed forward to see if her sister was hurt, watching her, feeling helpless as she cascaded through the air, completely off balance.

As she fell, with Lizzie diving over to grab her, she managed to make a punching motion out towards Krystanza's left leg. Fatally unbalanced, the blonde started to totter forward, just as Penny hit the floor and Lizzie landed on top of her. Like a tree falling (someone even shouted '*Timber!*'), with crashing slowness, Krystanza's nipples, followed by the rest of her, collapsed on top of the girls.

Lizzie felt as if she was being squashed beneath two giant spacehoppers as the place erupted into applause.

When they finally disentangled themselves, Krystanza was led off by an overly handsome man looking concerned, and the DJ was calming the crowd.

'I think *both* these lovely ladies deserve a bottle, don't you?'

'Yah!' Minty was shouting.

The DJ looked at Lizzie, who had managed to rip her top in the melee and was conscious that her hair was doing that frizzy thing again.

'Uh . . . yeah,' he said, glancing past her. '*both* our lovely cat-fighting ladies!'

Penny retrieved her top, panting, red in the face and somehow looking devastatingly sexy. Already footballers and the sons of once famous footballers were beginning to circle around her.

'You are crazy,' said Brooke, in a voice that sounded admiring.

'Yah, Penny, you're so wild,' said Minty. 'That girl, fighting in public. *So* common.'

'I started it,' said Penny happily.

Bottles of champagne seemed to keep appearing from somewhere, but nobody had asked Penny for any money, so it was quite all right. Lizzie, a bit wobbly from her trip and long day, sat quietly in the corner with no one talking to her except every so often, when they'd say something and she'd perk up and try and look happy and interested and raise her eyebrows expectantly, and they'd ask her if she'd mind moving so they could go to the toilet. So she drank too much and wondered unhappily why, if this place was so incredibly expensive, they couldn't spare some peanuts to put on the tables. She slurred this to Brooke before she left, who looked at her with an eyebrow raised and said, 'Darling, you know, I have this little dietician fellow you really *must* meet,' and Lizzie had lurched backwards like she'd been slapped. She couldn't bear to have her weight mentioned.

Suddenly it was after three-thirty: it was *so* late, and everything was winding down. Lizzie only just realised she was horribly drunk. People had been turning up with drinks for them all night and, madly, she'd just kept going. Their new neighbours had disappeared ages before – whether on to another club or just sensibly home to keep their perfect skin and glossy hair, Lizzie didn't know. There was hardly anyone left when Lizzie finally managed to drag Penny off the dance floor, where she was half dancing, half swaying with an incredibly sleazy fellow with slicked-back hair and shiny shoes, who obviously thought his luck was in and looked annoyed at Lizzie dragging his pissed-up dancing partner away, until he saw the determined set of her jaw.

'Home,' said Lizzie. If only they'd gone with Brooke and the others they could have cadged a lift in their cab, but Penny had been dancing and Lizzie had been standing up to let someone go to the toilet and they'd missed them.

'I've had a *fabulous* time,' said Penny. 'Everyone really liked me. And I've got . . . this!'

As they fell through the front glass doors, she held up her trophy, a long blonde lock of synthetic hair.

'I'm definitely going to be a Chelsea girl,' slurred Penny. 'I think I'll just stick this in my hair right now.'

Lizzie shook her head as she felt the cold morning air in her face, freshening her up considerably.

'Look at me,' said Penny, lifting up the hair. 'I'm Krystanza and I'm a great big fucking slut, slut, slut. Ooh! I'm a slut! I'm a slutty slutty slut . . . with my stupid big tits and my tiny wee butt I'm a skank, I'm a ho, I'm a slut slut . . . '

Her last word, which Lizzie suspected might have been 'slut', never had a chance to escape her mouth as the woman in front of them, waiting for a taxi, turned round and pounced.

'Hello, Krystanza,' attempted Penny, as the other girl tried to pick her up by the throat. In the next instant they were rolling around on the ground again, as the few remaining paparazzi started flashing away wildly with their cameras.

'Oh God,' said Lizzie. 'Will you two stop that?' And she waded in to try and separate them.

'*Get off!*' shouted one of the photographers.

'Yeah, get out of it, podge,' shouted another one. 'We've got shots to get here.'

Lizzie's head shot up. They couldn't mean her, surely?

'Yeah, get out of it. Shit, that arse is obscuring my lens.'

There was coarse laughter as Lizzie stumbled backwards, face flaming, to try and get out of the way. She lost her footing a little on the step and fell horribly, inevitably, her ankle vanishing from underneath her as she catapulted downwards and landed on her bottom on the pavement.

Stunned, feeling drunker than ever, she sat there trying to regain her equilibrium, the chortling of the photographers ringing in her ears. The heel of her shoe had broken off. She noticed it had fallen in a dirty McDonald's cup. This was possibly the most excruciating night out she'd had since her and Penny's joint twenty-first, when she'd pulled a virgin and they'd sat on her single bed for four hours drinking Nescafé with milk that tasted slightly off.

Maybe she should just stay here, in the gutter, and go to sleep. Maybe she could lie down and put her head in a puddle and find some more fast-food wrappers and stick them to herself to keep warm. She didn't think it could be any more humiliating than the way she felt already. After all, nothing could get any worse.

'Uh, hello?' came a voice from above her. It sounded kind and concerned. This wasn't what she wanted right now. Kind and concerned was bad, in fact, because it implied she'd done something ridiculous that required patience and pity. Grudgingly, she looked up . . . and her night deteriorated even more.

'I *thought* that was my new employee. I was right!' said Georges. He held out a helping hand. 'Are you OK? Have you been mugged?'

Lizzie realised how she must look, with the evidence of two fights all over her. She shook her head. 'No.'

He shook his hand at her and she took it and scrambled up. 'Having a good night?'

Lizzie swallowed, suddenly feeling very drunk and awful. She wobbled a bit in only one shoe and had to lean against him. He held her elbow.

'Are you OK?'

'I am absolutely fine,' said Lizzie, concentrating on not slurring her words. 'Are you?'

'Me? Yes, I am great. I go to the fish market, there may be some lovely red snapper. Early bird catches the fish, yes?'

'But it's the middle of the night.'

'Or very early in the morning. It's good. You should come, er, sometime.'

'What about now?' said Lizzie. Penny could still be heard

yelping behind her, and she felt like getting away.

Georges looked pointedly down at her missing shoe.

'I think you should probably get some sleep . . . I hear you start very important job tomorrow, no?'

Lizzie hung her head and leaned into him a bit. After all, he'd seemed to like her today, hadn't he? For a bit at least.

'Please?' she said, trying to sound a bit flirtatious.

'No,' he said, gently extricating himself from her boozy hold. She felt him pushing her away.

'Go home now,' he said. 'Get some sleep.'

'I didn't want to get off with you anyway,' she said, upset.

Georges coughed and looked startled. 'Er, excuse me?' he said.

'You're not my type,' said Lizzie, thinking in her befuddled state that this would make her seem cool and unbothered. 'I just don't have enough money to get home.'

Lizzie bent down to fish her shoe out of the McDonald's container. For a second it looked like she was about to topple over again, but Georges grabbed her by the waistband – sadly elasticated. She wavered for a second before righting herself.

Georges smiled at her, concern in his eyes. He stuck up his hand and hailed a taxi, handing the driver a tenner.

'Is this enough to get this lady back to Chelsea?' he asked the cabbie.

'I don't know, is she going to be sick?' asked the driver.

'Are you going to be sick?' asked Georges.

Lizzie shook her head miserably.

'Off you go then,' said Georges.

'I have to get my sister,' said Lizzie. 'I have to get her.'

'Where is she?'

But Georges didn't have to wait long to find out. Able to sniff out a free cab from five kilometres away, Penny was flying down the steps, with what looked like half a wig in her hands.

'Fly! Fly!' she yelled, as she hit the pavement. 'Who's this?' She looked at Georges without the faintest flicker of recognition that she'd met him less than twenty-four hours previously.

'It's Georges. I don't fancy him,' said Lizzie.

'Oh, that doesn't matter. Is he rich?'

'Goodnight, ladies,' said Georges. And he shut the taxi door and marched off down the street.

'Well, what a fantastic night,' said Penny. And, like a cat, she stretched herself out on the back seat of the cab and promptly fell asleep.

# Chapter Five

'Well, there's no point in crying,' said Penny, already making herself up very efficiently in the tiny square of bathroom mirror that wasn't completely obscured by boxes of pinned butterflies.

'You don't know how bad it was,' said Lizzie. 'I'm not a hundred per cent sure myself when it comes to it.'

'How bad could it have been? Wasn't he just sleazing you up a bit?'

'No,' said Lizzie, through painfully hiccuppy noises as she tried to prevent herself from bursting into sobs. This was why she didn't like getting drunk very often. 'I was sleazing him up. Oh, Penny, I'm a disgrace.'

'You threw yourself at your new fat boss?' Penny raised an over-plucked eyebrow.

Lizzie sniffled to herself.

Penny looked at her pityingly. 'So what are you going to do – move jobs?'

Lizzie shook her head. 'I can't . . . it was hard enough to find this one.' She groaned. 'I'll just have to do the whole thing without looking at him. Unless he sacks me, of course.'

'Is that a big zit on your nose or did you fall asleep on a Jammy Dodger?' said Penny.

How anyone could look quite so perky when they'd been ten seconds off getting a police caution only a few hours previously was a mystery to Lizzie. Penny strode briskly up to the newsagent's on the corner and picked up a copy of a tabloid.

Sure enough, there she was, on page eleven. 'Big Bust's BIG Bust Up!' ran the headline. 'Page Three stunner Krystanza's night came to a shocking close at Boujis when she was set upon by a jealous fan. "This girl was making a real fool of herself all night," said a friend. "Then when Krystanza went to leave she couldn't stand it any more and jumped her. It was pathetic really."'

This was emblazoned over a large picture of Krystanza, breasts akimbo, twisting alarmingly on the steps. Penny's fingernails could just be seen outstretched towards her bosoms.

'It's me!' said Penny. 'I'm famous!'

Lizzie studied it, momentarily distracted from her funk.

'It says you were making a real fool of yourself all night,' she said. 'I didn't think it was *all* night, just the bit when you were taking your clothes off and that.'

'Thanks,' said Penny. She studied the newspaper closely. 'I don't see a bit where it says, "The beautiful mysterious stranger is still being sought as she disappeared into the night".'

'Maybe they had to trim that bit for space,' said Lizzie.

'Maybe I should call the paper and put my side of the story.'

'What's your side of the story? She stood up and you tried to fight her.'

'She tried to nick my champagne!'

'She had the biggest tits in a "Who's Got The Biggest Tits" competition!'

'She cheated!'


Penny was still feeling mildly exuberant when she rocked up to the gallery. Sloan was outside, opening up.

'Shocking hangover,' he said. 'A few too many brandies at the Officers' Club with an old guardsman, ahem, chum.'

'Me too,' said Penny. 'Well, similar.'

She showed him the newspaper and he shouted with laughter.

'You are a hoot,' he said. 'What a girl.'

Penny smiled happily. At least someone approved. Why couldn't Lizzie understand she was only trying to have a little bit of fun, for goodness' sake, and nobody had got hurt. Well, maybe Krystanza had got a *little* bit hurt, but she'd be grateful for the column inches – Penny had done her a favour, really.

'Right, a gentle morning then,' said Sloan. 'You fire up the coffee machine over there and I'll leaf through *Harden's* and consider my luncheon options.'

Penny went over and looked at the strange hissing contraption. She didn't know where to start.

'Don't you have any Nescafé?' she shouted.

'Are you sure you've lived in Chelsea all your life?' said Sloan.

'Of course,' she said. 'We just always had maids to make the coffee. And stuff.'

'Of course you did, dear,' said Sloan, smiling. He couldn't help it: wherever she was from, he admired her chutzpah. 'Watch carefully.'

As he started to talk about steam pressure and grinding beans, Penny looked round the gallery – she'd glanced at the paintings yesterday, but Sloan had seemed so interested in her false nails that she hadn't really had time to take them in properly. Now as she did so, she realised they were actually rather nice. Large landscapes. They looked like photographs from a distance; only up close could you see the beautiful detail in every painting.

'Not challenging,' Sloan barked when he noticed her examining them, 'but they sell well and look gorgeous. The painter isn't bad-looking either, which always helps. Much better than those chaps who bring in their stuff made from piss and monkey dung.' He shivered, whilst he did something complicated with some filter paper and a tube that whistled. 'Practically sell themselves. So all you have to do, sweetheart, is sit pretty and smile widely. And *I* get my bloody lunch hour back. You know, I worried that when Maud left I would only get an hour or two!' He shook his head. 'What way is that to get business done? See,' said Sloan, pointing at the newspaper. 'I can tell you are definitely the right person. If someone tries anything, feel quite at liberty to challenge them to a fight. Nothing like a little bit of scandal. They'll be *flocking*.'

Penny wasn't entirely sure that being allowed to fight sexism with violence was quite the way they ought to be going about things, but Sloan seemed thoroughly satisfied, and so far this job seemed to involve a lot more sitting on her arse than being pinched on it, so perhaps this wasn't quite the time to bring up any human rights legislation.

'Ah, lunch,' said Sloan, looking misty-eyed. 'Now. Look here. If a painting has a red dot on it that means it's sold and you can't sell it again, OK?'

Penny nodded.

'However, if they really like it, tell them you might be able to have a word with Will, the artist. He can basically photocopy it and we'll sell it twice. Bingo!'

This wasn't how Penny had thought the art world worked, if she'd ever thought about it at all. But she could probably get used to it, she figured, as Sloan wobbled out the door at quarter to eleven, and she sat back with the paper.

Forty minutes later the door clanged open. Penny shoved her *Daily Mirror* under the desk pronto and tried to look smart. Lizzie had tried to stop her from using the lipliner this morning but she'd ignored her. Now she wished she'd listened; she felt far too pouty. Surreptitiously she tried to wipe it away.

'Hello,' came a posh voice. 'Are you eating a jam sandwich?'

She looked up. A man had entered. He was wearing a beaten-up old leather jacket at least thirty years out of date which somehow conspired to look great on him. Fair, with floppy hair over long-lashed eyes and an equally long jaw, he needed a haircut and had a twinkle in his eye. Rogue, thought Penny immediately, cheering up.

'I was,' she said. ' But now I'm all yours.'

The man looked around the gallery. 'What are these pictures? They're all crap.'

Penny glanced down at her desk. Sure enough, there was his picture on the glossy folder that accompanied the exhibition; this was Will Brown, the artist.

'I know,' said Penny. 'We're kind of selling them for charity. I think it's for the mentally handicapped or something.'

The man stifled a rather shocked snort. 'That is a very strange thing to say,' he said, looking at her more closely. 'Where's Maud?'

'I wanted her job so I had her killed,' said Penny, wondering if this mode of flirting was going to work or not. She figured that this cute-looking artist probably had women coming on to him all the time so she should probably look to stand out.

'Well done,' said the artist, looking round. 'So are you selling much of this rubbish then?'

'We give them away, mostly,' said Penny. 'Sometimes we use them as wrapping paper for other paintings.'

The artist looked confused but slightly pleased, which Penny reckoned was probably the right way to go.

'I'm Will Brown,' he said finally, holding out his hand.

'Penny Berry,' she said, smiling and taking it. 'Would you like a painting?'

He looked even more confused.

'I . . . er, those are my paintings. Do you talk to everyone like that?'

Penny decided to let him off the hook sharpish before he had her fired. 'I know.' She gave him the benefit of her widest grin. 'We've sold loads. I think they're lovely.'

Will held her gaze a tiny second too long, then dropped his eyes. Bingo, thought Penny.

'You've got lipstick on your teeth,' said Will. Bugger, thought Penny.


Lizzie could feel herself beginning to sweat as she put her hand on the door to the café. Oh bugger. How could she have disgraced herself like that? She would love, love, love to blame it on Penny, but for once she couldn't quite see how. She sniffed. Was that pure alcohol coming out of her pores? Oh bugger. So as well as being a shiftless party girl and part-time slut, she smelled of booze in the mornings. Her new life was going just great. It took quite a lot of Lizzie's meagre supply of courage to push open the door at all.

'Uh, hello,' she said, staring at the floor and blushing furiously as usual.

Georges peered out from behind the counter where he was deftly flaying fish.

'Hello. Is that Paris Hilton?'

'I'm very sorry about last night,' said Lizzie in a rush.

'I am amazed you are here,' said Georges. 'How is your head?'

'Terrible. And I don't remember a thing,' she said quickly.

'Oh, well,' said Georges, still looking severe. 'You have nothing to apologise for then.'

Lizzie winced.

'Would you like a coffee?'

She nodded.

'That is too bad. You've got lots to do. Come on then, get started. There's the bread – I need you to make a start on the sandwiches, and slice up the new ham that is just delivered, and I'm making risotto so you need to grate the Parmesan.'

Phew, thought Lizzie. She'd got away with it.

'Oh,' said Georges, 'and you must please scrub the bottom side of the cooker.'

Lizzie nodded and resignedly pulled on an apron from behind the door.

In a way, the hard work was helpful; cathartic. She still felt sweaty, but she was getting so unbelievably dirty it didn't matter much anyway. She scrubbed the whole place down, washing up everything before she started on the food, trying to lay everything out in a good place to make it as easy as possible for Georges when the lunchtime rush came around.

At eleven Georges popped his head round into the little washing-up area. He looked carefully at everything, quite impressed, then nodded.

'Good job,' he said. 'You can have a coffee now.'

'Thanks,' said Lizzie huskily. 'Do you mind if I have a Diet Coke?'

He laughed. 'You are far gone. Do your joints hurt?'

She nodded.

'You have a proper English hangover.'

She followed him through as he tossed her a can from the fridge.

'So every day you will be like this, Lizzie?'

Lizzie shook her head. 'It was—'

'Your sister?'

Lizzie nodded, surprised.

'Very naughty sister. Do you blame everything on your sister?'

'It was her fault!' said Lizzie, conscious she sounded about eight years old.

'So do you have much experience in the art world?' asked Will, suspiciously looking into the terrible cup of coffee Penny had just made him.

'Yes,' said Penny. 'No,' she added quickly in case he suddenly decided to give her a quick quiz.

Will smiled. 'So Sloan didn't take you on for your amazing history of art degree?'

Penny shook her head.

'Your marketing and design experience?'

'Nope.'

'Your brilliant financial acumen?'

'Yes. It was that.'

'Not your lovely smile and friendly manner?'

'I was only pretending to be friendly at the interview,' said Penny. 'I'm slightly worried about that.'

'Do you think maybe your friendly skills need working

on?' said Will. 'Your coffee definitely needs improving.'

'I'm a highly sophisticated art dealer, not a tea dolly.'

'I forgot,' said Will. He scratched his ear. He hadn't met many girls like Penny before – her hairspray alone was nearly choking him – and he was quite scared. But, on the other hand, he thought she was pretty sexy too. Very sexy in fact. She looked like the kind of girl who might wear a thong.

Most of the girls Will met wore footless black leggings with gamine dresses over the top of them and headscarves and wanted to talk about Cartier Bresson and Sartre. Which he would, drearily, until he managed to get them into bed, where they would usually want to talk about what a spiritual experience they were having. Sometimes they'd cry. The girls he usually liked wore Chanel earrings and expensive shoes, but they tended to be trickier.

'So,' he said, mustering his best suave-artist manner. 'Those friendly skills of yours . . . do you think they'd like a tutorial over lunch?'

'I got hired so someone else could go to lunch,' said Penny, delighted. 'So, no.'

'See, you're failing the tutorial already. That's not a friendly response at all.'

'What happens if I fail? Do I get punished?' She smiled a tad suggestively.

'See, there, that's too friendly, spilling over into frightening.'

Penny smiled to herself.

'It's my first day. I'm just trying to stay out of trouble.'

Will looked at her.

'Honestly?' he said. 'You look like the epicentre of trouble.'

The lunch rush went past so quickly Lizzie nearly forgot to eat a meal herself. She'd already forgotten her morning

KitKat and prawn cocktail crisps. Oh well, she thought sadly at three o'clock, there was probably a coleslaw roll left over somewhere. She hadn't seen a KFC in Chelsea.

'Ta-dah!' said Georges, plonking a plate of risotto in front of her. 'I saved you some.'

Lizzie looked up at him gratefully.

'I thought we would not see you today but you did a good day's work.'

'This is delicious,' said Lizzie. 'I don't think I've ever had it before.'

Georges looked utterly shocked. 'You've never eaten risotto?'

She shrugged sadly.

'But what do you eat?'

'You know,' said Lizzie.

'I do not know,' said Georges.

'Well. Quick things mostly. Stuff you can microwave. Pizzas and things.'

'You can't microwave a pizza,' said Georges.

'You can, kind of,' said Lizzie, mumbling a bit.

'What else?' said Georges.

'Curry and things.'

'You microwave this curry too?'

Lizzie nodded. 'And lasagne.'

'Ah. The easiest thing to make. You can't make that in a microwave, can you?'

She nodded again. Georges looked absolutely aghast. He sat down beside her.

'Ooh, Lizzie, Lizzie.'

Lizzie was blushing furiously. She knew her eating habits were terrible. There never seemed any point in cooking as Penny didn't eat anything. So she'd grab something and heat it up. On the pictures on the packets they'd usually have a serving with something green or some lettuce next to it, but she never bothered with that. Her mum had always just brought home some stodge from school and heated it up, and they'd never progressed really. She kept telling herself she'd lose the weight when she was ready, when something happened that would be worth losing it for. So far, nothing had happened like that.

Not unkindly, Georges reached out and pinched a little of the wobbly flesh on her upper arms. Then he took her hand and placed it on his big belly. Lizzie flinched. She knew Mediterraneans were more touchy-feely than Brits, and she knew she was more uptight than most. This was the first time a man had touched her, she thought suddenly, in over a year, and that was a regrettable accident, after she'd run into Felix in Coasters. She hadn't been entirely sure he knew they'd broken up. Georges felt warm, and more solid than she expected. She felt her face turn scarlet.

'Now this,' said Georges. 'This tummy. You feel it?'

She nodded.

'This tummy is made from good chèvre, good goat's cheese, and calamar, and baklava, and tagliatelle with a wild boar sauce, and best chorizo, and potato cakes fried in the new oil, and good wine, yes? Every kilo of me is made from quality food and happy days and nights. So I am fat but I have many friends and much good food inside me. But Lizzie, you eat slop, yes? You heat up slop and eat it and taste nothing and watch television and this is not good, is it?'

Lizzie suddenly felt as if she was about to cry. She put down her fork.

'Thanks, Gillian McKeith,' she said.

'I do not know who this is,' said Georges. 'Come now, eat.'

'I don't feel like it.'

'Of course you do. This is good Parmesan and good rice and good squids and—'

'Squid?'

'Calamar. Squids. Yes, of course.'

'I'm eating a squid.' Lizzie peered at it. 'Isn't there supposed to be ink everywhere?'

'You've never eaten squids?'

Lizzie shook her head. 'It was on a menu when we were in Spain once and we thought they were joking. We thought it was a right laugh, like eating donkey or something.'

Georges looked pained. 'But you are eating it and finding it good, yes?'

Lizzie looked at her plate. 'Well, I suppose.'

Georges winked at her. 'You have a long way to go.'

'Is it time for my lunch now?' said Penny a tad sulkily, when Sloan rolled up at ten to five. He was clearly pissed as a fart and in a terribly relaxed mood.

'Of course, my dear girl . . . did you sell anything?'

Actually, Penny had. It was rather embarrassing. A poised young woman had come in with two large men and pointed to a frame. The men had taken it down and the woman, with barely a word to Penny, had left a card on her desk. Penny was hoping fervently this was a regular customer Sloan could send a bill to rather than a thief with a gimmick.

'Well *done*!' said Sloan overenthusiastically, spotting the card. 'You must have perfect sales lady skills. This is one of our very difficult to please people. Russian oligarchs, you know.' He said the last bit in a murmur, as if someone could overhear.

Penny emphatically did not know, but it sounded interesting. 'I had to talk her into it. Do I get a commission, by the way?'

Sloan snorted. 'No! You get to sit in my nice warm gallery out of the cold and read *Hello!* magazine and drink free tea. The fact that I'm paying you at all is a bonus when you think about it. Now, darling, shall we go for a little cocktail hour drinkiepoo?'

But Penny was already outlining her lips in the mirror. Having taken it off earlier, she had a shrewd suspicion that Will might rather like a slightly tarty look. Not that he'd admit it, of course.

'I've got a date,' she announced. 'You don't mind if I pull one of your artists, do you?'

Sloan looked slightly pained. 'I'd rather you pulled one of our big spenders. No chance of that, is there?'

Penny shrugged on her short jacket. 'Introduce me to a few of those Russian Olive Marks.'

Sloan raised a single eyebrow. 'I shall.' He steadied himself and focused on her for a minute. 'And go easy on that William now, won't you? He's a gentle soul.'

'We'll see about that,' said Penny. And she winked at her boss and hopped out into the crowded evening.

Lizzie looked around her on the bus. They'd been in London three days: it was time to pay her respects to the architect of their good fortune.

Barnet was as end-of-the-line as it was possible to go, endlessly long street after street of suburban houses. Their mother had sent the address, written on headed notepaper in a very theatrical handwriting full of loops and squiggles Lizzie had never seen before. But somewhere here, there was a nursing home. The good weather had not stayed; it was back to early spring drizzle. Conscious of not missing her stop, she squinted repeatedly at road signs and tried to follow her progress on the *A–Z*. She was on the very top page of the *A–Z*; she hoped they didn't make any sudden left turns or she was done for.

No, that must be it, the building at the top of the road. Lizzie rang the bell to get the bus to stop, hopping up nervously. She suffered from a conviction that if she got on a strange bus in a new place, the bus driver would attempt to trick her and drive her all the way to the depot.

'Uh, yes, stop here, please,' she barked.

There was no one else on the street as she stepped down, just rows and rows of houses and parked cars, televisions casting blue shadows from behind the curtains. Lizzie pulled herself together and headed up the tilt of the road to the large building at the end.

The Larches was a huge Victorian house with netted windows. On the brochure it was shot in bright sunlight with a lawnful of daffodils in front of it and it looked rather like a stately home where you might take tea in the garden. In the early evening gloom of a London March, however, it looked forbidding and chilly. The windows were lit, but with strip lighting, not lamps.

Approaching the front door she smelled the nasty institutional smell of boiled veg, and too much bleach swilled into too many corners, a smell masking a far nastier, occasionally whiffed undercurrent.

'Hello,' she said to the grumpy-looking fat nurse sitting behind a reception grille. The foyer was sparsely decorated, with large emergency exit signs, six different types of fire extinguishers and one grey chair with a defeated-looking pot plant next to it.

'I'm here to see Mrs Willis.'

She nervously fingered the lilies she'd bought, half expecting the nurse to tut that she couldn't come in without an appointment. The other half of her thought that the nurse might give her a radiant warm smile for being such a nice caring girl as to come out all this way to visit her mad old granny.

The nurse did neither of these things, simply nodded and pressed a buzzer. The glass door separating the foyer from the rest of the house clicked open.

'Uh, which room?' said Lizzie. The nurse looked up, completely confused, then started tapping at the computer.

'Four, eleven,' she said finally, annoyed to be caught out.

'Thanks,' said Lizzie. 'I'll try not to steal any old ladies while I'm up there.'

But the nurse didn't respond, and Lizzie went through the door alone.

To her left was a room wreathed in smoke, from which a television game show was blaring. Glancing in, Lizzie saw a roomful of old people, mostly in night clothes, staring straight ahead, not necessarily at the TV. It was like *Day of the Dead*. A shiver went down her spine and she rushed to the lift, which was big enough to get a bed in and out of. For all the dead people, she supposed, getting more and more creeped out as it ascended.

The room was down a winding corridor distorted by oddly shaped protuberances, like any old property adapted for a lot of extra plumbing it wasn't designed for. The door was tightly shut.

'Uh, hello?' said Lizzie, rapping her knuckles lightly against the wood. There was no answer. She gently pushed the door.

The old lady was lying on the bed with her eyes closed. She was tiny, a little bird-doll. Lizzie remembered her, from her brief visits in childhood, as being big; big and smelly. But she couldn't be, this tiny frail thing. Her hair was so thin Lizzie could see her white scalp.

The old lady opened her eyes and fixed them straight-away on Lizzie, who jumped. 'Who are you?' she said. Her voice was stronger than her appearance.

'Uh, I'm Lizzie,' said Lizzie. 'Your granddaughter.'

The woman craned her neck, staring at her for a long time, and let out a sigh. 'The little twin?' she demanded querulously before falling silent again. 'You're a bit of a chunky one, aren't you?' she said finally.

Lizzie let the door bang shut behind her. 'Actually,' said Lizzie, 'if I want to get insulted about my weight, I can easily do it at home.'

The old lady grunted and slowly pushed herself further up on the pillows. 'I'm not being insulting,' she said. 'I'd love a bit of weight on myself.'

'Exactly,' said Lizzie. 'Compared to you, Nicole Kidman looks like she should be cutting down on the pies.'

The lady beckoned her over. 'Who did you say you were again?'

'I'm Lizzie. Penny and me are staying in your house.'

A look of worry passed over the old lady's face. 'I want to go back to my house,' she said. 'Why are you in my house?'

'You told us to stay in your house. We're the twins, Gran. Gran.' She realised she'd never said the word out loud. 'You're our gran.'

'The little twins?'

Lizzie nodded.

'Someone's let the little twins run my house?'

'I'm one of the twins, Gran,' said Lizzie, starting to despair. 'Here. I brought you some flowers.'

The old lady looked less confused when she picked up the flowers. She buried her nose in them for a long time, breathing up their rich scent. Finally, when she looked up again, she seemed much clearer.

'They give me lots of drugs,' she said. 'I get mixed up.'

'I know,' said Lizzie. 'That's why you're here.'

'Why are you in my house?'

'You said we could stay in your house while you were in here.'

'Why would I let the little twins stay in my house . . . Oh. Because you're not little twins any more.'

'Would you like a glass of water?'

'Are you looking after my house?'

Lizzie nodded vehemently.

'They're terrible here, you know. They take the newspaper away as soon as you've read it.'

'That does sound terrible.'

'And they keep cleaning up after you.'

'Awful.'

The old woman looked around. 'I'm not happy without my things about me.'

She beckoned to Lizzie, who approached the bed. Her grandmother grabbed her wrist, holding on to it with surprising strength. 'Don't throw out any of my things,' she hissed loudly.

'I won't,' said Lizzie.

The old lady's eyes misted over. 'Oh, I miss Chelsea. This place is a foetid shit house. You should have been there during the war. All the bombs falling, but we still went out dancing all the time. Misbehaving, too. Not much time to be hanging about during a war. Not many men around either.'

'I'm not sure life's changed that much,' said Lizzie.

'Hmm.'

'How did you meet Grandfather?' asked Lizzie eagerly. She knew so little about this side of the family.

'Who?' said her grandmother. 'Sorry. Who are you again?'

'I'm one of the twins,' said Lizzie sadly.

'The little twins? The little twins are in my house?'

'So, apart from being bats?' said Penny. She was lying on the sofa painting her nails with a dreamy expression on her face.

'Nope, that was it, mostly. Apart from fessing up to being a bit of a slut in the forties. Then I read her *OK!* magazine for half an hour.'

Penny returned her attention to her nails.

'So, aren't you interested?' asked Lizzie.

'In what?'

'In whether Dad's been in.'

'Has he?'

'No.'

'Imagine not even going to see your old mum.'

'Prick,' said Lizzie absentmindedly, from years of habit. Her father not exactly cutting the mustard as a family man wasn't what you'd call news.

'So anyway, aren't you going to ask me how my day went?' said Penny, a smile creeping onto her lips.

'I ate a squid,' said Lizzie, cheering up momentarily. 'It was nice. Like a chewy fish finger.'

'Ugh,' said Penny. 'That sounds rank.'

'Well, it wasn't. It was nice.'

'Well, I suppose I'm going to have to be prepared to eat lots of exotic foreign food from now on,' said Penny, rolling over on the sofa and pushing out her nails to dry. 'Now I'm going out with an international artist and jet-setter.'

Lizzie sat down. She was starving, but this news was too good to wait.

'You're what?'

'Oh, you know. Dating the artistic aristocracy, that kind of thing.'

'No, I don't know. What kind of thing? Your last boyfriend owned fifteen lock-up garages. Spill.'

Penny had been feeling good walking into the bar, despite the night before. She was made up, and she'd backcombed her hair so it bouffanted up high on her head, and tugged down her shirt a little.

Once she entered the crowded noisy wine bar, however, she felt a bit different. The place was heaving with men in expensive-looking pin-striped suits and very polished shoes, and the women were tiny, frail almost, with flat, very straight, glossy blonde hair – more honey colour than the Barbie shade she favoured. These women's nails were done, but with short French manicures, not long fakes. And they all had perfectly shaped, but quite full, eyebrows. Penny had been drawing on her eyebrows since she was fifteen.

She suddenly felt out of place, and wondered if it was safe to tug her skirt down. It had been all right last night when everyone was dressed to impress, but here the women were in cashmere overcoats and cream shift dresses. Always fascinated by money, to Penny this was a new breed altogether.

A few of the men started ogling her as she walked in on her three-inch heels. Normally confident, she almost stumbled as one of them leered at her. She remembered suddenly the extra layer of lipliner she'd put on to wind up Will. None of the women here were wearing lipliner like that. She looked towards the bar, where the barman lifted an eyebrow. Shit.

From the corner Will watched the whole scene, feeling for her. Here she was, the little rich girl up in the proper city for the first time. What presumably ruled the suburban footballers' nightclubs and tanning salons wasn't working here at all. He went from imagining her as hard as nails to seeing the vulnerability in her and, somehow, he found it an incredibly attractive mix.

'Over here.' He waved confidently. He stood up. 'You look wonderful,' he said loudly. Some people next to him rolled their eyes and stared at him rudely.

'This is a nice place,' said Penny, as Will brought back her vodka and tonic. Penny had wanted a Bacardi Breezer, but had forced down the impulse.

'Come here a lot?' said Will, amused.

'Oh, yes, all the time. I think their vodka and tonics are just to die for,' said Penny, wondering how Brooke and Minty got that kind of flick in their voices when they said 'to die for'.

'So. Tell me about you,' said Will.

Penny had been dreading this.

'Well, I live in Chelsea and I work in an art gallery. For fun, you know?' she added hastily.

'But of course,' said Will. 'Where were you born?'

'Chelsea,' said Penny quickly. 'Lived here all my life.'

'Right.'

Must be one of those self-made daughter types, thought Will. Cardboard-making dad gets lucky, that kind of thing. Probably a daughter of the much more attractive second wife. That accent was weird though. You'd think school would have rubbed it off a bit.

'Where did you go to school?'

'Are you investigating me on behalf of MI6?'

'No,' said Will, smiling. 'Sorry. Just making conversation.'

Penny took a swig of her drink.

'I didn't go to school. I had, you know, a governess, nanny-type thing.' Penny hoped they still existed. 'She came from Chelmsford.'

Will nodded. That explained the accent then. 'You're lucky,' he said. 'I hated school.'

'Were they always beating you up and calling you gay and that because you liked art?'

Will frowned. 'Um, no. I was head of the art club actually. Used to organise gallery tours and stuff.'

'Ooh, head of the art club. Ooooh,' said Penny sarcastically, unable to help herself, until she remembered she wasn't meant to have been to school at all and thus would have no view.

'That sounds really interesting,' she added quickly. 'Sometimes I feel I missed out, I really do.'

Will smiled. 'I'm not sure about that. Another drink?'

Penny realised hers was finished while Will was only half way through his. Whoops. She must try to remember to be ladylike in a Chelsea manner, not swig like someone who might later on misbehave with a wine bottle on national television. She looked at his long lean back as he went to the bar. Nice. She just had to get him to stop talking about schools before she got herself found out completely. Anything about the local turf in fact was probably best avoided.

'So tell me about your paintings.'

The amazing thing, as Penny explained to Lizzie later, was that it wasn't dead boring at all. 'Most blokes, right,' she explained to Lizzie as if Lizzie had never had a date before, 'most blokes, you ask them about their job, and they can bore the crap out of you for ages. And they'll start talking about some bloke that you don't know who's their boss and who's a complete prick for some reason, and they'll go on and on about them, and who really knows best and how they showed them and how if they weren't in an office they'd give them an arse-kicking they'd never forget.'

Lizzie nodded.

'And you just have to listen and nod and go, like, "Wow, you're really brave" and "What a bastard".'

'They must see right through that though,' said Lizzie.

'You'd think,' said Penny. '*Anyway*, the thing is, when Will was talking about his pictures, it wasn't boring at all. He was interesting. And he didn't hate his boss because he didn't even have a boss. He just did what he liked.'

She lapsed into a reverie again. Lizzie looked at her sharply. This wasn't like her sister. Usually Penny wanted a credit check and a cost/benefit analysis.

'So has he got tons of money, then?' asked Lizzie.

'Well, he must have, mustn't he?' said Penny. 'He's an artist and he went to nob school. But we didn't really talk about money.'

This was a first.

'We just talked about the countryside and our lives and pictures and things. It was lovely.'

Penny threw back her head and cackled heartily at a well-timed crack Will made about Sloan. At the table next to them, very well-dressed people who looked on their way out to a stultifyingly boring dinner, tutted to themselves and one of the women rolled her eyes. Will made up his mind.

'Come on,' he said. 'Let's get out of here.'

'Uh, where?' said Penny. She'd been having a good time – a surprisingly good time – sitting here with Will. She hadn't had to feign interest or anything, and he seemed genuinely interested in talking to her rather than, for example, talking about how much money he was making and how powerful and respected he was at work whilst simultaneously trying to fondle her kneecaps.

'It's a surprise,' said Will. Penny's super-thin eyebrows twitched. Surprise? What did he mean? She thought longingly of *The Thomas Crown Affair*. Maybe he was going to whip her into his helicopter and they were going to go to the Bahamas for a drink. She smiled happily.

'OK!'

But when they were outside he didn't immediately summon a chauffeur or nod her over to the back of a big shiny motorbike. Instead, he led her down a maze of back lanes towards the Embankment.

'Is this where you live?' she asked curiously. Will sounded like he was suppressing a giggle. 'Uh, no. I live in east London. Where the artists live,' he said, seeing her enquiring look. 'Round Hoxton.'

'Oh,' said Penny. 'So where are we going then?'

'Are you always this impatient?'

'Yes,' said Penny. 'I've found it speeds things up.'

'What things?' asked Will.

'Important things,' said Penny. 'Getting served in bars, getting the best of the sale bargains.'

'Ah. Important things,' said Will. 'You're a very urban creature, aren't you?'

'A what?'

'A city girl.'

'Yeah. Compared to what, cows?'

'A bit of natural beauty.'

'I don't see what's so brilliant about natural beauty,' said Penny, critically checking out her nails as she clopped along in her high shoes, trying to keep up with Will. 'I think it's overrated.'

'Can you climb in those shoes?'

Will had come to a full stop in front of a high, pink, brick wall that stretched on for a long way.

'I can do anything in these shoes.'

'Excellent. Hup! It's a soft landing.'

And with that, Will, half pushed, half lifted her up onto the top of the wall.

'Wh-aa!' screeched Penny.

'Shh,' said Will. 'Just jump. Trust me.'

'Trust you? I just met you . . . ahhh.'

Penny found herself on the top of a large compost heap, the setting sun reflected in her eyes from the river. She looked around, completely confused and shocked, until, with a scrabbling noise, Will made it up and over the wall, and bounced down past her.

'Come on,' he said, holding out a hand.

'What the hell are we doing?'

'Just . . . just get down, then you'll see.'

Penny worried about her ruined shoes as she tentatively clambered down the hill of manure.

'What the hell . . . '

'Shh,' said Will. 'I bet you've never been here at this time of day, have you?'

'I've never been here at all. Where the hell are we?'

Will looked at her, confused. 'This is the Chelsea Physic Garden.'

'Oh, yeah,' said Penny rapidly, trying to cover her mistake. 'Course it is. I've never been here though.'

'Why not?'

'Uh, my sister . . . gets hay fever and that.'

'Oh. Well . . . '

Penny looked around, and gasped. She was in a huge, beautiful garden. The trees were in full blossom, and the evening sun caught their delicate petals as they shimmered to the soft green grass. There wasn't another soul there.

'Oh my God,' she said. Will looked at her undeniable delight and grinned.

'I can't believe you've never been here. Come on, let me

show you around. I've spent hours drawing the botanics.'

Penny didn't know what he meant, but she followed him anyway as he motioned her down the wide gravel path.

'That's when I found out about the manure thing,' he said. 'Not very romantic, I know.'

'It's not bad,' said Penny, looking at the long rows of perfectly labelled plants and flowers. It was extraordinarily beautiful.

'They used to train doctors here,' said Will. 'That's why it's called the Physic Garden.'

'So do you bring all your girls here?'

'No,' said Will. 'I come here a lot on my own. I prefer it when there's nobody else here at all, just me. But I thought . . . I thought you might like it.'

She smiled at him, and he thought again how gorgeous she was.

'Come on,' he said. 'Let's go look at the cornflowers.'

'Why?'

'I don't know. I just like them.'

Will had liberated a bottle of wine from the wine bar and, with the aid of his palette knife, they eventually got it open and, as the sky darkened into a deep blue, they sat, then lay down, on the grass by the cornflowers, talking about – well, almost everything, thought Penny later. She told him about her sister and her mum. But perhaps she had implied that the family was wealthier than it was – he did ask lots of questions about them, and, emboldened by the attention, she had embroidered them so far that they had spent too many summers in France and winters in the Caribbean to have ever heard of the Physic Garden, and she was only working for the fun of it.

But he laughed when she told him about the restaurant (contracting eight years to a week), and she laughed when he told her about his terrible school, and by the time he reached over to kiss her gently in the deserted garden, she realised she'd forgotten even to find out how many paintings he sold and what kind of car he drove, and even more weirdly, she didn't even care. When he walked her to the door of the flat (at which point she panicked about asking him in and having her cover blown completely), he merely told her he loved her street, kissed her again – rather spectacularly this time – took her number and walked off down the road.

'*And* he paid for all the drinks?' said Lizzie, lost in admiration.

'Well, duh,' said Penny. She examined her newly perfect nails, no longer bright cerise, but a delicate shell pink. A smile kept tugging away at her mouth. 'He's minted, isn't he? He's an artist, with stuff in a gallery and that.'

'So there's just one question left,' said Lizzie, looking at the microwave lasagne she'd taken out of the freezer and, for some reason, not feeling like it just at the moment. 'Why are you here and not in his swish flat, knobbing his brains out?'

Penny blew on her nails and a most uncharacteristically shy smile crept across her face. 'Oh, Lizzie,' she said. 'Us Chelsea girls, we just don't behave like that.'

# Chapter Six

'Let me see you,' Georges commanded Lizzie the second she walked in. She jumped a little, flustered, as he stared at her. Just like yesterday, his Mediterranean sense of personal space meant he crept in closer than she was used to.

'What?' she demanded.

'I want to look into your eyes.'

Lizzie couldn't help it: her heart fluttered. Oh, for goodness' sake. What a daft pushover she was. She'd probably be like this if a traffic warden said something nice to her. Had anyone ever been more susceptible to a bit of male attention?

'Why?' she said, conscious of her pulse speeding up.

Georges crouched down gravely. His huge arms against his legs were like hocks of ham.

'They're clear,' he said, with some surprise. 'Yesterday they were red like tiny tomato pips.'

Lizzie backed away. 'Well, that's because I didn't go out clubbing last night. In fact I never go out clubbing. That was a complete aberration.'

Georges nodded.

'In fact, I was visiting my sick grandmother.'

Georges let out a guffaw.

'Ah, Lizzie, so close was I to believing you!'

'It's true!' maintained Lizzie. 'I promise!'

'Could you start on the peppers and mushroom? I'm planning something good with chickenses.'

'Chickens,' said Lizzie.

'And I don't want to tire you out too much for tonight, when you have to go and tend orphans.'

'Shh.'

'Or for tomorrow, when you have to go and put bandages on the feet of small slightly wounded ducks.'

Lizzie picked up her knife and set to work.

Three hours later the café was a smoothly running machine of organised chaos, full of contented-looking punters, and Georges was wiping sweat off his brow as Lizzie's phone rang. It was Penny.

'I just got into work,' she squeaked.

'Glad to hear it,' said Lizzie, wiping some sweat off her forehead too.

'Two wonderful things have happened!'

'Only two?' said Lizzie crossly. She could almost hear Penny smiling down the line.

'So, first thing this morning I run into Brooke in the hallway . . .'

'First thing, eh?'

'Well, ten-ish, you know.'

'Mmm hmm.'

'And she says,' at this point, Penny attempted to launch into an imitation of Brooke's amused drawl, not entirely successfully, '"Darling, we're having a little party on Saturday night – do join us!"'

'Why are you putting on a Welsh accent?' said Lizzie.

'So, we're going to be really good friends now.'

'Well, that's great,' said Lizzie. 'You can tell me all about it when you get back. Or maybe I'll just lie on the carpet with a glass to my ear.'

'Oh, you're invited, you idiot.'

'Really?' said Lizzie, annoyed to feel her heart leaping, despite herself.

'Well, I asked her how she defined "little" and she said, "Oh, darling, bring everyone you know."'

'I suppose the fact that she didn't then say, "Except for your chunky sister" means I should take that as her begging me to attend,' said Lizzie.

'Don't be so chippy,' said Penny. 'I think they're really nice and good fun.'

'I think they're evil and quite frightening,' said Lizzie. 'But I'm willing to be a bit more open-minded about women with scary gaps between the tops of their legs, and white jeans.'

'Fabulous,' said Penny. 'We'll find you a lovely Chelsea boy yet. Yes, Sloan, ten-thirty *is* time for a cocktail. Everyone knows that.'

Lizzie rolled her eyes. 'What was the other wonderful thing?'

'No, I don't want one, thanks. I don't know what pre-prandial means.'

'Penny?'

'What does pre-prandial mean?'

'I have no clue. Pregnant?'

'OK, got to go.'

'What was the other thing?'

Lizzie could hear Sloan squawk over the top of the telephone. 'Could you move these bloody flowers, darling? They're giving me hay fever. It's like Kew fucking Gardens in here. Who sends cornflowers anyway?'

'I think I'm seeing Will again,' said Penny, with a little glow to her voice. 'I think I might ask him to the party.'

Parties made Lizzie anxious, possibly even more anxious than nightclubs. At least in nightclubs there was usually a dark corner to hide in. And if you hid in the toilets in a nightclub nobody tried to bang the door down and accuse you of ruining everyone's evening.

And a posh party. What was that going to be like? Maybe they'd have little cucumber sandwiches with the crusts cut off. Lizzie groaned to herself. And now Penny was going to fall madly in love with some gorgeous rich artist and they'd spend all evening cooing and being all cuddly-wuddly in the corner. And they'd get married and buy their grandmother's flat and live in Chelsea and raise lovely posh Chelsea babies and she'd have to go back to Essex and look after their mother. She heaved a great sigh.

Georges popped his head round the door.

'What's the matter with you? Are you worrying about all those koala bears you are going to save in Bosnia?'

'No,' said Lizzie.

'You look tragic.'

'I have to go to a party.'

'That is tragic. That is the saddest thing I have ever heard. Watch as I start crying immediately – boohoo, boohoo. When is this party? Is it tonight? Will you need someone to pick you up and carry you home?'

'No,' said Lizzie. 'It's Saturday. And it's just downstairs from my grandmother's . . . I mean, my flat.'

'So why don't you want to go?'

'Because I won't know anyone and my sister will have her new boyfriend.'

Georges squared himself round.

'It's OK,' he announced gravely. 'I shall escort you to this party. No funny stuff. Just for friendliness. I am a very friendly person. I shall make some friends for you then I shall go.'

Lizzie almost giggled. She could just see big fat foreign Georges walking into that immaculate snooty sitting room. Her and Georges, the gruesome twosome. They'd be the cabaret.

'No, it's OK,' she said. 'I'm sure I'll be fine.'

'But I don't mind!' said Georges.

'Really, it's all right,' said Lizzie.

Georges turned back to his chickenses and started chopping them up with unnecessary force.

'So, I feed you, employ you, save you from falling in the gutter, yes, but you are ashamed of me? I am, what, too fat to go to a party with you?'

'No!' said Lizzie plaintively.

'You are prejudiced, yes? Against foreign people?'

'I would love you to come,' said Lizzie, as more hungry customers started to march through the door.

'Hey.' Penny had been uncharacteristically nervous about calling Will to thank him for the flowers and ask him to the party. Normally she didn't give a damn. But normally they weren't quite as handsome as Will.

'Hey yourself,' he said, smiling. 'Would it sound cheesy if I told you I was drawing cornflowers?'

'It would sound a lot less cheesy if you were drawing me amongst them.'

'Uh, would it?' said Will.

'Oh yeah. Umm, I called to ask you something.'

'Good. I like things. Ask away.'

'Would you like to come to a party with me?'

'I would like to do anything with you.'

'Really? I have a dental appointment next week.'

'I'll hold the spitbowl.'

'I don't really.' Penny hadn't been to the dentist since school. She'd been lucky. So far.

'So, do you have a real party or was it just an excuse to phone me?'

'Yes. There's a party.'

'Double date!' Penny was smugly doing her make-up in the bathroom mirror.

'It's not a double date,' said Lizzie. 'It's more . . . he's kind of escorting me. In case you and whatshisname want to sit in a corner all night playing suck face.'

'I would never behave like that,' said Penny.

'You strip in public for a bottle of champagne.'

'Don't mention that.' Penny flicked a perfect line of black eyeliner to the very corner of her eyes.

'Don't mention it? Isn't that why Brooke's invited you? Because you're the amazing naked party girl from upstairs? I think you're the professional entertainment.'

Penny put down the liner pen. 'Well, that doesn't matter, does it? They're not going to get it, and I am going to get a lovely boyfriend whom I actually like for a change, so butt out, would you? You bloody hate seeing me happy.'

'That's not true,' said Lizzie, wondering about it. She'd occasionally like her to be a little less troublesome, that was all, surely.

'Well don't ruin it for me,' pouted Penny. 'Oh, I forgot,

you did already, you're bringing Ape Face.'

'Don't call him Ape Face,' said Lizzie. 'It's just five o'clock shadow.'

'Chins and chins of it.'

'Anyway, maybe everyone will think he's a shipping magnate or something.'

Penny raised her eyebrows. 'A shipping magnate that smells of cooking oil? Let's have a drink.'

Lizzie obediently fetched two Bacardi Breezers out of the fridge.

'Where are you meeting him?' Lizzie asked.

'Down there,' said Penny, looking around. 'I don't know, I'm just not sure he'd enjoy the taxidermy collection.'

'I'm sure that's a rat,' said Lizzie, looking unhappily at the small furry stuffed animal in the corner. 'But why would anyone stuff a rat? It doesn't make sense.'

'Plus, he thinks I'm rich,' said Penny. 'He might not get too involved if he knew the truth.'

It was nine before the girls felt they'd heard enough doorbells and screamed greetings to feel they could risk heading downstairs. Penny looked slightly odd. She'd shrugged off her Jordan-style micro mini, and stuck to a fuchsia pink minidress she'd worn as the winner of Butlins lovely legs competition five summers ago. But to make it look not too tarty she was wearing jeans under it, with stiletto shoes. Lizzie could see what she was aiming for, but she wasn't entirely sure she'd succeeded. This wasn't like Penny. Parties were her life blood. Which could only mean one thing – who *was* this chap? Despite herself, and the Bacardi Breezer for Dutch courage, she even felt a little nervous herself.

She was in her black cross-over top that Trinny and

Susannah decreed was the right way to go if you had 'wonderful big handfuls of cleavage', which she knew actually meant 'are a big fat pig'. She was equally doubtful about the cheap bottle of rosé they'd bought, but who'd notice?

'Just chill, OK? It'll be fine.'

'I know,' said Penny irritably. Then she softened. 'Do you really think so?'

Lizzie nodded. 'You're irresistible.'

Lizzie's buzz disintegrated the moment they pushed open the large heavy door into the noisy thronged apartment. Two gorgeous specimens were chatting each other up in the doorway, and looked absolutely insulted to be interrupted just because some people wanted to walk through the door. The huge sitting room was full of tall, attractive, confident people, sipping drinks and laughing loudly. Lizzie suddenly felt as dumpy as a wombat in a deep submarine.

Penny swallowed loudly and tilted her head up.

'Right,' she said, and marched straight ahead. There was, amazingly, a small woman there holding a tray with glasses of champagne on it. Lizzie stared at her. She didn't know people actually did this outside of *Sex and the City*. Penny immediately swept up two as if this was the most natural thing in the world, and handed one to Lizzie, before she took off into the throng. Not having the faintest clue what to do, Lizzie rather apologetically followed her.

'Brooke!' said Penny, marching up to her. Brooke's hair shone in a long tawny mane. Her backless top showed off her flawlessly even tan. She had the cutest, most petite nose Lizzie had seen.

'Hello!' said Brooke, looking slightly surprised as Penny launched over to kiss her on both cheeks. She stood back from the two tall men she'd been whispering to.

116

'Sven... Rob... this is my upstairs neighbour I was telling you about...'

The boys' eyes widened.

'Well, hello there,' said Rob, the darker of the two. 'Hey, you've forgotten to take your jeans off.'

'Maybe later, eh, Penny?' said Brooke. 'She is *such* a party girl.'

'Excellent,' said Sven. 'Another glass of champagne?'

'No thanks,' said Penny. 'Actually, my boyfriend's coming. He's an artist.'

'Really?' said Brooke.

'I'm your boyfriend?' came a voice behind her.

Penny whipped round. Oh, bollocks, she'd messed that up fast. There stood Will, in that same beaten-up leather coat, looking absolutely gorgeous.

'Will!' screamed Brooke. 'My darling! How *are* you?'

'Hey, Brooke,' said Will, suddenly looking a tad uncomfortable.

'Oh. You all know each other,' said Penny, feeling her face flush.

'Well, of course... Will here was up to all sorts of naughty business with Minty last year, weren't you?'

Will flushed too. And suddenly Minty was standing beside them, looking stiff and annoyed.

'Hello, Will,' she said, in an elaborately casual tone. 'Fancy seeing you here at *my* party.'

'I didn't realise it was your party,' said Will.

'You just hate missing a Chelsea party, right?' Minty's face was tight.

'Uh, yeah, right,' said Will, staring furiously at the floor. Penny looked at him, momentarily discomfited.

'Have a cocktail!' squealed Brooke. 'They're wicked!'

Everyone immediately grabbed a glass from the passing

117

tray and slugged it as quickly as possible. Penny slunk her way out of the group, making it extremely obvious she thought Will should follow her.

'Do you know her?' she hissed, from the corner.

Will shrugged. 'Hardly.'

'Look,' said Penny. 'When I said boyfriend just then—'

'You didn't mean me? You meant your six-foot marine boy who's on his way over to smash my brains out?'

'No,' said Penny. 'I just didn't want those guys . . . you know.'

'To hit on you? Quite right too. You look luscious.' Will glanced at Brooke and Minty. 'Look, do you want to get out of here?'

Penny looked around. The room was really full now, with girls laughing hysterically, men in Pink shirts, waiters balancing full trays of champagne; while the cigarette smoke and expensive perfume made the place seem hazy and slightly hyper-real. She wanted to stay, to become the life and soul, to be standing next to Brooke, throwing back her head and laughing at the nice, charming people who wanted to be her friend. In one room . . . here . . . this was the life she was after.

'Can't we stay for a little while?' she asked. 'I've just got here.'

'But they're all idiots,' said Will.

'How do you know? Have you been out with all of them?' asked Penny. 'Is there a terrifying revelation about your past at every step?'

'Maybe,' said Will, softening a little and taking a sip of his extremely strong drink. 'Why don't you ask your boyfriend, Andy McNab?'

'Who?'

*

On the other side of the room, Lizzie felt herself sinking in quicksand. She had, nominally, ended up as part of the group that included the two tall boys, Rob and Sven, but they were patently talking over her head as if she wasn't there. Worse, they were speculating on the qualities of the other females present, as if she was a dog or something.

'What about that one over there?' said Rob, pointing out a supermodelesque Russian-looking girl with legs as thin as pins.

'Fat arse, wouldn't you think?' said Sven.

Woof, thought Lizzie sadly.

'Do you know who I'd like a crack at? Saw her at Ascot.'

'Who?'

'Elle Macpherson.'

'Ooh yes. Ding dong.'

Lizzie made a quiet cough.

'Are you wearing a smock?' said Sven suddenly, in a rude way Lizzie hadn't encountered since the school bus. 'Are you a lesbian?'

'Yes,' said Lizzie, tongue-tied and short of something to say. Immediately she realised her mistake.

'Are you?' said Rob, looking at her for the first time. 'Cool. Do you, like, snog women and feel their knockers and stuff?'

'Yes,' said Lizzie, feeling herself sinking into a deep hole with no clear way of escaping. 'Obviously.'

Sven looked fascinated too.

'Very naughty,' he said in an approving tone of voice. 'What else do you do?'

'Oh, mostly we go to wholefood shops, that kind of thing,' said Lizzie, looking around desperately for an exit.

'No, in the bedroom.'

Well, this had backfired badly; now two strange chaps

119

wanted her to talk dirty to them. Why couldn't she just get over her shyness and be herself with people?

'Sorry,' said Lizzie. 'I have to go over there to chat up a girl.'

'Can we watch?' said Rob.

Looking at Will, Penny realised how much she wanted to kiss him. Not marry him, or take him for a ride, or shag him – yet – or get him to take her out to dinner, or show off to Dwaneesa about who she'd managed to pull, or even tell Lizzie about it, which was usually half the fun. She wanted to kiss him, for hours and hours on a park bench, like they were teenagers.

'Why are you looking at me like that?' said Will. 'You look like a wolf licking its chops.'

'No I don't,' said Penny, hastily finishing her cocktail.

'So your place is just like this then?' he said.

'Yeah, it's the one above. Exactly like this,' said Penny, looking at the gleaming modernist chandeliers, huge paintings, expensive mirroring and halogen lighting. 'Just like this.'

'Maybe you could show me round sometime,' said Will, and Penny cursed herself for falling into the trap.

'Cheeky!' she yelled, in a tone that came out much louder and brasher than she'd intended.

'Uh, sorry, I didn't mean it like that,' said Will, backtracking desperately, as Penny hurriedly pulled another couple of cocktails off the tray. Free drink; who knew when it was going to run out?

'That's OK,' said Penny, her mind working furiously. Well, she'd just have to pretend to be very, very pure and make sure he never got back there. Plus, he must have some really funky pad in Hoxton, surely. Somewhere really cool, a big loft with all-white walls and huge blown-up photographs on his wall and polished floors and sunny spots for the cat to lie in.

'What's your place like?'

'It's all right, you know,' said Will, and he gave that self-deprecating grin that made her insides go all wobbly.

Minty came up to them, her legs looking like a baby giraffe's on long spindly heels.

'Will,' she said, in a voice that she obviously thought sounded calm. 'Could I . . . could I have a word with you, please?'

'Uh, no, he can't,' said Penny immediately. Her hackles rose. She wasn't going to have this anorectic cow smelling of Diorissimo and gin slobbering all over him.

'What's the matter, Minty?' said Will, looking concerned.

'It's private,' said Minty, glaring at Penny with a barely hidden snarl in her voice.

'Well, I can't really . . .'

'It's very important. It will take only five minutes. I think you owe it to me, Will.'

Minty was looking really tragic now.

'Well, if she's *begging* you,' said Penny nastily. She was giving Minty major evils, but she was clearly not a girl new to this. Minty immediately began examining a nail and looking coyly up at Will as if Penny had vanished into thin air.

'OK,' said Will. 'Five minutes.' He turned to Penny. 'Then we really should go somewhere that isn't full of people taking coke, vomiting up canapés and telling each other how expensive their hairdressers are.'

'Fine,' said Penny, only just resisting the urge to stick her tongue out at Minty. Not that it would have mattered, as Minty had immediately grabbed Will's arm and was leading him somewhere Penny suspected was the bedroom. Penny checked her watch. Well, they really *were* getting five minutes, then she was going in. There were some circumstances where subtlety would get you nowhere, and this was definitely one of them.

'Aha,' said Rob, appearing to her right with a fresh cocktail. 'There you are. We've just met the most *extraordinary* midget lesbian.'

This was more like it, Penny couldn't help thinking. Now there were chaps around, who'd attracted more girls, and there was a big group around them and she was quaffing the absolutely delicious cocktails and having a hilarious time, telling stories about other nightclubs she'd been to and the third-division footballers she'd met – everyone seemed so impressed – and her fight with Krystanza and how you could see her fingernails in the paper. The boys in particular were laughing heartily and refilling her glass. Will was nowhere to be seen, but that didn't matter because as soon as he came out he'd see how popular and pretty she was and be incredibly impressed and realise that she was a Chelsea girl; it was completely obvious that she couldn't fit in any more.

She'd forgotten about Lizzie completely.

Lizzie was trapped in a corner. She'd gone to the toilet as usual, to give her something to do, and heard lots of whisperings following her, along the lines of 'the new lesbian in the building'. When she emerged, an enormous woman wearing a purple hat and huge, flowing robes was blocking the landing.

'DARLING,' she said, swooping down and giving Lizzie an enormous kiss that reeked of Poison. 'I hear we must welcome you to Chelsea!'

'Well, that's nice,' said Lizzie, but her voice was muffled as she was still under the woman's armpit, jammed next to her vast bosom.

'Always lovely to get a bit more LOCAL COLOUR,' the woman boomed, then held Lizzie at arm's length – which meant Lizzie still had her head in her breast – and examined her. 'Well, better than nothing, I suppose,' she said. 'Now, sister, tell me. Did you know? Sylvia Plath used to live just around THE CORNER?'

'I did not know that,' said Lizzie, looking around desperately for her drink.

'Terrible story. Spent her life with a man, you see. Could have sorted it out MUCH BETTER, don't you THINK?'

There was no way past this lady. She was the only person at the party wider than Lizzie was.

'Here,' said the woman. 'Try this. I brew my OWN WINE.'

Lizzie gave up and sank down slowly on to the chaise longue.

Penny couldn't quite focus on who she was in the bathroom with. That was confusing enough in itself. Also, the bathroom was massive, clean, white and airy, with candles flickering along the window ledge and a claw-foot bath lined with Jo Malone smellies.

'This one bathroom,' she pronounced with some difficulty, 'ish nicer than my entire house. Was. I mean, a house. In a dream I had.'

'Never mind that,' said the man, a rather foxy-faced character who had slipped into the group as Penny had been loudly debating whether or not to take her jeans off underneath her minidress, and the boys were voting vehemently in favour. 'Here, try this.'

Penny lurched around. The man had wracked out two lines of white powder on the toilet cistern.

She'd seen it around, of course, but had never had the cash to indulge; nor the desire, come to that. They usually ran to a few cheeky Vimtos, the odd spliff and the occasional E at holiday times. But a different life . . . different tastes.

The man proffered a rolled-up twenty-pound note. In for a penny . . .

Lizzie realised she'd just agreed to apply for a shared allotment when she saw Penny reel out of the bathroom. Her eyes were wild, her pupils huge.

'Lizzie! Lizzie! My darling Lizzie,' she squealed. 'Oh, I must tell you, I think you look absolutely fabulous. And I think isn't this just the most amazing party? It's just amazing, I'm having such a fantastic time and . . . do you like this lipstick? What do you think, I wasn't sure, but . . .'

'Stop chewing your lips for a second and I'll try and tell you,' said Lizzie, annoyed.

'Ooh,' said the woman, whose name was Beulah. 'Is this your other half?'

'My sister,' said Lizzie.

'Whoo,' said Sven, passing through on his way to the champagne bin. 'Sisters!'

'Why don't we go now?' said Lizzie, ignoring them.

'Don't be ridiculous,' said Penny. 'I've just started to have a great, really brilliant time. I need a drink. And a cigarette.'

'You don't smoke.'

'And my bloody boyfriend. Where's my boyfriend?'

'Who?'

'You know. Will.'

'Are you sure he's your boyfriend? You don't seem to be spending lots of cosy nights in together.'

'Well, I'm just going to find him right now. He better not be cheating on me.'

'Your serious long-term boyfriend, whom you've known for all of ten minutes? Penny, no. Don't. Let's go home, you're a mess.'

Penny had discarded her jeans now, and her minidress was far too high in the leg and low in the breast for the tottering stilettos she was wearing, particularly coupled with her crazed stare and slowly meandering mascara.

'Please, Penny. Come home,' said Lizzie, begging.

'Shut up,' said Penny, tottering over. The foxy-faced man came up behind her. 'Looking good,' he said, cupping her bottom quite openly.

'Yeah, going to give us a strip?' shouted Sven.

'*Penny*,' yelled Lizzie in exasperation. 'No more stripping!'

But Penny stepped away, letting the horrible foxy man keep on groping her, and did 'ta-dah' hands. Lizzie looked around desperately for Will. If he saw this, he'd be out the door faster than a greased otter, and her poor sister would be mortified.

'I'm having fun,' said Penny. 'Will's fucked off, hasn't he? He's back there copping off with his old girlfriend, isn't he? No nice blokes for me.' She gyrated to the music playing. 'But that's OK, because I feel just fine.'

Lizzie watched her in horror as she stretched up to undo her dress top. Over on the sofa Brooke was sitting watching complacently, with a cream-licking smile on her face.

Suddenly the doorway was blocked by a large, bear-like figure. Lizzie glanced over in desperation.

'What is this?' came the accented voice. 'This is a kind of seedy party, is it?'

Penny turned round and focused unsteadily.

'Ah,' said Georges. 'The famous Lizzie's sister. You are cold, yes?'

And just as she let her hands – and the top of her dress – fall to her waist, Georges whipped off his coat and pulled it around her shoulders.

'Much warmer now.'

The boys started to boo, until Georges silenced them with a lift of one of his heavy brows.

'You live upstairs?' he said to Lizzie. 'Shall we go there?'

'I'm not going home!' said Penny, struggling with the coat. 'I have to show Will what a good time I'm having when he doesn't give a toss.'

'No, we will go home,' said Georges. Lizzie looked at him, and felt a little thrill in her stomach.

'Yes, Penny,' said Lizzie. 'Let's go home.'

'While Will is fucking some fucking slut in the back bedroom?' said Penny. The room fell silent.

'While I'm doing what now?' said Will, leaning against the wall. Minty slipped out behind him, looking sulky and petulant.

Penny's face crashed. This wasn't how it was meant to be at all. This wasn't her lovely party. Now everyone was looking at her like she was making a fool of herself. She stared at Will's gentle face one more time.

'Come on,' said Lizzie. 'Let's just go.'

And for once, Penny knew when she was beaten.

'Don't bring your girlfriend to our allotment,' yelled Beulah. The three of them left the party in silence.

Upstairs, Georges looked aghast at the apartment, as Lizzie moved a collection of broken dog figurines off a broken chair and set about making tea.

'This is your home?' he asked incredulously. Looking round, Lizzie realised how quickly she'd got used to it.

'It's not really,' she said. 'It's our grandmother's. She would go crazy if we moved or touched anything.'

She noticed Georges looking askance at an enormous open tea chest filled to the brim with macramé owls.

'Crazier.'

She put the kettle on for tea. Penny was sitting glumly at the table, completely deflated and most of the way through a pint of water.

'My head hurts,' she said.

'Don't take drugs,' said Georges.

'It was an accident,' said Penny. 'My nose fell on them.'

Georges shook his head. 'You girls are a real teapot of fish.'

Lizzie nodded, just as the doorbell went.

'Oh, God,' said Penny. 'It's downstairs, for sure. You know they want to be evil about me. In fact, I think I need a glass to hear what they're saying.'

'I don't think you want to know what they're saying,' said Lizzie.

'Don't answer the door. If it's Brooke asking about the carpet . . .'

'What did you do to the carpet?'

'Nothing. Red wine. Whatever. Oh God. I hate my life,' said Penny.

'You are a very unusual person,' said Georges.

'I'm sure loads of people hate their lives,' groaned Penny.

'I think he meant "evil" person,' said Lizzie. The knocking at the door sounded again, more vehement now.

'Oh God, I'm not evil,' said Penny. 'Am I? Maybe that's why I don't get what I really want. Why a lovely bloke like Will won't talk to me. Maybe I should change my ways, be a bit less selfish. Do you think I'm selfish, Lizzie? Maybe it is all my fault.'

Lizzie returned from the doorway.

'It's Will.'

Penny leapt up, a huge shiny grin spreading over her face. 'Fantastic.'

She hurried to the door, shrugging up her dress, leaving Georges's coat pooling in a pile on the floor.

Penny put on her best contrite face as she closed the door behind her and stepped into the well-kept hall. She was definitely going to play modest; no way was he going to get into her apartment tonight. It was simply too grim. She'd have to pretend it was lovely then move into his groovy artist's pad as soon as was humanly possible.

'Hi,' she said, hanging her head.

'Hi,' said Will, looking equally contrite.

'I wanted to apologise,' said Penny. 'I was jealous and acted like an idiot.'

He looked at her, amazed.

'But . . . ' he said, 'I came to apologise to you. We were meant to be on a date and I completely deserted you.'

'Well, there is that,' said Penny.

'Minty is . . . well, she wanted to tell me about how depressed she was and how she'd become dairy intolerant and stuff, and all about her parents' divorce, and every time I tried to get up she'd start crying, and . . . girls cry a lot, don't they?'

'I never cry in front of boys,' said Penny.

'I bet,' said Will. 'Anyway, I am sorry. The whole Minty thing was . . . a terrible mistake. So don't be surprised if she disses me a bit.'

'Apology accepted,' said Penny cheerfully.

'Although, you know, if the reverse were true I probably wouldn't have started stripping then screeching like a fish-wife.'

'Oh, yeah, course you would have.'

'And I think Minty wants to kill you,' he continued.

'OK, well, if she comes at me, I'll blow at her and she'll fall over and get carried away by a high wind.'

Will smiled and looked a bit embarrassed. 'Can I come in?'

'No,' said Penny.

'Good,' said Will.

'Why's that good?'

''Cause if you didn't want to get off with me you wouldn't give a toss about whether I came in or not.'

Penny paused for a minute and thought about it. 'Bollocks.'

Will looked around. 'This hall's pretty nice though. Soft lighting, carpet, pictures on the wall . . . '

But Penny was already kissing him.


Georges and Lizzie sat in the kitchen, looking at each other.

'This is a very exciting fun party,' he said. 'I'm having a wow time.'

Lizzie stared into her teacup, too embarrassed to answer. What on earth must he think of them?

Georges looked at the array of shocking junk piled up in the kitchen.

'You have lived here for a long time, yes?' he said. 'Maybe one century. Are you a wampire?'

Lizzie giggled. 'I'm not a wampire.'

Georges smiled. 'That's better, huh? You look so worried all the time. Which is how I would expect a wampire to look.'

'It's *vampire*.'

'Wampire. That's what I said.'

'Yes,' said Lizzie. 'That's what you said. Well, I'm not one.'

'So. This is your grandmother's house?'

Lizzie nodded. 'We're staying here while she's sick.'

'And then you're going again?'

Lizzie shrugged. 'I suppose.'

'Back to where?'

'Brandford, I suppose. If, I mean, when she gets better. She's very old.'

'You like Brandford?'

'I hate it,' said Lizzie savagely. 'I mean, there's nothing wrong with it. I suppose. I just . . . I mean, it just doesn't suit me.'

'But here in Chelsea you feel much better?'

'I don't know. Maybe I don't fit in anywhere.'

Georges tutted. 'Oh, Lizzie. Do not be so stupid.'

'I know,' said Lizzie. 'I can't even do self-pity right.'

Georges looked at her for a second and she felt most uncomfortable under his scrutiny. This was ridiculous. He was a chubby café manager who couldn't pronounce his V's. Why should she always feel she wasn't quite living up to him?

'I think it is time for me to go,' he said. 'I am up early, of course.'

'Thanks for coming,' said Lizzie, getting up.

'Not at all, it was . . . '

He let the end of the sentence trail off as he opened the door and saw Penny and Will literally all over each other in the hallway. Panicked, Penny immediately pushed the door back shut again before Will could turn round and see into the flat.

'OK,' said Georges. 'Well, maybe I didn't really want to leave yet anyway.'

'Sorry about that,' said Lizzie. Georges looked towards the windows.

'Second floor,' said Lizzie. 'I wouldn't jump. More tea?'

'No,' said Georges. 'I would like to go home. Could you tell your sister to take her boyfriend in or out or somewhere else, please?'

Lizzie twisted uncomfortably in her seat. 'I'd rather not.'

'She bites?' said Georges.

'No,' said Lizzie.

'Then you can just tell her, no?'

'I don't want to get in the middle of something . . .'

'Have you got a water hose?'

Lizzie twisted in embarrassment. She'd never hear the end of it if she ruined Penny's night.

'OK, we sit here waiting for Penny to finish doing exactly what she pleases? Are you a welcome mat, Lizzie?'

'You mean doormat.'

'Yes.'

'No. I'm not.'

'OK,' said Georges. He looked at his watch complacently. Lizzie was suddenly furious with him and leapt up. She flung open the door. Penny and Will had vanished.

'Just go!' she yelled. 'Happy now?'

'Lizzie, I just . . .'

'The doormat says goodnight!'

Georges left, giving her the same aghast look he had when he'd found her in the gutter. Bugger, bugger, bugger. Nobody could ever understand. She had to look out for her sister, that was all. Which meant that sometimes people . . . not anyone in particular, just sometimes . . . people should pay attention and notice that just because she was being sisterly didn't automatically mean she was being a doormat.

The doormat went to bed, thought about her terrible social skills, thought about being sad and lonely for the rest of her life, thought of the four thousand canapés she'd consumed at the party even though no one else had eaten any, and cried herself to sleep.

# Chapter Seven

Spring was definitely springing, and as far as Penny was concerned, the sap was rising. She bounced to work in the morning, then Will, with his delightfully relaxed artistic schedule, would come and hang around at closing time and they would go off and wander and have chats and talk about things. It was so unusual, and so delightful.

Not only that, but she was discovering a previously undiscovered knack for selling paintings. Years of hard pushing to the front of nightclub queues and shameless yelling had given her a certain tough edge when it came to alternately charming and bullying customers, men in particular. And the added incentive of Will's face every time she sold one of his pictures meant she was, for the first time in her life, in a job that didn't make her want to kill everyone in the place with a blunt instrument.

The only thing confusing her and slightly getting in the

way was the fact that she and Will hadn't . . . done it yet. There'd been long sessions of snogging, cuddling, a bit of wandering hands here and there, but just as she'd expect him to invite her back to his place, nothing had happened.

It crossed her mind briefly that maybe there was someone else at home, but he didn't seem at all as if he had something to hide, or give any indication that he had something better to be doing. He didn't hide his mobile or glance at his watch or say, 'I was out with . . . uh, nobody really.'

'So what's your place like?' she asked him, as they wandered through Hyde Park one unseasonably warm evening in March. Everywhere couples were waltzing through the daffodils, and throwing bread to the ducks. Jumpers were being shrugged off; anoraks tentatively spread on the still wet winter grass.

'What's yours like?' he countered immediately.

'You've seen it,' she said.

'I snogged you outside of it. That's not the same thing at all.'

'I'd like to see your place.'

'Why? Do you want an ice cream?' he asked as they passed a van.

'Of course.'

'Excellent. They do Loseley.'

'What? Can I just have a ninety-nine?'

'But that's their horrible aerated stuff. They've got tubs of proper ice cream.'

'But I want a ninety-nine!'

'OK,' said Will.

'I want a ninety-nine and I want to see your place.'

Will smiled. 'Oh, it's nothing really.'

This wasn't going according to plan. Penny took her ice cream and stuck her tongue in it in a very suggestive fashion.

'A mystery, huh?' she said. 'Are you on day release from prison?'

'No!'

'Are you gay?'

'Yes,' said Will. 'I'm gay. That's why I just bought you that ice cream. I was hoping you might set me up with Sloan.'

'So . . . ' said Penny. The sun was setting over the far side of the Serpentine Gallery. It was hard for her to believe she was within walking distance from home, just about. That London could be so beautiful, rather than filthy and dangerous and noisy . . . it was amazing, she thought. She'd already forgotten about her grandmother, really. She was such a distant figure. Lizzie was off visiting her again, thank goodness. They were spending their evenings playing Boggle. It was great Lizzie had something to do. And meanwhile, this . . . *here* . . . was home.

She flashed Will her widest smile.

'Well,' she said, 'pardon a girl for being forward. I just . . . I just wondered, you know, if you ever felt like being alone with a woman.'

Will raised his eyebrows at her. The evening sun was making her gold hair gleam, and she looked absolutely gorgeous. Why on earth hadn't she invited him home? How hard to get was she trying to be? He hoped she wasn't after an engagement ring or something equally ridiculous. But, goodness, he was desperate to . . .

'I beg your pardon?' he said.

'Oh, nothing,' said Penny, giving her ice cream a big lick. 'I was just thinking about something grown men and women do . . . in private. In the privacy, in fact, of their *own homes*.'

'What's that, then?' said Will, moving towards her.

'Uh, you wouldn't like it,' said Penny.

'Perhaps you could show me now,' said Will. He grabbed

her hand and pulled her off the path and into the shadow of a huge oak tree. Then he took a huge lick of her cheap ice cream and started to kiss her long and hard, sharing it between them.

'Who are you?' The old lady was staring at her again. Lizzie wouldn't have thought it possible, but this place was worse on a glorious evening like tonight than when it was pouring with rain.

'I'm Lizzie, Gran. I'm Stephen's daughter.'

'One of the little twins?'

'That's right. I'm one of the little twins.'

The old woman glowered and peered at her closer. Lizzie geared herself up to explain the whole thing twice more. Maybe next time Penny could visit. Lizzie laughed hollowly to herself. She was exhausted. For the last few weeks, she had worked her head off in the café. To her utmost annoyance, Georges, whilst paying her hardly any attention at all, had started taking loads of time off. OK, it was his business and everything, but he'd come in in the morning, start things off, then disappear. As she'd vowed to behave frostily towards him it was frustrating to say the least.

Slowly, and grudgingly, she was bloody well having to learn to cook. And Georges said he was going off on business somewhere but she didn't believe him. He was just mooching about, enjoying her hard work, which was still netting her only the minimum wage, plus the odd pound some of her regulars slipped her here and there.

The fact that it was about a hundred times more interesting and stimulating than the stamp importers hadn't cheered her up that much.

'Are you a happy little twin?' asked her grandmother.

Funnily enough, she had caught herself feeling something close to happiness just that morning. Georges had shown her how to make a wonderfully fresh-tasting bruschetta – which she'd never tasted in her life; she'd thought it was just garlic bread showing off – and pretty much every customer who'd sampled it had mentioned how delicious it was. It had taken her a second or two to realise that she felt proud of herself.

'I'm all right,' she said stiffly.

'Just all right? Not enjoying Chelsea, then? Your dad used to love it.'

'Did he?' said Lizzie eagerly.

'Oh, yes. I used to take him down the Embankment, you know, and we'd watch the boats go by. They still had the barges then. After he lost his daddy . . . '

Lizzie knew about this; that her grandfather had died in an industrial fire. His settlement had bought the flat. Secretly she wondered if this meant it was cursed.

Gran was musing. 'He was all I had, little twin. You'll understand one day when you have your own, how much you love them. And he was all I had left. I spoiled him. Yes, I spoiled him. Then I lost him.'

'We lost him, too,' said Lizzie.

'Aye, I know that,' said her grandmother. There was a long pause.

'Well, to other matters,' said Gran eventually. 'Have you got a nice young chap?'

'No,' said Lizzie.

'Have you got a horrid old chap?'

Lizzie looked at her grandmother for signs of smirking.

'No,' she said.

'Quite right,' said her grandmother. 'Don't settle.'

'Let's face it though,' said Lizzie. 'I'm going to have to settle, aren't I? Everyone says don't settle, like there's a million fabulous blokes out there looking for slightly below-average women. There's no doubt about it at all. I blame Colin Firth. He's an actor, Gran . . .'

'I know who he is,' said her grandmother suddenly. 'He's a spunk.'

'Oh, OK,' said Lizzie, 'well, it's his fault. In *Bridget Jones's Diary* he says he loves Renée Zellweger just the way she is. But he doesn't really. In real life, his wife is really, really, skinny and looks like a model and speaks nine languages. And in real life Renée Zellweger is super thin and gorgeous. I don't think spunks really do have to settle or love someone just the way they are.'

'Renée Zellweger settled down,' observed her grandmother.

'Hey, I thought you were crazy and a bit out of it and stuff,' said Lizzie, surprised by her gran's grasp of celebrity gossip.

'I am,' said her grandmother. 'Why do you think I have to sit about all day taking drugs and reading *People's Friend*?'

'Hmm,' said Lizzie, shaking the Boggle box. 'Well, anyway. Now I just have to decide how low to lower my standards. Every year they have to drop about five per cent, I reckon. Every year and every pound over eleven stone.'

Her grandmother looked at her. 'Is Wayne Rooney free yet?'

'I could never pull Wayne Rooney,' said Lizzie. 'Why am I depressed about that? I don't know. I find something constantly depressing in being unable to pull people I don't even fancy.'

'How's your sister?'

'She's madly in love with a gorgeous successful artist and adores her new job,' said Lizzie. 'Apart from that, you know, just about all right.'

The old woman sniffed. 'Nice of her to come and see me. Or maybe she did come before – was that her?'

'No,' said Lizzie. 'That was me.'

'You're not identical? Are you the little twins?'

Her grandmother's eyes were closing.

'Yes,' said Lizzie. 'Yes, we are.'

Penny was in heaven. Minty and Brooke had asked her out on another drinks night too. This time Lizzie, strangely, had declined. Penny had felt quite at home relaxing on the large brown sofas of the Sloaney Pony, letting boys in stripy shirts buy them champagne and make remarks. The girls had been very interested to hear all about Will, and she'd been delighted to talk all about it until, on their way out, Minty had cornered her in the toilets.

'So, it's all going swimmingly,' said Minty, touching up her flawless skin with a tiny amount of rose blusher. Penny was thwacking the bronzer on as usual, and wondered, for the first time, if she was going about her make-up quite right.

'Yes,' said Penny, smiling.

'Well, be careful,' said Minty, smacking her lips. 'I'm only telling you this for your own good, Penny, but that Will's a user.'

'What, like Pete Doherty?'

Minty swung her golden ponytail disdainfully. 'I'm just warning you, that's all. He's trouble. Bad news. Stay away. That's all I'll say.'

Poor Minty, thought Penny. So jealous. Will had dumped her and she'd never got over it. Well, the two of them were different.

Lizzie, meanwhile, was finding that between work and visiting Gran her world was, if anything, shrinking – she didn't even see her old friends now, it was all too much for them to make the trek. She had had one night out with Grainne, in a too-loud pub on the King's Road, music thumping around them, and gorgeous teenagers copping off with each other. It hadn't gone well.

'God, everything sucks,' said Lizzie as a conversation starter, gingerly helping herself to another prawn cocktail crisp. She'd been off crisps for a bit – Georges wouldn't have them in the café – and she couldn't believe how strong and fake they tasted.

'Yes,' Grainne had said. 'It really sucks, living in a castle in Chelsea and running a restaurant. I'd hate to live in Chelsea and get off with celebrities and be a millionaire.'

Penny grew rosy and happy with love – for the first time, as far as Lizzie could see. There were outdoor assignations, weekends away, parties which Lizzie, after the horrors of Brooke and Minty's, refused to go to.

Lizzie worked hard, ate fresh food, went to bed early. Penny danced all night. Georges left Lizzie to her own devices more and more, which she supposed was a compliment of sorts.

Penny and Will were lying entwined near the Serpentine. It was a perfect evening in a perfect park. People were feeding ducks and flying kites; taking strolls and generally, Penny suspected, feeling pleased with themselves and the world.

'I think,' said Penny, lolling. 'You should paint me in the nude. You know, like Kate Winslet in *Titanic*.'

'Like who?'

'You know. In *Titanic*. Everyone's seen it.'

'I haven't,' said Will, eyeing the ducks.

'You must have,' said Penny, shocked. Lizzie had cried so hard snot had come out of her nose. Dwaneesa had called her pathetic in front of everyone. Penny had laughed. She felt slightly ashamed of that now.

'Nope,' said Will.

'OK,' said Penny. 'Well, what happens is a boy takes a girl to a nice room, and she gets naked and he paints a really beautiful picture of her in the candlelight.'

'Really,' said Will, leaning over to give her a quick tickle. 'Why did I think it was about a big ship sinking and lots of people descending to their watery deaths?'

'Well, those are the kind of detaily things that happen later on.'

Penny peered up at him and gave a hopeful look. Will sighed. He would like to take her home, he really would but . . . it just wasn't the right time. He had to be careful. It was such a big step. He changed the subject.

'So, what do you like?' Will was saying. He was playing with a stick, watching the clouds and trying to work out what colours he'd use to paint them.

'Raindrops on roses and whiskers . . . hang on, that's not right, is it?' said Penny.

'No,' said Will, smiling. He couldn't get over how much fun Penny was, how much he enjoyed being with her. She wasn't like any of the other girls.

'I mean, what do you want? Out of life.'

Penny smiled. 'Like a Rolex watch? Or true love.'

'Or both,' said Will.

'Both then,' said Penny. 'A big house and a garden and a lovely home and a lovely family and, you know. Normal stuff. Not having to worry. That kind of thing.'

'But you've got a big house,' said Will.

'Oh, yeah,' said Penny. She should come clean, she really should, but her feelings for him had grown so strong. She wanted desperately for things to work out, she wanted to

141

meet his posh family, and spend time in his gorgeous apartment and meet more of his friends and ... but to her amazement, it wasn't just about that, about what he drove and how wide his television set was. It was about how he made her feel – pretty, yes, but she was used to that. Smart, funny and, more importantly, safe. Nothing bad had ever happened to Will, it was obvious. He was comfortable everywhere. He had money, and ease, and had always been sure of himself, and treated her as if she were just the same.

He'd never had to steal for a bus fare, or pretend to have been on an expensive holiday with his dad (Lizzie had loyally refused to deny it, even with Dwaneesa's taunting about her pasty skin still ringing in her ears). Will was secure. He made her feel secure. He was everything she'd never known she wanted. And it was scaring her to death.

She had to convince him she was the girl for him because ... well. Because she thought she was. Because she wanted to fit in. Because she didn't want to be rejected.

She swallowed suddenly. The ground seemed to be shifting under her feet. Or was the sky tilting? Suddenly she felt incredibly light-headed.

'Oh, Will,' she said.

'What?'

'I don't know, I just feel a bit ... '

She stood up, but that was worse. She felt terribly sick and bleary.

'Oh, Will, I think it must have been that hot dog.'

'I can't believe you ate a hot dog from a man in the park.'

Penny had bought one, and wolfed it down – she'd been starving – without even noticing Will staring at her, aghast. Well, now she knew. Smart people didn't buy hot dogs from a stand in the park. She filed it away as a mental note, just as she suddenly, definitely, knew she was going to be sick. And soon.

'Will, I've got to go,' she said.

'Well, let me come with you.'

'NO! I mean, no, don't, I'll be fine.'

'But I'll need to get you home to see you're all right.'

'No, you don't . . . ' she was practically running out of the park now. 'See you later . . . '

Lizzie was attempting to dust round the fourteen ornamental toilet-roll holders on the floor of the bathroom when she heard Penny enter.

'Pen?' she yelled. 'Are you still doing it outside all the time? It's disgusting, and it's getting grass all over the silver dog bowl collection.'

'Out of my way,' said Penny, only just managing to push past Lizzie and make it to the toilet in time, where she threw up copiously. Lizzie watched her in silence.

'Oh, OK,' said Lizzie. 'Forget what I said about the *grass* being disgusting.'

Penny ignored her, continuing to hurl down the lav. Lizzie went over and patted her on the back.

'What's the matter with you, then?'

Penny shook her head. '*Bleeaarrggghhhh.*'

'Dodgy pie?' said Lizzie.

'No . . . *Bllleeeaaggh.*'

'Dodgy foie gras? Bad glass of champers?'

Penny didn't answer and Lizzie handed her a towel.

'Here you go, sport. Don't tell me, Will peeled back his perfect skin and revealed he's actually a lizard?'

Penny shook her head vigorously.

'Is he here?'

The shaking was even more vigorous.

'OK, OK. Are you finished? Would you like some water?'

But Penny waved her away.

Twenty minutes later she emerged, looking sheepish, into the sitting room.

'How are you feeling?' said Lizzie, looking up from *Hello!*, which she'd borrowed from her grandmother.

'Really terrible. I ate a hot dog in the park.' Penny sounded shocked, like she couldn't believe something as strange as feeling bad could happen to her. She slumped down onto the couch.

'Ah, well,' said Lizzie, who considered herself quite hot on health and safety these days. 'If you will . . . '

'Yeah, yeah,' said Penny, smoothing down her fitted vest. 'I wouldn't normally. It's just not like me, but I was so bloody starvin'.'

Lizzie raised an eyebrow. 'Did you miss lunch?'

Georges believed sitting down to lunch was a hallmark of a civilised society and that the plastic-wrapped all-day-breakfast sandwich was an abomination. Sloan believed in the lunch break too, though only for him, and for different reasons.

'Well, I have to, don't I? Will's hardly going to want to go out with some porker. No offence.'

'There wasn't any,' said Lizzie, 'until that bit at the end, just there, where you said "No offence".'

Penny propped herself up on a weak arm. 'Is it just me, anyway, or are you looking a bit thinner?'

'That's because I've been puking my guts up,' said Lizzie, still stung. 'Oh no, that was you.'

'Stavros is obviously having a good effect on you.'

'His name is *not* Stavros,' said Lizzie. 'And I've hardly seen him.'

'Whatever,' said Penny. 'Oh God, I feel awful. I'm going to bed.'

*

The following morning Penny crept out into the sitting room, looking, if anything, worse.

'Oh God, I still feel terrible.'

Lizzie, making a lemon tea, looked up as Penny jumped up and ran through to the bathroom again.

'There's nothing coming up,' she said when she came back in. She was pale and white-faced, with beads of sweat showing on her forehead.

'Oh dear,' said Lizzie. 'Sit down.'

Waiting for the kettle to boil, Lizzie glanced through the huge windows over into the houses opposite. Those houses were beautifully furnished; polished tables and Persian rugs and untouched pianos in orderly rooms, and often empty as their owners flitted to the south of France, or skiing, or the Caribbean, or anywhere else Lizzie imagined they went. A minor chord was striking in her breast.

Penny was staring at the floor, a small island of pink pyjamas amidst the sea of junk. She couldn't look up and meet Lizzie's gaze; her heart was beating a million times a minute and her hands were feeling clammy.

'Well,' said Lizzie.

Penny blinked rapidly. She couldn't, couldn't . . . I mean, it was so ridiculous.

'I wonder,' said Lizzie, still looking out of the windows, 'I wonder if there's some kind of test you could buy from a chemist if you were throwing up in the morning.' She looked at Penny, who grimaced back at her. Lizzie noticed her eyes were red.

'Of course not,' said Penny. 'I mean, almost certainly not . . . I mean, it would be really unlikely . . . '

'Haven't you been doing tons and tons of alfresco knobbing?' said Lizzie.

Penny looked guilty.

'You know, scientists have discovered you can get pregnant doing it standing up.'

'Is this the time for jokes?'

'You were careful, weren't you?'

'Yes. Yes. You know, mostly. Nearly all the time.'

Lizzie looked at her.


Boots on a Saturday morning on the King's Road was heaving with beautiful young tourists. Lizzie couldn't quite believe she was doing this. The only time she'd even had a scare was one night with Felix when they'd had sex so stupefyingly dull that afterwards neither of them could remember a thing about it, including the contraception.

The queue was incredibly long, as they stood trying to look innocuous while carrying a big blue box.

'You're going to be fine,' said Lizzie. 'We're probably infertile anyway.'

'What makes you say that?'

'I don't know. The papers keep saying everyone's infertile, don't they?'

'Well . . .'

'And we're nearly thirty. And we drink cocktails and live in a built-up area with fumes and sleep with boys who've been drinking water that the pill gets flushed away in and stuff. I think we missed our chance to get pregnant when we were fifteen.'

'D'you think?'

Lizzie nodded fiercely and, even though it was stupid, Penny felt comforted.

'It's true,' said Lizzie. 'The only way we're ever going to get pregnant is via IVF. Everyone knows that. It costs thousands of pounds and makes you really moody.'

'You do that for nothing,' said Penny, smiling weakly.

'Oh, yeah,' said Lizzie, glad to see a ghost of a smile return.

'Yeah?' said the disinterested checkout girl, chewing her gum slowly in their faces. And I couldn't find a job, thought Lizzie to herself.

Penny held out the pack, hand shaking.

'Thirteen ni-ee nine,' said the girl. The twins stood there.

'Go on then,' whispered Lizzie.

Penny turned to her. 'What?'

'Pay her.'

'What with? I don't have any money, do I? Sloan hasn't paid me yet this month, and I owed Dwaneesa sixty quid.'

'Well, I don't have it, do I?' said Lizzie, exasperated. It cost her more than that in bus fares up to Barnet, and she only had twenty pounds to get her through till Monday. Which she hadn't brought with her.

'You got it or wot?' said the checkout girl. Penny gave Lizzie an anguished look. 'I don't, OK?' said Lizzie. 'Can't you put it on your credit card?'

'They chopped it up in Argos.'

Behind them the queue was getting distinctly restless. Lizzie hoped Penny wasn't going to do something embarrassing, like ask them all for a quid.

But then she saw Penny's face, and it didn't look tough at all. In fact she looked as if she was about to cry.

'Come on,' said Lizzie. 'Let's just go home.'

'You put that back,' said the checkout girl.

'Really,' said Lizzie, dumping the test on the counter and manhandling Penny out of the store with uncustomary vigour. Maybe all these rude Londoners were having an effect on her after all.

*

Back home, Penny was quiet at first.

Lizzie sank down beside her on the sofa and put her arms around her.

'Sweetie.'

From Penny came a great racking sob.

'How *could* I . . . how *could* it? I know I am. I just know it.'

Lizzie patted her gently on the shoulder.

'I mean, this is just bollocks . . . this isn't how it's meant to happen at all.' Penny, bleak with despair, shook her head then covered her face with her hands.

They were startled by the phone as it rang. Lizzie couldn't help thinking, It's for Penny, it always is.

'Hey,' said Will. 'How are you? Are you feeling OK? It's going to be a gorgeous day. Absolutely wonderful. I propose a picnic, with smoked-salmon bagels, cream cheese, and some diet Fanta for you. You can read *Heat* magazine then I'll snog you in the long grass. How does that sound?'

It sounded like heaven.

'Uh, I'm not sure,' said Penny. 'I'm not feeling too well.'

'Really?' He sounded concerned. 'Would you like me to come over and look after you?'

Penny glanced around.

'No!' she ordered, panicked. 'I'll . . . I'll call you later, if I'm feeling better.'

'OK, sweetie pie.'

Penny put the phone down and turned to Lizzie.

'What . . . What am I going to do now?'

Lizzie looked at her, helplessly.

'I don't know, Penny. What, you think this is the kind of thing that happens to me every day?'

'Maybe I should ask Brooke.'

'That's right,' said Lizzie. 'Posh people are much better at dealing with life's problems. That's why they're always going

148

into rehab and insane asylums. Why don't you just ring Mum?'

Penny winced. 'I don't . . . you know, I don't get on with Mum like you do. And it's the last thing I want . . . she'll just be so disappointed. Sometimes I feel like she's been waiting for me to do something like this my whole life.'

Lizzie tried not to show how true this was. 'She'll be OK.'

'Look, she's happy for the first time in her life, doing this stupid drama school thing.'

Unbelievably, RADA had deigned to allow Eilish in. She had taken to wearing coloured headscarves and large earrings, and talked about becoming the next Brenda Blethyn. Penny had found it embarrassing, and had barred her from coming in the shop without several hours' warning so she could get Sloan out of the way before he was rude about her.

Lizzie looked at her. 'You know,' she said gently, 'we're being very negative about this. How do you know he won't be . . . you know, pleased? I mean, you guys are in love and everything, aren't you?'

Penny swallowed. 'Pleased?'

'Yes, you know, happy. Maybe he loves you, and you might be having his baby and that will be a good thing.'

Penny looked away as her worst fears surfaced.

'Lizzie, he doesn't even know me. I'm supposed to be a rich bitch working for fun,' said Penny, looking as disconsolate as Lizzie had ever seen her. 'I mean, I'm just so different from him . . . he reads the *Telegraph*. He thinks . . . he thinks he's going out with someone else.'

'No, he doesn't,' said Lizzie. 'You're his gorgeous Chelsea girlfriend, aren't you? And I'm sure he doesn't care a fig either way. You're his Chelsea girlfriend, who just happens to have his baby. Move into his flat, or just pretend you're . . . uh, an eccentric messpot. Who's to be any the wiser? You could sort the rest out later. As far as he knows you're just a nice girl. None of that shit matters anyway. You know, what spoons to use and stuff. Nobody gives a toss.'

'You think?' said Penny, unwilling to admit to the world she'd described to Will. But she thought of the way those women looked at her when they went to bars and restaurants. Why had she never met his mother? What on earth would his mother think? Boys didn't care as much about these kinds of things but women . . . women knew straightaway.

Penny looked at her stomach sadly. How could she be so foolish, so ridiculously undone by a handsome face and a roll in the hay? This wasn't what she'd planned for herself at all.

But Lizzie's words had inspired a small hope. What if he did want to take on responsibility? They had had fun together, but it was so sudden, so soon.

She closed her eyes and imagined his face, spreading wide with delight.

'Oh my God! A little baby!' he'd say, then he'd pick her up and fling her around and spin her in the air, then put her down gently and carefully as if she was made of china. Then he'd take her to meet all his friends and his parents and they'd love her and . . .

A single tear ran down her face.

'Would you like to eat some French toast?' said Lizzie, who'd almost subconsciously started whisking eggs to calm her nerves. 'Otherwise I'm going to eat it all, and I was rather near to getting into my old black trousers.'

Penny paced up and down, still staring at the phone. There had been several cute and enquiring text messages from Will. Each one made her head for the door, determined to confront him head on, her heart full of hope. Every time she'd stop and wonder at the implausibility of meshing her life to his.

'I've got to know,' she said. 'I've got to know. There's no point putting it off.'

'He loves you,' said Lizzie loyally. 'And what a beautiful baby it will be.'

'Shh,' said Penny. 'That's not helping.'

The phone rang again.

'Oh, come on, Penny,' said Will. 'It's gorgeous out there. I don't want to be stuck at home.'

'I need to come and see you,' said Penny. 'At home.'

There was silence on the other end of the phone. She had it on speaker so Lizzie could hear.

'Uh, are you sure you wouldn't rather go to the park? It's lovely.'

'No,' said Penny. 'I want to come round.'

There was another long pause.

Will hadn't been expecting this; usually girls were all too keen to get him to theirs; cook for him and show him how lovely they were around the house. He counted on it. But Penny was different: so mysterious.

Still. She was different. She was special. Maybe the time had come. Will blinked rapidly and took the plunge. She'd look after him . . . wouldn't she?

'All right,' said Will finally. He sounded quiet, decided, rather muted. Penny looked at Lizzie expectantly.

Will gave an address in east London.

'I suppose you'll hop in a cab,' he said.

'Uh, yeah . . . ' said Penny, who was already fingering one of their grandmother's many, many bus timetables.

'What do you think?' she said to Lizzie the second she was off the phone.

'I think he knows already,' said Lizzie. 'He's a young

bloke, his girlfriend is sick and now she wants to come round to discuss something. What else is it going to be?'

'I think I'm going to be ill again,' said Penny, sprinting for the toilet door.

The journey from Chelsea to Clapton was one of the longest of Penny's life. She watched as the beautiful mansion blocks and pastel houses gave way to the formidable square structures of Belgravia and Mayfair; along the tatty bustle of Oxford Street and beyond; past Centrepoint and on past the bookshops of Charing Cross Road, along the Strand, and Fleet Street and on to Liverpool Street, to change and get on an older, tattier bus. Why buses serving cheaper postcodes should be nastier than those serving nicer ones she didn't understand at all, but just sat upstairs, her head leaning against the window, trying to keep the nausea down.

One second she would imagine a world where she inhabited Will's trendy loft, maybe sitting cross-legged on the floor, a neat baby bump in front of her whilst all their trendy friends (faces mostly blurred) came by and teased her, and Will announced she was getting more beautiful with every month that passed. And they would have a little girl and call her Chelsea. Or maybe that was common, she couldn't decide. Well, Bill Clinton's daughter was Chelsea, and so was that girl who used to date Prince Harry, so it couldn't possibly be.

And then she saw herself, pregnant, huge, lumbering through streets inexplicably covered in snow, crying to herself. Then she realised she was thinking of the film *Oliver!*. Or a cold hospital room, filled with other silly girls, looking at a pair of howling twins . . .

125b Nitclose Road wasn't at all what she was anticipating. She was expecting a converted school house. Or maybe just a huge warehouse, like the man from the old 'Easy Like Sunday Morning' adverts, with an open wall, and an industrial lift. Or a vast studio with great vaulting windows.

In fact, 125b Nitclose Road was a side entrance to a gloomy-looking Victorian terrace. It was filthy with soot, and the front garden was covered in black bin bags and an old sofa that sagged, looking soggy and disconsolate. Bits and pieces of various bicycles cluttered up the path.

There were five doorbells, all unreadable, by the small door. Penny picked up her phone to call, but just as she did, the door swung open, and Will stood there, at the bottom of a grimy flight of stairs littered with pizza delivery leaflets and brown envelopes.

He stood there, staring with a strange, apologetic look on his face.

'Well,' he said. 'Hmm. Have you heard of the new Bohemians?'

Penny felt as if she'd been knocked out by her second major shock of the day. Unsteadily, she followed him up the filthy stairs and into a tiny bedsit. There had obviously been a last-minute tidy up – several pairs of trainers had been lined up underneath the cheap MFI wardrobe – but there was no disguising the shabbiness of the brown carpet and green curtains.

Will winced. 'So,' he said, 'welcome to my, uh, humble abode.'

Penny looked at him, too shocked to speak. 'But I thought . . . I thought . . . but you're a successful artist.'

Will started boiling the small kettle in the corner. 'Coffee? I've only got instant, I'm afraid. And powdered milk. I, uh, don't have a fridge.'

'You don't have a fridge.'

Will rubbed the back of his neck nervously. 'Look, Penny, I know I've put off having you over.'

'I can see why,' said Penny, feeling chilled inside.

'But I thought . . . you should know the truth. I really like you and—'

'You're actually a tramp.'

Will looked ashamed. 'Well . . . I sell one picture every month or so . . . then there's materials and I have to pay off my student loan, and, you know, I like to use my money to socialise . . . '

Penny thought of all those expensive dinners she hadn't eaten, those nights out where he'd taken care of everything; his suave manner. She looked at his battered brown leather jacket again, hanging on the back of the door, and had a sudden flash of realisation. It wasn't battered because it looked better that way. It was battered because it was all he had to wear.

'Oh my God,' she said.

'I really like you,' said Will. 'So I thought . . . you should know . . . I'm not quite in the same league as you, financially speaking . . . '

She looked at him. Now she knew why Minty had been trying to warn her off. She'd thought it was jealousy, but it wasn't. It was something else altogether.

'You were sharking me,' she said quietly.

'What?'

'You're a shark. You go to nice bars to pick up rich people hoping they'll fund your art. Aren't you?'

And boy, did she know how that was done.

'No!' said Will, his face reddening. He wasn't a shark . . . he didn't mean to, but he'd found his looks and his accent made things easy and . . . well, otherwise, how was he going to live? He didn't want to live in Nitclose Road all his life, and was it so wrong?

'I mean, I go where, you know, patrons of the arts hang out, I suppose . . . '

Penny backed away cautiously. 'Were you looking for a meal ticket?'

'No,' said Will. Oh God. Agreeing to her coming here was the worst decision of his life. He gestured around slightly despairingly. 'Well. I don't want to lie to you, Penny. I mean, it would be nice to be able to work somewhere . . . you know, get my own real studio, something like that.'

He looked slightly ashamed for a moment.

'And, Pen, I really, really like you. I mean, I think I lo—'

Penny realised she was shaking. This could almost be funny. Two grifters, grifted. Well, it could have been funny. If it wasn't for . . .

'Uh, Will,' she said. He stopped what he was saying and looked up. 'You know, I don't have any money either.'

He looked confused. 'What do you mean?'

'I mean, I'm looking after my grandmother's flat while she's ill. That's why we've never had you over. She's my dad's mother and my dad was never really part of our lives and we don't even know him. It just came out of the blue. I'm from Brandford. Mum's a dinner lady.'

Will stared at her, as if she was the one who'd just dropped the bombshell. 'But . . . but . . . ' he said. 'You knew all those places to go.'

'I read magazines all day.'

'And you work in an art gallery.'

'Sloan thought it would be good for business,' said Penny. 'You know. Little market-stall worker stuff. He thinks it's hilarious.'

Will's mouth was actually hanging open.

'I don't believe this,' he said, although of course, it

explained everything. He'd just thought her money was a bit crass. Plus, she'd been willing to do things in parks that posh girls didn't mind doing either; it was only ever his middle-class girlfriends that were a bit uptight. It hadn't occurred to him for a second that it wasn't brash money; that it was no money at all.

I know something else you wouldn't believe, thought Penny, but all her protective instincts kicked in and she didn't say anything, just looked at him closely.

Will was fumbling with the neck of his T-shirt as if it was constricting him. He'd given up any pretence of making coffee, and had gone bright red. Penny swallowed hard. When she spoke, her voice was quiet, without its hard edge.

'But you still really, really like me, right? We're still, you know. In lo—'

Within a tiny millisecond, the space of a blink, there it was. It took him just a tiny sliver of a moment too long to look at her.

'Of course,' he said. But everything had changed.


Lizzie made salami with fennel on pasta and took it in to Penny, who ignored it. Lizzie eyed it hungrily.

'Are you going to stay in bed for ever?'

'Yes,' said Penny, sobs still racking her frame.

'You know, it might be fun,' said Lizzie. 'Having a little baby.'

'Being a single mum back in Brandford and raising a baby,' said Penny. 'Maybe I could get a job in a school. You know. Cooking. Hey, maybe I'm going to have twins.'

Lizzie patted her on the shoulder. She'd never asked this question before.

'Did you . . . were you in love?'

Penny looked up. There were four hundred sodden tissues littering the duvet.

'Uh-huh!'

Through the day, Penny didn't get out of bed, and Lizzie was beginning to feel like a full-time carer. On Saturday night the doorbell rang just as she was taking Penny another mint tea. Lizzie's eyebrows shot up.

'Don't get excited,' said Penny. 'It's Brooke and Minty. I invited them up. Told them what's happened. People love to hear about misery and maybe they'll give some advice. Or cheer me up or something.'

'Or something,' said Lizzie definitely, as she jumped off the bed and went to answer the door. Brooke and Minty were standing there, both in jeans so tight they could have fainted and not fallen over. Minty looked almost triumphant.

'POOR Penny,' she said loudly. 'I'm SO sorry for her. I did try and warn her you know. Gold-digging rat.'

'He's a cad,' said Brooke. 'We knew it, I'm afraid. Is this your place?' She peered into the room with a look of unfeigned horror on her face.

'It's industrial chic,' said Lizzie.

'This smells like that old lady who lived here,' sniffed Minty.

'Would you like to come in?'

'I can't stay long,' said Brooke. 'Charles is taking me to dinner at the Wolseley.'

'Oh, how boring,' said Minty. 'We're going to Crazy Bear. It's so loud there, I haven't the faintest clue what Oscar is banging on about. It's great.'

'Follow me,' said Lizzie. 'Uh, would you like a snack?'

She thought sadly of her lovely fennel and salami, which she'd hoped to tempt Penny with then polish off.

The girls sniffed loudly.

'I'd like a *cocktail*,' said Minty, striding into the room with her shiny boots.

'Ooh, yah,' said Brooke, marching in too and yelling to Penny. They bustled through leaving Lizzie feeling like the waitress. The doorbell rang again.

For crying out loud, thought Lizzie. This better be good news.

Amazingly, her Brandford friend Grainne was standing in the doorway.

'Hi,' said Grainne dully, staring at the floor.

'Hey, there,' said Lizzie. 'Come in. What brings you to this neck of the woods?'

'I thought you'd be in,' said Grainne.

'On Saturday night. Well, that's good,' said Lizzie. 'I'm glad that's the kind of thing you'd be quite happy to rely on and come all the way from Brandford without a phone call or anything. You know, just to make sure.'

'I'm very lonely,' said Grainne. 'Have you got anything to eat?'

'Salami and fennel?' said Lizzie weakly.

'I don't really like salami,' said Grainne. 'And I don't know what fennel is. Is it some pretentious new thing you have now you live in Chelsea?'

Lizzie shrugged.

'But it'll do, I suppose.'

In the sitting room the girls from downstairs were sprawled about, long legs up on the sofa and coffee table, cigarettes dangling, as if they'd never had to worry about spilling or breaking anything in their lives. Which they hadn't, of course.

'Hiya, guys!' said Penny. Somehow Penny had managed

to leap out of bed, squeeze into her super-tight jeans and a halterneck top – and a pair of heels for Christ's sake – and clear enough space on the sofa to lounge on it, looking nonchalant.

Brooke tilted up her indoor sunglasses and inspected her closely.

'God, Penny,' she breathed. 'You look like you've had a tit job.'

Penny had noticed that her breasts felt a little bigger. She supposed this was part of it too.

'Lucky cow,' said Minty. 'I had ten days in hospital after mine.'

'And you told us all you'd been having a torrid affair with an Argentinian gaucho,' said Brooke accusingly.

'Oh, I was fifteen,' said Minty. 'What was I supposed to tell you?' She patted her neck-height crystal-ball tits affectionately.

'Yes, well,' said Penny, giving a slightly fragile giggle. 'There have to be some side benefits.'

'God, yes,' said Minty. 'Count up the side benefits. There's the big tits and . . . ' She fell quiet. 'Um, not having periods,' she added. 'That'll be handy.'

'You still have those?' said Brooke scornfully. 'God, how much do you weigh?'

'Of course I don't,' said Minty quickly. 'No one who's anyone has periods.'

'So anyway, darling,' Brooke said to Penny, 'join the club.'

'You're pregnant too?'

For an instant, Penny had an image of them bowling around with matching three-wheeler buggies, having a great time.

'Good God, no; whatever gave you that idea? No, darling, three abortions at the last count.'

Penny was amazed. '*Really?*'

'Oh, yes. Know this excellent chappie. It's like having a haircut.'

Penny didn't think it was anything like getting a haircut.

'I can't believe you got knocked up. Will is *such* a bugger.' She stifled a chuckle.

'Although of course if he'd been a bit more of a bugger you wouldn't be in this situation! Haaw!' said Minty.

'Minty, that's not very helpful.'

'Of course not, darling. OK, hang on, I've got the doc's card in my purse . . .'

Penny squeezed her eyes shut, horrified that they both carried an abortionist's card in their wallets.

'Ah, here we go, darling.'

Penny wrote the number down on a piece of paper and stared at it.

Lizzie came in from the kitchen area with a freshly mixed jug of cosmopolitans. Grainne stood by her side like a suspicious toddler waiting for a vaccination.

'This is Grainne, everyone.'

The girls couldn't have looked her up and down faster if she'd been a piece of dust.

'Hmmm,' said Minty, possibly the lowest form of actual conversation ever invented. The other girls saw this as good enough to cover them too and didn't say anything at all.

'Can I sit here?' said Grainne, making Lizzie wince.

'Course you can,' Lizzie said quickly. 'Make yourself at home.'

'This sofa is bigger than my entire flat,' said Grainne.

'Really?' said Minty. 'That's a shame for you. Are you terribly poor?'

'Well, you know, London's so expensive,' said Grainne, purple with embarrassment at being singled out.

'So it's actually smaller than the sofa,' said Minty wonderingly. 'Do you have to curl up really small to sleep? How do you wash?'

'Well, it's nice really,' said Grainne.

'It's very nice,' said Lizzie.

'Oh, sorry,' said Minty. 'I thought you just said it was really squat and tiny. My bad.' She helped herself to more cosmopolitan.

'So, D&G have started doing a baby line!' said Brooke tactfully. 'That's exciting!'

'It is,' said Penny. 'Oh, I hope I get a little girl. So cute to dress. If I have it . . . ' she tailed off.

'Little boys are cooler, though,' said Minty. 'Look at Liz Hurley.'

'Little boys are definitely the way to go,' said Brooke. 'You can take him everywhere and dress him up and let him help with your make-up and he'll grow up gay and love you for ever and never leave you. While girls, I mean' – she lifted her hands – 'I can't stand my mother to tell you the truth. And she's always bursting into tears when she can't fit into my clothes.'

'It's true,' said Minty. 'My mother's on her fifth facelift but her neck is a complete mess. She's holding on to Belgravia by the skin of her teeth and I just don't think husband number four is going to turn up any time soon. But she cries every time I mention this stuff. You'd think she'd be happy to know the truth.'

'Little boy it is, then,' said Penny. She reached out and popped a bit of Lizzie's precious salami in her mouth. Grainne had also been absentmindedly stuffing it away in a completely oblivious way, which went a long way to explaining her figure and her constant state of amazement at her size. ('But I hardly eat a thing.')

'You'll have to watch, though,' said Brooke, looking point-edly at the salami. 'Victoria Beckham managed to get back into her size six jeans this time in thirty-eight minutes.'

'Gwyneth's still fuming,' said Minty. 'Took her nearly an hour and a half.'

'I'll worry about that later,' said Penny, licking her fingers.

Brooke glanced at her Cartier Tank watch. 'Oh! Charles has been waiting . . . twenty minutes. Do I have time for another cocktail or not?'

'I'd better go too,' said Minty. 'Although if he hasn't got me an expensive present, he can whistle for that blow job.'

'You give blow jobs?' said Brooke. 'Ew, I can't believe you still do that. That is a very, very needy thing to do. It's so vulgar.'

'Of course I don't give blow jobs,' said Minty, standing up and tossing her long blonde hair over her shoulders. 'I sug-gest that I might use it as a lure for gifts.'

'God, your friends are *so* lovely,' said Lizzie as she finally shut the door.

'They're all right,' said Penny, letting her stomach out and kicking off her shoes.

'They're not all right! Grainne's a shaking puddle on the sofa!'

'I'm still here,' said Grainne. 'And my flat is bigger than the sofa, actually, it's just that it's a studio, that's all, and there's nothing wrong with that. It's sixteen by twelve, I remember from the plans. I'd be very amazed if you had a sofa that was sixteen by twelve, ha, ha, ha!'

'It's OK, Grainne, we didn't think that,' said Lizzie gently.

'I mean, OK, so my sofa is like my sofa and a bed as well, and I don't always remember to fold the bed back into the sofa,' said Grainne, 'and OK, so you have to climb over the

162

sofa to reach the sink. But it's not the same size as the room, no way.'

She shoved the last piece of salami into her mouth.

'Shh,' said Lizzie, patting her on the shoulder.

'And it's cosy, you know,' said Grainne. 'In the winter I don't really have to turn on the heating, cause I can feel my neighbour's radiator through the wall.'

'Grainne,' said Lizzie. 'You bought your own place. With your own hard-earned money. They'll never do that. You should be really proud of it and really proud of yourself.'

'Neh,' said Grainne. 'I hate it. Can I come and live here with you?'

'I don't want to go,' Penny was saying.

'Well, you have to.'

Monday morning and Penny was, if anything, worse. The visit from the girls had perked her up briefly, but when they'd dashed out on their glamorous assignations, leaving her in with Lizzie and the television, her misery had grown and grown. Also, the salami had made a speedy reappearance. She hadn't been able to keep anything down all weekend and looked terribly thin and weak and now Lizzie was sending her to the doctor's.

'You are taking the day off and you are going to the doctor's,' said Lizzie. 'Shut up.'

'But I have to go to work,' said Penny. 'Sloan's got some big lunch on.'

'He always has a big lunch on!' said Lizzie. 'As far as I can tell, that's all he does.'

'This one's really important, though,' said Penny. 'He's got to renew the freehold on the building or something, blah, blah, blah. I didn't really listen when he was telling me, but apparently it's absolutely crucial he takes them to Sketch

163

and gets them mortal, otherwise he's going to lose the shop.'

'Oh, Penny,' said Lizzie. 'Why didn't you mention this before? You must have known you'd have to go to the doctor's.'

'Well, madly, I've had one or two other things on my mind,' said Penny. 'I forgot. Also, I thought . . . I thought I'd be better by now.' She winced to herself. 'I keep thinking I'll wake up and it'll all be better, you know?'

Lizzie nodded. 'So, what are you going to do?'

Penny looked up at her. There were huge dark circles under her eyes.

'Well,' she said.

'Oh, no,' said Lizzie. 'Oh, no. No.'

'Lizzie, please.'

'I've got a job, too, you know.'

'Yeah, but you can twist that bloke round your little finger, can't you?'

'No!'

'And you haven't had a day off in ages. Jeez, when I worked in catering you were considered pathetic if you didn't dog it at least twice a week.'

'I can't leave him in the lurch.'

'You found him in the lurch. And Lizzie, if you don't . . . if you don't help me out the shop will go under and I'll lose my job anyway, and . . . '

'Could you be any more pathetic?' said Lizzie.

'Nope,' said Penny. 'God, I hate this.'

# Chapter Eight

The sun came up huge and warm as Lizzie paced her bedroom. She couldn't believe she'd agreed to this. And she realised, picking up the phone at seven-thirty, that she hadn't spoken to Georges for weeks. Not properly, nothing beyond 'we need extra peppers' or him passing over a recipe before he sped out the door. Not since the stupid night of the party when he'd made her feel like the world's biggest, most introverted idiot. Which, she noticed, she'd managed to change about herself, by doing nothing but staying in and sulking for the last two months.

Well, she had to do it. Her sister needed help.

'Yes?' He sounded gruff on the phone, harassed. She wondered what on earth he did when he wasn't in the café. Maybe some weird European thing she didn't understand, like marching in a saint's parade.

'Georges, it's Lizzie.'

His voice softened straightaway.

'Hello, Lizzie. How are you? I feel I hardly see you, no? But you are doing a very good job of looking after my restaurant.'

Well, restaurant was pushing it. Sandwich bar just about passed muster.

'I'm fine.'

'You know, takings are up. I think the customers like you.'

Lizzie couldn't help but feel pleased. She thought of her old job where, as far as she could tell, nobody at all had liked her.

'You gave me some good recipes.'

'Good food is not hard, Lizzie. Just some good ingredients, you know, a little bit of love . . . '

'I don't know about love,' said Lizzie, feeling herself go slightly pink.

'No,' said Georges. Then his voice grew hearty again.

'Are you still using your microwave? And going to parties all night?'

'I'm not actually.'

Seeing as she was welcome to take home the leftovers, Lizzie had been eating from the café every day.

'No? You are eating better? Ah, you will look beautiful. The tomatoes will make your skin bloom, and the spinach will clear your eyes and enrich your blood.'

'You talk a lot of rubbish,' said Lizzie. But it was true. She was looking better. The mirror kept hinting at it, and her waistbands were loosening. The other day she'd bought a smaller size in tights. From extra large to large, but it had given her a huge frisson nonetheless. And she wasn't sure, but she thought she was losing her microwave pallor a little too.

'Normally I am very serious,' said Georges, but he didn't sound serious when he said it.

Lizzie steeled herself and dived in.

'Georges, I need to take a few days off.'

Immediately Georges's light tone ceased. 'I see.'

'I need to . . . it's a family matter.'

'Your sister is in a scrape?'

'No! Well, ish. Well, it doesn't matter, I just wondered if you would mind. Like, having a holiday.'

'I understand "a few days off".'

'Uh-huh.'

'Well, I think. Do you mean a few days off or do you mean bye, bye, Georges, I am gone never to see you again?'

'The first one,' said Lizzie. 'I just need to help Penny for a few days.'

Georges made a *pff* sound with his mouth. 'This is not very convenient to me right now.'

'Me neither,' said Lizzie, quelling a very passing desire to say if it was convenient he could take his job and shove it up his portly bottom.

'OK. You will be back on Wednesday? When? I must come in and cover for you.'

'Are you always so cross when anyone wants to take a holiday?'

'I am not cross, Lizzie. That is you, huh? Now, I have to go.'

'Oh, Penny,' said Lizzie. 'What am I supposed to wear? What am I meant to do? What are my duties? Does *Sloan* know I'm coming?'

'Yeah, yeah, yeah,' said Penny from the bathroom. 'You'll be fine.'

'*Penny!* You need to help me!'

There wasn't another sound from the bathroom.

'*Pen!*'

Silence.

'OK, I'm coming in.'

'No! No, no, no, no, no!'

Lizzie cursed manfully under her breath and headed back into her room.

OK. Deep breath. Not to worry about it. It was just Penny's stupid job, that appeared to require the brain power of a four-year-old. No panic. What the hell was she going to wear? It didn't matter to Penny, she spunked all her money on designer shoes and bags in the sale, then wore pure black and white the rest of the time. Anything looks OK in a size eight.

Usually at work she wore . . . well, an apron.

But this place – God, they practically sold paintings on the smartness of some ditzy girl's buttocks. The keyword she was really looking for here was pert. Pert was not something ever applied to Lizzie. Pear, maybe.

OK, breathe. Black. That was it. Arty people loved black. Well, she had plenty of that. After a bit of rummaging she found a long black skirt she'd last worn to a Mission reunion concert with Felix. OK, fine. And maybe a white T-shirt . . . nope. It wasn't that white, and she looked like a waitress. Black again. Not the ironic Iron Maiden, that was never going to work. And didn't look ironic on her anyway, it made her look like one of those girls that follows heavy metal bands around the country in the hopes of finding a boyfriend through the law of averages. Which, it occurred to her, she should look into trying one of these days.

She finally found a basic V-neck top and slipped that on and stared at herself in the mirror. She didn't look like an arty boho chick. She looked like a plump girl trying to blend into the background.

She stomped through to Penny's room and used some of

her expensive and patently shoplifted face cream.

'I'm just *accessorising*,' she called out. There came a muffled grumble which may well have been discontented annoyance mixed with an inability to prevent anything happening.

Inside Penny's jewellery box was some cheap silver and gold and a couple of tiny diamond baubles given to her by the slightly less cheap but still not exactly fabulous, dodgy men of her past. Lizzie picked out a large brooch and pinned it to her bosom. There we go; arty eccentricity, and it drew attention to her best feature, which would surely be a good thing to do in the world of paintings. Emboldened, she glanced around. What next?

Penny's bedroom, over the rubbish, was a mishmash of clothes and sparkly things that attracted her like a magpie. Lizzie caught sight of a black fur beret hanging on top of the cupboard door. Aha! She grabbed it and clamped it down on her unruly hair, then squinted at herself in the large mirror.

There she was. If you squinted (quite hard) she looked boho, arty and a tad frisky with the hat at a jaunty angle. This was perfect.

'OK,' she yelled. 'I'm ready.'

'What are you wearing?' groaned Penny.

'Never you mind,' said Lizzie. 'It's perfect.'

'Oh, God.'

'What do I have to do in this stupid job again?'

'Just sit at the desk and look pretty.'

They both paused.

Lizzie checked herself out again in the mirror. Perhaps some bright red lipstick, she thought. She picked up Penny's highly sought-after Chanel Red Bus, which Penny had always claimed to have found in the toilets at the All-American New York Diner, and started applying. Putting on lipstick wasn't as easy as she thought; she'd always made do with gloss. Oh well, no matter. She made a kissing face at herself in the mirror.

'OK. OK. I'm going to do this,' she said. 'Are you going to be all right?'

'Hhnnn,' groaned Penny.

'OK. Keep your phone on so I can contact you with any artistic emergencies. And, you know. Call me the second . . . '

'Uh-huh.'

Lizzie took a deep breath. She felt strangely excited. Maybe being an arty boho chick was the kind of person she really was after all. Maybe she could bring lots of art into Georges's café and turn it into a hip happening joint where people paid in paintings and got terribly famous.

'You know, I think I might even be glad you talked me into this,' she said. 'And, Pen . . . I don't know quite what this means, but – good luck.'

There was still no sound from the bathroom.

Lizzie had been to Penny's gallery once before, for an exhibition where they had free wine. She'd stood beside Brooke and Minty, who'd practically ignored her, until Will had come up to say hi, whereupon Brooke and Minty had come over all friendly with her to freeze Will out.

Chelsea was coming to life all around her. Deliveries were being made to smart restaurants; beautifully dressed shopgirls hurried past, tall, smart-suited bankers stamped along briskly. Every single one of them glanced at Lizzie's hat. Admiration, undoubtedly.

Finally she turned up the little cobbled street and found herself outside Penny's workplace, the name of the gallery beautifully scripted in an elegant white font against a racing-green frontage. It was an ocean of tranquillity and breathed money and peace. Lizzie wondered why on earth she hadn't considered working here earlier.

In the window was one of Will's huge landscapes that Sloan had put on display. Oh God, what if he came in? What if she tried to say hello and accidentally shouted, 'Penny's pregnant! Penny's pregnant! Penny's pregnant!' straight in his face?

'Uh, excuuuuuse me,' came a ludicrously over-the-top voice interrupting her unhappy reverie. 'Can I *helllp* you?'

Lizzie slowly turned around and found herself face-to-face with Sloan. He was wearing a large cream fedora hat and pastel bow tie that somehow contrived to look incredibly smart.

'Where did you get that *terrible* hat?' he said, then stopped himself. 'Sorry, I really shouldn't be rude. But in your case . . .'

'Terrible hat yourself,' said Lizzie, without thinking. 'Uh, I'm sorry too.'

'No, no, no, no, no,' he said. 'You're missing the point.'

He took out a huge old-fashioned key and unlocked the heavy outer door to the shop.

'You see, my hat is beautiful, exquisitely tasteful and suits me. Whereas you have a dead otter on your head. Do you see the difference? Beautiful garment' – he indicated himself, then pointed to her head – 'rotting maggot-infested carcass. Do you see?'

Lizzie followed him into the shop. What was with this posh/rude thing? Would she ever learn?

'Are you following me?'

His self-confidence was galling, and Lizzie was remembering the circumstances she'd lost her last job in, still unconfident.

'Uh,' she said unconvincingly.

'You know, there's a hostel round the corner.'

'I'm not a bag lady!' said Lizzie in annoyance.

'That's not what your hat's telling me.'

'You're the rudest man I've ever met.'

'In that hat? I'm amazed.'

'Shut up about my hat!'

She calmed down as he stepped into the shop.

'I'm Lizzie. Penny's sister.'

Sloan eyed her carefully. 'Are you *really*?'

'You've met me. Tons of times.'

'*Have* I?' he sounded doubtful. He stared at her, hard. 'I meet a lot of people. So, what are you doing here?'

Lizzie wasn't quite sure how to approach this. Maybe mention that Penny was taking one day sick then take it from there.

'Penny can't come in today.'

Sloan rolled his eyes. 'Oh, my goodness, that's ridiculous. I've had some ditzy dollies work here before but your sister takes the biscuit. She knows this is a big day for me.'

'No, don't say that!' said Lizzie. 'You see, you can take me instead! I'll do it!'

Sloan's face cracked into a smile, showing brown and orange teeth. 'You'll do what?'

'I'll fill in,' said Lizzie, looking around. 'How hard can it be? I've worked in shops before.'

Sloan's smile looked, on closer inspection, more of a snarl. 'Are you those psychic twins one hears about?'

'Nope.'

'You sound nothing like her.'

'She puts it on.'

'And you look nothing like her.'

'I do if I go like this.'

Lizzie sucked her cheeks in as far as they would go and rolled her eyes. Sloan's mouth twitched.

'And you think you're just going to stand in for her?'

His phone rang. The ringtone was a little classical diddly number.

'Yes? Sketch? For nine people? Of course I made the booking. Uhhh . . . hang on a minute.' He looked at Lizzie. 'Is this a prank?'

'Is what a prank?'

He gestured impatiently. 'Are you really here to work?'

Lizzie nodded fervently.

Sloan shut the phone with a slam. 'I think I may just have made a very big mistake.'

'Nonsense,' said Lizzie. 'I'll be good.'

They were both facing each other as someone entered the shop. It was a tall blonde woman with a Nicole Kidman nose and superior air, as if just having a Nicole Kidman nose was enough to make you feel superior. Maybe it was, thought Lizzie.

'Hello!' she said cheerfully. 'Can I help you with anything?'

The woman stared right through her as if she was made of invisible dust. Lizzie glanced at Sloan, but he was looking at her in exactly the same way.

'Well, I'll just be over here,' said Lizzie, 'if I can get you anything.'

The woman made a tiny moue with her highly glossed mouth. She glanced airily around the gallery.

'Are these all you have?' she asked eventually, with a slightly European accent Lizzie couldn't identify.

'Uh, no, not at all, madam,' said Lizzie, bouncing forward. 'I'll just check in the back. What kind of colour are you looking for?'

The woman stared at her. 'What *colour*?'

'You know. To go with your walls . . . on your yacht or

173

whatever . . . ' Lizzie's voice trailed away. The woman was staring at her in disbelief.

The woman's eyes flicked to Sloan, who jumped forward. 'What this person was *trying* to say was that Brown's extraordinary use of colour is truly what sets him apart from other artists in this area.'

'But half of these are black and white.'

'Are they though?' said Sloan. 'Are they *really*?'

The woman peered more closely at the pictures in front of her.

'You. Champagne. Now,' hissed Sloan at Lizzie out of the corner of his mouth.

'Thanks,' said Lizzie. 'But it's only ten-thirty in the morning.'

'For *her*.'

Lizzie stumbled into a large messy back room that was quite a contrast with the immaculate gallery next door. Frames were stacked in corners and a desk was completely submerged with paperwork. In the corner was an ancient fridge, held together with string, and inside were about twenty mini bottles of Moët. She grabbed one and looked around for something other than a chipped mug standing by the sink to put it in. There wasn't anything. She checked everywhere. Oh God. Maybe this was some kind of fashionable east London thing where it was cool to drink out of big builder's mugs. She poured it quickly.

Back in the gallery the woman and Sloan were deep in an animated discussion of just how many colours they could both see in the grey tones of Will's work.

'There's definitely some pink,' said the woman.

'That's amazing,' said Sloan. 'You know, there is, but only a very highly developed eye could have picked it out. I couldn't – the artist had to show me.'

'You know him well?'

'He's a very good friend of mine,' said Sloan.

'Champagne?' Lizzie said, holding out the chipped cup which, she now noticed, had a cover of the *Sunday Sport* printed on it.

The woman recoiled. 'Excuse me?'

Sloan immediately grabbed it.

'I washed it,' said Lizzie as he pulled her to one side.

'I could smack you,' hissed Sloan, and he looked like he meant it. 'Go get another one of those little bottles, open it, put a straw in it, give it to the nice lady, then get the fuck out of my sight for evermore.'

'What about Sketch?' said Lizzie bravely.

'I would rather have a robber's dog look after this store while I'm out than you. I think I'll just go down to the cellar and bring up some of the many rats who live there and invite them to take over. There's a chap in Shepherd's Market who looks after the prozzies with a razor and sells crack. I might ask him to step in for a couple of hours. After which I'll call up Ronnie Biggs, the great train robber, to do the stock check . . .'

'OK, I get your point.'

'Following which I'll see if Pol Pot is available to do the totalling up and get the resulting accounts audited by Enron. Am I making myself clear?'

Lizzie nodded.

'Where . . .' came the woman's voice from over their heads, '*did* you get that hat?'

'There's nothing wrong with my hat!' shouted Lizzie, finally pushed beyond endurance. 'If you bloody upper classes weren't so obsessed with things like bloody hats you wouldn't all be going inbred and mental.'

The woman had moved forward, not listening to a word.

'It's really terribly chic.'

They all paused.

'Uh, this hat?' said Lizzie finally.

'Yes. It's got an ugly chic to it. I like it.'

Lizzie squinted at her.

'Please, madam, do take it if you like,' said Sloan obsequiously.

'No, you can't!' said Lizzie. 'It's Penny's.'

'"Penny's", eh?' said the lady. 'I've never heard of them. Is there a waiting list?'

'Yes,' said Lizzie.

'Fabulous. Well done you, I'll get my PA to look it up right away.'

She swept towards the door.

'Oh, and Sloan, get those two big landscapes sent round, will you? The ones with the pink in them.'

And the discreet bell of the shop politely twanged and she was gone.

'Stop it,' said Sloan, after a time.

'Stop what?' said Lizzie, who was trying to compose her face whilst staring out of the window.

'Stop trying to keep that stupid smug grin off your face.'

'Why should I have a stupid smug grin?' said Lizzie. 'I've just made you tons and tons of money after being here for five minutes but you're still going to throw me out on the street.'

Sloan's mobile went off again. He listened to it intently then hung up.

'Did you know,' he said, 'that if you don't take up your lunch reservation at Sketch they charge your credit card anyway on what they think you might have eaten?'

'Is that the kind of thing a West End art dealer's assistant ought to know?' said Lizzie.

'Mmm,' said Sloan. He wandered into the back room. Lizzie heard him throw the china mug against the wall. It shattered with a crash. Eventually, he came back in, with a new, freshly straightened cravat.

'I'm temperamental,' he said. 'Do you think you can handle that?'

'I'm temperamental, too,' said Lizzie.

'Tough shit. Are you going to sell a few of these bloody paintings?'

'Yes!'

'OK then.'

Sloan whooshed out of the shop and slammed the door, shaking his head to himself as he did so.

Penny sat in the waiting room of the local doctor's surgery looking round with some interest, even as her left foot twitched uncontrollably. It was much smarter than Brandford community health clinic. There were pictures on the wall that nobody had twocced, and a couple of smartly dressed businessmen, fiddling with their BlackBerries whilst waiting to go in. This might not be a bad place to look for men. Then she remembered why she was here and groaned to herself. Oh, for goodness' sake. It may look a bit smarter, but she was still having to wait. Although they did have the latest issue of *Vogue* rather than a five-year-old *Reader's Digest*. That was something. Her fingers were a little shaky on the keys of her mobile when she called her sister.

'So how's it going?'

'I realise why you spend so much time on the phone,' said Lizzie. 'There's really fuck all else to do.'

'Yes, but when I spend time on the phone it's networking. You're just arsing about.'

'Any news?'

'Nope, still waiting. Although, Lizzie, you should tart yourself up sometime and get down here . . . '

Sloan would be back soon from his liquid lunch, and she hadn't sold anything else. Was this normal? She knew when she walked past these places (which wasn't very often, and even then only on the way to John Lewis to buy thread with her mother), there never seemed to be anyone in them, browsing or purchasing. She'd kind of assumed people bought over the phone or something, but the phone hadn't rung all day. Penny's job was just literally sitting. When she thought of how busy she was in the café, running about, chopping, cleaning, serving and chatting to the people coming in, she decided she had the better deal. OK, she had to start early in the morning, and she certainly got her hands dirty, and she didn't have a second even to glance at *Metro*, but her day flew by, and she got the pleasure of feeding people; of giving people things they liked. It had seemed that woman earlier hadn't even liked spending thousands of pounds on a huge treat like a painting; that it had been a chore rather than a pleasure.

But even just by being here, Lizzie could feel some of her suppositions falling away about these people. They weren't, as it turned out, any less mean or ignorant than the people she hadn't liked on her estate. They had the same expensive footwear (although shoes rather than trainers), flash motors and an unearned sense of entitlement. But this, oddly, made her feel less intimidated. She really didn't care.

Lizzie let herself slump over on the desk, not even worried now about the state of her hair. Oh God, and she really, really had to go and visit Gran too. Excellent, a two-hour bus journey on top of this day of hell. She let out a huge sigh, just as the door to the shop pinged.

'Aha!' came the loud voice dramatically. 'I guessed it! You are betraying me! But Lizzie, working for me is much, much better, no?'

Lizzie looked up and could not stifle a smile, even though she'd intended to treat Georges coldly the next time she saw him, after he'd been so short with her about taking time off. He was, for the first time, wearing a suit rather than a stained T-shirt with a striped apron tied round his middle or, at the party, a black shirt which simply screamed 'I am a black shirt donned solely for my apparently slimming qualities'.

Now, however, he was wearing a very well-fitting grey pin-stripe, with a cream shirt and a darker grey and yellow tie.

'I'm just covering for Penny,' said Lizzie. 'Just for a couple of days. She's sick.'

'You have not left for ever?'

'No. Not at all. You look very smart.'

'I am a very snappy dresser,' said Georges. 'Don't you think?'

Lizzie looked at the heavy gold ring and the little tufts of dark hair escaping from the cuffs of his immaculate shirt. Oddly, she found it rather sexy; the contrast between the pristine cloth and the animalistic man underneath made her shiver.

'Yes, you are. How did you guess I was here?'

Georges waved his hands. 'Well, I recognised that drunk man. Sometimes he comes in and asks me if I have any wines and I say no, we don't have any wines, we are a lunchtime shop with no wines and he says, OK, and then he forgets and comes back the next week and asks for wines.'

Lizzie nodded sagely.

'And I am on my way to see my bank.'

'Oh.' Lizzie felt concern. There was nothing wrong with

the business, was there? She hated to think of other places, who didn't care so much about their ingredients or how they threw their food together, getting the better of Georges by being cheaper.

'Is everything OK?' she asked worriedly, thinking of Sloan's meeting.

Georges smiled broadly. 'Lizzie, it is OK. You do not need to worry yourself about us.'

Lizzie rather liked him using the term 'us'.

'Oh good,' she said. 'It's a very good café.'

Georges looked around. 'What are these? They look like holiday pictures.'

'They're paintings,' said Lizzie. 'Those ones there are by my sister's evil ex-boyfriend.'

Georges raised his shaggy eyebrows encouragingly. There was no sign of Sloan in the street; perhaps he'd taken his meeting on to the Arts Club where, according to Penny, he could sit in the corner smoking with a cigarette holder and discourse on contemporary art for hours despite being absolutely whizzbanged. 'It's so boring it makes you want to kill yourself,' she'd said. 'I think that's why he gets drunk all the time. Otherwise he'd have to bash his own head in.'

Lizzie told Georges the whole sad story '. . . and that is why she's at the doctor's.'

'I know this word,' he said, holding up a finger. 'It is bounder. That is the word, yes?'

'Yes,' said Lizzie. 'That's it. And what he didn't think was, we don't have any money. He didn't realise.'

'He didn't see your kitchen,' said Georges.

Lizzie shook her head.

'I've seen your kitchen,' said Georges. He looked grave. 'And you work for me. Very few rich people work for me.'

'Well, quite,' said Lizzie. 'Can I have a raise?'

'A raise? While I am in here talking to you while you are working for somebody else?'

'Oh, yeah,' said Lizzie.

Georges walked around looking at the pictures closely. Lizzie wondered where he'd got a suit to fit him so well. Their mother's old lodger had had a suit, but he'd bought it at Burtons and it looked as if he was going to court, and not as a lawyer either.

'You know,' Georges said finally, 'I am a little sorry for Will.'

'Sorry for *Will*? How can you be sorry for him? He got my sister pregnant then dumped her because we're poor! Be sorry for *us*!'

'He doesn't know she is pregnant, no?'

'She didn't want to blackmail him into anything,' said Lizzie.

'That's good.'

'Plus she thought he still might not care. And that would make her feel worse.'

'That's bad.' He looked meditative. 'You know, Penny will be all right. She's a survivor.'

Lizzie let out a sigh.

'But to be a leech, to try to live off women's money, to pretend to make love . . .'

'He didn't pretend to make love,' said Lizzie. 'That's what got us into this mess.'

'Well, I think that is a very sad thing for a man to do. Or do you think I'm old-fashioned?'

'Georges, you make your own bread and you don't use a microwave. I *know* you're old-fashioned.'

Georges smiled. 'I think I want to buy one of his paintings.'

\*

181

The doctor was a woman clearly younger than Penny, which made her sullen.

'You can just buy a test in Boots, you know,' said the doctor crossly. 'They're just the same and much quicker.'

Penny looked at the floor. 'I couldn't afford to,' she mumbled.

'What was that?' said the doctor, as if the concept of not being able to afford something was entirely new. Which it probably was.

'Nothing,' said Penny.

'Well, now I have to send it away to the lab. It'll take five days. Should I write down that this is a wanted birth, or do we have to discuss our options?'

Penny wondered if being told off by a sixteen-year-old virgin was some kind of cosmic punishment. As was, it seemed at the moment, the whole of the rest of her life.

Lizzie was so shocked she burst out laughing.

'You want to *what*?'

'Buy a painting. Then Will can give some money to Penny if she has the baby. From himself, not from playing kissy with a woman. And look, he is very talented.'

'You're serious.'

Georges nodded.

'Which painting?'

'You choose.'

Lizzie almost giggled.

'Georges, they're thousands of pounds.'

Georges shrugged.

'But . . . '

'Lizzie! You are working in a shop selling paintings! Sell me a painting! You are worse at this than you are at cleaning the big brass pot!'

'I hate cleaning anything bigger than me,' said Lizzie. 'Uh. OK. Now, I have to write it down then we send it to you . . . I think . . . ' She disappeared under the desk and started ferreting about.

'This isn't the kind of service I expect in an expensive Chelsea art gallery,' said Georges. 'Is that your hat? I like it.'

Under the desk Lizzie smiled to herself. And found the invoice book.

'OK. What about this one?' She headed straight towards the smallest and cheapest, a tiny delicate seascape.

'That is the smallest! You think Georges Dos Santos takes the worst? Huh? No.'

Lizzie looked around desperately. Georges pointed at the far wall, to a painting of a canopy of trees over an avenue stretching along a desolate landscape, with only the hint of a steeple in the distance.

'I will take this one. I like it. It says the road is long, but shady. And at the end of it there is home. Very nice.'

'You're quite the romantic when you get going, aren't you?' said Lizzie.

'You'd better believe it,' said Georges.

'But I don't understand,' said Penny. She was sitting on the sofa, hunched up, working her way through a box of tissues on her left and Milk Tray on her right.

'I think he was just doing a really nice thing for you,' said Lizzie. 'I mean, the café can't make that much.'

Penny looked confused. 'Maybe it does.'

'I cash up the till. I'm telling you it doesn't. Georges buys really good ingredients and has no portion control.'

'Well, that much is painfully obvious.'

'Be nice; he was trying to help you out.'

'Did you say he goes out all the time?'

'Yeah.'

'There you go, then. Maybe he does something else. Bets on the horses or something.'

'How would that make you rich?'

But Penny didn't say anything. Her face crumpled up and she felt for the tissues again.

'Will'll be so happy,' she moaned, 'when he finds out he's sold a painting.'

'A big one too,' said Lizzie.

Penny sobbed. 'And he'll use the money to take out some bint, with diamond earrings and a tiny nose. I know he will.'

Lizzie patted her gently on the shoulder. 'Are you any closer to deciding what you want to do?'

'Yes,' said Penny. 'It's the obvious thing. And everyone keeps telling me there's nothing to it.' She sobbed harder. 'I've got to wait five days to get the results.'

'Ah, well, no, you don't,' said Lizzie, drawing the Boots package from her bag. 'What does petty cash mean anyway?'

As Penny sat there, stunned, Lizzie stepped behind the coffee machine Georges had said he was finished with and let her take home. It was taking her quite a significant amount of time to learn how to use it and it was still liable to blast her with super-heated steam when she wasn't paying attention.

'Oh God,' said Penny. 'Either my life is a hundred per cent ruined or . . . no, I think it's a hundred per cent ruined. I didn't even know that it was possible to cry this much. How come I'm crying this much? I don't think there's any fluid left in my body. I've been squeezed dry, like an old lemon in last night's Bacardi.'

Penny snatched the test from Lizzie's hand and dashed out. A second later she reappeared.

'It's the bloody crying! There's no moisture left in my

184

body, I can't pee! There's no water in me at all.' She grabbed a cup of Lizzie's coffee and sipped it furiously. 'Bloody hell. Right, back in a minute.'

Lizzie looked at the machine. As its pressure built up, the boiling water made a 'wheee!' sound, as – from the bathroom – did Penny.

# Chapter Nine

'I'm not pregnant!' Despite what she'd said about being drier than the Sahara, some new tears were dripping down Penny's face.

'Great! I'm giving Georges his money back for that stupid painting he bought.'

'No, don't do that,' said Penny, 'Sloan'd kill me. Just tell Georges he has to burn it.'

Lizzie rolled her eyes. 'Well,' she said. 'No harm done.'

'No harm done?' Penny threw back the duvet she'd been sheltering under for the previous five days.

'NO HARM DONE? My relationship is completely screwed up . . . which was obviously going nowhere now I come to think of it, you've made me realise my new friends don't necessarily want the best for me and it's made me give up drinking. How can you call that no harm done?'

'Well, at least I won't have to deal with your rude creepy

boss any more,' said Lizzie, sitting next to Penny and patting her gently on the arm.

'Sloan isn't creepy,' said Penny. 'Not as long as you give him plenty of Midori to drink.' She heaved a great sigh. Hot dogs, hot dogs, hot dogs. *Pff.* 'What do you think it was with the tits?'

'The power of positive thinking,' said Lizzie.

They sat in silence for a while.

'I just . . . you know, I thought for one tiny minute . . . just when I was on that bus to Will's house. I wondered what it would be like, you know. Me and him in –' she cast around – 'in a nice apartment. With a little baby.' She snuffled again.

Lizzie comforted her. 'You hate babies.'

'I don't hate babies. I just didn't want to be another one of the Evergreen Estate girls, you know? I just didn't want three babies, by nineteen, with different dads, and nowhere to put them and no money and not able to do anything with them and dressing them in England shirts and things. Those are the babies I didn't want.'

She looked at Lizzie, blinking rapidly.

'And when I saw Will's place . . . it was such a dump, Lizzie, honestly. It made this place look like the Ritz. And I thought, even if he wasn't a gold-digging bastard, Liz . . . even if he'd been nice and good and kind and everything – I still wasn't sure I could do it. I still wasn't sure I could have the baby and live in that shithole and have absolutely fucking nothing all over again when I've had absolutely fucking nothing up until now.'

Lizzie patted her gently on the arm again.

'Does that make me a bad person? I'm sick of it, Lizzie. I'm sick of scrimping on every fucking thing, then I look at what Brooke has got and what Minty's got and what bloody Sloan has got and just feel like shit all the time.' Penny shook her head. 'I'm sick of being poor. And that makes me just as bad as him, Liz.'

A quiet week limped into a quiet weekend – Lizzie stayed on at the gallery (in case Will came in, but he didn't), until Saturday, when Penny forced herself out of the house ('I can't help it, Lizzie, I'm starting to smell of old lady') to the amateur pole-dancing night Brooke and Minty were going to in Shepherd's Market.

'Come with us, Lizzie,' Penny had said. 'I've got to get back on the horse and you . . . you've got to get *on* the horse. Come on. I'll pay. To say thanks.'

'You want to take me pole dancing to say thank you?'

'It's something to do. And apparently lots of men go.'

'I'll bet they do. No thanks.'

Penny had sighed. 'Up to you then.'

The club had been great fun, full of daft girls up for a laugh. Penny had watched Brooke and Minty carefully though, especially Brooke. She watched how she refused every other drink, and encouraged other people on to mischief whilst never getting out of control herself. They'd been pleased to find out she wasn't pregnant, although Penny suspected Minty wouldn't have been that fussed. And now Brooke was pointing out the chaps to her.

'Look,' she said. 'Always check the watch. If it's too big it's almost certainly fake.'

'And the shoes,' said Minty. 'They must be wearing shoes, not trainers. If there are tassles on them that means middle management and golf. Run, run, run.'

'OK,' said Penny. She'd had a couple of vodkas on her shrunken tummy and was feeling defiant.

'And the car,' said Brooke. 'That's important. You want

flashy but not too flashy. If it's too flashy he's probably been saving up for it since he was six and still lives with his mum.'

'After all,' said Minty after a pause. 'You did try falling in love, didn't you?'

'Yes,' said Penny.

'And, did it work?'

'It bloody didn't.'

'Exactly. Darling, you've got to go for what lasts.'

'Money,' said Brooke. She raised her glass. 'To fun and money. And, darling, can we have a teeny tiny word about your miniskirt?'

Penny didn't look like their other friends, and Brooke had privately wondered about her, but Minty had never met anyone who hadn't been to boarding school before and was prepared to take Penny on trust. 'She's probably from one of the minor counties,' she'd said to Brooke sympathetically. 'Somerset or somewhere equally preposterous. We should feel sorry for her really.'


Lizzie was so bored by Sunday lunchtime – Penny wasn't up yet – that she'd started moving piles of things around slightly. She realised this was strictly *verboten*, but her grandmother certainly didn't seem to be getting any better or look like she was coming back, and she could always move them again later, and if she could just get to the window to clean it, the whole place would look better immediately.

She surprised herself by getting into the work, and having vigorously had a go at the window she decided to attack the sink unit too. There was something satisfying about lifting up endless layers of gooey gunk, which somehow suited her mood, and as she swilled yet another bucket of soapy water down the drain she felt a little better, so she wasn't really paying attention when the doorbell rang.

Assuming it was the girls downstairs looking for sparkling water ('You still drink milk? I think milk is common,' 'Yuh, all dairy is definitely common'), or the young gentleman callers on the girls downstairs who often got confused (Minty thought locking men out was a hilarious prank), she went to answer it without taking off her rubber gloves or removing the old pair of tights she'd wrapped around her head to keep her curls out of her face, singing a Sugababes song to herself rather tunelessly.

'Hello,' said Georges.

Lizzie nearly dropped the mop.

'What are you doing here?' she demanded. Georges stared at her.

'Hello. Welcome, traveller, to my home, where I shall show you kind hospitality and shower you with warmth, as I am a human being with normal human instincts, even when, as now, I resemble a frog wearing a pair of tights on top of my head.'

Lizzie flushed.

'Well,' she said. 'It's a reasonable question.'

Georges was wearing a suit again, but a different one this time, a lighter-weight khaki that made him look darker than ever. His bushy eyebrows came together.

'And I was taking my little sister to Mass, then she wants to go to Topping Shop. Is that enough or do you need a paper signed by many expert witnesses and the mayor? And I need to know if you are coming back to work tomorrow or will I have to get Marina to work instead, which I think will cost me much money in Topping Shop.'

'Come in,' said Lizzie. She was extremely pleased to see him, although mortified by the way she was dressed. 'Would you like some coffee?'

'I'm very hungry,' said Georges.

'Cheek!' said Lizzie. 'I cook for you all week and now you want me to cook for you for free!'

'You look to me,' said Georges, 'well, you dress like that . . . '

'You are the most sexist dinosaur in the world.'

'I am not,' said Georges. 'If I was sexist I would say, "You do not look like you are dressed for cleaning and cooking, you look like you always dress like that and are a sad girl."'

'Is that what you would say?' said Lizzie. 'In that case you certainly get no breakfast.'

'Ah, but when you smile . . . everything lights up and is happy again.'

Lizzie couldn't help it. She smiled.

'See! Now any man would forget tights on head. What do you have? Eggs? Peppers?'

'Yup,' said Lizzie proudly.

'We will have Portuguese omelette,' said Georges. 'It is like Spanish omelette, only good and not filthy and covered in rat hair and evil Spanish blood. Sit down. Where is your unfortunate sister?'

'I'm here,' said the voice, not nearly as weak and tear-stained as it had sounded before. Penny rounded the doorframe of her bedroom and Lizzie nearly gasped. She hadn't been privy to Brooke and Minty's little directional fashion chit-chat that Penny had taken to heart, so the effect was completely out of the blue.

Penny looked different. She looked dewy, and clear-eyed, with shiny pink lips and rosy cheeks. She was wearing a billowy, expensive-looking white shirt and a pair of soft faded jeans. Her bare feet were still quite brown, and the toes were perfectly manicured. She looked fantastic, like a black and white photograph of an American film star romping on the beach. Where was the fake tan? The five layers of mascara? Even the nails were shorter.

Lizzie's gaze shot to Georges. Sure enough, his eyebrows, which always betrayed exactly what he was thinking, had shot up.

'Penny,' he said, and there was a new softness in his voice, 'I should not know but I do know and I hear that congratulations is in order. You look like motherhood is going to suit you. Having a baby is always a wonderful thing, even if it is not always in the best of circumstances, no?'

Rather than contradict him raucously, Penny gave a shy smile.

'It was a mistake,' she said, sitting down demurely on a chair and looking at Georges, eyes wide. 'A silly mistake, I suppose.'

Lizzie was incredulous. What was this with the 'I suppose'? She'd just had the most narrow escape of her life!

'I am sorry,' said Georges. 'Maybe you are a little sorry too, no?'

Penny tilted her head in a Princess of Wales fashion, craning to see if she could get a glimpse of Georges's watch.

'Maybe,' she said. Maybe nothing, thought Lizzie. What had happened to Penny? What was she up to?

'I am going to cook you a good meal,' said Georges, leaping up.

'Wow,' said Penny, looking straight at him. 'I love a man who can cook.'

Georges disappeared into the depths of the kitchen annexe, occasionally making disappointed noises as he pulled out antiquated and shockingly dusty kitchen appliances.

'What are you up to?' hissed Lizzie to Penny. 'I thought you were getting over your heartbreak by being all sluttish and stuff.'

'I was,' said Penny, making her downcast face again. 'But

you know, Lizzie, I think I've changed. I think this happening has made me see things differently.'

'Differently how?'

But Penny just smiled infuriatingly and padded over to the kitchen.

Georges was cooking with his usual élan, tossing the pan, letting the bread hop out of the toaster and doing five things at once.

'That's amazing,' said Penny, watching him as if he was the most wonderful thing she'd ever seen.

'It's not that amazing,' said Lizzie. 'I can do it.'

'Not like that though.'

'Yes, I can. It's just every time I offer to make you something you say, oh, boohoohoo, or you go and be sick or something.'

'Don't be silly!' said Penny. She laughed a tinkling little laugh that sounded a lot like Brooke. 'You're such a joker.'

'Is Lizzie a joker?' said Georges, his bottom lip overlapping his top lip. 'This is interesting. I did not know this.'

Lizzie went to the bathroom to take the tights out of her hair. Then she decided that taking the tights out of her hair would be a really obvious thing to do and they would probably both pass comment on it so she'd better not take them out in case . . . well, in case Georges . . . anyone . . . thought something of it. She rubbed under her eyes in the mirror to get rid of any old mascara tracings which seemed to congregate there and took a scout around for Penny's make-up, but couldn't see any trace of it, the hoarding witch.

Penny's peals of laughter echoed from the sitting room just as Lizzie knew that if she hid in the bathroom any longer everyone would assume the absolute worst.

'This is *delicious*,' Penny was enthusing, scooping up the

omelette and – this was a first in a while – actually putting it in her mouth. 'You're so clever.'

'I listened to my mother,' said Georges, grinding some black pepper.

'So did we,' said Lizzie. 'That's why I was such a bad cook.'

'But you get better,' said Georges. 'That is the important thing. And you work hard. That is good too.'

'So,' said Penny, looking mildly discomfited to find the attention moving off her, 'you bought Will's painting.'

Georges shrugged. 'I like paintings.'

'You didn't have to do it.'

'I know.'

'It's quite expensive.'

Georges shrugged.

'I wanted to say thank you. I know it was kind of for me.'

'Not at all. I like paintings.'

'Do you buy many paintings?'

'Sometimes.'

Georges glanced at her, his face unreadable. Penny changed tack.

'So, how long have you been running your lovely café?'

'Well, my father started running it when I was a boy . . . I came here when I was twelve, and I helped him with the shop. Then he retired and went back to Portugal.' He pronounced it Por-too-gal.

'Uh-huh,' said Penny, forking her food into her mouth.

'So I opened a few more shops, you know. It was good, my dad was happy when the business grew. And he could build a house in Portugal for my brothers and buy land for my mother to have her horses, and he was very happy about that.' Georges smiled even when he thought about it. 'So, you know, poor old Georges, I have to stay here and work and always open the cafés and work hard just so my mother can have horses, and my sisters can have these designer clothes, huh? It is a dog's life.'

'I didn't know you had lots of shops,' said Lizzie.

'You didn't ask,' said Georges, buttering himself another slice of toast. 'You say, Ah, Georges, I have dropped the mustard on the floor again. Ah, Georges, where is the taramasalata? Ah, Georges, once more I have cut open my finger and we must throw away the good meat.'

Penny laughed again. Lizzie wanted to throw butter at her.

'That's amazing,' Penny said, 'to come to this country with nothing and build up a whole chain. You're quite the tycoon!'

Georges noticeably puffed up. 'Well, I don't know,' he said. 'You know, I work hard.'

'Well, I think it's amazing,' said Penny. 'I think you're so clever.'

Lizzie was staring at her in disbelief. She couldn't mean it. Penny couldn't be serious, trying to pretend she liked someone like Georges. And Lizzie couldn't believe Georges had money. She'd thought he was just the fat sandwich-maker guy, who made her laugh and made her embarrassed and cheered her up and told her off. She realised as she thought this that she had begun to think of him in a proprietorial manner which wasn't exactly appropriate. It's just, Georges was *her* . . . friend.

'You must take me round some of your places some time,' said Penny. 'Mind you, if I can eat that well everywhere, you may have to roll me around!'

'I'm sure you would never get fat,' said Georges. 'Fat is only for old idiots like me.'

As Penny laughed her high tinkling laugh, Lizzie realised her teeth were gritted.

Two days later Penny 'popped in' to the café. Lizzie was furious. After everything she'd done for Penny . . . the help, the care. And now Penny was muscling in on the only part of her life she really enjoyed, that was hers. She spent her life looking out for her mum, her gran, her bloody headstrong bloody sister. Georges and the café were *hers*. Well, not hers, not like that but . . . how dare she? What a pig-selfish way to get over a broken heart.

'*Hello*,' Penny said to Georges. 'I thought you were never here!'

Georges shrugged. 'I like to visit all my shops.'

'Quite right. Very shrewd. I said to Sloan, we must see if you're interested in catering for any of our launches . . . we've got a very big exhibition coming up—'

'Oh yes?' said Georges. 'We might be interested. Canapés, goat's cheese, that kind of thing is good, yes?'

Lizzie watched how enthusiastic he was getting over the new idea.

'We could take some small sunblush tomatoes and stuff them with rice and . . . '

'And pesto,' said Lizzie. 'That would be good.'

'That would be very good,' said Georges. 'And take some pecorino cheese and—'

'Hang on,' said Penny. 'I did say it. But Sloan said, no, if you handed out food nobody ever ate it, and it interfered with good drinking time and the drunker people got, the more paintings they bought.'

'Oh,' said Georges.

'It would have been good,' said Lizzie loyally.

'I know,' said Georges.

'Anyway,' said Penny briskly. 'What's good on the menu today? It all looks so delicious.'

'El Bullitt,' said Georges proudly. 'Portuguese stew. To our secret recipe.'

'As long as it's dairy free,' said Penny. She'd been saying

this for years, ever since she'd read in a magazine it was a good way to avoid eating fatty foods. Georges looked genuinely upset.

'But no cheese? No fresh milk? No hot lattes or Greek yoghurt?'

'Uh, I seem to be OK with yoghurt,' said Penny.

'Oh, well, if you can eat yoghurt you can eat Parmesan.'

'Just a juice, please,' said Penny. 'So. Georges. What do you do to relax?'

Georges stopped chopping up aubergines for a moment.

'What do you mean, relax? I do not understand this English word. Aha, that is me making a very funny joke.'

'Well, you came out partying,' said Penny. 'So you can't be all square.'

'I am all round,' said Georges. His English, Lizzie had noticed, seemed to deteriorate a little when he got nervous. 'I must stop with the very funny jokes, I will cut myself like with a knife.'

'Me and the girls,' said Penny – nothing ventured, nothing gained, she was thinking, 'were going to try out a new restaurant tonight. Would you like to join us?'

That was fast, thought Lizzie.

Georges looked at Lizzie.

'You are going to try out new restaurant?'

'I'm not invited,' said Lizzie, trying to busy herself with something.

'Of course you're invited,' said Penny, sounding irritated. 'Do I have to send you a golden ticket to get you to do anything? No wonder you never go out. It's a celebration to, you know, start off the rest of my life and all that. Plus, Brooke's got us into an opening, so the food will be free.'

'Well, I promised to go see Gran.'

'Join us later then. Sheesh.' Penny looked conspiratorially

at Georges. 'And next time I'll remember to send the footman with the engraved scroll.'

'No, almost any invitation would do for me,' said Lizzie.

'It's tough, living with a martyr,' sighed Penny.

'I'm not a martyr!' said Lizzie, brushing out her grandmother's hair. The journey up had been worse than ever and she'd had to sit next to a group of giggling scrawny teenage girls. Lizzie remembered when the only thing you had to worry about with teenage girls was that they would take the piss out of your clothes. Now, according to the papers, they were also into happy slapping and general physical violence, so she had trained her eyes out of the window and kept them there.

'You are a little bit of a martyr, little twin,' said her grandmother. She'd seemed a lot more lucid today. Lizzie wondered, deep down, if she mightn't be getting better. Could that happen? She'd have asked one of the staff, but there was rarely anyone to be seen, and anyway, she was slightly frightened of them.

'You do complain a lot. Especially now you're not looking so, well . . . bountiful. And you should go out more. You don't need to come and see me every night . . . I know I'm just a boring old lady. You're young and should be going out and having fun.'

So even her old gran, half crazy and confined to a bed in Barnet thought she was a loser, pondered Lizzie gloomily, in what she realised was a martyr-ish manner.

'Do you know, I'd like to see my son,' said her gran, out of nowhere. 'I think he'll come to see me. Don't you?'

Well, seeing as he had disappeared without trace almost twenty-five years ago, no, thought Lizzie. Maybe she was overestimating Gran's improvement.

'Yes, I would like to see him,' her gran continued dreamily. 'Anyway, why aren't you getting ready for dinner? They're going out to dinner? You must go. You like the man, you have to chase him.'

Lizzie stared at her hands.

'There is a man I like,' she admitted quietly.

'Oh yes?' said her gran.

'But I think Penny maybe likes him too . . .'

Her gran leaned over and patted Lizzie's hand. 'I liked a man once. But I didn't chase him. Then he died in the war. So, the moral is obvious.'

'Chase a man or he'll die in a war?'

'Exactly.'

'Like, the sex war?' said Lizzie.

'Oh, any war,' said her gran. 'And you can tell me all about it the next time you come. But not too soon, all right?'

# Chapter Ten

The new restaurant was everything Lizzie had expected it to be, and worse. She had always dreamed, when she was working in the stamp firm, of what it would be like to come to a place with real napkins and mood lighting. She remembered for their seventh birthday their mother had brought them up to Leicester Square and taken them to Garfunkels and they'd been allowed to eat as much ice cream as they wanted; Lizzie had eaten so much she'd been sick in a Technicolor fashion all the way down the toilets (something which hadn't seemed to surprise the staff).

At the time she'd thought this was the pinnacle of fine dining and had continued to do so for a long time. But no, she saw every day now, pin-thin women on the streets of Chelsea slipping into restaurants where a bowl of spaghetti cost twenty pounds. Genuine ladies-who-lunched then slipped back into cars after two glasses of mineral water and a leaf. What would it be like, she wondered, to go out for lunch, right in the middle of the week, to just wander in and sit and chat to your friends for two hours? What would they even talk about? Handbags probably. She couldn't really talk to Grainne about much these days.

Still, she was looking not bad in a simple black wrap dress she'd bought from Hennes, now she'd finally been paid. It was cheap, but it didn't look it. Well, it didn't look *that* cheap. And it suited her, which was a first, and, she thought, twisting around and examining herself from a few different angles, she looked definitely 'curvy' rather than 'plump'.

The restaurant, just off the Fulham Road, was called Daffodil, for no earthly reason Lizzie could work out, but its food was, according to the invite Penny had left for her on the kitchen work surface, a new fusion between raw foods and Mongolian cuisine. There was a sample menu, but from the looks of it, it mainly involved uncooked carrots and porridge. The aim of the restaurant was stated to be 'leaving mind and spirit in a harmonious spirit of freshness' rather than, she noticed, feeding you and making you satisfied and happy.

Across the front was a strip of smoked glass, and the lighting inside beautifully gleaming, making it extraordinarily soft and flattering. Only the heads and feet of punters were visible through normal glass, so it looked like lots of disembodied golden mannequins laughing and screeching. At the doorway, several wafer-thin girls were hanging about smoking furiously and giving each other dirty looks through smoky dark eyes. Into the monkey pen, thought Lizzie, handing over her card to a ridiculously well-dressed bouncer person and squeezing her way inside.

'Lallie,' said Brooke, waving happily. Lizzie went over crossly. She didn't want a nutty posh-o nickname like everybody else, thank you. After her little stint in the gallery, she'd resolved to stop letting people treat her like a pushover. Well, like so much of one.

'It's Lizzie, actually,' she said, as stiffly as she dared. 'I live upstairs. We've met. My hands smell of garlic, I never get any post and my sister's a tart.'

Brooke paused for a minute, then broke into a smile.

'Here, try this, *Lizzie*,' she said, handing her a glass. 'It's a thistle cocktail. Disgusting, but effective.'

Lizzie accepted the proffered drink and took a hearty gulp. She couldn't believe that had worked.

'Jesus. That's repulsive.'

'I know,' said Brooke. 'But apparently it gets you drunk whilst performing a full body detox!'

'Great,' said Lizzie. Rob and Sven passed by, looking sharky as usual. They appeared to be wearing zoot suits.

'*Sven*,' said Brooke fulsomely. 'You remember *Lizzie*, don't you?'

Sven tried to look as if he did. Obviously, thought Lizzie, this dress wasn't quite doing the job. Or, if you looked at it another way, it was.

'Have you tried the canapés?' he said, making a face. 'It's, like, black pudding served with a radish, and spinach and cream and shit.'

'Excellent,' said Brooke, patting her tiny hips. 'Inedible canapés. This place is going to do fantastically.'

Penny swung round. Keeping to her new simple regime, she was wearing a white top with subtle diamanté sewn into it, so it glinted in the light.

'Hey, Lalls! How's Gran?'

'She's fine, *Pens*,' said Lizzie. 'You'd know if you went to see her.'

'Yes,' said Penny. 'Imagine, me going to see someone who

wanted nothing to do with us, whose son abandoned us and who has never given us an iota of support or encouragement throughout our entire lives. My bad!' She scooped up another cocktail from a passing waiter and took a large swig. 'Oh God, I thought these things might get better, not worse.'

'So, Penny,' said Minty, flouncing up and kissing Sven on the lips, 'where's the new man then?'

Penny shot a quick glance at Lizzie. She wished she hadn't mentioned Georges to the girls. But it was like they said – she had to get back on the horse, decide what she wanted and go for it. Just because Lizzie was making this big deal of not approving of her behaviour so soon after Will. Well, Will was different. Penny had thought he was special, then he'd turned out to be a gold-digging fink, and she wasn't going to let herself go through that again. She was *not* going to be one of those women, like her mother or her classmates, who just assumed all men would let you down, who sang 'I Will Survive' on the karaoke down the social after too many rum and Cokes.

Penny was going for security – real security – and Lizzie could stop getting her knickers in a twist; you'd think *she* fancied the hairy shortarse.

'Don't be stupid,' she muttered. 'There's no new man.'

Lizzie stared at her. She couldn't mean . . . she couldn't be serious. I mean, a mild flirtation maybe, but surely not enough to tell her friends about him. But Penny was definitely looking pink, as Georges, dressed in a smart black polo neck that did nothing to hide his girth but went extremely well with his black hair and blue eyes, pushed his way through the revolving doors.

Fuck, thought Lizzie. Fuck, fuck, fuck. And she even chucked back another cocktail.

'Hello, Lizzie,' said Georges, looking, as always, delighted to see her.

'Yeah, hello, whatever,' said Lizzie, feeling sulky and awkward.

Georges looked confused. 'You look nice tonight. Though I miss the frog tights.'

'Ooh, what are the frog tights, Lizzie?' said Brooke, bursting into the conversation.

'Nothing,' said Lizzie, feeling even more sulky and annoyed at herself. She bucked herself up. This wasn't what her grandmother had meant. It wasn't Georges's fault. 'You look nice, too.' She smiled at Georges.

'You think?' he grimaced. 'You know, I must go on diet. I went to Borough market today and ate so much cheese I think I am blowing up like giant balloon. Ooh.'

He grabbed two canapés off a passing plate and stuck them in his mouth, then his eyebrows made a comic twitch of disappointment.

'Now, this is not food. You must come with me to Borough market, Lizzie. You would love it there. Everything is so fresh, and good. And they let you taste it. Too much, maybe. They know me there, so they say, "Georges, cheese!" They know I am a soft touch.'

'If you had me there I wouldn't let you.'

'You wouldn't? You would be worse, I think. You would say, "More cheese!"'

'I would not! I would be discerning!'

'You would say, "Ah, orange cheese. Yellow cheese. Green cheese. Yes please!"'

'OK, that's enough, Dr Seuss,' said Lizzie.

'Perhaps I need to appoint a cheese consultant for my business. I wonder, would anyone here be interested?' He squinted around the room, as if confused, whilst Lizzie giggled.

'GEORGES!' yelled Penny, although she was only about a metre away.

'Penny,' said Georges. 'Hello.'

Penny pushed her chest out a little and smiled a dazzling smile.

'You know, Rob and I here were just talking about cars.'

Rob nodded. Lizzie didn't think they had been talking about cars at all, but a man couldn't deny talking about cars in case it made him look homosexual or something. Brooke nodded at Penny approvingly.

'Lizzie and I were talking about cheese,' said Georges gravely.

'Yeah, whatever,' said Penny. 'So, anyway, Georges, what are you driving these days?'

Georges looked perturbed. 'Uh. I don't drive.'

Lizzie felt a small stab of triumph. For sure, they were barking up the wrong tree with this one. She could see what Penny was trying to do, but Georges wasn't rich. He didn't behave like someone rich.

'Oh,' said Penny, trying to keep the disappointed tone out of her voice. She could already tell Brooke and Minty weren't exactly impressed with his looks.

Georges looked at the floor. 'I have a service. I am too lazy to drive, yes?'

A service? That meant, what, a chauffeur? Lizzie's face fell. The other girls perked up.

'Oh, yah,' said Minty immediately. 'Much easier.'

'Definitely,' said Penny. She moved closer to him and, as if on cue, the other girls took a step back.

'So, tell me more,' she said, leaning into him a little. She looked beautiful, Lizzie thought wistfully, as her perfume reached her. Georges couldn't help it. He looked dazzled, as Penny gazed at him – they were about the same height – with wonder in her eyes.

'Well,' said Georges. 'I thought about buying a car, then I

thought, Why not let someone else do the hard work, eh? And I don't care much about cars. I think they are silly boys' toys. Not important.'

Penny nodded. 'I think that's really true,' she said, a tad breathlessly. 'There's a lot more important things to think about.'

'Yes!' said Georges.

'Like cheese,' said Lizzie. But nobody heard.


Of course, it was her fault, thought Lizzie, licking her wounds in the corner. Even the cocktails had started to taste better. If she'd told Penny or asked her to back down she would have. They did *not* have a history of having the same taste in men. But protecting her sister by letting her take anything she wanted – that wasn't right, was it?

Penny was steeling herself. She'd done this before. It was the only way for her. She wasn't calm and grounded like Lizzie, or full of confidence like Brooke. She had looks, cheek and about three more birthdays to do what she could with them, or she'd be spending the rest of her life in the All-American New York Diner, and no mistake.

And she was getting somewhere. Georges certainly seemed surprised, and a bit fascinated. I mean, surely she could get used to his . . . build. She looked around the room. It was full of gorgeous skinny tall women with little fat men. That was the way it worked. Nobody got everything. If she did manage to pull one of the four good-looking rich straight men in London they'd be too busy forming an orderly queue of other women to spend any time with her. Plus, she knew her limits. She couldn't ski, couldn't ride a horse, her accent probably wasn't fooling anyone. So. Time to get on. Be pragmatic.

'So I like to take the car to the strawberry-picking fields.'

Oh God, did this man never talk about anything other than food? No wonder he was so gross.

'Wow,' said Penny. 'That sounds fabulous.'

Suddenly her eye was caught by a movement near the door. Someone was skirmishing with the black-clad bouncer. Inclining a little towards the noise, she could hear a familiar voice.

'I'm on the list! I'm sure I'm on the list.'

She moved nearer the door.

There, struggling his way through the revolving doors, looking very gaunt, still wearing the beaten-up leather jacket, his handsome face looking strained, was Will.

The gold-digging fink had been pacing the pavement for a long time. He'd heard of the party on the grapevine, and knew he had to see her; had to see Penny. He couldn't sleep, couldn't eat and, most importantly, he couldn't paint, which meant his loss of appetite was about to become less of a problem when he couldn't afford to buy any food.

Finally he scrambled through and, conscious of the entire room staring at him, instantly tried to dust himself off and look inconspicuous.

'Well, look what the cat dragged in,' said Minty loudly.

Will stared at the crowd until he found Penny.

'Penny,' he said.

Penny leaned back into Georges.

'Penny.' He strode towards her. A waiter offered him a cocktail, but he waved it away angrily.

'Penny.'

She stared at him. He looked gorgeous, and so tired. Her heart felt as if it was cracking in two.

'I've been thinking,' he started, 'I know . . . I know we're two of a kind, you and I.'

'I don't know what you're talking about,' said Penny, considering whether to take Georges's arm.

'You know . . . looking for an easier life. But Penny. I've never . . . I've never felt about anyone the way I feel about you. It's different.'

Lizzie heard Minty give a large tut.

'Please. Come back to me. We'll . . . I don't know. Live off canapés or something. In fact' – he turned round to the still-hovering waiter and grabbed two of his prawn concoctions off the tray, proffering one to her – 'come to dinner with me?'

Penny stared at him, taking in the glowing ambience of the restaurant; the chink of expensive glassware; the scent of expensive perfumes. Then she looked into Will's kind, desperately worried-looking face and thought about love.

'You're hesitating a long time,' said Will nervously.

She knew she was. But . . . could she change everything and settle – settle for less, even, than she'd left behind before? Could she trust *him* to? She thought of everything she'd longed for and everything she'd dreamed of. Then she looked into his face and . . .

Minty couldn't take another second. '*I'll* tell him,' she screamed. She threw her cocktail into his face. 'How dare you dump our friend just because she was pregnant!'

Will looked comically outraged, covered in sticky stuff.

'*What?*' he bellowed.

'You chuck her because she's pregnant and she might cost you money you don't have. Well, she doesn't need you, so you can just piss off.'

'How was that?' she said to a shell-shocked Penny, patting her on the arm.

'Uh . . . unexpected,' said Penny, staring at Will, who was staring back at her. His forehead was creased, trying to understand it all.

'But. But . . . '

Then his face hardened. He'd misunderstood. This had all been a complete waste of time. How could she do something like that? Just because of *money*?

'Not good enough for your baby, was I?' said Will coldly. 'Knocked it on the head as soon as you saw I wasn't quite the meal ticket *you'd* been hoping for?'

'Of course not,' said Penny. 'Of *course* not.'

He looked at her with narrowed eyes.

'I'd thought maybe we were just two of a kind,' he said. 'And that, you know, I loved you, so it wouldn't matter as much as all that. But now I see . . . I don't . . . '

His face seemed to crumple. Will trying to be an ice-cool man of punishment wasn't something he could sustain for very long.

'A baby . . . ' he said. Then he turned round and pushed his way out through the crowd into the bustling street beyond.

Penny immediately turned to follow him, but Minty held her back.

'He's not worth it,' she said. 'Let him go.'

'No!' said Penny. 'You don't know what you're saying.'

And she dashed after him, elbowing past women who tottered on their needle-thin heels and turned their sharp eyes to watch as Penny pushed at the heavy gold crossbar of the door.

'Will! Will!' she shouted on Fulham Road, which was full of dressed-up women, drunk men, confused-looking foreigners, smoking waiters, youths trying to look hard, couples worrying about starting times, European students knocking one another with backpacks: everyone in the world, it seemed, except the one person she was looking for.

# Chapter Eleven

Summer flattened into its dog days. Chelsea, Lizzie discovered, went quiet in August as everyone took off to their yachts, or their other houses, she supposed, or went on their international grand tours, or to the moon perhaps.

Georges was gone; back to Portugal to see his family. On the one hand, Lizzie was pleased. It stopped Penny hanging around and asking after him all the time. On the other, she missed him horribly. He'd left her in charge of buying, and she couldn't even feel an aubergine without remembering him yelling, 'Baby's bottom, Lizzie! What must it feel like? Hairy camel bottom? No! Big monkey bottom? No! You must listen to me. I am good teacher. And also, you must teach me something. For good balance.'

'I don't know anything,' Lizzie had protested.

'Lizzie!' He was shocked. 'You must do. I wish to know how much is one stamp to Por-too-gal, please?'

'I don't know,' Lizzie had giggled, blushing as usual.

'Uh-huh. My stamps experts. Now, you must tell me then, what is happening in *EastEnders*. I must know.'

And she'd giggled again, but oddly, had rather enjoyed telling him, and they'd both got quite engrossed in her retellings as they chopped the veg in the mornings (he'd started coming into the café again, more and more), and now Lizzie couldn't put on the television without thinking of him, and instead tended to take long walks on the nights she wasn't visiting Gran.

She'd never looked so healthy. So why did she feel so dull?

Penny was refusing to discuss Will in the slightest, but seemed to be dressing much more in her old style when she went to work. The skirts were getting shorter, the lips larger. It was with a certain sigh of relief that Lizzie felt the light winds of September come and the freshness in the mornings.

Gran, whilst always pleased to see Lizzie, seemed no better and no worse, and had stopped mentioning Redmond Street at all. As a result, Penny and Lizzie had gradually begun to feel that it was their own. They still didn't dare throw anything out, but had started adding their own touches.

As the weather turned colder, Lizzie noticed that none of last year's huge winter woollies seemed to fit her; they were massive, baggy black things. In fact, she thought, looking at them, they were horrible. She suddenly felt the urge to get moving, do something new with the way she looked. Georges had given her a pay rise too, and no longer having to pay even the tiny amount of rent to their mother definitely helped. Maybe she could get Brooke and Minty to help out... show her how to be a little bit more stylish.

Obviously she hated stupid fashion and everything stupid that went with it but, she thought, looking at herself in the mirror . . . it couldn't hurt.

She mentioned it one Saturday to Penny, whose face lit up. Lizzie'd been waiting for this for a long time. It was the most animated Lizzie'd seen her in weeks.

But Lizzie changed her mind just as Penny started hustling her out of the house.

'No, no, no, no,' said Lizzie, clinging on to the banister.

'Come on. It's a makeover! It'll be fun.'

'How will it be fun, again? Standing naked and being judged in front of a bunch of emaciated strangers. How will that be fun?'

'Because they're going to help you look better. And feel better. It'll be great.'

'Great as in undeniably humiliating?'

'Come on!' said Penny. 'You need to be getting a life, stop staying in and watching *Celebrity Gay Partner Swap on a Crocodile-Infested Island.*'

Lizzie stuck out her bottom lip.

'Oh, yes, what I'd much rather do is watch you parade around in size six *Footballers' Wives* outfit for three hours whilst nobody gives me any food.'

'Trying on designer outfits and eating lots of food just don't mix, how many times do I have to tell you? If you're that desperate, make like your friend Grainne and bring some crisps. But don't get any greasy fingerprints on stuff.'

'I won't do that,' said Lizzie, 'because I don't eat crisps any more and because I've just decided *I'm* not coming.'

'Do you really not want to look glamorous just once in your entire life?' Penny said.

Of course she did. If she hadn't looked like a pig in a wig every time she'd run into or worked for Georges, might things have turned out differently? She couldn't stop remembering the way he'd looked at Penny that night at the restaurant. He was . . . bewitched. He couldn't help it, even if he thought Penny was nuts in real life.

But getting there felt like it would be terribly hard work.

'Well,' she said, twisting her fingers round the banister.

'Course you do,' said Penny. 'And you've got to start somewhere.'

'OK, OK,' said Lizzie. 'I just meant, forgive me if I'm not totally in the mood for lots of harsh personal criticism.'

'Then why are you wearing your shirt buttoned up wrongly?'

'Oh, shut up.'

Where did Penny meet all these people?

'Beautiful,' Rodrigo, the worrying personal shopper said. 'So curvaceous.'

Lizzie rolled her eyes. She'd been waiting for this. Next they'd say they didn't have anything in her size, and would she mind heffalumping the hell out of their shop?

'What?' said Penny, who had perched on a high stool sipping champagne whilst Lizzie stood in front of the three-sided mirror in the beautifully swagged personal shopping suite, slumping her shoulders and trying not to catch glimpses of her greying bra and slightly scuzzy pants. She'd looked for nicer ones in her drawer and it had hit her with a shock that she didn't have any.

Buzzing around them was a beautiful junior giraffe. Lizzie couldn't imagine what being a trainee personal shopper could possibly involve – maybe you started off on socks and worked your way up, but she seemed to have the sneer down to a tee. Who knew personal shoppers even existed in high street shops?

213

Rodrigo eyed Lizzie sternly through his ridiculous 1950s women's spectacles and leaned over and whispered something to Penny, who nodded her head seriously as if they were having a debate at the UN.

'What?' said Lizzie miserably. 'Stop whispering about me.'

'It is nothing,' said Rodrigo. 'Nothing which someone of your Rubenesque beauty should ever worry your lovely head about.' He stared at her. 'You must embrace the sensual,' he said. 'Feel the fabric. The rich, dark purples and deep jewel-green velvet.'

Lizzie recoiled in horror as the giraffe wheeled in a long rail of non-black items.

'I'll look like a sofa,' she said, gazing at a leather burgundy skirt.

'You won't,' said Penny. 'You'll be making a statement.'

'Yeah – "I shop at DFS",' said Lizzie, looking furiously around for her perfectly serviceable black skirt. She couldn't help it. Tears sprang to her eyes.

'Ah, you cry with the drama of fashion discovery. Happy tears, happy tears.'

The giraffe handed her a purple velvet skirt and a soft, small-looking grey top.

'Why don't you try it on?' said Penny.

Lizzie did as she was told.

'*Bravissimo!*' said Rodrigo.

She risked a glance in the mirror.

It was beautiful. The skirt had chic little French buttons that fastened down the side; it was less purple on, she noticed, more of a dusky lavender which, with the soft woollen top, enhanced the greys in her eyes. It was . . . she looked . . . for the first time in her adult life, Lizzie thought, she looked nice. Better than nice. Pretty.

And she could see behind her in the mirror Penny, both thumbs up, grinning like a Cheshire cat.

For some reason, she wanted to cry.

They bought the lot. Lizzie felt sick; but Rodrigo kept murmuring 'investment . . . investment . . .'

The hairdresser's was even better. Or maybe, Lizzie thought, she was just more used to being insulted by hairdressers.

'Who cut your hair before?' asked the snotty uninterested stylist, although, as it was a smart salon Penny had modelled for for years, the stylist was rude but also gave Lizzie a glass of champagne.

'A badger,' said Lizzie. Her inhibitions about responding to London rudeness had vanished for ever. 'I think he was drunk.'

'He shouldn't be cutting hair,' said the stylist, who hadn't listened.

'He shouldn't,' said Lizzie. 'Animals without opposable thumbs should very rarely be cutting hair. Can I have another glass of champagne?'

'I'll have to charge you for that,' said the stylist. Lizzie felt her traditional panic, like when she was on that cheap flight they'd taken to Ibiza and she hadn't known whether she had to pay for the drinks or not so she had to get up and get her wallet out of her bag and pay for it in euros and everyone on the plane had been looking at her. But it was OK. She had a bit of money. She deserved to be here. She was fine.

Then she glanced at Penny, who was having new ultra-blonde super-Gwyneth highlights put in. Penny waved over the bottle and put her thumbs up. Of course. It was OK to have champagne.

'Now are you sure you don't want to go blonde?' said the

stylist. 'Only, that's kind of what we do here. For most people. Most people want to go blonde.'

'I'm not most people,' said Lizzie proudly.

'Only, cause your hair's a bit pubic, you know, and if we dyed it it wouldn't look quite so frizzy, you know.'

'Well de-frizz it then,' said Lizzie, less proudly. But the stylist still stood there, hovering unhappily.

Penny came over to help. 'They don't know what to do without colouring,' she whispered to Lizzie. 'Everyone's got coloured hair.'

'Everyone?'

'Everyone in the country. Every single person.'

Staring into the mirror, Lizzie realised uncomfortably that her hair was very mousy, really. She didn't, she supposed, look in the mirror that often. Not that carefully anyway, otherwise she got depressed. She stared harder. For all this time she'd just thought her hair was a particularly flat colour and everyone else's was shinier, just as Penny had got the lovely straight hair and she'd got the frizz, even though it had been similar when they were children. Now she had an uncomfortable sensation.

'*Everyone?*'

'No,' said Penny sarcastically. 'Everyone in the country has sun-lightened highlights and we're a nation of natural blondes and shiny redheads. Oh, and burgundy hair is real.'

'It's a lot to take in.'

Lizzie stared at herself.

'Oh, and everyone has really straight hair naturally,' said Penny.

'Well, you do,' said Lizzie.

Penny gave a do-you-believe-this? look at the stylist, who shook her own poker-straight scarlet locks.

'Eh, Lizzie.'

'Yes?'

'We're twins, remember? We have the same hair.'

'We're not identical.'

'No. But, trust me, we have the same hair.'

Lizzie stared at her sister.

'Oh, God.'

'Do it,' said Penny to the stylist. 'Just some light streaks, don't scare the horses.'

Lizzie shook her shining, straight, gently streaked hair in the mirror. For the nineteenth time.

'Yes,' said Penny. 'It's lovely.'

'But how am I going to keep it this way?'

'With a bit of care and attention,' said Penny.

'I was afraid you were going to say that.'

'And some nice expensive hair products.'

Lizzie screwed up one eye and looked at Penny.

'Which you buy,' said Penny hurriedly.

'Hmm.' Lizzie went back to flicking her thick hair in the mirror. 'So. That "invisible make-up thing" . . . ' she started.

'Yup. Tons of it,' said Penny.

'I thought as much.'

Lizzie couldn't stop looking at herself all the way to work. She was wearing a neat little grey woollen jacket over a slightly gathered jewel-green skirt, with soft make-up and her new hair. Penny had grinned widely at her.

'Go now, Grasshopper,' she'd said. 'My work with you is done.'

It was a perfect autumn day, and the red and brown leaves were lying on the ground for the four seconds they were allowed to in Chelsea before being swept up by smartly dressed roadsweepers. The sky was a bright chilly blue and

Lizzie had an absolute bounce in her step as she marched towards the door of the café.

'*Lizzie!*' came a huge roar from the other side of the road. And standing there, looking as merry and bear-like as ever, was Georges, getting out of the back of a smart black car.

'*Lizzie!* I am back! I am back! And you have not burned down the café! Truly, my happiness could not be more complete.'

His smile was so broad and his cheeks so rosy, Lizzie couldn't help but crack open a huge smile in return, and she dashed across the road to see him. As she stood in front of him, he regarded her gravely.

'Oh, madam, I am terribly sorry. I thought I was addressing Elizabeth Berry. But now I see that I was quite mistaken and you are a very beautiful model on her way to a high-fashion modelling shoot.'

'No, it's me, Georges,' said Lizzie, giggling and feeling ridiculously happy that he'd noticed. He peered into her eyes and she caught the sharp black spirit of him as he did so.

'So it is!' he said, standing back. 'You are a miracle.'

Lizzie kept looking at him and, slightly, his face seemed to change.

'A miracle,' he murmured, almost to himself. 'Well, well.'

Lizzie smiled at him again, more hopefully, wondering why his face suddenly looked a little sad. Then there came a noise from inside the car.

'Georges!' came a heavily accented voice. 'Georges! *Comece sobre aqui!*'

Lizzie didn't understand a word of the string of speedy high-pitched sentences that came out in a stream from the back of the car, but she saw Georges's face as he hesitated then put on a wide smile and extended a welcoming hand towards the back seat.

From the car arose a shortish, sturdy figure, dark hair, dark eyes and heavy-looking brows, which were presently pulled together in something approaching a scowl.

'Maria-Elena, I would like you to meet my friend and co-worker, Lizzie,' said Georges.

Maria-Elena glanced at Lizzie then let fly with another long flurry of Portuguese.

'And now we are in England,' said Georges gently, 'we should speak English, don't you think? Especially in front of our friends.'

'Hello,' said Lizzie timidly, wondering what was going on. Was this his sister? It could be.

'Hello,' said Maria-Elena, not sounding too thrilled about it. 'It is wonderful to be here in your very cold country.'

She looked towards the café. 'Is that your shop?' she said to Georges.

Georges nodded proudly.

'This is one of the cafés, but I must say,' and he smiled at Lizzie, 'it is my favourite.'

This provoked a new torrent. Lizzie had never had a talent for languages, but at a guess it wasn't an entirely positive critique. She looked at Georges, raising her eyebrows. Georges, uncharacteristically, looked wrong-footed. He coughed and cleared his throat, fiddling a little with his tight collar.

'Uh, Maria-Elena . . . she is my third cousin,' he said to Lizzie almost apologetically. Lizzie thought she knew what was coming. Maria-Elena was going to be her new boss. She was going to move into the café, start running it, she would never see Georges again and Maria-Elena would be difficult and shout at her a lot. Her good mood started to evaporate.

'So, uh, when I was in Portugal . . . ' started Georges, but stopped again, as if this wasn't quite right. Maria-Elena gave him an impatient look and fired a volley of Portuguese at him again.

'Yes, yes,' said Georges. 'Well, I spent a lot of time with my family and it is decided. Maria-Elena and I are getting married.'

Lizzie stopped dead and looked from one to the other. Sure enough, Maria-Elena was wearing a huge, almost grotesque ring on the fourth finger of her left hand. She smiled complacently. Neither of them, though, was exuding the obvious joy that normally accompanies such announcements.

'Well,' Lizzie said. Inside she shook herself for being an idiot. Of course Georges wasn't just swanning around waiting for someone like her to pull herself together and then, one day, magically notice her . . . of course he was going to get married and have lots of beautiful Portuguese babies. And, of course, it would never have been her anyway, it would have been Penny. In fact, Penny was going to take it even worse than she was. Imagine, the two of them being sad over some short fat sandwich maker. It was ridiculous. Except that he'd become so much more to her.

Lizzie swallowed loudly. Of course it was ridiculous. And it would always have been impossible, and by the looks of things he would never even have considered it: he would always have gone back to his town and married a nice local girl, of course. She was probably a virgin. She got a glimpse of Maria-Elena's slightly feral teeth. Definitely a virgin.

'Congratulations,' she forced herself to say. 'It's . . . it's wonderful news.'

'The family thought . . . ' said Georges. 'It is a very good thing.'

'Can you marry your third cousin?' asked Lizzie, in what she'd intended to be a playful tone but came out as slightly aggressive.

'But of course,' said Georges. 'Nearly everyone is third cousin in the world. You are probably my third cousin also.'

She looked at him for a moment then, but Maria-Elena was tugging his wrist.

'Also I am very good businesswoman,' she said in English. 'Will help with smartening up all the business. I want to look at . . . hmm, in English, how do you say? Profit margins. Yes. My English is very good also.'

Georges nodded. 'Exactly,' he said. 'It is very much a good thing.'

'So when . . . when are you getting married?' asked Lizzie.

'In six week,' said Maria-Elena. 'I will organise it magnificently.'

'Are you getting married in London?'

Maria-Elena snorted rather wonderfully.

'Yes,' she said. 'We are getting married in London. With the rain. And we would like to eat bacon and fried eggs for our wedding feast and we would like to drink beer and have a cup of tea, yes, please excuse me, I am so terribly sorry, thank you very much.'

'We will get married in Portugal,' said Georges. 'All our families will come.'

'Just the one then,' said Lizzie, but quite quietly.

'There will be four hundred people there,' said Maria-Elena. 'To watch Georges do his duty.'

'Your duty?' Lizzie couldn't help asking with a smile.

Georges looked slightly haunted for a moment.

'Yes. I have been away for too long. It is time for me to settle down and get married and have children and make a good family in Portugal.'

'And that's what you want?' said Lizzie gently.

'Of course it is,' said Maria-Elena. 'Now, let me see how

you work at this restaurant, please. Then, Georges, we are going to Harrods.'

'Bollocks!' said Penny. 'That is *so* unfair! I don't understand it. Every time I get hold of a millionaire, they slip through my fingers. Or turn out to have been ratbags.'

'The world is standing in the way of your true destiny,' said Lizzie, who to her annoyed surprise had stopped off at the corner shop on the way home (of course it was a Chelsea corner shop which meant it was hard to buy things that weren't Bendicks bittermints and vintage Pol Roger) and bought a whole loaf of cheap and nasty white bread and some Nutella. She was methodically working her way through the whole loaf, next to the toaster, and loathing herself.

'You say she's ugly?' said Penny. 'Maybe there's still time.'

'She's not ugly,' said Lizzie. 'She just looks a lot like Georges.'

'That's quite ugly,' said Penny. 'Especially on a girl.'

'No, it's not!' said Lizzie hotly, before quickly turning back to the toaster. Penny stared at her.

'Oh, no,' she said, realisation finally dawning. 'Of course, of course. Oh, Lizzie! I didn't realise! You've got a massive thing for him.'

'I do not!'

'You do! Oh my God, all this time I was pulling him . . . '

'You were not pulling him!'

'I would have pulled him. Oh my God, Lizzie, I had no idea.'

'I didn't . . . ' Her voice petered out. Was there even any point in denying it? 'Well, I thought . . . '

'What, you'd have pulled the millionaire?'

'I didn't know he was a millionaire. Not until he came into the art gallery.'

'Which is when you started fancying him.'

'No, it's not,' said Lizzie, hoping she wasn't about to cry. 'I fancied him a long time before that.'

'You can't have done,' said Penny. 'He's short and covered in hair, like an ewok.'

'You wanted to go out with him,' said Lizzie defensively.

'I didn't fancy him. I . . . uh, respected him.'

'And his big fat wallet.'

Penny rounded on her.

'And you think I'm about to start apologising to *you*.'

Lizzie moved backwards, slightly startled by the strength of the onslaught.

'What do you mean?'

'You of all people. You know what I've been through.'

'Exactly what I've been through,' said Lizzie.

'Which is why you should *understand*.'

'Understand what?' said Lizzie. Suddenly, she was furious. 'That you should get everything you want just because you're blonde? That you could treat Georges like a toy and play around with him just because you don't like working for a living? That you can't see what is patently obvious in front of your eyes – like your sister liking someone, which would have been *completely* bloody obvious if you'd ever paid attention – you know some twins have that secret communication thing? Maybe we should work on our *basic* communication thing – and even our grandmother who is one hundred and thirty years old and lives in a bed in an eight-by-eight room, which by the way you'd also know if you ever went to visit her, if you could take time out of your own selfish bloody lifestyle, even *she* spotted that I really liked this bloke at which point you went all out to ruin it for me, and for him and, well, it doesn't matter any more, OK? I'm used to coping with disappointment in my life. But don't you fucking *dare* to ask me to sympathise with you.'

When she finished talking, Lizzie realised she was completely out of breath and quite shocked by how much she'd said. Penny too was completely taken aback, mouth open.

'I didn't mean—' Penny started to say.

'Save it,' said Lizzie. 'Really. Save it for people who don't see completely through you.'

And she unplugged the toaster, picked it up, placed it under her arm and retired to her room.

Although they bickered a little – well, non-stop, Penny realised – they didn't actually have stand-up fights that often. And, well, she just wasn't used to seeing Lizzie so shouty. Bolshy, yes, but usually in a slightly low-key way, under her breath, which Penny could usually quite happily ignore. This whole Lizzie doing home truths thing was new. A lot of things about Lizzie were new. How could she not have noticed? But she hadn't realised Lizzie'd really had a crush on fat Georges. She supposed it made sense when she thought about it – the new interest in food, the losing weight, the fact that she hadn't complained *that* much when they'd given her her makeover – yup. It was all there.

But the fact that Lizzie fancied Georges suddenly made him much more attractive in her eyes. She could see why you might *like* Georges, as well as how you could *admire* him, and want the security and life he could provide. *Fancying*, she hadn't really figured on. But if Lizzie could see it . . . and had seen it even before she knew about the money. An uncharacteristic thought came to Penny – could she help?

Lizzie stomped to work the next day feeling sick and grumpy. Suddenly, without the chance of bantering with Georges and hearing him pronounce on things and teach her what to do with chilli peppers ('No! No, Lizzie, you want to kill all my customers stone dead?'), it was just another job. In a café, basically. She was coming up to thirty and buttering sandwiches for a living, whilst staying in someone else's borrowed apartment without even her stupid idiotic sister to talk to. Things didn't look good. Maybe she should call Grainne; hearing about her life always put things into perspective.

When she got to the café, she was surprised to see someone already waiting outside it. There were a few regulars who popped in for their excellent coffee, but they were well aware what time the café opened. She'd seen Sloan there a few times, apparently on his way home from the night before, but he was usually wobbling on the pavement enquiring loudly about the availability of wine, so it wasn't him.

'Hello?'

The figure, skinny and wan, slowly lifted up his head and she recognised him immediately.

'Will?' she asked incredulously. 'What are you doing here?'

Will didn't look terribly good. Well, thought Lizzie, if you weren't being too harsh, the stubble slightly suited him, and being so thin gave him the look of the starving artist, and his gaunt face made those puppy-dog eyes look even bigger. But on the whole he looked unkempt, uncared for, a million miles away from the confident charmer she'd met earlier that year.

He looked at her rather piteously as she opened up.

'Will . . . are you *hungry*?' she asked as he followed her in.

He shrugged. 'Well . . . ' he looked around the little restaurant, his eyes coming to rest on the panini toaster.

'Would you like some breakfast?'

'Why, are you having some?'

In fact, Lizzie was so ashamed of her previous evening's stress-related carb blow-out that she had vowed to stick to fruit until lunchtime.

'Of course,' she said encouragingly. 'Full English OK?'

Well, if that's what you're having,' he said, looking incredibly grateful.

Lizzie quickly stuck the frying pan on the burner and started chopping mushrooms.

'Where have you been? You look like you've been dragged through a hedge backwards.'

Will shrugged. 'Oh, I've been . . . about . . . not in this end of the woods, really.'

The first two pieces of toast popped up and Lizzie buttered them speedily and sent them over to him, just as the Gaggia squealed and the first espresso of the day squeezed out. Will immediately guzzled both down so quickly that at first Lizzie couldn't quite work out where they'd gone.

'You really are hungry,' said Lizzie worriedly.

Will shrugged. 'Well, my canapé diet has . . . uh, suffered a bit. I miss those mini fish and chips they used to do.'

'But Penny sold loads of your paintings,' said Lizzie. 'Even I sold a few.'

'I know,' said Will. 'Just covered my materials, really. And the two years it took to do them. Anyway, the exhibition is over now. And I don't think I can expect another one in a hurry; apparently Sloan's put the word out. I'm untouchable.'

Lizzie brought over some more toast and checked the frying sausages.

'That can't be true. Sloan can never remember to tell anyone anything.'

'Hmm,' said Will.

'What about your parents?'

Will straightened his back and spoke in gruff tones. 'You want to leave a perfectly good university and try and make it as an artist, boy, you'll be standing on your own two feet with no help from us, do you hear?'

Lizzie finished his fried eggs and flipped them up into the air artistically so they landed perfectly on the plate, feeling slightly pleased with herself.

'Thanks,' said Will. 'Where's yours?'

'Oh, I don't need it,' said Lizzie. 'Could do with losing a few pounds.'

'Really?' said Will. 'I think you look smashing.' And he bent his head to his food.

After ten minutes, he finished a second cup of espresso and mopped up the last of the egg yolk with the fried bread, letting out a big sigh of satisfaction as he did so. Noticing Lizzie watching him, he immediately pulled out a very bashed-looking wallet and started counting out twenty-pence pieces.

'Don't be daft,' said Lizzie. 'You just ate the staff breakfast. Don't give it another thought.'

'OK,' said Will, shaking his head in relief. 'God, you think good days are going to last for ever, don't you? I spunked it all away.'

He swallowed and went quiet.

'Literally, I suppose. Sorry, that's horrid.'

Lizzie took her own cup of tea, and a banana, and rounded the counter to sit at the table.

'Will,' she started. As soon as she did so, he looked up at her, his eyes shining.

'Lizzie,' he said, 'I didn't know there was a baby. I promise I didn't. I wouldn't make someone get rid of my baby in

227

a million years. I'd love to have a baby, really I would. Someday. But it would have been all right. We'd have got over it. It's just as soon as she came to see me we both realised . . . we both realised that it's not . . . it's . . . ' He couldn't finish and stared at the table, clutching his cup. 'I can't believe she killed my baby without even telling me.'

Lizzie stared at her fingers until he'd composed himself.

'Listen,' she said. 'You have to listen to me.'

'What?'

'There wasn't a baby. It was a mistake. A real mistake, not something to wind you up or anything. She just got a bit sick and we jumped to conclusions and, well, it doesn't matter now.'

'She didn't have an abortion?'

Lizzie shook her head. 'I don't think she could have. She loved you, Will. But when she saw how you lived . . . and Minty told her you were just after a meal ticket.'

'*Minty*,' said Will. 'That crazy bitch pursued me for months and wouldn't take no for an answer.'

'So you never slept with her.'

'Well. Just a couple of times, you know. But then she really got the knives out for me. Practically stalked me. She called me "Daddy".' He shook his head in horror and looked at his empty plate again. 'There never was a baby.'

Lizzie shook her head gently. She really thought he ought to know.

'So I messed it up all on my own?'

Just then, the door tinged, and Georges and Maria-Elena stepped in. Maria-Elena sniffed loudly.

'I see,' she said. 'This place . . . it smells very much like something in your country I have heard of that is called a transportation café, no?'

Georges shook his head. 'No, we do good food and . . . '

He looked at Will, then Lizzie, who shot him a warning look, whereupon Georges changed his tone and said, 'We do whatever is the best for the customer. Is that not right, my friend?'

Will stared at him. 'You're Penny's new boyf—'

'Nothing,' said Lizzie. 'That's what you were about to say, wasn't it? Nothing at all. Ha ha!'

'I do not understand,' said Georges. 'But here, this is my beautiful fiancée, Maria-Elena.'

'You know,' said Maria-Elena to Will. 'If you are to keep eating those English breakfasts you will get fat and die.'

'Good,' said Will.

'Shh, shh,' said Georges. 'We will have none of this talk.'

'Would you like an omelette?' said Lizzie. If she couldn't make Georges love her, she could at least make him an omelette.

'Yes, please,' said Georges, smiling at her.

'No!' said Maria-Elena. 'At least this man is thin. You are fat. Too fat. No more eggs before the wedding. You should be thin for a wedding.'

'I cannot do that,' said Georges as Lizzie stood undecided over the frying pan. 'I was a fat baby. Then I was a fat child. Then I was a tubby young man. Then I was a plump grown-up man. And now I am Georges! Thin and I are two things which will never be friends!'

Maria-Elena's brows knitted together and she muttered something in Portuguese.

'And if we have children they shall be fat little babies and podgy children and plump teenagers . . .'

Lizzie thought of having little plump babies with big dark eyes like Georges's and bit her lip a tad wistfully.

'No, we will not,' said Maria-Elena. 'You.' She was talking to Lizzie, who was staring into space and not noticing. 'You.

I would like orange juice, and make a fruit salad.'

Lizzie stared at her. Maria-Elena said something to Georges, and it wasn't necessary to have a word of Portuguese to know that she'd just said something along the lines of, 'Is your employee a retard?'

Georges looked cross, then his face cleared as he remembered something.

'Aha,' he said, pointing at Will. 'For you, a man suffering a broken heart.'

'I'm not suffering a broken heart,' said Will. 'Oh, yes, I am. I forgot. Can I have that omelette?'

'Of course,' said Lizzie. 'You'll have to be quick, though. I have to go and pick oranges or something.'

Georges dashed out and returned in moments with a parcel covered in bubble wrap.

'You're going to try and cheer me up with bubble wrap?' said Will.

'Ooh, I love bubble wrap,' said Lizzie.

'No,' said Georges. 'But I forgot it had arrived!' and he pulled apart the badly wrapped parcel to reveal Will's painting.

It was the avenue of trees, and the painting looked very delicate and beautiful in the brightly painted café.

'I am going to put it up here,' said Georges. 'So all my customers will see it and say, Georges, where did you get this fantastic painting as everybody knows you have the taste of a mountain goat. And I will say, you must NOT go to Sloan's terrible art shop, you must call my friend Will, and everybody will call you and make you a *milliadaire*. What do you think?'

Will merely shrugged his shoulders.

'It looks terrible,' said Maria-Elena. 'All the colours are wrong.'

'It's great,' said Lizzie. 'Put it up here by the clock over the door. People always look at the clock.'

'That is very true!' said Georges. 'Here. And now, we must open the shop.'

'What about the fruit salad?' said Maria-Elena.

'Ah, my bride, I am so sorry, no fruit salad today.'

'I'm making Georges a quick omelette aux fines herbes, though,' said Lizzie. She knew it was a little mean, but at the moment, she just didn't care. 'Are you sure you don't want one?'


'My dear,' said Sloan to Penny. He cleared his throat and tried again. He had somehow mysteriously woken up on the floor of the gallery again and, all things considered, had found it least painful if he didn't try to move. 'My dear, I sense you are sad. Or angry.'

'How did you guess that?' said Penny, who was marching loudly over him when she needed to get anything out of the back.

'Call it my feminine intuition,' said Sloan, who was trying to think of a polite way to tell her to stop stomping up and down like a baby elephant which wouldn't involve her redoubling her efforts and getting louder.

'How about making your old Auntie Sloan a bit of an eye-opener, eh?'

'You really are a hopeless soak,' said Penny, who wasn't exactly in the mood to do anything for anyone. 'Don't you think you should get help or something?'

'I think,' said Sloan, propping himself up on his elbow with some difficulty in order to extract his cigarette holder from his smoking-jacket pocket, 'help is for people who have difficult lives. Whereas my existence, a state, if you like, of near constant lunch, I find extremely pleasant. Now, if you look in the fridge I believe you will find some tomato juice, some Worcestershire sauce, one egg and a bottle of Grey Goose vodka. I wish you to mix these ingredients in the order your heart tells you to.'

Cigarette successfully lit, he returned to lying on the ground.

'Say what you like about that Will fellow,' he said. Penny snorted loudly. 'But at least you knew which way up to hang his paintings. Whereas with *these* . . . '

He indicated the new oil paintings hanging on the gallery walls. They were vast abstract canvases, covered with mustard-coloured geometric shapes spattered with blobs of grey and mushroom. In short, perfect for any office lobby in the developed world. Sloan was fully expecting to make a killing.

'Ah, thank you,' he said, as Penny returned with his drink. 'No straw . . . no . . . ?' He huffed himself into a sitting position. 'Ah. Worcestershire sauce as the primary ingredient. Interesting concept. Now, what did you say the matter with you was again?'

'My life is not going well,' said Penny.

'Indeed?' said Sloan.

'The only millionaire I know is getting married and the man I love is a penniless conniver who hates me. I need you to introduce me to some millionaires. Nice ones.'

'Funny you should say that,' said Sloan. 'Because I have just the job for you. We need to arrange a launch for the new pictures.'

'Uh-huh?' said Penny.

'The artist supposedly lives in the cloud forests of South America and never comes down to taint her life with civilisation, although she may make a special exception for cut-price champagne. Personally I think that's humbug and it's two blokes in a lock-up garage in Edmonton. But that doesn't matter now. Go through my Rolodex and invite everyone with a postcode starting W or SW, numbers up to eleven.'

He fixed her with a slightly rheumy eye.

'If you don't find a pushover banking millionaire in that lot, Penelope, there is frankly no hope for you.'

Penny smiled for the first time in three days.

'Thanks, Sloan!'

'Don't thank me,' said Sloan. 'You could get me a pillow, though.'

# Chapter Twelve

Lizzie had meant to tell Penny she'd seen Will, but they still weren't speaking. Fine, she could lump it then.

Penny was in whirlwind mode in any case. For the first time in living memory, she was working incredibly hard, dashing around to put the opening together. She'd designed the invitations – 'That's original,' Sloan had said, looking at the red devil-shaped card, most unlike the plain Smythson stiffy he usually sent out – that said, *Be a devil. Come see our most dangerous collection yet . . .*

'It's not very dangerous,' said Sloan.

'You have to know,' said Penny, 'that the concept of buying art is very scary to most people. So I'm playing on their fear.'

Sloan raised his eyebrows. 'What's scary about buying art? Oh, Christ,' he indicated a student walking past the window. 'Would you look at the shoes on that? Great legs and shoes like a carthorse.'

'Actually, that's what's scary,' said Penny. 'People like you checking out your shoes.'

Sloan pouted. 'People are terribly oversensitive.'

'So, I'm convincing all these business people to take a risk,' said Penny happily. 'We've had loads of yeses already.'

Sloan didn't tell her that few people were as likely to travel a great distance for a free glass of champagne as people who were already rich; it was one of the ways they'd got rich in the first place.

'Excellent work,' said Sloan. 'Now, what about the artist?'

'She's coming in today,' said Penny. 'To check the plass-mong.'

'The what?'

'I don't know. She said plassmong.'

'Place-*ment*, my dear,' said Sloan, chucking her on the cheek. 'You are so adorable.'

'Stop that,' said Penny. 'Just because I don't know your stupid posh German or whatever it is.'

'Quite right, too,' said Sloan, vowing to keep Penny and the artist as far apart as possible.

Unfortunately, as with so many of Sloan's vows, some old chums at the Reform Club and an excellent claret got in the way, and Penny was on her own, tweezing her eyebrows in the reflection of a particularly ugly steel sculpture which was supposed to represent womanhood but in fact represented something on the floor to bark your shins on, when the woman walked in.

At first Penny smiled politely, assuming a customer had just entered, and one of their more eccentric Chelsea types at that.

'Hello,' she said.

The figure stood stock-still, framed in the doorway with the light behind her, and stared at Penny.

'Oh,' said Penny jumping up. 'Do you need some help getting up the step?'

There came a loud imperious sniff from the doorway.

'Sloan Williams-Forsythe, please!' boomed a voice loudly.

'Er, he's not here,' said Penny. 'I'm sure he won't be long, though.' She always said this, hoping against hope that they wouldn't decide to wait for him. Most people, however, were aware of his lunching habits.

'I am Tabitha Angelbrain Dawson,' said the woman, moving into the full arena of the shop. Without the light behind her, Penny took a closer look. She was a heavy woman, draped rather than dressed in shades of violet and purple, including heavy eye make-up and a mouth that was lipsticked so dark it looked like a place cherries went to die. Her hair was stiff, and a very peculiar aubergine colour Penny couldn't have described, which gave her some respect for her artistic abilities.

'Hello!' said Penny. 'You're the artist! I'm organising your party.'

Slightly regretfully she remembered the last artist she'd met in here. Somehow she didn't think this one would put up with quite as much cheek. Mind you, she wasn't quite so desperate to get in this one's knickers either.

'I've just got you down as Ms Dawson, though,' said Penny, looking at the sheet. 'Sorry, I can change it.'

'Tabitha Angelbrain Dawson is my full name,' said Tabitha Angelbrain Dawson. 'Tabitha from my beloved daddy, God rest his soul, and Angelbrain came as a gift from heaven when no less than Sir Flinty Fortescue himself said, "Tabitha, dear, you have the brain of an angel."'

And the body of a brickie, thought Penny, but didn't let it show on her face.

'Dawson, well, what can one do?' Tabitha continued, looking slightly glum for a moment. 'It sounds like I run a pottery shop in rural Yorkshire. Anyway, no matter. Let me take a look at *le hanging*.'

She started pacing round the shop. In fact, she was loping, so deliberately Penny couldn't help thinking she wanted it noticed.

'You have a very graceful stride,' she said winningly. This party was very important, and it would be helpful to get Tabitha on her side, if at all possible, especially, as a general rule, she'd found fat women tended not to like her that much.

'Thank you,' said Tabitha, straightening up and beaming. This had obviously been very much the correct thing to say. 'My yoga teacher says that my spirit guide is almost certainly a big cat.'

'Perhaps a panther,' said Penny.

Tabitha nodded gravely, as if some huge secret had passed between them. 'And all cats, you know, they find me irresistible.'

Penny hoped that they hadn't hung any of the pictures upside down, but Sloan hadn't been in business for thirty years for nothing. Tabitha slowly completed her tour of the room, nodding occasionally in a cougar-like manner to show that she approved.

She stood in the middle of the room, finally, and closed her eyes. Painfully slowly, she lifted both hands out to the side, raising her fingers up until her arms were fully outstretched, her purple robes fluttering behind her, like a priest.

'I feel it!' she said. 'I feel the vibrations! I feel for my art, for my creation, from the angels, from the mother spirit, I declare this . . . uh, this is the correct place and everything shall be good. And. Er. Let it be.'

She kept her eyes closed for another twenty seconds or so and Penny squeezed hers shut too in sympathy, hoping nobody popped in and nicked the computer while she did so.

'Fantastic,' said Tabitha Angelbrain finally, when she opened her eyes again. 'I feel very strongly everything is going to go just fine. Got any tea?'

'Absolutely,' said Penny. 'But just normal tea, not chamomile or anything like that.'

'Really? OK, then. Although I try not to pollute my body with caffeine. Ooh' – she had spied Penny's secret stash of chocolate digestives – 'are those digestives? Can I have one? Absolutely starved. Can you think of anywhere good for us to lunch?'

'I'm not really allowed to take lunch,' said Penny. 'We have a strict one-employee, one-lunch policy.'

'Nonsense,' said Tabitha. 'You just tell Sloan the artist ordered you. Plus, I have some very funny stories about my cats that I think you'll absolutely love. You strike me as someone who's very in touch with their inner spiritual core. Am I right?'

Penny was firmly of the belief that people's inner spiritual cores only ever made an appearance when they didn't have to worry about paying the council tax, but considered it wise not to say so.

'Well, there is this one place . . . ' she said.

Penny stopped just before the window of the café, as Tabitha paused to smell the cooking on the air in the manner of a tiger.

Through the glass she could see Lizzie and Georges behind the counter. Lizzie was doling out food into containers which she was seasoning with parsley and tossing to

Georges, who then, with a chat and a smile, handed them to hungry customers. They weren't even looking at one another, but working entirely on instinct, Lizzie passing the salt or finding extra change; Georges handing her another tomato or reaching for the toaster without her having to ask him. They were a perfect ballet of complementary motion, and engrossing to watch.

Tabitha looked ready to head in, but Penny couldn't move. They looked so perfect, so absolutely right together. How could she not have noticed it before? Was she really that self-absorbed? OK, yes, so she was incredibly self-absorbed, what else was new? But she hadn't really been trying to be cruel to Lizzie when she tried to seduce Georges. She really hadn't appreciated how Lizzie felt about him.

Now it seemed unbelievable that she could have missed it.

At the side of the counter stood a dark-looking woman, scowling at the customers. It wasn't hard to work out who that was.

'My inner leonine element of femininity,' announced Tabitha, 'is saying that it is experiencing a primal hunger for the misty plains. That means lunch,' she added hopefully.

Swallowing quickly, Penny pushed open the door and marched in.

Lizzie wasn't in the slightest bit happy to see Penny. In fact, she was furious.

Here she is, thought Lizzie angrily, clop, clop, clop, on her little shoes, in to get the guy with the money. Make it even worse, the *engaged* guy with the money. Stupid cow. She ignored her, even when Georges looked up and smiled at the two women. Daft old Georges, she thought affectionately.

You could probably kill his mother and he'd still want to give you a welcoming hug.

'Two beautiful ladies!' said Georges happily, 'who look in need of a tasty aubergine Parmigiana!'

Tabitha bestowed on him a wide toothy smile.

'I like a man who sees inner beauty,' she said. 'And can cook.'

Lizzie sniffed. She hadn't noticed Georges's amazing ability to discern inner beauty when she was chunky and looked like a frump.

'Hi, Lizzie,' said Penny pointedly, but Lizzie just gave her a look.

'What's the matter?' Penny asked, just to be annoying.

'Nothing,' said Lizzie.

The woman who was obviously Georges's fiancée let loose a torrent of another language, that equally obviously said, 'Who are *these* women?'

Georges looked a bit haunted.

'Maria-Elena, this is Penny, Lizzie's twin.'

Maria-Elena's eyebrows shot up so fast she might as well have had 'I am a very rude lady' tattooed on her forehead.

'Hello,' she said. 'Georges, he has many female friends, yes? And you . . . ah, I see you dress in the "London" style. Interesting.'

This kind of talk didn't phase Penny at all, who'd been the victim of many a ladies' toilets backstab in her time. She stared Maria-Elena down until she took a step back.

Penny looked at Georges again as he flipped his tongs to get the nice corner piece of the Parmigiana for them. There was a wide sweat stain under the arm of his slightly grubby chef's whites, and sweat glistened on his low heavy brow. How on earth . . . I mean, obviously he looked a little better in his sharp suit, stepping out of a car someone else was driving, but you'd have to be really, really desperate . . .

'Who are you?' said Georges in a friendly fashion to Tabitha.

'I am Tabitha Angelbrain Dawson. I am . . . an artiste,' said Tabitha.

Georges nodded. 'Excellent. Me too. I am an artiste of Parmigiana. Here, try it.'

And he passed over two warm plates.

Wow, thought Penny, looking over at Maria-Elena, that woman really is evil. She suddenly had a flash of inspiration. She saw it clearly. Georges was a good bloke and Lizzie really liked him. But he had an evil fiancée standing in her way. She could handle her, make out that her and Georges were a big thing, piss the fiancée off all the way back to Portugal and then Lizzie would be free to settle down with Georges. And they would be so grateful they would buy Penny lots and lots of pairs of shoes, and Penny wouldn't mind a bit that she didn't have any boyfriends at all and Lizzie had a rich one. Penny felt so noble at her potential self-sacrifice she sniffed into her aubergine Parmigiana.

Tabitha reached out and placed a manicured hand, festooned with large rings, gently on Penny's arm.

'I see you too become emotional over a beautiful meal, breaking bread with kindred spirits,' she said. Penny noticed she'd nearly cleared her plate already.

'I really think we are kindred spirits, you know,' Tabitha continued, picking up some bread to wipe up the leftovers. 'Me and the spirit world . . . we're very entwined.' Penny picked at some lettuce – Georges placed salad on the side of everyone's plate as a garnish, but usually ended up throwing it out.

'Me, too,' said Penny.

Tabitha took a huge intake of breath, then looked dramatically round the room to make sure they were not being overheard.

'Penny, my dear,' she said in a near whisper. 'Can I trust you?'

'Of course,' said Penny, looking as serious as she could.

'Very well. Then I shall share with you ... I have certain ... certain gifts.'

Penny waited for her to continue.

'They are a burden,' said Tabitha, looking very sincere and sad. 'They bring great power and yet great responsibility.'

Penny was sure someone had said this in a movie, but didn't want to mention it.

'I have been told often by famous psychics and those who know of the spirit world that I must be very careful how I use my skills.'

Penny nodded respectfully.

'So, my dear, do you have a problem? Is it a matter of the heart? A love spell? Or revenge?'

Tabitha was so excited at talking about her magic powers that a little bit of spittle came out and landed on her plate.

Penny rolled her eyes. 'Do you know how to make a potion to see off a love rival?' she asked, glancing at Lizzie, who was watching her sourly whilst pretending to dry up.

'All love is beautiful,' said Tabitha gravely.

Penny sashayed up to the counter, feeling strangely calm and in control. Georges was still passing over Parmigiana to grateful customers. Maria-Elena was watching her with a beady eye, as was Lizzie (whilst manfully pretending not to). Penny knew what she had to do. She stroked down her eyebrows and slipped behind the display of sandwiches and cakes.

242

'Georges,' she purred, staring straight into his eyes – and, on the periphery, noticing Maria-Elena's eyebrows drawing together in a suspicious frown.

She placed a hand on his large forearm. 'That was the most *delicious* lunch I think I've ever had in my life.'

Georges looked at her hand with a slightly puzzled expression on his face. 'I make good food for everyone,' he said.

Penny gave a little flirtatious giggle, and gently touched the side of his face.

'I think you make it specially for me,' she said. She could swear she could feel the steam coming off Lizzie behind her. Ah, Lizzie. She didn't realise the self-sacrifice involved here. This was about Maria-Elena, not her. Once the Portuguese monstrosity was out of the way, she'd quietly withdraw. After all, all was fair in love and war.

Slowly, aware that the whole café was watching her, she leaned over and carefully placed an extremely deliberate kiss on Georges's slightly sweaty cheek. There was a *tchok* as Lizzie sliced her knife hard into the chopping board. Maria-Elena was looking absolutely furious. Georges couldn't have looked more surprised if she'd slapped him in the face with a wet halibut.

'I'll see you,' Penny murmured suggestively, 'later . . .'

She turned to go, then suddenly stopped in her tracks. For the first time, above the clock on the wall, she noticed Will's picture. She stared at it, open-mouthed.

'You . . . you're . . .'

This wasn't right. This wasn't right at all. What the hell was Georges doing putting that up?

'You've hung Will's painting.'

She could sense Lizzie behind her, concentrating intensely.

'Well, yes,' said Georges. 'I like it.'

'But I didn't think . . . I didn't think you . . . I mean, I assumed you would *burn* it.'

Georges looked slightly discomfited. 'But I thought . . . '

'You thought what? That I wouldn't mind? That I would like having to look at the fucking thing every time I came in here?'

'You do not often come in here,' said Georges, shrugging. 'And . . . well . . . '

A horrifying thought struck Penny.

'Does he?'

She spun round to look at Lizzie, whose face instantly gave her away.

'Oh, he does, does he? What, pops in from time to time, so all of you are lovely friends having a smashing time?'

'It's not like that,' said Lizzie. 'He just came in . . . '

'Really? What's it like then? Do you all just sit around having a good laugh at me?'

To Penny's horror, Maria-Elena had sensed the tide had turned, and had a mild smile playing about her lips.

'No,' said Lizzie.

'So, what? Is this some kind of crazy revenge thing? You're trying to seduce him?'

'No!'

'Just to make me miserable, is it?' Appallingly, Penny couldn't help but feel the tears well up. 'You've all ganged up on me,' she said. Then, blinded, she pushed past Georges and Tabitha and headed out of the door.

Lizzie looked around. What the hell had just happened? One moment her sister had been playing some mad game of 'Who's the biggest bitch on the block?' and all but un-zipping Georges's trousers, then next she was dribbling and mewling like a *Big Brother* contestant deprived of cake.

Georges shook his head.

'Ah, your sister. She suffers terribly in love.' He looked at Lizzie, with a sad expression on his face. 'You are running to her, yes?'

Oh, crap. Five seconds after Lizzie decides to let Penny stand on her own two feet, she immediately has a public nervous breakdown. How very convenient for her.

'Uh, yes,' she said.

Maria-Elena was looking disapproving as Lizzie undid her apron. 'You will have to look at your staff,' she said to Georges, very deliberately in English. 'They are hysterical girls in England, no?'

Lizzie rolled her eyes as she headed for the door.

Penny was half walking half running towards home when Lizzie caught up with her. She glanced at Lizzie but didn't speak to her.

'So what was that little scene about?' Lizzie said finally.

'I don't know what you mean,' said Penny, trying to keep the wobble out of her voice.

'Well, let's see. First you try to have sex with Georges behind the counter and the next you have a complete shit fit because of a picture of some trees.'

'I didn't . . .'

Penny searched desperately for a way of denying this version of events, but couldn't think of one.

'Oh, what's it got to do with you, anyway?'

'Quite a lot actually,' said Lizzie. 'Seeing as Georges is my friend and is getting married and doesn't exactly need to be mixed up with the likes of you.'

'The likes of me?' said Penny, sounding furious. 'What the fuck do you mean, "the likes of me"?'

'Nothing,' said Lizzie, worried that she might have gone too far.

'And what the fuck do you mean, *Georges is my friend*. Georges isn't your friend. He's the guy you'd like to get it on with. Don't pretend you wish him well with his wedding, you hypocrite.'

'I'm a hypocrite. That's fucking rich given that you rubbed yourself up against him like a dog on heat then caved like a fucking paper bag because of your ex-boyfriend's little drawing.'

'It's not a "little drawing",' said Penny. 'Like you know anything about art. Like you know anything about anything, you complete mouse.'

'I'm not a mouse.'

'You're a pathetic cowardly mouse that can't even chat up a bloke she stands next to for like nine hours a day.'

'And you're a gold-digging slut.'

'Mouse!'

'Slut!'

'Mouse!'

Without realising, they'd arrived in front of their building. Sitting on the step was a man. He was middle-aged and shabbily dressed, reclining against one of the white pillars reading a tabloid. He watched them with some interest, but for a short time Penny and Lizzie were too engrossed in shouting at each other to notice.

Finally, his attention made them turn round. He had a keen eye on both of them.

'Who the hell are you?' said Penny, who was in no mood for tramps, salesmen, Jehovah's Witnesses or anything else except getting upstairs and slamming the door on her fucking annoying sister.

The man smiled enigmatically and rather annoyingly.

'Well, well, well,' he said. 'The little twins.'

Lizzie drew in a breath and stepped forward. The last time she'd heard them called that . . . 'Who are you?' she asked, echoing Penny, but with a strange beating of her heart and a funny dry feeling in her mouth.

The man stood up, folded his paper carefully and put it in his pocket.

'Little twins,' he said, straightening and opening his arms wide. 'Don't you recognise your old dad?'

## Chapter Thirteen

They found a third chair buried under some newspapers and drew it up to the old kitchen table. They managed this without speaking to each other at all, except when Lizzie went to put the kettle on.

The man took off his coat, which was old and worn. Whilst Lizzie waited for the kettle to boil she studied his face. He was clearly attempting to look relaxed and unconcerned, stretching out in his chair, but he couldn't help his eyes flicking around nervously, taking the whole place in. This was, Lizzie supposed, where he'd grown up. He had fair hair, like Penny, now turned mostly to grey, and his eyes were blue like hers. But the wide mouth was Lizzie's, undoubtedly. She could see he'd probably been handsome once, but now he looked slight and nervous and pushed down by life.

They knew so little about him. Yes, a few stories they'd

pestered out of their mum and grandmother, but mostly Lizzie remembered her mother saying, 'Girls, if you get pregnant in your teens, I will cut my throat with this knife here. Now, who wants cake?'

And Lizzie would say yes, and Penny would say no.

Lizzie dished up tea, along with some grapes she'd bought.

'So,' said the man finally. Lizzie wondered what to call him. Dad was . . . unlikely. Out of the question. His name was Stephen, but that seemed peculiar too. Mr Willis? Maybe she'd stick to not calling him anything at all.

He looked very happy to be given a cup of tea. Maybe he'd been maligned, she allowed herself to think for a moment. Maybe despite everything it was her mother who'd caused all the trouble, made things impossible for him to stay so he'd had to go out and fend for himself, but he'd loved them all along . . .

Then she got a sudden mental image of her mother's dishwater hands, her swollen ankles as she rolled in from yet another day serving mush to ungrateful brats who gave her backchat and lip, and felt terrible. Her mother had held the whole thing together and she hadn't had a word of thanks nor an iota of help from this man.

Penny had already reached this conclusion and was eyeing him unfavourably. Why, she wondered, would he have come to find them now – a few months after they'd moved into his mother's flat? She folded her arms and waited to hear what he had to say.

'Girls,' said the man finally, after taking a long gulp of tea and looking suspiciously at the grapes. 'I never thought you'd grow up to be so beautiful.'

Penny rolled her eyes. 'I'm amazed you know we grew up

at all,' she said. 'We could have been thrown into the river in a bag without you noticing.'

The man laughed in a forced kind of a way.

'Not at all,' he said. Then he put his hands on his knees, as if he was about to come clean with them.

'Look,' he said. 'I've been a terrible father.'

Penny made a snorting noise. Lizzie shot her a look. Please, please, could Penny just hear him out? Of course he'd been a terrible father, but he was the only one she was ever going to get and, maybe, just maybe, he was here to make amends.

'But I've learned my lesson,' he said, looking at his hands. The nails were bitten almost down to the quick. It seemed a strange habit in a grown man.

'I've messed up so badly,' he said. 'You know, when me and your mother were together, I was so young . . . twins, you know. It was a lot to take on.'

'Which is why you didn't,' said Penny. 'Thanks for the birthday cards, by the way. Oh, no, hang on, we never got one.'

The man shifted uncomfortably. Lizzie noticed, though, that Penny hadn't asked him to leave or shoved him out. Penny wanted to hear what he had to say as much as she did.

'I had to move away,' said Stephen, looking bitter. 'My mother was crazy, I was trying to make it as an artist . . . '

'You were *what?*' said Penny quickly. Her face looked shocked. Neither of them had known that.

'Well, that doesn't matter,' said Stephen. 'Thought I'd make it, didn't I? Be the biggest thing since Andy Warhol. But life doesn't always work out like that.'

Penny's eyes were wide. Lizzie could see exactly what she was thinking. Her face was stricken and, without being able to help herself, all her rancour gone, Lizzie reached out and gently put her hand on Penny's shoulder.

'What kind of work did you do?' asked Penny.

'Conceptual,' said Stephen, still with the last dregs of arrogance in his voice. 'Installations, you know? Birds, shouting, and broken glass everywhere.'

He paused for a bit.

'Not enough people really want to buy an experience like that. Fucking cretins.'

'I work for an art gallery now,' said Penny.

Stephen smiled. 'Really? See, there you go. Runs in the family. Whereabouts?'

'Sloan's,' said Penny.

Stephen's face darkened immediately.

'That bastard,' he said. 'He would never exhibit me.' Nervously, he tapped his jacket until he found a crumpled packet of cheap cigarettes. Without asking their permission, he lit one up and drew on it deeply, screwing up his eyes.

'You don't smoke, do you, kids?' he said. 'Good,' he said as they shook their heads. 'Your mum didn't half do a good job. Much better than I'd have managed.'

'Sloan is a bastard,' said Penny, eyeing Stephen with distaste. 'But *he'd* probably have made a better job bringing us up than you.'

'No need to get nasty, sweetheart,' said Stephen, and there was an awkward silence.

'So, uh, what else have you been up to?' said Lizzie, trying to lighten matters up. Penny and her dad were glaring at each other, and looked ridiculously alike all of a sudden. Stephen broke his gaze first.

'Oh, this and that,' he said. 'Worked in, er, retail for a bit. Went to America. Tough place, America.' His short-stubbed nails rubbed the back of his neck thoughtfully. 'Then I worked on a few ventures with, uh, an acquaintance. Selling personalised plates for weddings. Door to door. Should have been a great hit, but, you know . . . people let us down and the, uh, production lines didn't function correctly. Anyway, after a short period of time as company director I've, er, recently resigned to look into other options. Back here, you know. Good old London town. City of my birth and all that.'

Penny and Lizzie watched him, waiting to hear what he was going to say. Lizzie just wished it would be something like, 'And I came in to say I love you. And would you like me to take you out for ice cream?' But somehow, she knew that wasn't about to be forthcoming.

Penny, though, was beginning to guess where this was heading.

'So, anyway, I thought, Wow, I have to look up my gorgeous girls. I wonder if they're as beautiful as I'd always dreamed. And you are.'

Penny still didn't say anything.

'And I called in on me old mum, you know. Still bonkers, of course.'

'She's not that bonkers,' said Lizzie. 'She's just eccentric. I like her.'

'So do I, of course, of course,' said Stephen. 'So I got talking to her, and I was saying, well, here I am, back in London for the first time in, ooh, twenty years or so.' He didn't sound like his mum. His voice was more aggressive mockney, like he thought he was in an old British gangster movie.

'Uh-huh,' said Penny.

'And, my Christ, hasn't the old town got expensive? Eh? Eh? Can you believe the cost of things in old London town these days?'

A line of sweat had popped out on Stephen's brow, and he looked around for something to stub his cigarette out on. As neither girl moved, he used his saucer.

'So, of course, she says, "Stephen, you're my only boy and I love you . . ."'

That didn't sound like Gran, thought Lizzie.

'Course you've got to go and stay in the flat, haven't you? After all, it's practically yours.'

He rubbed his eyebrow and attempted a grin that didn't succeed particularly well.

'I mean, she's not long for this world, is she?'

'I think she is,' said Lizzie. 'She just likes having a bit of a lie down, that's all.'

She was aware how feeble this sounded.

'So . . . ' said Stephen. He sat back in his chair as if what came next was obvious.

'So what?' said Penny immediately. Her cheeks were very pink. 'You want to move in with us?'

Stephen looked uncomfortable.

'I suppose there's the boxroom,' said Lizzie, trying to pour oil on the troubled waters. After all, he wasn't coming across so well, but he was her dad. Maybe he was just nervous; maybe underneath it all there was a good man, and they could all live together and get to know each other again and they'd all get on really well and she could reintroduce him to their mother and they'd fall in love again and . . . Lizzie sighed.

'It's got all the most obvious crap in it, though,' argued Penny, realising what Lizzie was thinking. 'If we take stuff out of there we won't be able to move around. Especially with three people here.'

'We'd find somewhere for it,' said Lizzie. 'Of course we would. This is a big flat, there's plenty of room for everyone.'

'I suppose,' said Penny, looking mutinous. 'How long would it be for?'

Nobody spoke for a moment. Then Stephen cleared his throat.

'The thing is, girls, you know, it's lovely to see you and everything, it really is. You're my gorgeous girls and I can't wait to get to know you again. But I'm a grown man, you know? I'm a grown man, with, you know, various business arrangements to set up, and there'd be various comings and goings, know what I mean? And a man needs a bit of privacy. Bit of, you know, space to get his head together. And, anyway, so I spoke to Mum, and she said – well, she said she'd only seen one of you by the way, wanted to know if you're identical and she'd just forgotten . . . ' Penny rolled her eyes, to cover up how guilty she felt suddenly. 'So, anyway, I think she wants me to live here now. Her son. On my own.'

And he stretched out his legs, revealing a stretch of slightly grubby-looking white calf and a pair of cheap brown shoes.

'No fucking way,' said Penny. They were in her bedroom, holding a council of war. Stephen was still in the sitting room; they could smell his revolting cigarettes. 'I'm not going anywhere. I'm squatting.'

'But what about when we go to work?' said Lizzie. Their argument was completely forgotten. It was them against the world.

They'd tried phoning their mother – although what she could do, apart from march round with a rolling pin and pound the crap out of him, which Penny couldn't see an earthly reason against at the moment – but there was a message on her phone about her being out at the zoo impersonating an antelope for drama class, and they were only to leave a message if they could bray it.

Lizzie was just miserable. For a second, a tiny second, her heart had inflated with the possibilities of having a daddy.

And then – well, he'd turned out to be just the shit her mother had told them he was. Hardly surprising, given their mother had never lied to them about anything in their lives. Which was why Lizzie's expectations had been so low. Whereas Penny's had been so much higher – had she taken after their father much more, with dreams of breaking free, becoming famous, being successful, which was why she seemed to be crashing to the ground so much harder?

'Well, our father's a prick then,' said Penny, sitting back against the wall. 'Do you think social services would do anything?'

'What, like take us into care?'

Penny winced. 'What about the police? What if we say he's not really our dad but an imposter that's trying to break into our house?'

'That would work brilliantly, until they lined you up and looked at you side by side.'

'Oh, for *fuck's* sake,' said Penny. 'When am I ever going to catch a break?'

Lizzie shrugged. 'When I do, I suppose.'

There came the sound of the television being turned on followed by the noise of the horse racing.

'Oh, good,' said Penny. 'John McCririck is exactly the person to make all this better right now.'

Lizzie sighed. 'Well, listen. We're not going to sort this out sitting in here.'

'We're not, eh? Oh God, I need to phone Sloan.'

'Sloan will understand it's a family crisis.'

'No, he won't. He believes in severing all ties with your family at eighteen and never speaking to them again.'

'Apart from taking money out of his trust fund,' said Lizzie. 'I suppose using your cashcard can be an act of love.'

'We wouldn't know,' said Penny, scowling.

'Well, what I was thinking was, we could go and see Gran,' said Lizzie. 'Just, you know, to make sure that having *him* around is what she meant.'

'She doesn't know what she means,' said Penny. 'Can't we just lock him in and run away? It's not like there's any food in the house. He'd die in about two days.'

'There is food in the house,' said Lizzie, peeved. She'd started to build up the basics of a cook's cupboard, and had been selecting olive oils, balsamic vinegars and various staples on Georges's advice, and was annoyed Penny hadn't noticed. 'You just don't eat any of it.'

Penny weighed things up. Going to see their grandmother was probably the most sensible idea. But what if – and she probably would – she told them that it was OK, her only son was looking after the house now, and thanks for the help?

She didn't want to go back, she really didn't. The commute, if she were to keep her job at Sloan's – and she really wanted to – would be about four hours a day. To go anywhere with Minty and Brooke would either cost her her entire wages in taxi fees or set her back on the night bus to hell. Her chances of life looking up would go. Maybe they should just sit tight. On the other hand, he was a man they didn't know anything about. Who knew what he was capable of?

Penny looked at Lizzie. 'I've never even met her,' said Penny. 'She's going to be really fond of me, isn't she?'

'Well, I did tell you when I was going,' said Lizzie.

'Yes, yes, all right, Saint Elizabeth. No need to point it out.' Penny shrugged. 'What about if you go alone and I go and try and save my job?'

'I don't think that will work,' said Lizzie. Penny heaved a sigh.

'OK. Are you absolutely positively sure we can't just kill him and dispose of the body?'

'*Penny!*' Lizzie was genuinely shocked.

'Oh, come on, we didn't even know for sure he still existed till ten minutes ago. And now he's clearly an idiot. Let's just kill him.'

'Shh.'

The girls tried to look insouciant as they walked back into the sitting room.

'Is that you off then, girls?' said Stephen who was trying to look relaxed on the sofa, though not making a very good job of it. 'Great. Well, see you later, maybe Christmas, yeah?'

'We are *not* off,' said Lizzie. 'We're going to visit Gran, actually.'

Stephen looked a bit uncomfortable.

'Oh, yeah? Great. Tell her I said hi, yeah? And I'll be off to see her soon.'

Penny and Lizzie stared at him.

'So I guess you'll need a couple of days to move,' said Stephen. 'So maybe I'll leave the locks till then.'

'That's it,' said Penny. 'I'm not going anywhere, you fucker.'

'Shh,' said Lizzie, trying to push her out the door.

'I'm sure Mum wouldn't like to hear you talk to your father like that,' said Stephen, an unpleasant smile playing on his lips. 'Would she, now?'

'You're not my dad,' spat Penny viciously. 'You're absolutely bloody no one.'

'And who are you?' shot back Stephen. 'I mean, you look like a tart, but it's so hard to tell these days.'

Penny finally stopped shaking after they'd waited for the bus for twenty-five minutes. Lizzie knew well enough just to let her be. It was the one benefit of being pessimistic, Lizzie thought to herself. You weren't quite so open to disappointment.

They travelled in silence, Penny staring out of the window. She wanted to vow that she would never travel by bus again; she had sworn it, she remembered, when they'd first moved there. And she was getting so tired of it all.

'Come on,' said Lizzie, getting up.

'Are we there?'

'No. We have another bus to get.'

'Of course we do.'

It was getting dark as they alighted at the end of the street. Penny found it just as spooky as Lizzie had done the first time she'd come.

'I want you,' said Penny, 'to shoot me before I ever have to come to one of these places.'

'OK,' said Lizzie.

'You're not meant to say that!' said Penny in despair. 'You're meant to say, "Don't be daft, how would you ever end up in one of these places? You'll be surrounded by family and friends and grandchildren before you painlessly slip off in your sleep one night like that old lady in *Titanic*."'

'Sorry,' said Lizzie. 'That's what I meant.'

'You don't say, "OK, I will take the gun and shoot you dead when you are lonely and mental which you definitely will be because you'll have inherited the mental genes from your gran and the evil genes from your dad."'

Lizzie patted her on the arm. 'Come on,' she said.

'There you are again!' said Penny. 'You could have at least suggested I wasn't evil.'

'You just tried to get me to help you to murder our father.'

'Yes, well . . . '

Lizzie said hello to the usual staff, who were getting to know her well enough that she occasionally almost got a grunt in return, and headed towards her grandmother's open door.

'Hey, Gran,' she said, knowing the old lady's closed eyes didn't necessarily mean she was sleeping, merely that she was unable to find anything of interest around her. 'I didn't have time to get any flowers, I'm sorry.'

'Little twin,' said their gran with a smile on her face. 'I get so many visitors these days! I think downstairs they think I'm the Queen.'

She glanced up and took in Penny, then looked at Lizzie enquiringly, waiting to be introduced.

'And this is Penny,' said Lizzie. 'The other little twin.'

Penny had the curious feeling of being looked up and down. She had no sense that this woman had lost her marbles at all.

'Hello, Gran,' she said. 'It's . . . uh, nice to see you again after all these years.'

'You look like Stephen,' said their gran almost instantly. 'So like him.'

'I'm not like him!' said Penny. 'Not at all. Well, you know,' she added, remembering he was Gran's only child, 'a bit.'

'So you've met him?' said their gran. 'Is that why you're here?'

'Well, and to see you,' said Lizzie.

'I know,' said Gran. 'How's that man you're in love with?'

Oh, great, thought Penny, bring that up. Even a senile old woman in bed knew more about Lizzie's life than her twin had noticed.

'He's engaged,' said Lizzie, going pink. 'To somebody else. But it's OK.'

'Well,' said Gran kindly, 'you tried your best. You look very lovely, little twin.'

'Thank you,' said Lizzie, biting her lip. 'I didn't try my best. But maybe next time . . . you know. If there's a next time. I could maybe try a bit harder.'

'There'll be a next time,' said their gran. Penny waited for her to ask a question about her, but she didn't.

'And my Stephen is back,' she said. 'I told you he would be, didn't I?'

'Yes,' said Lizzie. 'Well done you. Was it nice to see him?'

Her gran rubbed her eyes. 'You love your children, Lizzie. So much. One day you'll find that out.'

Lizzie doubted whether she'd ever get the chance, but she nodded and patted her gran on the hand.

'So. Did it feel strange to meet your father again?'

'Strange?' said Penny. 'Well, he tried to throw us out on the street.'

'What do you mean?' said their gran.

'He wants to live in your house and he doesn't want us to live there.' Penny's voice sounded accusatory.

Their gran pushed herself further up on her pillows. When she spoke again, her voice was much stronger.

'And you think . . . you, by the way, who I have only just met, who has only just come to see me . . . you think you have a right to my house?'

Penny swallowed hard. 'Well,' said Penny, 'I thought . . . '

'What did you think? Did you think, I don't care two bits for what that old lady tried to do for me, I don't ever have to see her, but I deserve her flat?'

'No,' said Penny. She looked down. 'I've been busy.'

'I haven't,' said their gran.

'We've loved staying there,' said Lizzie. 'Thank you.'

'That's all right, little twin,' said their gran. 'But, you know. Your sister . . . ' She looked harshly again at Penny.

Penny didn't say anything. Lizzie nodded.

'Thank you for looking after the flat for me. But now Stephen is back . . . '

She let her voice trail off, but it was obvious what

she meant. Penny slowly nodded. It was all her fault.

'Will you still come and see me, little twin?'

Lizzie nodded. 'Of course,' she said. 'It's an easier bus ride here from Mum's anyway.'

'"It's an easier bus ride from Mum's anyway",' mimicked Penny as they stood at the bus stop. She was feeling enormously guilty, and it was making her aggressive. 'You are such a complete dishcloth. She's just made us homeless!'

'She's an old woman. It's her house. And, by the way, she might not have been quite so happy to get us out if you had ever bothered . . . '

'I know, I know, I know,' said Penny. 'And you're perfect. What do you care? Grainne's waiting for you at home, you can get a job in any old caff – there's six thousand round the corner – and everything will be fine for you. It's just my life that's ruined.'

Penny looked at her sister, wanting a reaction, but Lizzie turned away and, in the rain-spattered light from outside the home, Penny noticed for the first time that she was crying. Great big tears were running down her cheeks, collecting in a puddle with the rain.

## Chapter Fourteen

'I'm not clearing my stuff out when he's there,' whispered Penny as they mounted the stairs.

'I'm sure you could leave it,' said Lizzie. 'It could just blend in and become part of the mess. I don't think Stephen's much tidier than his mother is.'

'Oh God,' said Penny. They were mounting the stairs to the apartment, possibly for the last time. Lizzie tried to take in the polished mirrors, the immaculate parquet, the works of art on the wall. Best not to think about that. 'Are you absolutely *sure* we can't kill him? Surely the world would be better off without him. I'm sure I didn't notice when he wasn't around.'

'Really?' said Lizzie. 'I always did.'

Penny stopped outside Brooke and Minty's apartment.

'Oh, no,' said Lizzie.

'Come on,' said Penny. 'I need to see some friendly faces.'

'Well, we should go somewhere else.'

'No,' said Penny severely. 'I need to find someone who'll make us a cocktail and talk nonsense about two-hundred-and-fifty-pound boots. And I think this is the best place for it.'

Lizzie, unwilling to head upstairs on her own, lingered behind her sister.

Brooke came to the door, fastening her earrings, obviously heading out.

'Darlings! How are you doing!'

'Great!' said Penny immediately. 'Fabulous, in fact. Where are you off to, you gorgeous creature?'

'Oh, some boring old hunt ball. Grosvenor House again.'

'Again,' said Penny, trying to sound sympathetic and keep the disappointment out of her voice. 'That sounds tedious.'

'Alarmingly so,' agreed Brooke.

'Great,' said Penny. 'Why don't you blow it out and we'll go and get drunk on Tanqueray and pomegranate?'

'That sounds good,' said Brooke. 'But I have literally hundreds of people waiting for me to be there.'

Lizzie rolled her eyes.

'All tedious, of course.'

'Of course.'

Brooke eyed herself up approvingly in the huge hall mirror.

'I wouldn't want to keep you from your public,' said Penny. 'Is Minty about?'

Brooke's gaze lowered and she moved towards them into the hall.

'Ah,' she said, 'rather a delicate matter.'

'What?'

Brooke looked round, but there was no sign of Minty behind them in the large room.

263

'Well,' she said, 'it's nothing really. Minty's just having one of her *turns*.'

'What kind of turn?' asked Penny suspiciously.

'Oh, usual stuff. When a man breaks up with her. She tends to go a bit . . . hmm, what's the word?'

'Psycho?' suggested Lizzie from behind Penny.

'Yes, that's it. A bit psycho. Wanders around in a daze, trails them to their house, phones them up a million times an hour, that kind of thing.'

For a moment Penny couldn't speak. Was that how it had been with . . . Then she found her voice.

'Does that . . . does that happen often?'

'Only all the fucking time,' said Brooke. 'It's all right, I'm quite used to it. We just say she's fragile, poor girl.'

Just then Minty wandered into view. She was dressed in a hideously stained dressing gown, which didn't conceal holey pyjamas that weren't buttoned properly. Her hair was a huge pile of straw, and her eyes tiny and red. She was carrying the telephone.

'Hello, Minty,' said Lizzie. She knew it was wrong, but she couldn't help it. 'You look tired.'

Minty grunted in their general direction. 'Men suck.' She sniffed.

'Of course they do,' said Brooke kindly.

'They do,' agreed Penny, nodding vigorously.

'I don't know enough to do a statistical sample,' said Lizzie. 'But I've heard . . . '

'I've been phoning him non-stop for forty-eight hours,' said Minty. 'There's no way he can't be in for forty-eight hours! And now it's saying that that phone has been disconnected from the network! So he's not going to know I've called!'

'I'm sure he'll know you've called,' said Brooke. 'Now,

hey, the trick is to play it cool and let him come running.'

'They never do, though,' said Minty, looking confused. 'They start running and then they go all funny. Why is that?'

'I've told you before,' said Brooke. 'You've got to stop buying them pets and calling them Daddy.'

Minty stuck out her bottom lip. 'I love my daddy.'

Penny and Lizzie looked at each other.

'Actually, we should get going,' said Penny. 'Call us if you need us, Minty.'

'I can't call you,' said Minty, as if explaining something really obvious. 'I'm calling Kieran. I love him, you see.'

'You don't think . . . ' said Lizzie as they mounted the next flight of stairs.

'Don't say it,' ordered Penny. 'You weren't there. Will's a gold-digger and having a run-in with Minty the nutcase doesn't change a thing. Oh, Christ.'

They had reached the top of the stairs. Outside the door were two old, stained suitcases, full to overflowing with their clothes.

Lizzie swallowed hard. 'You know what? I think I'd rather be the nutcase with the daddy who loves her.'

Penny banged hard on the door, then opened it with her key, which still worked.

'Hello, little twins,' said Stephen. He was sitting on the patched armchair, a cigarette flickering in his fingers. 'I thought I'd help you get a move on with packing. But you can leave a few things here, of course. In case you ever want to come and visit your old dad. How's the old girl, then?'

Lizzie's voice quivered as she spoke. 'You'd better keep going to visit her and be really nice to her.'

'Yeah, whatever,' said Stephen. 'Off back to your mum's, then? That's nice. Everyone lives with their mum and it all works out nice and tidy. Course Brandford's not quite so handy, is it, but then, I think it suits you two better anyway. You're more local girls than Chelsea types, don't you think?'

Penny looked at him. 'You're unspeakable.'

'Course I'm not, darling. I only want what's mine, don't I? We've all got our lives to lead.'

Lizzie had telephoned Georges, reasoning that if there was ever a reason to ask for a favour from a friend who had a car service, it was now, but she'd got Maria-Elena on the telephone. She'd tried to explain the situation, but Maria-Elena affected not to understand a word she was saying, so it hadn't got across. It had ended up with Lizzie hanging up in despair.

'That woman is—'

'Is probably going to turn Georges into a billionaire,' finished Penny, who was throwing tiny pieces of underwear into an ancient carpet bag with a fierce right hand.

Parkend Close had never looked quite as bleak as it did that night. They'd planned to spend a little bit more time in Chelsea whilst they figured out what to do, but it simply wasn't possible; Penny said she couldn't trust herself to spend a night in the same house as that man and not stab him with the bread knife, using the sleepwalking defence to help her get off.

It was getting on for midnight when the grimy, stinking bus deposited them, with their luggage, at the end of the road to the estate. It had been the journey from hell. Neither of them mentioned, or could bear to think of, their triumphant departure on that sunny spring morning, in the shiny black cab.

And now they were 'home'. They'd finally got through to

their mother, who was sad but, she said, not entirely surprised. Stephen had had a nasty streak then, and it didn't seem to have mellowed with the years. She didn't even show much interest in how he looked or what he'd been doing, which Lizzie found astonishing.

Oh, and she was going out tonight – an unmissable rehearsal, apparently. And the lodgers were still there and she wasn't going to be able to get rid of them for a week or two. Sorry, darlings, but not to worry, she'd cook them up a huge stew the next day and everything would be much better.

Neither of them was convinced.

'I can't believe we've both got to sleep on the living-room floor,' moaned Penny. 'You realise this means we really are officially homeless? If I had been pregnant we could have thrown ourselves on the mercy of the council.'

'Christ,' said Lizzie. And she heaved her bags up the stairs.

Has the house shrunk while we were away? wondered Lizzie, lying on the patterned carpet between the ancient worsted three-piece suite.

Penny was snoring quietly beside her in an old sleeping bag that smelled of mould, but there was a banging coming from the loud rap music one of the pale weedy student lodgers was playing upstairs, and their mother wasn't even back yet. Not to mention she was going to have to get up at five in order to reach the café in time. She could probably forget about sleep altogether. But she couldn't get up and do anything either. There was nowhere to go. Nowhere at all.

Things seemed slightly better in the morning. But not much. At least the acned lodgers didn't show their faces first thing, and the sun was peering, ever so weakly, through the dirty downstairs windows, and their mother was up, at the crack of dawn as always, making white bread toast and instant coffee.

'Hello, my girls!' said their mum, and at the sight of her face – still worn, but looking a lot less tired than the last time they'd seen her – kind and concerned, Lizzie felt like tucking herself inside her mum's strong arms and never coming out again.

Their mother put some eggs on to fry. 'Would you like some breakfast?'

'Uh, no thank you, Mum,' said Penny and Lizzie at the same time. Their mother looked up.

'So, changed with your new London ways?' she said pleasantly. 'I knew it would get you.'

She put another couple of slices of bread in the toaster, and sat down with her arms folded.

'So,' she said. 'Did you enjoy your experiment?'

The girls looked at each other and nodded.

'I didn't expect it to end so soon,' their mother said. 'But I'm glad you're back.'

She was, it was so wonderful to see them, especially with Lizzie looking so well. But she'd hoped that this would be their chance to fly the nest.

'It's good to see you again. Have you adopted lots of fancy ways?'

'I already had lots of fancy ways,' said Penny grumpily. 'I haven't changed at all.'

'Hmm,' said their mother. 'You look different to me. What about you, Lizzie? You look different to me too.'

Lizzie shrugged. 'Oh, it's nothing,' she said.

'It doesn't look like nothing,' said their mother. 'You're definitely different. Slimmer . . . more grown up.'

Lizzie swallowed. Well, she supposed she had learned a

few things. 'Not really, Mum,' she said, giving her a hug.

'You're not in love are you?' said their mother suddenly. 'My little Lizzie?'

'No!' said Lizzie. 'Of course not, Mum.'

Penny jumped in quickly. 'So,' she said, 'you never told us our father was such a prick . . .'

Their mother quickly turned back to the oven.

'I should have known something like this might happen,' she said. 'I should have . . . never trusted your gran really. But she's so old now, and he's been gone for so long . . . I didn't think it would matter. But when there's some money, Stephen will be around for a sniff. Leopards don't change their spots.'

She sighed and glanced out the dirty window.

'It's the only reason you haven't seen him, you know. Because I never had any money. Sometimes I think it's almost what's kept me down. On purpose, you know. If I'd won the lottery, well, your dad would have been round like a shot.' She turned to face them. 'And I'm not sure it would have done you any good.'

'No,' said Lizzie.

'He was a bad lot,' said their mother. 'I'm sorry, but it's true. You two, however, are my wonderful, gorgeous girls. And I couldn't be more proud of you.'

Even Penny sniffed.


'Sloan,' said Penny in what she hoped was a winning tone. She had just managed to sell one of Tabitha's paintings to someone who looked so suspiciously similar to Tabitha – and had swooned so extraordinarily over them, particularly when someone else had popped into the shop – that she could only be a relative or some kind of a plant. She hoped Sloan hadn't noticed: he didn't see so well in the mornings.

'Yes?' said Sloan. He was looking at his unrequested cup of tea and Penguin biscuit as if Penny were trying to poison him. She never made him anything without being asked, begged, then finally shouted at, and even then she usually disappeared into the back of the gallery and read *Heat* for half an hour while pretending to wait for the kettle to boil.

'What's *this*?' he held up the biscuit.

'It's a chocolate biscuit. I bought it for you myself. Well, out of petty cash.'

Sloan continued to look at it dubiously.

'I don't understand,' said Sloan. 'Has it got fish in it?'

'Oh, for goodness' sake,' said Penny. 'Ordinary people eat chocolate biscuits all the time, you know. Just because you're a big snob who only eats, I don't know, swan.'

'You can only eat swan if you're eating with the Queen,' said Sloan. 'So, of course I have.'

'When did you last have chips?' asked Penny.

'Game chips?'

'What are they? Like, chips with gravy?'

'Oh, my little Penelope. I do love you so.'

'Good,' said Penny. 'Because there's something I need to ask you. You live just round the corner, don't you?'

'Well, I just can't wait to see where this is heading,' said Sloan. 'Book me a cab to the Ivy, will you, darling, I feel the sudden urge to leave immediately and eat fishcakes.'

'I was just wondering,' Penny ploughed on regardless, 'if you'd be interested in a lodger.'

Sloan guffawed. 'You?'

'What's wrong with me?' said Penny, affronted. 'I'm tidy.'

'And I know how much you can afford to pay me,' said Sloan. 'Anyway, darling, of course I already have lodgers.'

'You do? Really?'

Sloan looked careless. 'Well, yes. I call them lodgers. Helping out the young men in the vicinity. Builders, brickies, plumbers, that kind of thing.'

'Sloan,' said Penny, genuinely shocked. 'You like a bit of rough!'

'Why do you think I hired you, my sweetness?'

'Bugger,' said Penny. The doorbell pinged and Tabitha glided in.

'Hello,' said Penny. 'Where do you live?'

'I am a citizen of the sun and the moon, my dear,' said Tabitha. 'I have no earthly shape nor form, and I sleep with the wild wind and the high seas.'

'Really?' said Sloan. 'Because I've got your VAT address down as Watford.'

'And Watford,' said Tabitha.

'How's that meant to help me?' grumbled Penny. 'Would you like a Penguin?'

'I believe so,' said Tabitha gravely. 'Now, tell me, my darlings. How is my party coming along?'

Sloan raised his eyes to the heavens. 'I *so* have to be somewhere else.' And he picked up his cane.

'If you're looking for a new lodger they're putting up scaffolding at the corner of Sloane Square,' said Penny as he left.

'What a terrible loss not to have you living with me,' said Sloan, sweeping out.

'So,' said Tabitha, 'do we have lots of people coming?'

'Loads,' said Penny. The party was only two days away and she'd been extremely busy, organising drinks and snacks – she'd gone for bright cocktails and sausages on sticks, with pineapple and cheese, also on sticks, pushed into oranges to look like hedgehogs, which she'd thought would be a nice touch, what with Tabitha being a nature-lover and

271

so on. Sloan had laughed his head off and told her it was delightfully retro.

'Excellent,' said Tabitha, clapping her hands together so the rings rang out and made a noise. 'According to my spirit guide it's a most auspicious day.'

She cast a look around the shop. 'But where is *The Daily Unfolding Meridian of the Sublime Abyss, II*?'

'That orange one?' said Penny. 'Oh, we sold it this morning.'

Tabitha looked cross. 'To a woman? Wearing a jewelled turban?'

'Do you know, I can't remember what she was wearing,' said Penny. 'Uh, yes, that was her.'

'Bugger,' said Tabitha. 'She was meant to buy it at the party. No matter. Anyway, I have something for you.'

She looked mysteriously to the left and right, then drew something out from under the voluminous folds of the cloak she was wearing. It was a small, hessian bag, which smelled strongly of herbs.

'Here,' she said.

'What's this?' said Penny.

'It is a potion. To see off a love rival.'

'A *what*?'

'Did you forget our little magic chat?'

'Uh, no. But I didn't realise you . . . you meant it.'

'You must slip it in the glass of the love rival, who will then appear spotted and horrible in the eyes of the beloved.'

'You are kidding?'

'Are you questioning the power of the spirits? Because, you know, they hate that.'

'No,' said Penny. 'No, really, no. Thank you very much.'

And she took the sachet and slipped it into her pocket. Of course it was completely ridiculous.

*

'You are so sad this morning, Lizzie,' said Georges eventually. He hadn't wanted to mention it. He felt slightly uncomfortable about why she might look this way, without quite admitting to himself why.

Lizzie had assumed he knew everything about it already from Maria-Elena, and hadn't mentioned it for fear of being insensitive.

'I'm all right,' she said. 'Well, you know.'

'I do not know,' said Georges. 'I know that frittata is not made better with tears, huh?'

'Well, you know about my dad . . . coming back and taking the flat . . . '

When she saw Georges's look of incomprehension, Lizzie realised he didn't know at all, he didn't have the faintest idea what she was talking about.

'I called you yesterday . . . when we had to move at short notice . . . I was wondering if we could have borrowed a car.'

'I did not get a call.'

'No, I spoke to Maria-Elena . . . but you didn't call back, so I presumed you were too busy or it was too rude a thing to ask you . . . '

Georges was still staring at her, so, seeing as they were quiet, he made them two cups of tea and they sat down while she told him everything. By the end, she realised her eyes were once more full of tears.

'Oh, Lizzie,' Georges said many times. 'Oh, Lizzie.'

He didn't try and tell her what to do, or give her advice, or suggest that she be angry or indignant at her father or her grandmother. He just sat and listened gently. At the end he patted her gently on the arm. It was like being stroked by a friendly bear. Lizzie wanted to collapse onto him and stay there for ever.

'This is a very sad story,' he said. 'And you had to take

the bus all the way to Brandford with all your things?'

'It wasn't so bad,' mumbled Lizzie. She felt like she was telling tales now.

'Why didn't Maria-Elena tell me?' wondered Georges.

'Well, you know . . . I thought, maybe she just didn't understand me . . . her English, you know . . . '

'Her English is perfect,' said Georges. The door opened as some customers came in, and he stood up, looking annoyed.

'You know, I have some places . . . some homes around. I will be able to sort you out, I'm sure. Somewhere not so inconvenient as Brandford.'

'No . . . No, Georges, it's all right. We really couldn't . . . I mean. We couldn't afford to rent a flat. At the moment. We'll be OK.'

'Ah, but I'm sure we could sort something out . . . '

The idea of living in one of Georges's properties for free as some kind of a favour was so awful and embarrassing, Lizzie couldn't countenance the idea. Imagine having to work for the person who was putting you up for free.

'No, thanks,' said Lizzie, a bit stiffly. 'We'll be able to manage perfectly fine on our own, thank you.'

Georges had to turn to serve a customer, and Lizzie headed through into the back to wash her face. She let the cool water run over her brow and into her hair, completely unaware of Georges who, having said goodbye to the customer, had turned to watch her.

# Chapter Fifteen

'So, you know. It was an interesting experience, I suppose,' said Lizzie. 'Like a holiday, really. But I suppose it's better to be back where we belong.'

Grainne stared into her glass of cider and chewed speculatively on a McCoys crisp. Lizzie remembered turning her nose up at the restaurant opening – really. And now, here they were back in Coasters. At least in the new restaurant her feet hadn't stuck to the floor, and there wasn't a bunch of feral thirteen-year-olds messing about with the darts. There weren't any darts.

'Miss Friss says hello,' said Grainne. She was being kind, Lizzie noticed, and sympathising rather than gloating that they'd been brought back down a peg or two.

'That's nice,' said Lizzie. 'Say meow from me.'

'She's sulking,' said Grainne. 'Doesn't like her new kilt.'

Penny arrived. She'd never usually come out with them,

but that hadn't seemed to matter so much recently. She was wearing a smart, sober, Victorian-style blouse, which looked completely out of place amongst the muffin tops and pink vests of the bar.

'I need to plan the party,' said Penny. 'There's too much Biactol in the house and nowhere to sit.'

'Where's Mum?'

'She's at some play in an old match factory. It's about worker exploitation. Why can't she be the kind of actress that gets friendly with Sienna Miller and gets us invited to West End openings?'

'Because we're Berrys,' said Lizzie. 'Nothing good can happen to us, remember?'

'So how are you, Grainne?' said Penny after she got back from the bar.

'Good,' said Grainne. 'I slept with an Australian at the Walkabout bar.'

'Well done,' said Penny. 'I've heard that's really difficult to do.'

Grainne looked pleased.

'So, how's the party going?' said Lizzie.

'A party?' said Grainne. 'Can I come? Will there be Australians there?'

'Not just Australians,' said Penny. 'We're also having crisps.'

Grainne looked even more pleased. Lizzie couldn't believe Penny was inviting Grainne. Six months ago she pretended she could never remember her name, even though Lizzie had known her for years.

'It's a shame,' Grainne said finally. 'About you having to lose your big London flat and your dad turning out to be a bastard and that,' she said.

Lizzie nodded in agreement. 'I know.' She looked around.

Maybe she could work here. No, she couldn't do that. But she knew, now, for absolutely certain, that she couldn't carry on working for Georges. It wasn't just the commute, although that was impossible; it cost her about ten per cent of her wages as it was, and they put the bloody fares up once a fortnight. It was the thought of seeing Chelsea, and everyone they'd met there, drift further and further away from her. Georges and Maria-Elena would get married, and either move back to Portugal or stay away from the shop and have beautiful, chubby, dark-eyed babies and laugh a lot and things, and Penny . . .

Lizzie regarded her sister with a wry smile, watching Penny as she tried to be polite and listen to a confusing story Grainne was telling her about a dog taking a poo in her communal hallway. Penny would make it out of here. Not this time, but one of these days, with one bound she'd be free. Parkend Close was just too small for her. Lizzie had no doubt she'd keep working for Sloan, and she'd meet someone, or one of Minty's crazy friends would turn up, or . . . well, something would happen. But for her, well. Maybe not.

Lizzie smiled at Grainne when Penny went to the bathroom.

'Penny's changed a lot, hasn't she?' she said.

Grainne shrugged. 'Hmm. A bit maybe. She's still the same underneath.'

Lizzie wondered if this was true, watching Penny catching the eyes of several men lined up against the bar. Oh well. And she was back to being dependable old Lizzie.

'Actually,' said Grainne suddenly, 'the one who's really changed is you.'

Later, when they were getting ready for bed, Lizzie told Penny that she thought Penny would escape, that she would still be a Chelsea girl.

Penny stopped brushing her teeth for a moment.

'Do you really think so?' she asked.

'I don't think it's possible that you won't,' said Lizzie. 'You'll probably meet someone at the party and you'll be away.'

Penny grimaced and put the toothbrush down. 'I'm sorry,' she said. 'I'm really sorry. About Georges, I mean. You know, it was . . .'

'Don't worry about it,' said Lizzie. 'I was kidding myself anyway.'

'No, you weren't,' said Penny, fiercely. 'Stop underestimating yourself. You look brilliant, you're, you know, great. I know I cock things up but I just never want to . . . you know, get chucked out of my house again. I want security. Do you understand?'

'Yes,' said Lizzie. 'But it still seems high risk to me. Money over love and all that.'

'I had love, though,' said Penny. 'And look where that got me.'

'You had it once,' said Lizzie. 'You'll get it again. And it made you so happy.'

'A car service would make me happy,' said Penny, spitting. 'Liz, you were great to me all through my . . . well, my little difficulties. And you looked after Gran and everything, even though she's a vindictive old bitch.'

'Who's looking after her family,' pointed out Lizzie.

'Yeah, the evil bit of it anyway,' snarled Penny. 'Stop bloody underestimating yourself. I bet Georges is kicking himself. With his big, hairy podgy feet.'

'Stop it,' said Lizzie, but without rancour.

'You've changed, Liz. You really have. For the better, with or without Ape Face.'

They headed into the lounge and turned in. Lizzie was so

knackered she was about to fall asleep despite the pounding Snoop Dogg coming from upstairs and the musty smell of the carpets. Just as she was nodding off, she heard Penny say, very quietly, 'When he came into the café . . .'

Lizzie didn't have to ask who she meant.

'Did he . . . I mean, how was he, Liz?'

'Shocking,' said Lizzie.

There was a silence.

'Good,' said Penny. 'He deserves to be. Doesn't he?' She didn't sound entirely convinced.

But Lizzie had already fallen asleep.


'You would never think I was from Brandford, would you, Sloan?' said Penny, at four-thirty on the day of the party. She had been bouncing about on nervous energy all day, fiddling with the tiger lilies that had been delivered, on Tabitha's instructions, at eleven on the dot so they would be opening perfectly by seven.

Revved up by Lizzie's belief that she'd have another chance, Penny had gone to town with her outfit. She was wearing a grey tweed dress she'd found in a charity shop, which fitted her like a dream, and looked like something out of the forties. She'd applied bright red lipstick and, as a finishing touch, the beret. She looked marvellous.

Sloan regarded her through half-closed eyes. He'd tutted over the wine Penny had ordered in ('Well, you did set me a budget of two ninety-nine,' she'd pointed out. 'And when I asked you if Chateau Loup was OK you snored at me'), and popped out to get his own, just to get them in the mood.

Penny had one glass but no more. She'd learned her lesson. Plus the last thing she needed was to do something really atrocious and lose this job. Mind you, she wondered what she could do that was so awful Sloan would sack her. It would really have to be pretty bad.

'*Crisps?*' said Sloan suddenly, noticing a pile of garishly coloured packets piled up in the back room. 'What on earth are they doing there?'

'Well, you said we couldn't have any food,' said Penny.

'Yes.'

'But I thought, if people can have a little snack they're more likely to stay longer.'

'*Crisps*, though.'

'Well.'

'Penelope, having crisps in this shop is a sackable offence. Get rid of them, you guttersnipe.'

'*Sloan*,' said Penny. 'What am I meant to do with two hundred packets of crisps?'

'Feed some of your illegitimate children by different fathers, I shouldn't wonder,' said Sloan.

Penny tutted and threw a bag of Skips at him. They hit his wig and knocked it slightly askew.

'Can*not* get the staff these days,' said Sloan. 'Now, pour me another glass and get the music sorted out. The music has to be loud. Then people lean over to shout in each other's ears and sometimes they end up accidentally snogging, which is always good for a party. And also, if some fartypants critic turns up and starts bellowing about how shit they think the artwork is, no one can hear them.'

'Can do,' said Penny. 'I've put together a compilation. Of cat-themed songs.'

'Oh, yeah?' Sloan raised a sceptical eyebrow as Penny brought out the CD.

'Here we go . . . "Lion Sleeps Tonight", "Lovecats", "Tiger Feet" . . .'

Sloan snatched the plastic box out of her hands.

'*I'll* handle the music,' he said. 'God, I really do have to do everything myself around here.'

By seven, people were already gathering outside the doors, and by five past, the place was filling up, buzzing merrily.

'That was fast,' said Sloan. 'Even for Rentamob.'

Penny was standing next to the door, greeting people with a big smile. She looked fabulous, she knew, partly because people kept telling her so, and partly because she was standing next to Tabitha, who was wearing a lime green muumuu with a yellow feather in her hair.

'*Namaste*,' Tabitha was saying to everyone as they walked in the door. Most people said 'bless you', thinking she'd sneezed.

Lizzie arrived at seven-thirty, nervous but excited. She was wearing a simple, belted dress she'd found in the Jigsaw sale, which she knew looked good on her, and she'd used Penny's lipstick. It was far bolder than she was used to, but as soon as she'd put it on she'd realised it suited her perfectly.

'Hey, look at you two,' said Rob and Sven, who'd just arrived. 'You look like twins.'

'We are twins,' said Penny. 'We've met before, remember?'

'I'm sure I'd remember you,' said Sven to Lizzie's breasts. Lizzie and Penny looked at each other and grinned.

Grainne sidled in looking nervous. She was wearing a black skirt and a white shirt, out of which her breasts spilled alarmingly.

'Hey, there,' said Lizzie. 'How are you?'

'Terrible,' said Grainne. 'I wore this just in case I'd misheard you and you actually wanted me to be a waitress.'

'No,' said Lizzie patiently. 'And here. These two men are desperate to meet charming young ladies.'

'They don't really have to be charming,' said Rob. 'Just handy.'

'Are you Australian?' asked Grainne.

'Nope.'

Grainne thought for a moment. 'Ah, that doesn't matter. Do you like crisps?'

'Who doesn't?'

By eight the party was really starting to move. Tabitha was standing in the centre, letting people come to her and allowing copious amounts of raw red wine to be poured into her glass. Sloan was sitting behind the desk, deep in conversation with several young men who appeared to be models of some sort. Penny had been grabbed by a bunch of enthusiastic young money men from a Mayfair office who were asking her to explain the history of art whilst attempting to pinch her bum. Normally this would have been a perfect state of affairs, Penny was thinking. Why did it feel so hollow?

Lizzie was nursing a glass of wine, happy to survey the clearly successful party – there were already red stickers on the smaller pieces, and Tabitha was gaily instructing people to buy immediately, otherwise she would do a large tiger roar at them.

Minty and Brooke had arrived with some of their louche friends, and despite spending at least twenty minutes explaining how they couldn't possibly stay long, they had much more exciting plans elsewhere, they were still here, listening to the ridiculous pop music Penny had finally managed to get on the stereo, and clearly enjoying themselves. Minty was in a corner with Sven, tossing her shiny blonde hair meaningfully and giving him a slightly unhinged wide-eyed smile. Lizzie wondered how on earth she could ever have been scared of her. Even Krystanza had turned up, with a photographer in tow so he could get pictures showing how cultured she was. Unfortunately her bosoms were obscuring the view for the other punters, but it couldn't be helped.

Then a sleek black car drew up. Of course. Lizzie nodded her head. If it was up to her, Georges would walk everywhere, not sit in the back of a big car, getting podgy.

But it wasn't, of course.

The doors of the car opened and Georges and Maria-Elena got out from opposite sides. It was odd, mused Lizzie, eyeing them from her vantage point at the window, that they didn't talk to one another at all. Their body language was extremely frosty. Maybe they'd had a row about something. She didn't think it would be difficult for Maria-Elena to pick a fight with someone. Probably didn't want to come to evil Penny's party, and she supposed she couldn't blame her, after the terrible display Penny had put on.

Nonetheless, Georges, courteous as ever, stood on the outside edge of the pavement, and made sure he opened the gallery door for his future bride. Of course he would, thought Lizzie, going forward to say hello. She was going to have to tell him she was leaving. In fact, she should tell him sooner rather than later. The faster she stopped having to pay these ridiculous bus fares the better, and he had plenty to do with organising the wedding and whatnot.

'Lizzie,' he said, his face, as always, bursting with warmth. 'You get more . . . well.' He stopped himself. 'What a lovely party.'

'Hello, Maria-Elena,' said Lizzie. Maria-Elena raised her eyebrows and handed her coat to Georges without looking at him. She grabbed a glass of wine and went off to look at the paintings.

'Actually, I have to talk to you,' said Lizzie.

'Oh, yes?' said Georges.

'It's about . . . well, I have to . . . '

Just then, Tabitha Angelbrain Dawson rang her fork sharply against her glass and made a loud 'huhhummm'.

Sloan, who'd looked to be dropping off to sleep, raised his head. 'Oh, Christ,' he said. 'What is this, a fucking Cheshire wedding?'

'I just wanted to say, thank you all so much for coming to my party,' began Tabitha in very loud, imperious tones.

'Who's that?' Sven could be heard asking plaintively over the crowd.

'Well, of course, I say my party, but I like to think it's really the spirits' party. They have guided me – I am merely the vessel. A toast. To the gods of creativity; of animalistic spirit, and of course, to the inner-leonine passion which has guided us all here today.'

She raised her glass impressively.

'To the gods of creativity . . . animal blah blah, spirit, blah blah, mmm mmm,' said the rest of the crowd, raising their glasses too.

'And buy lots of the damn things,' said Tabitha. 'There's a free packet of crisps with each one.'

There was a huge round of applause at this, then everyone went back to quaffing their wine, throwing it back quickly before it peeled the enamel off their teeth. The chat level increased commensurately.

'What?' said Georges urgently.

'Sorry?' said Lizzie, who'd got slightly sidetracked by trying to work out what exactly Tabitha had stencilled in gold on her fingernails. They looked like claws. Also, the woman with the Nicole Kidman nose from her first day at the gallery had just walked in, and had bypassed Lizzie without a second glance.

Lizzie wasn't certain whether to be pleased or slightly annoyed by this. Even Sloan hadn't insulted her or anything. She supposed she was fitting in around these parts, just as she was about to head on the long way home. And there, she reflected, wherever she ended up, she was going to be completely out of place again. God, life was annoying. She sighed.

'Lizzie,' said Georges, snapping his fingers. 'You are in a dream.'

'Oh, sorry,' said Lizzie. She swallowed hard. She wasn't looking forward to doing this, but there was no way around it. She had to be brave, and upfront, and all the things Georges and her gran kept telling her to be. Get it over with.

'Georges,' she said. 'I have to . . . I mean. I resign.'

There. She'd said it now. It was out of her mouth and out of her hands.

'No,' said Georges. 'No, you cannot! I need you, Lizzie.'

'Of course you don't,' spluttered Lizzie. 'I think you're doing OK, don't you?'

She looked meaningfully at his expensive watch.

Georges blinked rapidly.

'But . . . you know, I say already, I can help find you somewhere to live and . . . '

'Georges, I'm not an abandoned dog. I can look after myself.'

'I know that, Lizzie, but . . . '

His face was stricken. 'But . . . ' He seemed to be searching for the words.

Penny had been listening to a monopolies manager trying to explain to her what his job entailed. He'd lost her about ten minutes ago, but she was nodding politely and trying to look alert and interested. She glanced sideways; Lizzie and Georges seemed deep in conversation.

'Excuse me,' she said with her most professional smile. 'I have to go and look after all my clients.'

'Of course,' said the man charmingly. 'I'm sorry to have monopolised you. Ha, ha, get it?'

Penny composed her features into a look of surprise. 'Oh! Aha! You're so funny! Now, excuse me.'

And she sidled up to Maria-Elena to size her up.

'Hello,' she said coolly. 'Having a good time?'

'What do you expect?' said Maria-Elena. 'This town is no good for Georges. Is full of whores who want his money.'

'You think?' said Penny.

'The women here . . . they are tarts, they drink, they cannot dress. I heard Chelsea was a smart part of town. Hah! It is disgusting. How anyone could live here I cannot imagine.'

Penny felt down into her handbag. Goddamn it, if all Tabitha's potion did was give someone a nasty stomach, this witch was getting it right now.

'Here, give me your glass. I'll refill it,' said Penny with her smoothest smile. 'Maybe you can forget for a few hours your life of terribly upsetting luxury.'

'No!' said Maria-Elena. 'What, you think I want to drink more of that gut rot and get staggering and vomit like the English girls?'

'Just a bit,' said Penny desperately, seizing the glass. 'Who knows, it might melt your iron knickers.'

She poured some wine from a nearby table then turned away slightly to get the herbs in.

'What are you doing?' screeched Maria-Elena, loud enough to be heard above the hubbub. 'What are you doing with my glass?'

'Nothing!' said Penny, jerking suddenly and spilling the contents all over the floor.

'What is this? Georges! Georges! She is trying to poison me!'

'I'm not trying to poison you,' said Penny, desperately trying to force the herbs back into her bag. OK, as whims went this one was really dumb. 'Stop being stupid.'

Georges came over. 'What is it?'

'Nothing,' said Penny, putting her hands behind her back.

'Show me that glass!' ordered Maria-Elena. 'Georges, she is trying to poison me. Phone the police immediately.'

'Of course she is not trying to poison you,' said Georges, adding something sharp in Portuguese. In response, Maria-Elena merely pointed at Penny, who still had her hands defiantly behind her back.

Georges looked apologetic. 'Penny, please, can you show us the glass? So we can sort this out.'

'No,' said Penny. 'Uh, I mean, what glass?'

'Don't be silly, please,' said Georges. His face was imploring. 'You know Maria-Elena is a little . . . how should I say, highly strung.'

The entire room now (except for Sloan, who had vanished) was watching the scene in silence. Penny looked around feeling cornered, and slowly brought the glass round. Sure enough, traces of the herbs were very clear on the rim.

'See!' shouted Maria-Elena. 'See!'

Penny rolled her eyes. 'I'm not trying to poison her.'

'But what is this, Penny?' asked Georges, looking grave.

Tabitha swooped in on them like a vast purple eagle.

'Ah, my dears. You tinker in the dark arts at your peril.'

'What?' said Georges.

'This is a little potion I made up for Penny . . . you are very naughty, by the way.'

'It was only a joke,' said Penny sulkily.

'What kind of a potion?' demanded Maria-Elena.

'I am gifted by the spirits in many ways,' said Tabitha, 'and Penny asked me to do a love potion. It is to see off a rival.'

'Yes. *Poison!*' screamed Maria-Elena.

'It's not poison,' said Penny. 'Plus it could hardly make you any uglier,' she added, not quite quietly enough.

'I *knew* you are after him!' Maria-Elena's face had gone completely puce. Georges just looked bamboozled. Penny looked embarrassedly at Lizzie, who was also looking completely disbelieving.

'So did I,' said Lizzie. 'For Christ's sake.' And she turned away.

'But I did it for you, Lizzie,' shouted Penny. 'You know I did. I mean, if it really worked. Plus it would only have been a few boils or something. Enough to postpone a wedding, anyway.'

'You don't do anything for anyone else,' said Lizzie. 'Just yourself.'

'You've got to believe me,' said Penny.

'You've got to get over here while Georges calls the police,' said Maria-Elena. 'Call the police, Georges. Now. *Now!*'

'Do not speak like that, please,' said Georges. 'I will not call the police. This is all very silly.'

'Call the police, you *grande cabrao!*'

Georges looked shocked, and Penny bounded for the door. Bugger them, she thought. Bugger Lizzie, bugger Georges, bugger Chelsea, bugger London, bugger the world. She was getting out.

She reached the door and pulled it open, not noticing the trembling figure on the other side of the glass.

Standing there panting, damp, agitated, filthy and emaciated, with a desperate look in his eye, stood Will.

# Chapter Sixteen

'Penny!' shouted Will. 'You have to come with me.'

He stepped up into the doorway of the gallery.

'To live with a gold-digger under a bridge?' said Penny. 'No I fucking don't.'

She tried to push past him, conscious that it absolutely was not beyond Maria-Elena to follow her and grab her by the hair, in preparation for a good slapping.

'You do. You have to come. It's your house.'

'What do you mean, my house?'

'Your house. In Chelsea.'

'That's not my house,' said Penny. 'Oh, you haven't been keeping up, have you?'

'Shut up!' said Will. 'There's no time for that. It's on fire!'

For a second nobody spoke. Then there was a yelp from the back, as Brooke realised that if the twins' place was going up in smoke, theirs would be too.

'My Birkin bag!' she yelped. And immediately everyone started to move.

Lizzie and Penny tore down the streets with Will, who was exhausted, falling behind them. The rest of the gallery stood watching, Maria-Elena spitting blood oaths as Georges immediately shouted that he was phoning for a fire engine.

'I can explain,' puffed Penny as they rounded Redmond Street.

'Don't,' said Lizzie, her face clouded in pain.

Sure enough, smoke was billowing from the second-floor windows. They halted, inhaling the unfamiliar burning smell.

'Oh God,' said Penny. 'It must have been Stephen.'

'Those bloody cigarettes,' said Lizzie. 'You don't think . . . '

They turned to each other, the same thought in their minds. Was he still in there?

Just as they thought this, Lizzie caught sight of it. At the kitchen window. A white smudge, banging hard. Their father's hand.

'Look!' she screamed. 'Look! He's up there!'

They looked around. The fire engine hadn't arrived yet. There was nothing else for it.

'Have you still got the keys?' yelled Lizzie, rushing to the door.

'Oh God,' said Penny again. 'Well, yes. I like to look at them sometimes. Not for sentimental reasons or anything.'

'Quick, then,' said Lizzie. Penny would rather have waited for the fire engines, but couldn't help being impressed by Lizzie's all-action stance.

Even from outside the front door they could feel the oppressive heat; cautiously they went in.

'We've got to put something over our mouths,' said Lizzie

as they inched upwards holding the banister, which felt warm to the touch.

'Why?' said Penny, who was trembling with adrenalin.

'I don't know, do I? Saw it in a bloody film.'

With no small heartbreak, knowing this was likely to be the last of her nice dresses for quite some time, Penny pulled at the neckline of the antique frock until most of the top came away, and tore the paper-thin material in two.

'Here you go.'

'Thanks. We're meant to wet it or something.'

They were outside the door to their flat now. Although the big thick door was holding the flames back, they immediately had a sense of the terrifying force of the heat that was behind it.

'Oh God,' said Lizzie. 'Oh God, Oh God.'

'Are you sure you saw him?' said Penny. 'Why hasn't he broken the window?'

'I don't know, do I? OK. We should probably push open the door, then run backwards.'

'I like the running backwards.'

'In case the flames jump out or something. Why did I spend the whole of *Backdraft* thinking about William Baldwin naked?'

Penny shrugged. 'I dunno, I spent it snogging Fingall McStankie because he had a motorbike.'

'OK,' said Lizzie, fitting the key in the lock. 'One, two, three . . . ' She turned the lock and they both pushed the door then jumped back into the stairwell. Immediately the flames burst out with a roar.

'Shit,' said Penny. There was a sound of sirens, but it was very far away in the distance. Now they could hear, 'Help! Help!' very faintly from inside.

'Bollocks,' said Lizzie. She peered in. Everywhere in the

huge apartment, crap was burning: timetables, newspapers and macramé. The entire place had always been a fire hazard waiting to happen.

'OK,' she said to Penny.

Penny looked at her. 'We're going in, aren't we?' she said, her teeth chattering.

'We have to,' said Lizzie. 'Unless, you know, you still want to kill him and everything?'

Penny, the choking smoke already getting to her eyes, shook her head.

'OK,' said Lizzie. 'Down low. He's by the kitchen window. We'll take an arm each.'

Penny nodded.

'Shall we do it on three again?'

'Yup.'

They looked into the burning apartment.

'OK,' said Lizzie.

'I just want to say . . . ' Penny started.

Lizzie looked at her. 'Don't be stupid. One . . . ' said Lizzie.

'I know,' said Penny. 'But I love you.'

'I love you, too, you idiot. OK. Two . . . THREE.'

They burst into the flat on all fours. Lizzie half shut her eyes and relied on her memory to locate the sink, Penny followed on her heels.

'*Dad!*' shouted Lizzie. '*Dad!*'

'I'm over here,' came the voice, followed by a lot of coughing and choking. Peering upwards Lizzie saw him. The kitchen cabinets had caught now, and he was crouching down, underneath the sink. The tap was running, and he'd drenched himself and the ground around him.

'I'm burned!' he shouted.

'Follow us!' said Lizzie.

'I can't move,' he said. 'I can't. I just can't.'

'Of course you can,' said Lizzie, looking around worriedly. There came a roar from the far side of the room as the old dusty curtains went up.

'I can't,' said Stephen. 'I'm not brave like you two.'

'Yes, you are,' said Lizzie, starting to panic. If he didn't move, they'd all get stuck here and they'd all die.

'I can't!'

'*Please!*'

As Lizzie shouted, choking on the smoke, she realised that this was something she'd been screaming to her dad since the day he left, and great heaving sobs threatened to overtake her in the burning room.

'I can't,' Stephen repeated.

Penny scrabbled up next to Lizzie, giving her a push on the knee.

'Of course you can,' said Penny. 'You're just a complete old prick. Come on. We have to go. We *really* have to go,' she said, as the smaller panes of glass on the windows started to shatter. She linked her arm under his and Lizzie grabbed the other one, and in a strange, crab-like manoeuvre, they scrabbled their way out to the door, chests heaving with the effort.

They cascaded directly into Georges and Will, who'd just reached the top of the stairs.

'Lizzie!' screeched Georges.

'Penny!' yelled Will, as Penny went crashing straight into him. Unbalanced, all five of them collapsed down the stairwell. They rolled over, cushioning each other, until they landed with a bump outside Brooke and Minty's door, where Brooke and Minty had formed a human chain with willing bankers from the gallery and were passing out a line of expensive shoeboxes.

Penny disentangled herself and leapt to her feet, the

adrenalin causing her to ignore the bumps and bruises all over her body, and screamed to be heard over the deafening sirens.

'Is it just me, or is this building on fire!' she hollered. 'Get out of here.'

Minty looked at her. 'You know water damage is the worst, don't you?'

As if on cue, the sirens ceased, and the first, huge, tumbling deluge of water came piling through the windows, dripping down on top of their heads.

'Out! Everyone out!' bellowed Georges, and those who could, ran, and those who couldn't were helped out of the building and onto the street below, which was now filled with rubberneckers and hundreds of hunky-looking firemen. Minty's face brightened immediately.

Lizzie couldn't quite piece together what happened next. She had a vague impression of her dad being whisked to hospital, of lots of people talking to her – but she couldn't hear what they were saying. Or, they were saying something, but she didn't understand what they were talking about, or what language it was in. She had no idea how much time had passed, as the water was trained on the building, which took on the appearance of a bedraggled and ruined wedding cake left out in the rain. It wasn't falling down, though. The firemen were smiling, and kept giving her thumbs up, so she guessed that maybe it wasn't going to burn down to the ground. In fact, there weren't even any flames any more. A friendly policeman gave her a cup of tea, and a neighbour came up with a small tot of brandy and a foil blanket to go round her shoulders.

'There, there,' they seemed to be saying, but their voices didn't quite match their words. Suddenly she noticed

Georges was kneeling beside her, holding her hand, which seemed nice enough, so she didn't move a muscle, just watched Penny and Will, who seemed to be silently yelling at one another.

'I'm not yelling,' said Penny, who was still coasting on adrenalin and felt massively, hugely invigorated by what had just happened.

'That's good,' said Will. 'Could you whisper with a little less volume, then? And really, please, will you sit down, have a drink of something.'

'No,' said Penny. 'And I don't want a silver blanket either, thank you.'

'It's very you,' opined someone from the crowd.

'And your bra is showing,' said Will. Penny remembered she'd had to rip up her dress, and accepted the blanket – and, while she was at it, the brandy.

'I just want to know . . . what were you doing lurking outside my house?'

'I wasn't lurking,' said Will. 'I didn't know you'd moved.'

'So what were you doing? Stalking?'

'No,' said Will. He looked around, then, from behind one of the trees, picked up his art materials.

'Actually,' he said, 'I was doing this. It was for you. To say sorry.'

He pulled out the canvas. It showed a beautiful, exquisite watercolour of their building. Every elegant window, every curlicue of the builder's art was there, every shade of the trees on the road. At the front door was a figure, small, but recognisable. With the blonde hair and the combative stance, it was Penny, clearly, slipping out of the building and into the autumn light, a huge bunch of cornflowers in her arms. She wasn't naked, or on a sinking ship. But it was beautiful.

'I was going to give it to you. But not in a stalking kind of way. Just to say I was sorry. I knew you wanted to pose for me. Then I was going to be a very good, tortured-artist type and disappear for ever, I promise.'

'But, instead, you set my house on fire.'

'No!' said Will, looking shocked. 'That wasn't me.'

'Looks like a cigarette, love,' said a passing policeman. 'Usually is. Did anyone in the house smoke?'

'Uh, just a bit,' said Penny.

'Just as well you two were here, eh?'

'Do you know,' said Penny, 'I think that's the first time that would ever have occurred to him. Is he going to be OK?'

'Should be,' said the ambulance man. 'Bit of smoke inhalation, third-degree burn to the leg. Made a hell of a fuss. I'm a bit worried about your sister, though. I think she might be in shock.'

Penny looked over to where Georges was kneeling on the ground, oblivious of the water cascading over his expensive trousers and shoes.

'She's in good hands,' she said.

'Oh, my *gawd*,' Minty was saying. 'Look at this painting! It's our house! It's fab. I want one! I'll buy it with the insurance money! Quick, Brooke, hide those shoes! Insurance! Is that me, Will?'

'No,' said Will.

'Are you sure?' Minty's bottom lip was pushed out in time-honoured fashion.

'I can do you one, if you like,' said Will. 'With you in it.'

'It'll be very, *very* expensive, though,' said Penny.

Will looked at her. 'What are you talking about?'

'You know. When I become your business manager.'

'What do you mean?'

Penny rolled her eyes. 'Well, you may want to live in that garret for ever, but I certainly don't.'

She watched him carefully, gauging his reaction.

'Do you . . . uh, what do you mean?' said Will, trying to disguise the wobble in his voice.

'Look,' said Penny. 'There wasn't any baby. It was a mistake. Not a trick, or blackmail, or a test. Just a mistake.'

'I know,' said Will. 'Lizzie told me.'

Penny's eyes went wide. 'You *knew*? And you still didn't bother coming to see me or anything?'

'I thought it was too late,' said Will. 'Even though there wasn't a baby, I'd still behaved so badly . . . You looked so angry at me at the damn restaurant.'

'I was . . . I was confused,' said Penny. 'Then you started yelling and . . .'

Will was gazing at her. 'Could you bear it?' he said. 'Never being rich, I mean?'

Penny stared at him, her heart in her throat.

'You know, about twenty minutes ago,' she said, 'I wasn't entirely sure I was even going to be alive. So I don't know how bothered I am really. As long as I'm with you, I mean.'

'Are you sure, Penny? Are you sure?'

Penny looked at Will's gorgeous open, honest face and thought of the stupid ideas she was leaving behind; the scheming, and the jostling and manoeuvring into position. Life could go up in a puff of smoke.

'God, yes,' she said, and rushed into his arms, kissing him passionately, even though they both tasted of charcoal.

Lizzie stirred. Someone was speaking to her, she could hear it now. It was a lovely voice, a kind, sweet, gentle voice, one she loved very much. Was it her mother? No, it was a man, definitely. She let it tinkle on, like a wandering stream, and felt herself come back into herself, back together. She remembered why she was here, and what had happened, and that everyone was all right, and that the person talking to her was – Georges.

'. . . and so,' finished Georges, an intense look on his face. 'After all that, that is why I am asking you, will you marry me?'

Lizzie shook her head and blinked hard. 'Sorry?' she said. Georges was kneeling on the wet road in front of her. '*What* did you just say?'

'Ah, well, it was a long speech, you know, Lizzie. I do not think I can repeat it again. Especially, you know, now, with all this weight on my knees.'

He looked at her face. 'But for you, of course, I will repeat. To say, this: I do not love Maria-Elena. That was a mistake to please my family. Sometimes you cannot always please your parents, huh, Lizzie? Well, what would you know about this?'

'Uh-huh,' said Lizzie. Her heart was going pitter-patter. Fortunately she could not see the dirt and soot covering her face. Even though he was facing her, and gazing deeply into her eyes, Georges couldn't see it either.

'It was a mistake. She told me so, too. She will go. She thinks we are all disgraceful.'

Lizzie nodded.

'And, you know, when you said you would not move into one of my houses, my heart was broken. And when you said you were leaving, I thought, this cannot be. I spoke to your sister, OK, I think maybe she is crazy.'

'She is crazy.'

'But she says that you maybe have feelings for me too and she was pretending to like me to get rid of Maria-Elena. Although this I do not believe. Who could not like me? And also that I am a big idiot elephant.'

298

Penny and Will had come dashing over, hand in hand, full of the joys. Eyes sparkling, Penny came up behind him.

'You are,' she said. 'You're a big idiot elephant.'

'Lizzie,' said Georges. 'You know me. I am not a man of half measures. I am not a man who says what he does not mean, or wastes time. All I have, is yours. My heart, my soul.'

'His car service,' muttered Penny, as Will took the executive decision to take her away to the side of the road and quietly snog her up a bit.

'So, Lizzie, I ask. Would you like to be my wife?'

Lizzie squinted at him. 'I think I must be concussed.'

'That is why I choose my moment now. You know. Take advantage of you while you are in a weak state.'

Lizzie looked at him. 'Oh, Georges. Oh, yes. Oh, yes, please.'

And she jumped up, shrugged off the silver blanket and threw her arms around his big strong shoulders.

## Chapter Seventeen

They moved slowly and carefully, one twin either side as their gran was taken out of Georges's car and into the waiting wheelchair. Only two people per bed were allowed at visiting time, but the hospital was making an exception for the twins and their gran. It had been a long process picking her up from the old people's home. Lizzie had managed with ease to persuade Georges to give her the day off – in fact, they were both taking far too much time off, seeing as they had spent most of the last two weeks staring at each other – and Penny had left Sloan hanging Will's new exhibition – a collection of Chelsea town house paintings, which seemed likely to sell out as fast as he could finish them, both to the residents and the aspirationals.

The hospital smelled just like Gran's room. 'Ah, home,' she said, as the double doors opened automatically.

'Which ward?' said Penny.

'Honeysuckle,' said Lizzie. 'Down here.'

Lizzie had expected to feel more nervous about going to visit her dad, but she wasn't. Partly because he didn't scare her any more – he was just a man, a weak man – and partly because she was wrapped in such a cloak of happiness, very little could penetrate it. She had moved into Georges's flat right away – it was very tidy and practical, and she had set about trying to make it a little more homely and comfortable. Maria-Elena had left no traces at all, except an invoice which had arrived for her first-class flight home and other expenses. Georges had laughed, and paid it straightaway, apologising fulsomely to Maria-Elena for wasting her time.

Since then it had been a blur of food and sex so unlike anything Lizzie had associated with the words before it made her go pink even thinking about it.

Only once had she asked timidly, in bed one morning, 'Georges . . . when I started working with you and I was, you know, fat and a bit spotty and stuff . . . did you like me then?'

'Ah, *cara*. Of course I like you. I think you are very nice girl. But when you become beautiful, when I come back from Portoogal. That is when I fall in love with you. I cannot help myself, I am a man, and I love beautiful things. You want an Englishman, huh, who does not care and wears sports pants with lager on them and goes on television on *Trisha* to shout in the mornings?'

'No,' said Lizzie, but still felt oddly insecure all of a sudden.

'Of course, now I love you for ever,' said Georges, turning over to face her. 'So you can grow fat, grow moustache, I don't care.'

'I don't want to grow a moustache!'

'Fine, grow goatee. Maybe some sideburns, huh? And an ear, here, on top your head. And a tail.'

'Georges!'

'A tail, very useful for many things. You can pick fruit, peel bananas.'

'Come here.'

Penny had almost the opposite conversation, lying naked on the ancient couch she'd covered with a new throw, watery sun coming through the windows, showing up the motes of dust in the room as Will sketched.

'Of course I fell in love with you when I saw you,' said Will. 'Well, I thought you were a fox. Then I filled the rest in about six hours later.'

Penny grinned ruefully. 'And my postcode. You loved my postcode.'

'Oh, shush. You were at it, too.'

She smiled at him. 'I don't think I even knew what love was. Till you went away.'

Will, very carefully, put the paintbrush down.

Penny couldn't care less about visiting the hospital. But that was good. It meant she didn't hate him any more. She didn't hate anyone. It was done, and she was through with it.

In fact, Penny was privately full of the not unpleasant – but unfamiliar – sense of self-sacrifice that came with pretending not to mind that Lizzie was living in a duplex in Eaton Square while she was commuting back to a bin liner in Clapton every night. But every time she got on that daft old bus, her heart leapt with joy. She couldn't help it. Knowing Will would be waiting at home with a dirty brush stuck behind his ear, ready to tease her and make her laugh – and, if they didn't learn to be a little bit more careful, probably make a real baby one of these days, and then what kind of a pickle would they be in?

They turned into the ward and asked the Sister which bed he was in. She indicated the fourth one down, which had the curtains drawn around it.

'OK,' said Lizzie. 'Deep breath.'

Penny pulled back the curtain, patting her grandmother on the shoulder at the same time.

'Hello,' she said. But the bed was empty.

'Well, the doctors didn't sign him out,' said the Sister, after the ward staff and security had been alerted. 'But you know, we're not a prison. We can't keep anyone here who doesn't want to be here.'

'I know that,' said Penny. 'Was he OK?'

'Perfectly recovered, yes.'

'And he didn't leave a forwarding address?'

The ward clerk shook his head. 'Sorry, miss. I think he's just gone.'

'Oh, Gran,' said Lizzie, reaching down to give her a hug. 'I'm so sorry.'

'That's all right,' said their gran. 'I'm . . . I'm used to it.'

She looked up at the two girls.

'I backed the wrong horse, didn't I, my dears? With you two lovely girls. But families . . . you know how it is. You love them and hate them all at once.'

Lizzie and Penny traded a glance. Yes, they knew how it was.

'Take me back to the Larches,' said their gran. 'I'm so tired. Everything tires me so.'

'I know,' said Lizzie, 'shall we stop for tea first?'

Their gran put up her hand to touch Lizzie's face. 'You saved his life,' she said.

'I helped!' yelped Penny.

'You're such good girls, little twins,' said their gran. 'Even you, the slutty one. I want . . . I've made up my mind. I want to turn the flat over to you two. It's for you. I hope you have more luck there than I did. Or Stephen, for that matter. I'm giving it to you. I've got my solicitor's number back at the Larches.'

She looked wistful for a moment, then snapped out of it.

'That's my home now. And do you know why I like it? Because it's so *tidy*.'

And she let out an old-lady cackle as they wheeled her back towards the automatic doors.

They walked with trepidation towards the front door. What if Stephen was back? What would it look like inside? The insurance money would turn up, but most of that would go on restoring the plasterwork and exterior of the building, there was so much to do.

The hallways had just about dried out, but there were big patches of damp here and there, with strips hanging off the wall. They mounted the stairs carefully.

On the landing, the door opened. It was Brooke.

'Thank *God*,' she said. 'You're coming back, aren't you?'

The twins shrugged.

'It's boring as *anything* without you. Same old, same old premieres, yah? Bloody red carpet, I am just so *fed up* with it. Plus Minty's in love with a fireman and driving him absolutely bloody crackers as usual.'

'I'm glad to hear it,' said Penny.

Brooke eyed her. 'There's something different about you,' she said.

'Just being myself,' Penny smiled, as they continued up the once-beautiful stairwell to the front door. Now it was blackened, peeling.

'Here goes,' said Lizzie. They pushed open the door together and stared into the room.

The entire floor was knee-deep in ash, rubble and water-stained debris. Everything small and flammable – all the papers, all the pictures, all the collections, all the bric-a-brac, all the baskets, all the macramé. It was all gone. There was none of it left, just ash upon the floor.

The table was still there, but the nasty mismatched chairs were a pile of charred sticks on the floor; the horrid filthy curtains mere scraps of material at the top of the windows. Apart from the smaller kitchen panes, which had been blown out, the huge sitting-room window was intact, and, thanks to several thousand litres of water, blasted clean. It let huge swathes of light into the room, now huge, open, and practically empty. The girls stood and stared.

'It's . . . it's beautiful,' said Lizzie. Penny just nodded, overcome by emotion. Will could have a studio here . . . it would be so perfect for him. And her. They would be back. And everything would work . . . if Lizzie still wanted to live with Georges, of course. They were planning a wedding already. Penny couldn't have imagined her safe, dull, quiet sister doing anything quite so crazy as agreeing to marry a man she'd never even kissed. But somehow, two weeks later, she couldn't have imagined her *not* doing it.

'So . . .' said Lizzie.

'So,' said Penny. 'Once this place is done up it's going to be . . .'

'Yeah,' said Lizzie.

'So, do you . . .'

They were both being incredibly polite to one another.

'Penny,' said Lizzie. 'I . . . I'm going to live with Georges. I love this place, but I think you should live here. If you want. You know, it's yours.'

Penny nodded, her brow furrowing. It definitely sounded like there was a 'but' on the end of that sentence. And, looking around she realised what it was. Of course. The person who'd done everything for them. Who'd never complained. Who'd always looked out for them.

'Yeah, yeah,' she said. 'It's not all that. You know, Clapton's a really up-and-coming place. I wouldn't move from there for anything, really. I think Will and I are making it fashionable all on our own.'

'Really?' said Lizzie. 'I mean, it's OK for me, I'm sorted, but . . .'

'No, don't be an idiot,' said Penny. 'What do you take me for, some kind of spoiled, shallow princess?'

'Never,' said Lizzie. 'Never in a million years.'

Penny picked up her phone. 'Mum? We've got a surprise for you. How do you feel about launching your West End career from . . . well, the West End?'

# OPERATION
# SUNSHINE

*For someone due out the same week as this book –*
*we cannot wait to meet you.*
*Well, two of us can't wait to meet you. The other one would*
*probably prefer a new bicycle and some apple juice.*

# Acknowledgements

Huge thanks and respect to Ali Gunn, my sensational agent, of Gunn Media, and Jo Dickinson, my brilliant editor. Both of you were right about everything, as ever!

And thanks to everyone at Little, Brown, especially Tamsin Kitson, Antonia Hodgson, Helen Gibbs, Alison Lindsay, Louise Davies, Peter Cotton, Hannah Venn, Ursula Mackenzie, and all the sales team who've done so much and worked so hard – thank you.

To all the yachties who have been so friendly and kind to me over my years of hanging about and getting in the way, particularly the crews of *M/Y Golden Cell*, *M/Y Leander*, *M/Y Jo* and *M/Y Deniki*.

Jonny Popper, whose excellent and lucid poker game was too long to make it in here, but will somewhere else; AMELISA and Roni for being such great friends during our year abroad, and Jojo Moyes for chocolate and sanctuary on so many occasions; Mrs Doctor Karen, Katrina, Wesley, Dan and, of course, everyone on the board, as well as a big shout out to Feb Mums.

Huge thanks to Marina, and the staff of Kozie, de Drukkery and Zeeuwse Bibliotheek.

Thanks to my wonderful family for everything, and special thanks to Mr B & wee B, my two favourite people in the whole wide world.

# Chapter One

'Holidays suck,' Lydia was proclaiming loudly, stabbing her straw into her drink to make her point. We were in a new West End bar which had been recommended in *Time Out*. Places like this normally intimidated me, but Lydia loved them; her dark eyes flashed at the cheesily good-looking barman, and her movements got more emphatic. You'd notice her.

'They SUCK!'

'Well, that's your opinion,' I said, a little stiffly under the circumstances. But I was the one who had brought up the subject of holidays, and now I was being told that, therefore, my dreams and desires were effectively a big pile of steaming dog turds that I'd just deposited between us on the bar.

'It's not an opinion,' she said. 'It's a fact. Everybody

1

knows. You've got to fly in a shitty plane, which is always shit, sit on some stupid bus for nine hours, sleep in some stupid room that's nothing like as nice as your own, listen to other people shouting all night, get sunburnt, get hungover, spend all your money, have a shit time, get knocked over by a car, remember you forgot to buy travel insurance, get your leg amputated and get flown home on a cargo plane to face three years in debtors' prison.'

'And that's what always happens, is it?' I said.

'Pretty much.'

I sighed. This wasn't going exactly as planned.

You always see, don't you, other people's holiday snaps, where they're patently having the most fabulous time somewhere incredibly exotic, and you ask them about their holiday (if you have a lot of time on your hands at work, which I do) and their faces go all slack and dreamy and they get a faraway look in their eyes and say something stupid like, 'Well, we'd get up early in the morning and go running along the surf on the empty pink sand, then pick coconuts and fruit for our breakfast in the hammock.' And you think, Eh? How come I got vomited on by a child all the way from Gatwick to Fuerteventura and ate chips every night for a week?

Or they organise massive gangs of chums.

'Oh, yes, thirty of us are going sky hiking in the Peruvian Andes, then we've taken a luxury villa for a month in a cloud forest.'

How do people do that? Do I have the wrong friends? I

can't get any three of mine to commit to going to the cinema on the same day without two cancellations, one cancellation retraction, one falling out between two people who then refuse to sit together, a skirmish over the M&Ms and nobody paying me for the booking fee.

'My last holiday,' said Lydia, tossing back her long black hair, 'I copped off with a bloke who lives two doors down from my mum. Ten years of my life getting away from that place, and then what happens?'

'Well, if you knew that, why'd you cop off with him?'

'Durr! Because ON HOLIDAY they make you drink big goldfish bowls full of spirits until you're nearly unconscious, that's why. Chalk another one up to "why holidays are shit" by Lydia Li.'

'Well, THAT is why you have to listen to me,' I said.

I was doing my best to be assertive, whilst not being blinded by the retro disco lighting. It's important to be assertive with Lydia. Not that she's the most insanely competitive woman that ever lived. OK. She's the most insanely competitive woman that ever lived. If *you've* broken your leg, *she* was once skiing in St Moritz with Prince William and she did the world's highest ski jump and broke her neck and the doctors said it was a miracle and they gave her the Nobel Prize for prettiness.

You never ever wear new clothes if you're going to see Lydia. If she likes them she'll say, 'Oh, I like your outfit – very WAG.' (Even if it's, like, a grey sack made out of plasticine.)

3

And if she doesn't, she'll say, 'Oh, that was seventy per cent off down the King's Road – is that where you got it?'

We work next door to one another. We're receptionists on Harley Street in London, where all the plastic surgeons reside.

Lydia is 50 per cent convinced that one day a rich man is going to come and pick his wife up from surgery but instead get blasted by a lightning bolt and fall in love with her instead. I've told her this is both unlikely – rich men NEVER bother to pick up their wives, and their wives wouldn't want them to – and immoral, but she won't be moved. Her other 50 per cent is convinced that she's going to pull a young doctor. She doesn't date very much. No wonder she went mad on holiday.

So being assertive, my friend Bailey says, would help me no end. Growing up with three evil brothers in a very small house meant I had to develop a very loud mouth to even get fed, or rescued when the horrid beasts I had to share a home with, also known as John Jr, Patrick and Cassandro (Mum went a bit mental at the end), had alighted on some new form of torture involving holding me down whilst they shut the automatic door of the garage on my head, or setting fire to one of my pigtails, or threatening my pet rabbit with dire dismemberment whilst tying me to a tree. It wasn't what you'd call idyllic. I'm only stunned (and occasionally disappointed) that they're all now rational adults roaming free and not in some prison somewhere.

We didn't go on foreign holidays when I was young, partly because we didn't have much money for all six of us, but mostly because Mum and Dad knew the boys would behave so unbelievably badly that we'd all end up getting deported.

So we always ended up in a caravan park in Wales, where the boys would instantly turn feral and run free, returning only for frequent top-ups of sausages and ice cream. We always stayed one week in one place and one week in another so that the boys didn't get enough time to form an international criminal conglomerate with all the other children on the site.

I'd sit inside with my parents and we'd eat crisps and play card games as the rain beat against the window whilst I indulged my fantasies of being a cosseted only child. It wasn't bad, but it wasn't the same as returning to school sporting a suntan and ankle bracelet with ribbon braids in my hair, and talking about mysterious dark waiters and romantic young men on motorbikes and staying out all night, like the other girls in my class.

When I was seventeen and just about to start college, I had my first all-girls' holiday, to Malaga. I looked forward to it for months. I stuck the tickets above my desk and fantasised solidly with my friends about the gorgeous boys who were going to fall madly in love with us, and spent every Saturday going in and out of Dolcis and Ravel choosing exactly the right pair of white stilettos. Tanya and Claire promised that we'd get free drinks everywhere and that it would be sun, sea and snogging all the way. I pored excitedly over letters in *Jackie* that said, 'I fell in love on holiday but now I don't know if I'll ever see him again,' and vowed to take the problem page's wise advice, and not put too much hope into a holiday romance when it probably wouldn't work in the rainy days back home (although I was sure mine would).

So it did come as something of a disappointment when it turned out that our one hundred and twenty-nine pound special was a room in a grubby white building next to a small pool filled with pissing children and surrounded by bull-necked families who'd brought their own packets of lard and deep-fat fryers.

This wouldn't have mattered if we weren't chased around by tragic-looking reps effectively begging for a huge share of our holiday money to take a 'party cruise', which we duly did. Tanya pulled one of the reps, who it then turned out Anne-Marie, another, slightly plumper girl, had a thing for, precipitating an enormous row which split the camp and lasted the whole of the rest of the holiday. Which hardly mattered to me, I was so shivery and shaky with sunburn (I had covered my mousy locks in Sun In and sat out through the heat of the first two days) I couldn't think straight, and Los Animalo's only disco, the Slutty Slug, gave me a pounding headache the first five thousand times they played the 'Macarena'.

Between hugely intense levels of secretive bitching, dirty

looks, Anne-Marie showing how over the club rep she was by snogging a different bloke every night, until they started hanging around outside our apartment like stray dogs, it was not what you might call the holiday of a lifetime, particularly after I got home and my finkish brothers developed a new game called 'Peel the Skin Off Evie'.

Since then I'd kind of sworn off holidays. At college, whilst other people went off Interrailing and trying to make it through Italy on five quid a day, I worked in the local pub and tried to look interested when people showed me pictures of the lions they'd seen on safari in Namibia, or of the Tuscan villa they'd hired, or of them falling hilariously off a big yellow banana and I'd think glumly about the night Anne-Marie got sangria sick on Tanya's new coat and they went for each other's hair.

And now, well, I was older, Bailey had got me a job in London working for some very grumpy doctors on Harley Street, which sounds a lot more important than it actually is, and I have some new friends, which, post-holiday, seemed the best thing to do under the circumstances.

And I wanted a holiday. I hadn't been away for two years, apart from to visit friends who were working overseas which was less of a holiday (they never wanted to take you to the tourist attractions) and more of an extended piss-up. I'd been single for eighteen months. Eighteen months. I felt like a born-again virgin. It was a desert out there. Or at least it was if you didn't have tiny thighs and a modified nose, like the clients I saw every day. They seemed to do all right.

And it hadn't exactly been wine and roses before then. My last boyfriend, Bill, had . . . well, it had never really progressed to the right moment to go on holiday. There isn't really a right moment, sometimes. With Bill I always felt like I was saying, 'Fancy going on holiday?' and he'd hear, 'Fancy getting a mortgage and getting married tomorrow and having nine children and you're never allowed to go out ever again and I'm about to put on four stone?'

He once condescended to take me on a long weekend barge trip with his unpleasantly sporty friends. It was the most boring thing I've ever done in my life. Travelling at two miles an hour whilst getting up and down to open locks isn't a holiday, it's exercise for a sixty-year-old recovering from a heart attack.

Maybe it's me. Maybe holidays and me are just not destined to go together. Maybe I'm designed to spend the rest of my life waking up at 7.40 a.m. and eating Weetabix for breakfast, even though I hate it, because apparently it means I won't feel hungry again until lunch, even though I always do and have a KitKat at eleven. With four fingers if it's raining. I'm not allowed to eat them in front of the clients though, we do a lot of liposuction, and they might turn wild and tear the wrapper out of my hands.

Back in the bar I toyed with my white wine. The rain was lashing down outside. I wasn't sure it was just about a holiday. I think I need more excitement in my life. I shouldn't get so excited, for example, when a new flavour of Pringles comes out. I'm twenty-seven. I feel I should be exploring the world; having mad passionate love affairs; dancing in the surf.

The city is fine, but it's hard to feel truly free with an Oyster Card. There must be more to life than magazine day (Tuesday – my favourite day. I especially like it when the stars tell you their diet and exercise secrets when we've had them in two weeks before).

'What if . . .' I said to Lydia. She really is intimidatingly beautiful, which makes the clients think they'll end up looking like her. I'm 'approachable-looking' according to Dr Bennet, which I think means they hired me so that even if an operation goes horribly wrong, the patient will still come out thinking, Well, at least I still look better than the receptionist. 'What if I organised a holiday so fantastic, you came back totally relaxed and had the best time you'd ever had and it was in paradise?'

Lydia looked at me sceptically. 'What, and it's free?' she said.

'No, of course it's not free. What are you talking about?'

'Oh. The way you're talking about it made it sound like it would be free.'

'No. But I'd organise it and do all the legwork.'

'Who's going? It'll have to be somewhere fancy.'

'Like all the really fashionable places,' I said casually, as if I was totally au fait with where those might be.

'They don't have to be fashionable.' She sniffed. 'They just need to have rich people in them.'

'Which makes them expensive,' I said.

'Well, duh.'

'OK, so do you have a secret trust fund I've never heard of? Are you not really a receptionist, but actually an heiress slumming it for a reality TV show?'

She shrugged. 'You asked what it would take to make me go on holiday with you, when it's a given that all holidays suck. And I'm telling you – somewhere posh and full of rich blokes but not too expensive for us.' She looked at me. 'Actually, I'm not sure we should go together after all.'

'What's wrong with me?'

Lydia didn't say anything, just played with her glass. 'Nothing. Oh, I don't know. Maybe I should take a busty blonde, you know? For contrast? Enhance my prospects?'

And she wasn't even joking. Proximity makes you some funny friends.


I wasn't downhearted. Yet. Next stop Bailey. I've known Bailey for ever. We grew up on the same street, and spent a lot of time hiding from my brothers.

His mother, in the manner of a zookeeper feeding fish to sharks, kept throwing him together with the beasts in the hope that they'd all become friends, rather than Bailey becoming Chump.

I think of Bailey as my backup. He's not gorgeous, but he

is funny, well off and really smart. Lydia keeps going on about wanting to meet him. I do my absolute best to keep them apart; I don't want her getting her talons into him.

It didn't help that he was very small and very clever and absolutely refused to know when he was beaten – even the time John Jr buried him headfirst in the sandpit he still came out spitting mud and threatening to curse them unto the third generation (he was going through a *Lord of the Rings* period at the time).

To escape the sheer brute force he took to hanging about with me, even when I made him spend an entire summer as a patient whilst my girlfriends and I played *Casualty*. I was always fascinated with medicine. It was one of the biggest disappointments of my life when I entered my third year of physics, chemistry and biology, hoping to romp into a fabulous career as an emergency doctor (this was pre-*ER*, but nonetheless I think I already had George Clooney in mind before he was even invented), only to discover to my shock and horror that I didn't understand a word of it. Not wave forms, not Boyle's law, not photosynthesis.

How I was ever going to perform emergency transplant surgery when I couldn't even remember the parts of the flower I did not know, so I switched to business administration instead. Mind you, there's not a lot I don't know about healing times for bhleroplasty (that's your upper eyelid). Sometimes I think if I work at the Saint Harley Clinic for long enough I'll become a plastic surgeon by osmosis, another scientific concept Mr Gahery failed to explain adequately to me in Year Nine.

Still, I do get to do quite a lot of interesting stuff at work – I've sat in on various ops, so I'm not the least bit squeamish, even for pus. And I run the back office too, all the paperwork. Well, most of it; Dr Bennet has a secretive streak. It's a more prestigious job than Lydia's, which drives her crazy.

Bailey came and found me a couple of years ago when I was drowning in a hospital basement on this ludicrous temp job I'd picked up, coding people's injuries in their medical files. So: hit on head, 310. Hit on head with brick, 310-12; hit on head with fish, 310-96; hit on head by flying saucer, 310-977, etc. It was doing my brain in.

'I've found a job for you,' he'd said, observing me over the top of his lunchtime hummus sandwich. 'It's got windows and daylight and everything.'

I liked it when Bailey did things like this for me. Made me think he cared.

'Oh, yeah?'

'Harley Street.'

'I don't believe in private medicine,' I'd said snootily.

'Do you believe in . . .' and then he'd mentioned a figure nearly twice what I'd been gritting my eyes up for.

'I also have very flexible moral standards,' I added (unnecessarily), thinking about Top Shop's new collection. Bailey briefed me for the interview too, to make me appear a bit classier than I actually am, and I was in.

Anyway. Bailey, being a mini-genius – he really plays up this angle, too much I think – wears shirts with buttons on the collar that he gets in America, and John Lennon glasses, like he's in the Geek of the Month club. Anyway, he took to the summer of *Casualty* too, and is now head of development for a cutting-edge hospital design company who build really big things, and he's always flying all over the world with a briefcase chained to his hand and being extremely important and constructing the world's largest MRI scanner or something. I always make sure I mention it to the beasts at Christmas time. Patrick says, 'Well, it's no wonder he's building big things, he's such a tiny fellow,' and John Jr pretends not to remember who he is, even though he hit him with a spade every day for nine years.

I met Bailey near his office in Fitzrovia two nights after I saw Lydia. There were lots of other zippy people in the pub looking clever and explaining things to each other using rulers. I know it's nerdy, but I secretly think it's also quite cool. Plus, lots of blokes work for Bailey's company. I think it's very rude of him not to devote more time to finding a man for me.

'Let's go on holiday,' I said, almost before we sat down. Bailey looked up at me, blinking in surprise behind his glasses. When we were sixteen we snogged in Clissold Park. For four hours, even though up until then I'd only ever thought of him as the brother I could push around. It was a really mild night in early spring. The next day neither of us said a word about it. But it's nice to think it's there. I often think we should have one of those Julia Roberts 'if we get to thirty without meeting anyone . . .' pacts. Just to formalise things.

'Why?' he said. 'I'm always on a bloody plane and you hate holidays.'

'Well,' I explained patiently, 'I hated asparagus too, until someone made me some in butter sauce and told me not to eat the bottom bits.'

'So you think you'll like holidays if you just avoid the bottom bits?'

'Exactly!'

'Well,' he said. 'What kind of holiday are you going to have?'

'A *good* one,' I said emphatically. 'With lots of nice people all having fun together.'

'Are your brothers coming?'

'Are you listening to me or what? I said nice people. People we like.'

'Is it going to be a sun, sea, sand, paperbacks kind of holiday? They're quite boring.'

'No, they're not! That's my dream!'

'Sounds boring.'

'OK, well, what if it were a sun, sea, sand and lots of interesting activities holiday?'

'Hmm. Cambodia's very interesting right now.'

'The place with all the skulls?'

'It's interesting. It's a country in transition.'

'I don't want a country in transition! I want a completely stable country with sun, sea, sand and cocktails.'

'Wouldn't you rather do something that helps indigenous peoples and increases your cultural understanding of our planet?'

'No, because that would be annoying and make me feel guilty and I spend my life being annoyed and feeling guilty. That's why I need a holiday.'

'So you're going to spend a lot of money on the holiday of a lifetime but endeavour to make it as banal as possible? Where are you going? Does it matter?'

'Not to you,' I said grumpily. 'You're not coming.'

'Oh, come on, Evie!' he said. 'I'm only teasing. Anyway, I know what this is about.'

'What do you mean?'

'This sudden push for a holiday.'

'What?'

'You're jealous.'

'Of what?'

Bailey just drummed his fingers on the table and waited for me to catch up. 'Well, all your brothers got married in the last two years . . . you're just feeling left out, in need of adventure.'

I stuck my lip out.

'Well, it's not fair, is it? John Jr is a big fat bastard, Patrick thinks he's God's gift . . .'

'Well, his marriage only lasted four months.'

'Yes, and that bronze bridesmaid's dress monstrosity will take twenty-four thousand years to decompose on a land-fill . . . I can't believe he chatted up the lady vicar.'

'Mmm.'

'And Cassandro . . . I mean, he's younger than me.'

He'd married a girl from my year at school. They'd dis-appeared to the Caribbean on holiday and called us when the deed was done.

But I'd seen the photos – the pink, clear sky, the soft yellow sand and Jilly and Cassandro looking so absolutely blissed out and beautiful and tanned. Jilly had a simple white cotton shift on and a huge flower tucked behind her sun-bleached hair, and she looked radiant. Cassandro had pale trousers rolled up over bare feet which made him look not quite as much a dick as it might have done. They looked like they were part of a perfect, romantic world, miles away from the grey streets and the everyday and the commute and the dirt I had to put up with. Why couldn't I get a bit of that?

I was jealous. I was jealous of their obvious, sun-kissed happiness. They looked part of a scene straight out of a movie, and I wanted a bit of it.

'Is that the rain again?' said Bailey, sighing heavily and staring out of the window.

'What happened to this drought we're supposed to be having?' I asked moodily.

'Well, no, it still rains, but it all runs off people's decking because nobody can be bothered to cut grass any more, so it doesn't soak into the soil and therefore people use more water to . . .'

'Yawn, yawn, yawn,' I said. 'Glad you're not coming on my luxury holiday. I'd say it was girls only, but that wouldn't necessarily rule you out.'

'Doesn't matter,' he said infuriatingly. 'I'm off on a big luxury secret junket anyway, and it's all paid for, and it's somewhere gorgeous. So there.'

I walked into work the next day downhearted but determined not to be put off by a few negative reactions and, well, the fact that my credit card statement had just arrived.

I'd left it on the mat, jumping over it quietly as if it were a poisonous snake I was praying hadn't noticed me. It's my fault, of course: in a moment of impassioned clarity I decided to transfer my balance onto one of those zero interest credit cards, the way you're meant to. Then, of course, I didn't either pay it back or transfer it onto *another* credit card, which meant 3000 per cent interest or something kicked in and I realised I'm the sucker who's funding everyone else's free credit cards. Which I wouldn't be, I suppose, if I didn't leap over my credit card statement as if it were a poisonous snake.

Anyway, I'm not exactly sure what's in there, but I know it's not pretty. So the absolute last thing I should be doing at the moment is planning luxury holidays. Or planning anything, in fact, apart from, obviously, getting a night job and moving into a shed until I've paid the damn credit card off, which I suspect, unless I win the lotto/marry a millionaire (not likely until I, at the very least, get my roots touched up) or invent something great (like, for example, the way to tell the difference between black and navy tights when it's dark and cold in your bedroom first thing in the morning and you've still got sleep in your eyes), is a very, very long way off.

So, I thought, heading into the office. Just to recap. I want to go on a fabulous holiday with my friends, except nobody wants to go with me and I don't have any money.

'Good morning,' said Dr Bennet. He's very handsome and smooth and he makes all the ladies fizzy. Doesn't do much for me; I've seen his toupee flap in a high wind and met his terrifying wife, but he smells nice.

'Dr Bennet, where would you go on holiday if you wanted to go somewhere nice?' I said.

He tried to wrinkle his brow thoughtfully, even though he can't: it's shot full of dead cow stuff and doesn't move.

'A nice holiday?'

'A fabulous holiday.'

'Aha. Well, you don't have a private jet, do you?'

'I do actually,' I said. 'I just park it in the mews.'

'Well, you should fly with British Airways first or Virgin upper class. Obviously you would think first would be better, but, you know, I don't always like the stewardesses, and the food is a little frilly for my taste. And, in fact, now you mention it, somewhere I visited for a wedding, Necker. You know, Richard Branson's island? He has a private island in the Caribbean; nobody there except people to look after you. Oh, it's beautiful. It's in the Balinese style, and it's so quiet, and the food, oh my God, I can't even begin to tell you about the food . . .'

His large brown eyes looked a bit melty as he stared out of the window into the grey and red-brick surroundings of Harley Street.

'Of course, it's expensive, you know? It's forty-five thousand dollars a day.'

'OK.' I said, sitting down at my desk. I did some quick addition in my head. 'Uhm. Can I have a raise of three hundred and fifteen dollars?'

Dr Bennet smiled. 'Well, OK. But you did ask me for fabulous. That is fabulous. Maybe I should be a plastic surgeon in America. It annoys me that I can't afford Necker myself.'

'I'm really, really sorry too,' I said as sincerely as I could manage. He can't be that far off, anyway, the amount of loaded old bruisers that march through the doors. And I'm not calling them that to be mean. Well, I am, but trust me, they are *really*, *really* mean to me first.

'Yes,' he said, picking up his case list for the day. 'Well, anyway, if you have not got much money, Venice is always nice.'

'Oh, yes?' I said, but without enthusiasm. I did want to go

to Venice, madly, but I had a secret life plan for Venice which involved, ideally, a flashing-eyed lover who would call me *cara* and we would run over picturesque bridges together and fall madly in love and feed each other spaghetti, like in *Lady and the Tramp*. So Venice was out. For now.

'Spain?' he said.

'Oh, no.' I shuddered, remembering my teenage Spanish experience.

His mouth twitched. 'Really? You have seen all of Spain? Much of it is very beautiful, don't you think? Have you been to Bilbao?'

'I don't like Spain,' I said firmly.

'Oh, well. There is only one place. The South of France, huh? Beautiful, warm sunshine, expensive Orangina . . . you would like it.'

The bell pinged, and one of our regulars, Zephyr, an ageing model (she calls herself a supermodel in the press, but I don't think there's anything terribly super about getting your tits out for *Nuts* magazine twice a week), came in for a top-up of fillers. It's not Dr Bennet's fault, he only does what she demands, but she's getting very weird-looking. Her top lip is now so pronounced she has to drink through a straw, and the very top touches her nostril, which can be extremely off-putting while she's talking to you.

'Hello, my dear!' Dr Bennet launched himself at her, charm personified. 'I'm terribly sorry, we don't treat under-eighteens here.'

20

Zephyr attempted what might have been a smile, but, hampered by the thick layer of plastic that now made up her face, came out more like a twitch.

'Hello, Yuri,' she hissed in a bad transatlantic lisp. Really, knowing your plastic surgeon by his first name. Is that sad or what? 'I need you to get to work.'

'Indeed, my dear. Although I am weak in the presence of beauty,' said Dr Bennet. I rolled my eyes. 'My dear, why don't you come through for a cup of herbal tea?'

'Got any champagne?' said Zephyr. It was ten past nine in the morning.

'But of course. Evie,' said Dr Bennet, 'see to our guest, will you?'

Zephyr didn't even bother glancing at me as I led her into Dr Bennet's office and made her comfortable with a copy of French *Vogue* on an armchair that cost more than my annual salary. I didn't think much of her shiny tight skin, but I couldn't help myself admiringly glancing at her long giraffe legs, carelessly clad in skinny white designer trousers. What must it be like to be able to wear tight white trousers? If you had legs like that did you think about them, or did you not even notice the elegant way they folded up under you without spilling out at the sides? The first and last time I tried on a pair of 'skinny' jeans, my legs looked like parsnips.

'There you go,' I said cheerily. A sniff came from Zephyr's suspiciously hollowed-out nostrils.

'Tell me,' she said as I reached the doorknob, 'what's Dr Bennet's wife like?'

I considered telling her she was ninety and had no teeth, just to see if she would try to seduce him, but I'm not a horrible person. Well, I have horrible thoughts, but I don't *think* that's the same thing, is it?

'She's absolutely bloody terrifying,' I said kindly.

Zephyr nodded her head a fraction – gratefully, I think – and went back to her magazine, as Dr Bennet entered the room.

'Now, my beauty. How can I improve on perfection today?'

Zephyr sighed. 'Oh, God, I have to fly to Barbados *again*. Sort me out, they don't even run Concorde there any more.'

'It's a scandal,' said Dr Bennet seriously. And I think he meant it.

I knew I hadn't got long to check holidays online, because Fanny Eleanor Moncrieff was coming in at 9.30, and she always brought her four tiny yappy dogs. Naturally dogs aren't allowed in a health centre, even one as lax as ours, so guess who has to take them out and round the block regardless of the weather? I wouldn't mind, I like dogs, but these aren't dogs, they're rats wearing coats, and they hate me, and each other, and spend their time getting their Chanel dog leads wrapped up with one another. Fanny Eleanor Moncrieff is ninety but, thanks to the wonders of Dr Bennet, looks eighty-five.

The door pinged as Dr Maitland marched in, head down as usual. He's not one for good mornings. In fact, I've worked here for three years and Dr Maitland's lack of interest in the niceties borders on the completely weird. He's not interested in charm, but he's unbelievably good at what he does. I can tell the difference between his work and Dr Bennet's in a minute – not that Dr Bennet is bad, but he gives a definite plastic surgery 'look'. Which, weirdly, some women actually prefer, in the same way platinum blondes don't really expect you to think their hair is that colour.

Anyway, if I needed anything done (ha ha, ha ha! More like, if I decided to start to tackle, over a period of some years, the pug-nosed freckle factory that is my face), it would be to Dr Maitland I'd go. Which is why he annoys me so much. It's OK for Dr Bennet, he's got family to support (as well as a sports car habit). But I don't understand why Dr Maitland is wasting his time, and his talent, injecting goo into stupid women who park their SUVs in the middle of the street then shout at me when they get a parking ticket. Why isn't he at Great Ormond Street repairing burns victims, or working in a plastics unit for people who get their faces eaten by dogs or something? Even helping kids who get teased at school for their huge ears would be more worthwhile than this. Which is just my opinion, obviously. And I realise the money is good – for all I know he's supporting ten thousand orphans through university. I just can't help feeling it's a bit of a waste of a very good doctor.

Anyway, he walked through the outer office, grunting as usual, and taking off his hat. He isn't old – not older than forty anyway – but he dresses like he's about a hundred. He always wears a hat and a bow tie. I asked Dr Bennet about the bow tie and he said it's so your tie doesn't drop into the mucky stuff when you're operating, which makes sense I suppose. Despite Dr Maitland's complete lack of personal charm, he's always busy because he's so good. In fact, he gets more celebrity clients than Dr Bennet, because you can hardly notice his work and because he's extremely discreet, or, possibly, lost his tongue in a climbing accident (I imagined once in a dull moment).

'Morning, Dr Maitland!' I said in a friendly way. Technically, you were meant to call him and Dr Bennet 'Mister' as they were so eminent, but I always called them doctor (secretly, I think they preferred it. What's the point of swotting for all those years if you can't impress total strangers on the street). I know to make him a cup of very strong coffee very quickly. That's one thing we've all caught off Dr Bennet – I can only drink coffee now if it comes in a tiny cup with the spoon standing straight up out of it.

'Hello,' said Dr Maitland, rustling his *Telegraph*, grabbing his coffee and rustling past as quickly as possible. He makes the ladies fizzy too, actually – God, what is it about women and doctors? They've seen your guts, for goodness' sake. Do you really want to sleep with a man who spent his formative training years sticking his fingers up old ladies' bottoms?

'Ocean Consortium rang again,' I said, reading off from his messages list.

'Oh, bloody hell,' he muttered, almost to himself. 'This thing just doesn't quit . . .'

I had no idea who Ocean Consortium were, except that they kept phoning, that it was secret, and that Dr Bennet was always delighted to hear from them, and Dr Maitland was always pissed off. Sometimes I heard them arguing about it in the consulting suites.

'Who are these people?' I said. 'They're incredibly persistent.'

'Don't ask,' said Dr Maitland, disappearing into his office. 'Nothing good.'

That sounded interesting. I was just about to look them up on the Internet when I realised Fanny Eleanor Moncrieff, with dog entourage, was already standing right in front of me, and I hadn't even helped her up the steps.


God, it was freezing out there walking those bloody rats. I stomped around the block, calling in on Lydia to see if she wanted to join me. She laughed, pointing out that she was sitting in a nice, cosy, centrally heated office. Her place is much posher than mine; she works for three brothers from Tripoli who specialise in lunchtime lipo. But she has less to do – they have a practice manager for the docs; she just smiles and answers the phones. She's always pretending to be sympathetic about my horrible workload though. Plus, she added, she was getting her sneer ready for when the new girl band turned up in five minutes' time.

'Do they get a discount for doing all five at once?'

'Yeah, course. That producer sends all of them here. The only thing is, they don't get to choose what they get done, he does.'

'Yuk.'

'Oh, they're so desperate. You could say, "OK, we're just going to graft an extra ear on, here, over your tits," and they'd say, "Awesome! That's hot!"'

'You're very harsh.'

'I'm just a bit stressed out.'

'You need a holiday.'

She narrowed her eyes at me. 'I NEED you to close the door and stop letting the heat out. What are those things you're walking anyway? They look like mops.'

'Psychotic mops.'

'OK. That's enough. Shoo. Shoo!'


Back at the office Fanny Eleanor Moncrieff was being ushered out by our nurse, and I took over pronto to make sure her driver was outside to pick her up.

'Thank you, my dear,' she croaked through the white bandages. She peered at me suddenly, her eyes sharp, even though she must have been well under the cosh of the painkillers Dr Bennet doled out with a liberal paw.

'You know, you really are very helpful. Are you looking

forward to Cannes . . . ?' Her voice trailed off as her long-suffering driver opened the back door for the dogs, firstly, then helped her in.

'Am I looking forward to what?' I said. You never know, sometimes people get a bit woozy and think they have to tip me. Dr Bennet's warned me very seriously about it, but I don't see the harm.

'I love the place, you know,' she said, going a bit misty eyed. 'Lost two husbands' fortunes on the Riviera. Great days. Life on the ocean blue . . .'

And before she had the chance to go any further, the big black doors of the Mercedes had closed behind her, and the huge vehicle simply slipped away.

# Chapter Two

'That's strange,' I said, pulling my cardigan tightly around me as I bounced back into the welcome warmth of the office. Dr Bennet was ticking off the charts.

'What?' he said. 'You weren't soliciting for cash again, were you?'

'I do not "solicit for cash",' I said. 'One time that Arab princess offered me a small gratuity just for mentioning you couldn't even tell she'd had surgery.'

'While she was wearing her veil.'

I tried to look contrite. 'Well. That wasn't it. Miss Moncrieff mentioned something.'

'Did she indeed?' Dr Bennet raised one of his perfectly plucked eyebrows.

'About Cannes.' I pouted. 'Are you going on yet another jolly and not taking me?' It wouldn't be the first time.

Dr Maitland entered the office, silently as ever.

'The FDA turned it down again,' he announced gruffly. 'Now there's a surprise. A sensible decision.'

'Wilf, come here a second,' said Dr Bennet. 'I was just thinking about discussing Cannes with Evie here.'

Dr Maitland barely raised an eyebrow.

'Well, she'll have to know sometime.'

'What do you think? We could divert the phones, have a bit of a human face. And she was just telling me how much she needs a holiday.'

'I was.' I nodded emphatically. I didn't know what they were talking about, but it sounded promising.

'What would you think about her joining us in Cannes? We could do with the help on the paperwork.'

'That's hardly a holiday,' said Dr Maitland, running his hand through his thick hair. 'There's masses to do.'

'Well,' said Dr Bennet. 'It could be time we got some extra help involved, don't you think? For "Operation Sunshine"?'

Dr Maitland squinted a bit and lowered his voice. 'Whatever you think. Won't everyone else be taking those daft model dolly birds though?' He looked at me apologetically. 'I wouldn't want you to feel out of place.'

I was slightly insulted that he didn't think I'd be mistaken for a six-foot dolly bird, despite evidence to the contrary.

OK, so I don't look like Lydia and most of the other girls up and down Harley Street. But I'm not a gargoyle; if you saw me coming you wouldn't throw your hands up and shout, 'For the love of heaven, cover it up!' then light torches and come and burn me out of my house.

In fact, boyfriends have on occasion called me pretty. It's not my fault that at some point in the last five years freckles went from being cute to being considered a vile mark of global warming, or that curls are out and all hair must be straightened and ironed until it's as flat as a sheet of metal.

But this was just insulting. I knew that the docs didn't really see faces as faces per se – just as problems to be looked at, imperfections to be fixed. They had a picture in their minds of a woman's face: long, high of cheekbone, pointed of chin, tiny of nose, peculiarly flat of forehead, and anything that deviated from this presented itself as a series of problems to be fixed. *But I was standing right here.*

Dr Bennet leaped in, anxious to pour oil on troubled waters, as usual.

'No, we don't need any slutty types,' he said. 'Just some-one friendly-looking to help people if they're feeling nervous.'

Dr Maitland raised an eyebrow. 'I don't think anyone in Cannes is ever nervous.'

My heart, which had been beating too fast at the insult, suddenly skipped a beat. Cannes? South of France?

'Well, I think it's a good idea. You know this thing is about to go huge.'

'I suppose,' said Dr Maitland grudgingly. Gee, thanks boss.

Dr Bennet turned round to face me squarely.

'OK, Evie. Would you like to help us with Operation Sunshine and come with us to Cannes?'

*Would I?* My head filled immediately with visions of palm trees; red carpets; great big yachts; beautiful actresses dancing on the sand; sunshine and blue skies.

Dr Bennet smiled as he noticed my reverie.

'Now,' he said, 'it's not a holiday.'

'Of course not,' I said, shaking my head seriously. Dr Maitland rolled his eyes and went back to his office.

'It's this practice's latest project. We'll be working with and talking to some of the best doctors and richest financiers in the world.'

I nodded, but my brain was doing a little dance to 'holiday holiday holiday holiday'!

'I was going to use the admin company from the conference organisers, but Miss Moncrieff might just be right . . . why shouldn't it be you? You could make sure everything runs smoothly . . . book the flights, the hotels . . . take minutes.'

Ooh. Business-class seats were de rigueur when the docs travelled . . . I wonder, maybe we should book a private jet? And as for hotels, wasn't there a really famous one there?

Where George Clooney always stayed and you had to pay in cash even though it was a million pounds.

'I think separate accommodation for doctors and administrative staff,' said Dr Bennet hurriedly.

I nodded.

'Good. It's settled. We're quiet in July anyway. We'll just divert the phones. Now, come here.'

Dr Bennet handed me a thick file. On it was a picture of a beautiful woman in a striped bathing suit. TOP SECRET was stamped on the cover. Ooh! In big letters across the bottom it said: OPERATION SUNSHINE.

'Looks exciting,' I said. Then I opened it and saw it was full of boring-looking legal documents. Hmm, maybe later.

Anyway, just then the door pinged to admit Hank, an American actor who always comes by whenever he's in London, despite the fact that he thinks, correctly, getting stuff to make his face freeze is doing absolutely nothing for his emotional range (bloody doctor/patient confidentiality kills me; if my friends knew who I'd been having cosy little chit-chats with, and how gay he was, no way would they keep blowing me off for holidays). Dr Bennet slipped off to his consulting room, before I even had a chance to say thank you.

'Aha ha ha,' I messaged Lydia, who I could see was online. 'You know what you were saying about free luxury holidays? Well . . .'

Infuriatingly, the message came back almost immediately.

'Oh, that. Yes, my docs are going. I didn't want to mention it in case you weren't invited.'

I couldn't believe this. What kind of a work-based acquaintance was she, not filling me in on all the juicy trips? What else was I missing out on?

'So you're going then?' I messaged. 'Business class?'

This time it was my turn to receive the laughing smiley.

'I booked my ticket two months ago,' the message read. 'All the seats have probably gone by now. But the coach only takes thirty-six hours.'

Wow, Lydia really does kid around a lot.


'So, anyway, I won't be able to come to the all-night horror show at the NFT,' I casually dropped into the conversation, as Bailey and I sat with our noses in the trough at Wagamama. I didn't really like horror films, but Bailey liked someone to grab at creepy moments, and I didn't mind.

'I'm going to be in . . . oh, let me see, where was it again? Oh, yes, the South of France!'

Bailey looked up from his udon noodles. His glasses were steamed up.

'No way! Yuri's taking you?'

Yuri is Dr Bennet. Him and Bailey are thick as thieves; I've never really understood why.

'Don't sound so surprised,' I said. 'Can I have the last dumpling while you're staring at me with your mouth open?'

'You know I'm going to be there?' he said. 'It's my project.'

'Operation Sunshine?' I said, to make myself look in the know.

'Yes! What do you think?'

'Oh, fabulous.' I must read the brief. 'Amazing.'

I changed the subject as quickly as I could.

'So, everyone's going. It's going to be a proper jolly. Lydia's coming too. There you go, I asked for a holiday and look what's arrived. I think Noel Edmonds is right about that cosmic ordering.'

'Is Lydia the one who wants to meet me?'

'Oh, yes, I forgot.' I frowned. 'I think she wants to do it with you like they do on the Discovery Channel.'

'Charming.'

'I mean it. I think beneath her elegant exterior lies a sex-crazed maniac.'

Hang on, wasn't I meant to be putting him off her?

'You can see the tension in her ten-inch fingernails.'

This was a high-risk strategy to keep him away, all right. I wondered if it would work.

'This isn't a jolly, you know,' said Bailey. 'It's a big serious development.'

'Yes,' I said, slurping the last of my apple and ginger juice. 'Do you think polka dots are still in this year?'

'Who am I, your gay BF?' said Bailey crossly. 'Talk sensibly or I'm taking out *Practical Mechanic* and reading at the table again.'

\*

I'd tried – and failed – not to eat too much as Mum and Dad had invited me round for tea – I'd agreed to go only if the beasts weren't invited too. I called in on them and told them about the trip. At least Mum sounded genuinely pleased, even if she thought that meant I might be getting a promotion of some kind. I don't know how to tell her there's not much in the way of promotion in the medical reception field unless, like Lydia's evil plans, you get lucky and marry the boss and/or a client.

'I'll look out your old French book,' she said. Oh, yes. Suddenly something that had been niggling at the back of my mind jumped to the forefront. Well, have you ever met anyone who *doesn't* put 'French' on their CV? No, you haven't, have you? So maybe, just maybe, under 'other languages' on my application form, I'd written 'French' quite proudly because, 1) how often was I going to have to use that in Harley Street and, 2) if required I could order a cup of coffee with pretty much no problem at all. (Although was it *un* or *une café*? I could never quite remember.)

'So, the boys are coming round . . .'

'They're not, are they?' I said, looking around our beige sitting room like a caged animal. Mum and Dad got so used to all their nice things being destroyed or broken that they'd never got out of the habit of buying the absolutely cheapest of everything, and the room looks like it's been entirely furnished from the back of the Sunday supplements.

'Evie Esme, don't be silly. You've got to stop thinking like you're nine again.'

'That's like saying to a victim of torture that they can't go through life looking over their shoulder,' I grumbled, picking up a fruit scone and removing all the raisins from it in one practised move. 'I've got post-traumatic stress disorder.'

Sure enough, as I was doing this my mum quickly set eight places at the table. Why I hadn't noticed the size of the stew pot she was stirring I don't know. And then the doorbell rang.

'I can't believe this,' I said. 'You lured me here under false pretences.'

'We've got to welcome Cassandro's new wife,' said Mum. 'It was the only way I knew you'd turn up.'

'By telling lies to your only daughter?'

'Hello, hello.' John Jr's loud tones rang through the house. His horrible bullying ringleader ways when we were children have made him a highly successful manager of a car showroom, and he's got the trophy wife, Kelly, to prove it. Kelly's thirty-one and weighs about six stone, most of that gold jewellery and lip gloss.

'Just parked the new Lexus outside. Hope it won't get stolen, huh huh. Evie. How's it going? What are you driving these days.'

John Jr knows fine well I can't afford a car in London, but he always asks people what they're driving the second he meets them. It's like some knee-jerk thing he can't help, if I'm being charitable. If anyone (a man, usually) is foolish enough to venture an answer he will suck in his teeth and go,

'Oh. Happy with it?' Then, if they say yes, he'll raise his eyebrows, as if he can't believe they're such an idiot for driving that car, but he wouldn't like to mention it in polite company. Usually he'll work his way round to bragging about Lexuses (Lexi?) for hours. I don't know anything about cars but I do know that if I ever buy one it will never ever, ever be a Lexus, not even if it was free and delivered by George Clooney carrying a year's supply of jam.

'Hello,' said Kelly. Despite being incredibly pretty (if you like the bleached-blonde aerobicised look, and in my experience blokes really, really do, even if sometimes the girls are a *teensy* bit difficult to tell apart), she was incredibly insecure about her looks. She was always on at me to find out the latest procedures and peels, then went home and got her unqualified beautician to do them for her. I really wished she wouldn't, but she won't be told. 'What's new?'

I thought for a bit.

'Well, there's Radoflux 9000. Gives you baby skin apparently. But it keeps getting turned down by the FDA in America, and the BMA won't look at it. That means you can't use it. It's driving Dr Bennet demented. *Don't* try and buy some off a dodgy website.'

'Would I?'

'Remember that chemical peel?'

'It smelled like Cillit Bang.'

'Remember what we said? If it looks like Cillit Bang, and smells like Cillit Bang . . .'

'Don't use in the under-eye area.'

'Don't use in the under-eye area, that's right.'

She was all right Kelly. I don't know why she was so insecure; John Jr was unbelievably lucky to have pulled her in the first place. It would never strike twice.


'Ooh, what's for dinner, Anne? Smells gorgeous.' Kelly always says this, but never eats anything, and we all pretend not to notice.

'Stew,' said Mum. 'How are you doing, JJ?'

John Jr sat down on the best armchair and spread out his big beefy legs, like a visiting king.

'Yeah, great, Mum. We're thinking of building a swimming pool onto our conservatoire extension, ain't we, Kell?'

Kelly looked pleased. I wasn't surprised: wow, a swimming pool.

'Well, we thought what's the point, right? What's the point of even *having* a conservatoire if it ain't got a pool? Doncha think?'

As soon as John Jr made some money they moved out to Essex, and they live on a gated executive estate, or, as I like to think of them, wanker zoos. My mum blinked. Her and Dad have struggled all their lives – he's only a cabinet-maker, a good trade nobody wants any more, and she spent her life bringing us up, but they wouldn't dream of asking John Jr for a helping hand now and again, and he wouldn't dream of offering. Or me, of course, not that I give a shit. I just wish he wouldn't keep pointing out exactly how much money he makes, and asking me about my salary all the time.

The door crashed open and Patrick burst in, without a girl in tow for once. He's extremely good-looking, or so my female friends have always insisted. At least, he doesn't have a face like a burst pudding, like John Jr. He has a bad-boy swagger that's made the girls go all wobbly since I was twelve – he's also got a motorbike, wears leathers and sneers. It's amazing that still works these days, but it does. Anyway, by night he drinks cider and plays the bad boy, by day he goes to work in a surveyor's office with his hair combed down.

'All right,' he said sulkily, throwing himself down.

'Hiya, Patrick,' Kelly said. Patrick ignored her like he does all women, which usually makes them worse. I rolled my eyes and pointedly asked Mum if she'd like any help in the kitchen.

'Where's Mr Ball and Chain then?' said Patrick. 'I can't believe he got caught by a bird like that. Is she up the duff?'

'Patrick,' said Mum. 'It was very romantic, that's all. They just got carried away on a beach.'

'Yeah,' said Patrick. 'And then they had to get married.' He and John Jr sniggered. 'Got any beer, Mum?'

'Are you on that motorbike?' asked my mother. 'Because if so, no.'

Patrick tutted as my father came in and patted me

comfortably on the head. He's at least a head shorter than the boys and always looks slightly puzzled as to how on earth he could have produced them.

'All right, boys?' he murmured.

'Yeah,' said Patrick. 'Mum was just getting me a beer.'

'Dad, you going to get that wreck through its MOT?' said John Jr. 'You really want to think about upgrading, you know.'

My father muttered something and took his seat at the head of the table, looking around for his stew. My mother looked at the brown clock on the kitchen wall – it has birds that are meant to chirp every hour but they haven't chimed since 1978, when John Jr had a spectacularly high-reaching tantrum. In this case, I'm glad.

'I wonder where they are,' she said nervously. It can't be helped; Cassandro, by virtue of his being as slippery as a snake and not actually evil, is her favourite, and I could tell how nervous she was about meeting his new bride, even though she'd known Jilly since her knees were permanently skinned.

'Probably still at it,' sniggered Patrick.

'Stop that!' said Mum. 'I won't have that kind of chat at the dinner table.'

'Well, I'm not sitting down at the table yet, am I?' said Patrick.

'It's romantic though, innit?' said Kelly. 'A beach wedding. Just you and the one you love. Simple and gorgeous.'

Which is a bit rich, because they had three hundred

people to a sit-down in the world's most floral hotel and Kelly wore a dress so wide people had to brace their feet and heave to get her into the toilet.

'And cheap,' said John Jr. 'Nice one.' He heaved his fat bottom onto one of the creaking kitchen chairs. Because Kelly isn't interested in food, she doesn't much care about John Jr's diet, and I think everything that enters his body has to come wrapped in pastry. I sometimes think Kelly wants him fat and lethargic so that he won't have the energy to chase other women; and possibly so he'll have a heart attack.

My mother sighed and started dishing out stew and dumplings. Patrick tried Cassandro's mobile, but didn't get an answer. He then started texting someone at the table, until Dad gave him a very hard look.

'So,' said Mum. 'Anyone else got any news then?'

'Best February sales in three years,' said John Jr through a thick mouthful of stew. 'I'll be getting some kind of prize.'

'Oh, JJ, that's wonderful,' said my mum, genuinely pleased.

'Yeah, well,' said John Jr. 'Takes bloody thirteen-hour days, but it's worth it.'

'I've got news too,' I said. Everyone turned to me with concerned-looking expressions on their faces. Oh, for goodness' sake. Why do they assume my news is automatically going to be terrible, like I've been arrested or something?

'I'm being sent abroad on a business trip,' I said. That sounded pretty good, actually.

'Where they sending you then?' said John Jr. 'Timbuktu? Is it a one-way ticket?'

'No. The Côte d'Azure actually. That's in France.'

'"That's in France",' mimicked Patrick. 'Why are they sending *you* to France?'

'To administer to a major conference, *actually*.'

'Why, have doctors medically discovered a cure for farting, Evie?'

'No, it's about how to make surveyors more interesting. No cure's been discovered yet, sadly.'

Patrick went back to stuffing his face. I was just about to elaborate on my glamorous trip, now I'd got a word in edge-ways, when the doorbell rang.

'Here they are!' sang my mother, her face lighting up. And in swanned Cassandro and Jilly. Even on this dull rainy evening, they seemed to emit a glow – not just their light tans; their happiness and love seemed to light up the whole house. As they chatted excitedly about dolphin-spotting, barbecues on the beach and yacht parties, I felt my mood get lower and lower. Everything I wanted – excitement, change, adventure, sunshine. It was right here at the table, and none of it was mine. I got quieter and quieter and, as soon as I politely could, left to catch the tube, after swallowing a Battenberg cake that tasted like ashes in my mouth.

'Everything booked?' said Dr Bennet, bowling into the office the next morning. I'd got in early too. Three business-class seats (not for me, sadly – Dr Bennet's scary wife was accompanying him) was going to cost over two thousand pounds. For a two-hour flight and a sandwich! Despite my gloom, it felt fun to spend that much money. Yes, those were the circles I was in now. Two thousand pounds? No problem! Now, hotels. Christ, there were thousands. I didn't trust myself not to stick them in some underground dungeon by mistake, and decided to ask my supportive friend and colleague for advice.

'Oh, for goodness' sake. Just as well I didn't want to go on holiday with you. We'd have ended up at the Birmingham Novotel, but paying five times the rack rate.'

'What's rack rate?' I said to be annoying. Lydia was bringing me back down to earth.

'If I tell you, do you promise not to follow me around like a little puppy dog when we get to Cannes?'

'Well, I thought I could be your wingman.' I had, actually. I didn't mind pulling the good-looking guy's best friend; they're normally more fun anyway. Just call me Ms Brightside.

'Is that what you thought?'

'Yeah, you know, pinpoint the hot young docs . . . check out wedding rings . . .'

Lydia sighed and named two hotels.

'One for them, posh, lots of other docs there. One for you, not quite so posh, lots of PAs there so I won't be the only person you turn to when you need your shoelaces tied.'

Wow, Lydia was lucky my brothers had already softened

me up for lots of insults. Anyway, I'd already started dreaming about suntan lotion ... large oversized sunglasses (except they didn't make me look all weeny and young and fragile, like an Olsen sister, they made me look legally blind), acres of white sand and young Frenchmen with pert bottoms and a widespread knowledge of history, art, literature and the erotic arts.

# Chapter Three

The Saturday before we left I went to the drawer under my bed where I keep clothes I've bought by mistake, or for a special occasion, or that don't fit quite as well as I thought they might when I bought them. It's a big drawer. Normally I stay away from it as it just serves to remind me of stuff I've spent money on but haven't got around to wearing. Yet.

I pulled everything out one by one. OK, the ethnicy kaftan might be a bit last season (and made me look like one big square box from my shoulders to my thighs, where it cut off at a ridiculously high point) but surely it would be just the thing for pulling on after, let's say, a swim to the pool bar?

So yes, the kaftan was in. Now, swimwear. In my knickers drawer I had my swimming costume, which I'd had since school, and although it gave me a bit of hungry bum these days, it was still wearable. It was also, however, a plain black Speedo and did make me look like I was about to cover myself with goose fat and have a shot at the Channel, whilst wearing a nude-coloured skullcap.

This was no good. I needed at least one fancy bikini – Coleen McLoughlin always looks like she takes about fifteen on holiday. Mind you, her job is going on holiday. Why didn't I fall in love with a footballer?

I added to the pile an ill-conceived bright orange skirt, bought during that peasant frills fiasco we all went through a couple of years ago – maybe in Cannes they'd think it was retro chic. Anyway, from what I remembered from our school exchange, all French people wore skin-tight white denim and those women that didn't all wore black suits whilst smoking furiously and talking about pudding, and I wasn't going to be able to manage any of that.

Buying bikinis is such a hideous affair but it was either that or spend my weekend reading the briefing notes, and I didn't think I could take it. Also, I had forgotten it was half term and thus found myself in a department store with about a million unbelievably skinny teenagers moaning to their mothers. I wish my mum had taken *me* shopping for clothes when I was a teenager. But no, she was taking the boys to casualty while I was working in a handbag shop. Why didn't these moony whingers work? Then I wouldn't have to wait two hours to get into a changing room and feel sweaty and hot before I even tried anything on, then wondering how sweaty other people had been whilst trying on bikinis. Yikes. I was *not* in the holiday mood.

'Oh, for goodness' sake,' I exclaimed to myself, trying to turn around in the minuscule cubicle. I felt like a dog chasing its tail.

That reminded me, it was one of the few conversations Dr Maitland and I had had. Geneva Pitt, a horrid society stick woman who calls everyone 'girls' and pretends she's some kind of a dizzy lassie but is actually the most ruthless witch ever, had come in howling. Her face is so stretched and shiny it looks like she's made of pink chewing gum.

'Wilf!' she'd hollered, ignoring my greeting. For goodness' sake. He's your doctor. Just call him 'Doctor'. What, you think we're impressed that we bill your poor husband for tens of thousands of pounds a year?

'I've got cellulite!' she screamed. 'My life is over!'

Seriously, she was in tears. Must have nicked them off a spare crocodile she'd passed on Wimpole Street. Then, right in the middle of the waiting room (there was no one else there except me, and I'm invisible), she pulled down her incredibly tight leather trousers to reveal, just under her absurdly tight bum, one tiny, tiny bump which was only visible when she scrunched up her arse. Honestly, sometimes I realise how men can be completely confounded by women.

'There, there,' he'd said gruffly. 'Follow me, err. Mrs . . .'

He'd forgotten her name! What a boor. I quickly jotted it down in big letters on a piece of paper and held it up behind her back.

'. . . Pitt,' he finished. 'Come right in.'

Afterwards, he came up to me whilst picking up his hat.

'Thank you,' he said quietly, in his dignified way. He was right to thank me; the whole business relies on making women feel pampered and special, and it's hard to feel special when someone is calling you Thingy.

'That's OK,' I said. Then I added, 'Can I ask? Cellulite . . . What is it? I mean, really. Will it go away if you stop drinking coffee?'

'Oh, God,' he said. 'Professional ethics forbid me from talking about it.'

'OK,' I said, trying not to sound sniffy. Professional ethics seemed to stop him from talking about a lot of things, up to and including a 'How are you, Evie?' once in a while.

'Well,' he said. Then he looked around again. 'Can you keep a secret?'

I nodded heartily, regardless of the fact that this wasn't perhaps 100 per cent true.

'It doesn't exist,' he whispered.

I almost jumped. 'What do you mean it doesn't exist?' I said. 'I've got bloody masses of the stuff.'

He shrugged. 'Well, it's simply an aesthetic term. What you've got is fat deposits on your bottom and hips.'

'Thanks very much.'

'That's where fat deposits in females. And that's what it looks like. End of story.'

'But . . . aren't we supposed to be able to get rid of it with brushes and stuff.'

'You can get rid of it by stripping all the fat out of your body. Paula Radcliffe doesn't have any. Nor does Ms, ahem, Pitt, once you suck it out. Otherwise, well, that's it.'

'But all those creams, and potions . . .'

Dr Maitland shook his head. 'You think a cream can penetrate your skin and specifically dissolve fat?'

'I would like to think that.'

He almost patted me on the head.

'Bless you,' he said. 'I don't think you'd like liquid-permeable skin. Certainly not after the first time you took a bath. And, I promise, there are many, many more important things in the world to worry about than cellulite, a made-up money-spinner for the beauty industry.'

Then why, I thought, for the nine thousandth time, as he left to hop into his little MG, quietly closing the door behind him, don't you worry about any of them?

Reassuring though this had been at the time, well, it wasn't bloody helping me *now*, was it? I wrestled myself into another pair of 'boy cut' bikini bottoms. I'd asked all the men I knew (apart from the beasts) what they thought about cellulite and none of them knew what the hell I was talking about, except for Bailey and he said it didn't bother him, though what would he know about it seeing as he only dates supermodels? Or, at least, better-looking girls than I'd think he'd get without the platinum corporate Amex and the access to cheap boob jobs.

Then I turned around and saw 'it'. It was just hanging there, on the shelf full of stuff to be taken back into the store. Obviously one of the Keira Knightley-esque teens had tried it on and nearly drowned in it . . . but for me . . .

It was a dark red dress: not an in-your-face tomato juice colour, but a deep, shimmering silk that slipped on like a second skin. I wondered for a moment if it might look a bit like a nightie but, when I tried it on, it didn't. It looked like someone had sat down and designed a beautiful red summer dress, just for me.

Shopping moments like this almost never happen. When they do, your only choice is to grab them and run with it. Terrified in case the person who'd orginally tried it on realised they'd made a terrible mistake and came running back, I whipped it off, grabbed the first bikini that came to hand and charged to the checkout.

It's not that I didn't have anything to do that Saturday night *at all*. I would have had loads of offers, probably. It's just I happen to really, really like my mum's cooking, especially when she's doing lamb, that's all. My mother's roast lamb is so good it makes it worth sitting next to a bunch of disgusting animals in a zoo. Which is just as well.

I'd spent the afternoon curled up in my old bedroom with the pictures of ponies still on the wall, immersing myself in a guidebook on the Côte d'Azure and occasionally jumping up to try on my new dress again. I didn't want to show Mum; she had conniptions about anything that cost over £15.99, and this had cost quite a lot over £15.99.

Cannes looked incredibly thrilling. Miles of palm trees and golden beach, huge yachts tied up in the harbour at sunset; pictures of Chanel and Louis Vuitton shops. It wasn't actually that crucial for me to know the whereabouts of the Louis Vuitton shop. I suspected I may have bought the wrong guidebook – *The Côte d'Azure Guide For the Skint and Non-Beautiful* wasn't in stock, but *The Glamour Guide to Cannes* was.

*Don't miss*, it enthused, *the many glamorous parties and premieres of the film festival. Some prefer the Splendid to the Eden-Roc, overrun as the latter is at this time with movie stars and wannabes.*

Movie stars and wannabes sounded all right to me. And I would be delighted not to miss the many glamorous parties, if someone would only tell me where and when they were; I had the dress for it.

*Or of course just moor the yacht (but make sure you've got mooring sorted well in advance – tel: 06 55 43 32 10).*

I had definitely bought the wrong guidebook. Although I was tempted to call the number. 'Hello, *bonjour*, yes, I just need to reserve my yacht parking space. For the film festival, yes. My name . . . uh, it's Jennifer Aniston. A-N-I . . .'

*Dressing for dinner in Cannes is very dressy indeed – now is the time to wear your couture, and break out your family jewels. View the setting sun from the terrace of the Hotel Belles Rives, which shimmers nightly with crystal champagne glasses and diamonds.*

'Evie!' my mother yelled up the stairs. 'I need a hand chopping cabbage.'

I sighed.

'OK!' I shouted down. 'I'll just back up the yacht,' I added to myself.

Downstairs, sitting *right there* was John Jr, watching the sport.

'Oh, it's all right,' I said. 'You've already got John Jr to chop the cabbage.'

'Yeah, yeah,' said John Jr. 'Some of us are actually recovering from a hard week's work where you don't just sit behind a desk reading magazines.'

'I would do it, Anne,' said Kelly. 'But, you know. Fingernails.' She held up her hands apologetically. Her nails must have been three centimetres long.

'You do that on purpose!' I said.

'It's just grooming!'

'It's chore avoidance!'

'Because she's a lady,' said John Jr proudly.

I wielded the knife grumpily, wondering if he'd fancy the cabbage if I stuck some lipgloss on it.

'So, Anne,' Kelly was saying, examining her cuticles. 'Apparently in Cannes the champagne glasses and the diamonds shimmer in the setting sun.'

'That sounds lovely,' said my mum, who was sweating slightly, pulling huge trays from the oven. 'You're going to have such a lovely time.'

I turned round, shocked.

'What are you talking about?'

'In Cannes, you know?'

'Yes, I do know. Are you going there?'

'Why?' said Kelly in a teasing voice. She knew how I felt about John Jr. 'Scared we'll show you up?'

'Other way round more likely,' said John Jr.

Thing is, I do like Kelly – it was her choice to marry an unmitigated baboon, but she has to share an en suite with him, so it's her that's suffering. But I really, really didn't want them barging in on my holiday. This was my trip; my chance to be whoever I wanted to be. I didn't need someone creeping up behind me making farting noises while I was talking to Dr Maitland or, well, anyone really.

'I thought you said the French had arseholes for mouths, hated fighting wars and ate their own shit,' I accused John Jr, whose sentiments on the peoples of the world were often expressed.

'What my darling wants she gets,' he said, not taking his eyes off the television.

'Apparently it's really, really classy and lovely,' said Kelly. 'Chanel shops everywhere and that.'

'Yeah,' I said.

'Evie don't know what that is,' said John Jr.

'It's clothes,' said Kelly. 'And they do skis, like what Posh Spice has.'

'I *know* what Chanel is,' I said.

'Don't worry,' said John Jr. 'We're going high style, so I don't think we'll see much of you.'

Then he leaned over.

'But Kelly wants you to introduce us to all your doctor friends,' he said.

I looked at Kelly. 'No way. Really?'

She shrugged. 'Well, I was thinking of getting some more serious work done . . . I am nearly thirty-two.'

'Don't do it,' I advised immediately. 'I could tell you some stories that would curl your GHDs.' Actually, most of what we do is pretty safe, but even so, it's still a bit dumb that someone as pretty as Kelly would submit herself to the knife. And I can always tell.

'Not your guys, though,' said Kelly.

'No,' I conceded. 'My guys are very good. But you're gorgeous, Kell. What do you want to go messing with that for?'

Kelly leaned back, looking mollified. But she didn't take her eyes off the French brochure I'd noticed earlier in her lap.

'Any news from Cassandro?' I asked loudly, trying to change the subject. My mother's brow furrowed.

'Yes,' she said. 'He called to tell us they loved Antigua so much they're thinking of going back and opening a beach bar and living happily ever after.'

Oh, God, that sounded blissful. I could just imagine it – clear blue skies, soft blue seas, rum punch every day. Oh, God, I so needed to get away.

'Lazy bastard,' said John Jr. 'He should come back and get a job. In the rain,' he added.

'You never tell John Jr off for swearing,' I immediately pointed out to Mum.

'Cos I'm not a lonely spinster like you,' said John Jr.

I mouthed 'bastard' in the direction of his beefy shoulders but carefully, so Mum didn't see.

Heathrow early in the morning is a fearsome sight. The airport was so huge, mobbed with people and slightly imposing, what with the policemen carrying machine guns and everything. I looked at my scruffy green rucksack. It was inherited from the boys' turns at the Scouts, and smelled like it too. And it hardly had anything in it: a couple of suits and my orange skirt; my not-bad bikini, which wasn't too disastrous if you half closed your eyes and repeated very loudly 'cellulite doesn't exist' three times whilst tapping your heels together (it also struck me that the South of France might be somewhere you'd be expected to wear high heels with your bikini so I'd thrown in my party shoes too); one sun dress, slightly faded, bought the year I said I really was sick of never going on holiday and was going to go and tour India all by myself, then I'd crapped out at the last minute; and of course the new red dress. I'd caressed the material packing it. It felt so full of possibility. It was a pulling dress, if you were being vulgar. A romantic dress, if you weren't.

Lydia came striding towards me. She looked chic and striking in a black trouser suit and white shirt that you could tell was really well cut and expensive, rather than the white shirt I own, which make me look like a pregnant man painting a house. She was also wearing a positively gigantic pair of sunglasses.

'Did you know you've got two coffee cups stuck to the front of your eyes?' I asked by way of greeting.

'Nice jeans,' she replied. 'Are they those loss leader ones they do for five pounds in Tesco?'

'No.'

'Oh, how funny. I could have sworn the waist was elasticated.'

'OK, OK, truce,' I muttered. 'Shall we go and check in?'

She sniffed loudly as we made our way across the concourse. She was trailing a chic black bag with a completely indiscreet large gilt label on the top, just in case it got mistaken for the million other identical black bags out there.

I wouldn't have minded but, looking round the queue, there were certainly a lot of very slim-limbed women, and none of them was wearing jeans. They were wearing Gillian McKeith-style trouser suits in pale shades, or, occasionally, mini skirts. There was one girl in 501s, but as soon as a smart mother shouted, 'Magda! Toilet the children, please!' it became patently obvious she was the hired help.

'Well, this isn't right.'

I tuned in from my sulk to hear Lydia remonstrating with the check-in woman, who looked scared.

'I send a lot of business your way, and I have to say, it doesn't seem too much to ask.'

'Yes, but we have to keep those seats . . .'

'Yes, but I checked in online six weeks ago.'

The woman looked pink. Honestly, sometimes I don't know why Lydia's working on reception. She should be marshalling troops somewhere.

'I'll just go talk to . . .' the woman scuttled off. I forgot I was meant to be sulking.

'What's up?' I said. In reply Lydia looked at me like I wasn't there.

The woman came back from her secret office at the back. 'I'm going to be able to upgrade this ticket,' said the woman. Lydia bestowed a beatific smile.

'*Thank* you.'

'If you'd just follow me.'

Fantastic! Upgrade! Lydia was bloody marvellous! I'd never travelled swish class before. I looked at the rest of the queue with pity. So long, suckers! Enjoy the cheap seats! I picked up my bag to follow them. At that precise instant, they both turned to look at me and the expression on their faces was almost identical. It said, 'Not you, you moose.'

Crushed, I put my bag back down slowly.

'Well, nice to run into you, Evie,' said Lydia casually. 'See you later, yeah?'

I think it was at this point that it started to occur to me that Lydia maybe wasn't all that great a friend.

'Magda! Tell Jacintha to stop kicking,' came the voice behind me for the millionth time.

'Stop keecking, pleece, Jacintha,' said a low, tentative voice that I could already tell would have no effect on Jacintha, because Jacintha was right behind me and it was me she was kicking, and had been for an hour and forty-five minutes.

'NOOOOOOOO!'

When I'd seen the family group I'd wondered why on earth you'd take your nanny on holiday. Having become well acquainted with the feet of Jacintha, it was no longer such a mystery. Certainly didn't help me focus on the briefing notes, anyway. I couldn't read a thing.

Sighing I turned towards the window. We were descending – I'd had my breath taken away earlier, both by a Jacintha boot to the kidneys and the sight of the snow-topped Alps just below us, continuing on for miles. Now, though, I was looking at a long swathe of bright buildings lining the shore and glistening in the bright sunlight, framed by dark forbidding mountains rising up above.

As I watched, looking for the airport, we continued on past the beach and out into sea. This was odd, as we were definitely getting lower and lower. I could see the white wakes of the boats out on the open sea . . . now I could see their sails. Uh, I didn't want to cause panic, but was no one else aware that we were about to all crash into the water and drown?

I looked around for a stewardess but there was none to be found. Oh, no! They must all be up the front, huddling! Or maybe they'd all bailed out already. I found my fingers making a clawing shape as the wings tilted and nearly hit the water. Bugger! I was going to die before I had the chance to go to Cannes! I was going to be a terrible loss just as my life was beginning! I couldn't help it; even though my heart was pounding, I had a momentarily satisfying flash of my brothers all crying and being miserable and wishing they'd been nicer to me, and my mother would say, 'I knew we should have bought her that pony,' and they'd all be very sorry I was dead and would think about me all the time. I hoped I'd get to come back like that girl in *The Lovely Bones* and watch them all being sad and talking about how fantastic I was and how they wished they'd told me when they had the chance, and Bailey would throw himself onto my coffin and say I was the only girl he'd ever loved and now his life was practically over too.

I was just closing my eyes to prepare for impact – and hoping it was quick – when the plane wheels bumped down onto something solid. I realised, with a sense of mild disappointment, that we'd landed, and that the airport seemed to be in the middle of the sea.

My spirits perked up, however, when I heard the captain say, 'Welcome to Nice, Côte d'Azure, ladies and gentlemen . . . where the temperature is twenty-seven degrees Celsius.'

The terminal building looked, frankly, too clean for my manky old bag. It was last out too – maybe they'd temporarily mistaken it for a duster of some kind. God, Lydia better have waited for me. She would know how to get to Cannes, surely? Otherwise, if she'd left me on my own . . . well, maybe I should have prepared slightly better for when I got here, but obviously I'd had a lot of very difficult bikini issues to work out and simply hadn't had the time.

Oh, thank God, there she was, standing with her gigantic sunglasses on, next to a short man. A man with sticky-up hair. A man who looked incredibly familiar, in fact.

'Oh, there you are,' she said. 'I thought you'd got completely lost. Anyway, I just wanted to tell you, I'm getting a lift in this lovely gentleman's helicopter, OK? So I suggest you get the train or a taxi, if you can afford it. *Adieu!*'

'Hello, Bailey,' I said. Lydia's eyebrows shot up.

'*You're* Bailey?' she said, as Bailey came up and gave me a hug. '*Bienvenue*,' he said. It didn't seem fair to be annoyed with him because a) he'd not yet thrown himself on my grave in the event of my imaginary death, and b) he'd not got to know Lydia yet.

'I certainly do,' I said. 'What's this about a helicopter?'

'They've sent a helicopter for me,' said Bailey, half apologetically, half obviously unbelievably delighted. 'I am the chief designer, I suppose.'

'Oh, how boring. Helicopters again,' I said. 'Why don't you ask for the space shuttle like all the fashionable people?'

'Shall I see if there's room for you, too?' he asked.

'They do have quite strict weight limits,' said Lydia. Then she turned round. 'We were sitting next to each other. In business.'

'Oh, did you go business?' I said, trying to sound airy. 'I thought they'd led you off to put you in the hold.'

'Well, this is going to be fun,' said Bailey. He turned to a smartly dressed man and spoke a few words to him in rapid French. Lydia made a big show of widening her eyes and nodding her head along to show she understood, though I bet she didn't.

'OK, no problem,' said Bailey to me. 'I promise not to throw your horrible kit bag into the sea either.'

'Yes, I must swap it for a handbag, like you have,' I said. In fact, it was a man bag, but I smiled to show him I was genuinely pleased to see him.


Ooh, and I was. What a thrill. I instantly realised that this was the way I was born to live. The speed from which I could get from a manky high street changing room to going *flip flip flip flip flip* (helicopter noise, as experienced first hand by me) over the deep blue Mediterranean sea must mean something. It must register a change in my life; a fresh start, a new beginning. As I sat back in the (not very comfortable) seat and stared into the sun, it certainly felt like it.

# Chapter Four

Well, this wasn't exactly what I'd been dreaming of. A huge black car had been waiting at the helicopter pad (hurrah!) and, after whisking us through busy traffic, it had dropped Bailey off at some huge five-star joint on the front, where three little flunkies, actually wearing hats and white gloves, hopped down to take his luggage.

Then the car had dropped Lydia off at a nice smart white-washed place that looked more house than hotel, with bright green shutters, wisteria growing up the walls, overflowing window boxes, a lawn, a pool and a nice fat lady who'd greeted Lydia by name and with a kiss. 'Why didn't you recommend I book here?' I'd asked. 'Well, I can't give the name and address out to just anyone, can I?' said Lydia, as if this were reasonable.

Anyway, it was now forty minutes later and the driver was circling what looked like a housing estate in the back end of nowhere, looking grumpy and muttering to himself under his breath. I hope I wasn't meant to tip this guy. Well, even if I was, I only had twenty-euro notes, and not that many of those, and he certainly wasn't getting one.

The driver said something which sounded like 'vlah vlah GarRUMPH' and stopped the car, pointing towards a grimy-looking apartment block. I thanked him, considered offering him a pound coin but then scarpered before he had the chance to say anything to me I wouldn't understand. Hmm, maybe my French wasn't just 'rusty'. Maybe it was more like 'non-existent'.

This couldn't be right, though. It was just a big block of flats, and all the windows were covered in metal grilles. I turned round, but the driver had already whizzed off, obviously affronted that his beautiful car had had to pass through such upsetting surroundings.

Hoisting up my rucksack, the sun suddenly felt like it was beating very warmly on my head – I looked at my watch. It was noon, the hottest time of day. I moved to what had to be the front door. Sure enough, there written next to a bell was *Hôtel de Cannes (deux)*.

I sighed. Well, Hôtel de Cannes had sounded such a good bet. You know, like the best hotel in Cannes, thus the title. The fact that it was so cheap in the middle of conference season was simply a bonus. Now I suspected that the *deux* might actually be quite important, some kind of legal require-ment from somewhere. I rang the buzzer, which sounded deep inside the building, and sighed.

There was no answer. Actually, after a couple of minutes my heart lifted a bit. If the hotel was shut I'd just have to move – maybe to that place Lydia was in, that looked nice. Or maybe Bailey would have a spare bedroom in his luxury bloody hotel or something. But just as I was wondering where I could get a cab, the door creaked open. A small woman stood there. Very slender and with her hair fiercely tied back she did not look a single bit like the friendly woman with the rolled-up sleeves who had greeted Lydia.

'*Oui? Qu'est-ce que c'est?*' she barked at me, and various other sentences stuck on the end. I looked at her blankly.

'Uh, *bonjour*,' I said, my brain searching for the set phrase I'd learnt off by heart to ask for my room. But I wasn't going to get that far.

'Ah,' she said. 'Hell-OH.' She said it in a deliberately slow and simple way, I reckoned, as if by not being French it was clear that I was mentally retarded. 'Yes? What do you want?'

'Uh . . . the hotel?' I said, as if *she* wouldn't be able to understand more than a few simple nouns.

She raised her eyes to heaven and then pointed out some numbers under the sign, which I'd assumed were the address or something.

'*Fermé 12–14h*,' it said.

'*Fermé*,' she said. 'Closed. Until two o'clock.'

Closed? I didn't know hotels could close. I thought that was the entire point of why something was known as a hotel rather than, say, a youth hostel where you had to do chores.

'I can't get in till two o'clock?' I said.

'No,' she said. Then she turned her back on me and clip-clopped off down the road.

I love it. France. I do. I love travelling and going away and visiting new countries and having holidays in lovely places such as France.

These are a few of the thoughts that did NOT go through my head for the next two hours, as I sat on my gigantic bag. I thought about trying to go somewhere – anywhere – but I couldn't move the damn thing and I could only see apartment blocks in both directions. I called Bailey but got no answer and I couldn't bear to phone Lydia – after that little conversation about the hotel I didn't really trust her to help me, rather than, say, come and run me over with her hired car.

So I had to stick it out, listlessly reading *Heat* magazine for the ninth time and trying to work out what horrible thing I could do to this hotel room to get my own back. By the time I'd got to jamming up the plug sockets with egg sandwiches (a favourite trick of Patrick's, particularly when I had friends round at that awkward stage in my early teens, who very quickly became not my friends when they realised my room smelt funny) I was ready to scream.

Nobody passed me in the street at all, apart from a curious

fat woman who stared at me rudely. Where was everybody? Were they all getting ready for super-fancy cocktail parties? Asleep? I was in the middle of the buzzy Côte d'Azure. Puff Daddy comes here to throw Beyoncé into the sea. I'd arrived by bloody helicopter, for goodness' sake, didn't that stand for anything?

Nineteen hours later, at two minutes to two precisely, there came a clip-clopping up the road. I regarded the woman through narrow slits for eyes.

'*D'accord*,' she said. She didn't ask if I'd had lunch or been for a swim or even had a glass of water, simply eyed me as I heaved my enormous, stupid, smelly bag and traipsed wearily after her.

The Hôtel de Cannes (deux) was . . . well, it was cheap. It was up a flight of stairs and seemed to be built around an apartment block, which was a new concept in hotelling to me – I'd expected a swimming pool. It smelled of disinfectant, which failed to mask the odour of old cigarette smoke and cheap coffee. The walls were a horrible brown, with mirrors reflecting back more dismal brown.

The woman checked me in grudgingly, as if my sit-in outside her hotel was some kind of ruse to scam her out of a room. Finally, after laboriously photocopying my passport, and amidst many weary sighs – how could she possibly be expected to fill out these forms after a mere two-hour lunch break? – she handed me a slightly sticky key card and nodded me up to the third floor.

Here was a long corridor of brown once again. There wasn't another soul in sight. I stomped along, pulling the bag behind me like an errant dog. At room 317 I stopped and inserted the card. The cheap, brown Formica door swung open. It really did look quite a lot like the kind of room someone would get murdered in in an exploitation movie from the seventies.

Brown, stained lino. Shutters closed on a small window, rendering the place wreathed in gloom. Chipped cabinet with yet another brown-reflecting mirror.

I figured I'd have a shower and that would make me feel a bit better, but the water was brown and dribbly and luke-warm. I had to get out of here.

The hotel woman grudgingly pointed me in the direction of the promenade ('It is water. You just go *downhill*.' '*Merci*,' I said. We really were talking to each other like idiots) and I headed out into the bright afternoon light.

It was lovely. Fresh and clean under the bright blue sky and I slipped on my sunglasses as I walked down towards the harbour. The air felt warm on my skin and I began to forget all the indignities of the last couple of hours. There was street after street of apartment blocks, painted yellow and blue, with wrought-iron balconies draped with swimming trunks hanging out to dry, mixed with the high gates and walls of white-washed villas whose driveways curled up into the hills. Coming further into the town there were indeed the promised lines of shops: Louis Vuitton, Chanel, Gucci. Here it was absolutely thronging with people; emaciated women of a certain age, with huge powdered hairdos and tiny little dogs, picking their way through the cobbles on heels. Suave, Italian-looking men with slicked-back hair and pink shirts took telephone calls as sullen-looking model-y girls with Russian accents looked at incredibly over-the-top dresses in Nancy Dell'Olio colours.

Baby girls in big puffs of pink fluff were being pushed around in baby carriages that looked more like small convert-ibles, and gorgeous, tanned teenage girls showed off flat stomachs over low-slung jeans and Hi-Top Converse, chatter-ing loudly all the while. Quite obviously set apart from the colourful locals mooched groups of tourists: Brits, Dutch, German, all made obvious by their sloppy sports gear and bad posture.

At last I emerged at the water's edge. The soft Mediterranean waves – now with a hint of early evening pinkness on them – shimmered into the endless distance, whilst the boats bobbed up and down along the quay. There were huge white boats; huge blue boats; little boats that would look grand if they weren't tied up next to the huge boats. There was a massive grey boat that looked like a war-ship but, judging by the chandeliers, it was a big gin palace too. There was the easyJet cruise ship, stuck out in the bay miles from shore, looking like a big orange blob. Young, hunky men cleaned the sides of the boats while others carried crates of champagne on board. Huge Bentleys and BMWs purred up and down the road. I liked it. A lot.

I watched the most absurd little yellow sports car with a million-decibel engine roar by. People were congregating at pavement cafés and ordering carafes of wine and I suddenly felt a distinct desire to be one of them. I decided to go and get Bailey. I could do with a friendly face to go with the rosé.

Bailey's hotel was set right on the palm-lined seafront, past carousels and ice-cream stands and immaculate-looking couples strolling hand in hand, accompanied by their clean and beautiful children. It didn't remind me much of home.

The hotel looked like a cake that had been spun out of icing sugar for some ridiculous billionaire's wedding – layer upon layer of scallops and frills which resolved themselves, as you got closer, into balconies and crenulations. It was wildly over the top, there were turrets everywhere. I loved it.

As I clopped up the stairs into the huge lobby I started to wonder if I should have just thrown on the red dress straight away. That, actually, it was a little subtle. If the women on the street had been dressed up, the ones here were positively festive. Millions of sparkling lights from the chandeliers bounced off huge mirrors and onto glinting ear lobes, huge rings and heavy necklaces.

This was serious jewellery, and it all looked real. I tried not to stare too much, but I couldn't help it, and anyway, why would you wear this stuff if you didn't want people to stare at it? And they were all so thin. This wasn't just in shape, or gently toned, Coleen McLoughlin style. This was full on I-will-never-not-ever-eat-a-meal style. It was amazing their tiny wrists and necks could even take the weight of the precious stones. It looked like just wearing them would be all the exercise they would need that day. I saw some pretty high-glamour women at the practice, but even they weren't like this. This was a different realm altogether; it wasn't millionaire's wives looking for bigger tits. It was billionaire's wives looking to float away, and only the rocks were keeping them tethered to earth.

'Oh, my,' I said, out loud.

'Can ah 'elp you?'

I did find it mildly dispiriting that the beautiful young man in the smart designer uniform could tell I was English before I'd even opened my mouth or glanced in his direction. Damn you, Topshop, for making us all so completely identifi-able from thirty metres or more.

The receptionist was beautiful, though he had a look in his eye that implied that if I was only in here for a quick sniff around, he'd rather I left.

'Bailey Arnold, please,' I said in my best imperious tones, which aren't that imperious, frankly, and make me sound con-stipated.

'Ah, Monsieur Arnold. Of course.'

He nodded his head and made a quick call.

'Go right up – room 801, on the top floor.' I wondered if that was penthouse good or servant's quarters bad as I got into the incredible panelled lift, which had a small red chair and a small red man who pushed the button to '*numéro huit*', as deftly rehearsed by me.

The lift slid smoothly up and deposited me on a bright landing, with large windows at either end and thick, lush carpet spreading out in both directions. There were only two doors visible on the entire floor, which went on for miles: 801 and 802. I figured it probably wasn't the servant's quarters.

There was a proper old-fashioned bell outside the door so I pushed that. Bailey opened it immediately as if he'd been waiting for me.

'Come in!' he said. 'Come in! Learn why it was, in fact, worth getting my head kicked in by the beasts every day because they knew to lie in wait for me outside the technical library! Learn why, yes, CAD physics is worth giving up every Tuesday night for a year for. Yes, why—'

'Shut up, boffin-oh,' I said. I wanted to take in my surroundings in peace because, quite frankly, I'd never been anywhere so nice in my entire life.

You entered the suite via a parquet-floored hall in which stood a coat rack and various large pieces of marble art, until the room opened out into a vast living area. It had a vast, spotless cream carpet that felt like it could curl up to my ankles; it was like walking in moss. Three huge windows overlooked the pale blue sea, sails bobbing up and down in the distance. A huge fireplace had a fire dancing in it, even though it was hot outside, but the room still felt temperate. There was a glass table set for dinner with an enormous bowl of fruit on it, and several huge and comfortable-looking jewel-coloured sofas. In the corner was a fully stocked drinks cabinet with proper-sized bottles, none of your minibar nonsense (I didn't even have a minibar in my 'hotel'). Panelled doors led off either side of the living area, presumably into more rooms.

'*Mon dieu*,' I expostulated.

'*Mais oui*,' said Bailey.

'Fuck a duck,' I said.

'*Exactement*,' replied Bailey.

'I don't understand,' I said, looking round again. Bailey? Here? It was just amazing. 'I mean, this is for rock stars, or royalty, or . . . or . . . you know, VIPs. Not swots from St Michaels' whose hobby was "getting their head kicked in".'

Bailey sank happily into one of the other sofas.

'My dear,' he said. 'In the world of dynamic changing environments in healthcare, I *am* a rock star.'

I'd always known Bailey was a brainiac with a brainiac job, but this was something else. I'd clearly completely underestimated him. No wonder he went out with supermodels all the time. Imagine, a man in undying love with me having all this.

'Where's your robot butler? Can you have him bring me a gin and tonic?' I said looking round and trying to be casual.

'*Mademoiselle?*' and from one of the panelled doors came, I promise, a man dressed in a black frock coat. For a second I thought he really was a robot and nearly screamed. Bailey looked embarrassed.

'He comes with the room,' he whispered to me. 'I don't know how to make him go away.'

'Uh, a gin and tonic, please,' I said hesitatingly.

The butler glided over to the bar and started mixing drinks, the sound of which made me very happy indeed.

'I knew I should have copied off you at GCSE,' I said. 'Bugger. What have you actually done?'

'Well, you've read the brief?'

'Oh, yes, of course.' Well, I would. I'd hate to look unprofessional.

I opened the balcony doors, to be greeted with a sudden yell that sounded like it was coming from next door.

'You'd think they'd soundproof this place,' said Bailey. 'Seeing as it's a royal palace and everything.'

'Yeah,' I said. 'Can't the robot butler . . .'

Bugger, what was I thinking? I'd completely forgotten he was a real live man, standing there.

'*Immédiatement, mademoiselle*,' he said, and shimmied out of the room as if on wheels.

'That butler thing gives me the creeps,' I announced.

'He's a real person,' said Bailey. 'Do try and treat him like, you know, a humanoid. Now, do you want to see the rest of this place? I have to say, it's the nicest . . .'

But before he could beckon me over, the butler came hurtling back into the suite, looking terrified for his life, closely followed by a leering, menacing – why, it was none other than John Jr.

'Oh, for crying out loud,' I said, almost stamping my feet. John Jr was in full flow.

'So if I say best room in town oi MEAN best room in town and that means, buster, if oi want to have a bust up with the old trouble and strife you better keep your big nose aht of it, know wharra mean?'

The butler had recovered his composure somewhat and gave John Jr a look that said 'You will never order another dish in any restaurant bar or café in this town without someone I know personally peeing in it,' but he said nothing.

'John Jr, for God's sake.'

John Jr turned round at that. He got the shock of his life when he saw me; his already red face turned puce.

'Evie . . . Evie, for fuck's sake. Are you staying here?'

I sighed. 'If I say I am will you move?'

Kelly came out of the suite to see what the commotion was. Now I understood the noise; there'd obviously been some sort of incident with the hair straighteners. A large chunk of her hair looked distinctly singed.

'Ow, hello, Evie,' she sniffed, smiling bravely. 'I hoped we'd run into you.'

'Yup,' I said. 'Well, this was quick.'

'Now, I don't want to push in . . .'

'Uh huh . . .'

Kelly looked towards Bailey. 'But is this one of your fabulous doctors?'

I looked round at Bailey, who was retreating towards the

windows of his huge suite, away from John Jr. It was almost comical to see. He probably didn't realise he was doing it, just vestigial habit.

John Jr narrowed his piggy eyes. 'Hey. I recognise you.'

Bailey's lips twitched and he fussed with his glasses. I'd never mentioned at home that I still saw Bailey. Mum would have wanted us to get married and the beasts would never have let me hear the end of it.

'It's Bailey boy, innit? Ol' Bailey boy, Snaily Bailey.'

I could see the colour rise in Bailey's cheeks. I forgot sometimes, encased as he was in his great job and nice lifestyle, that it had been pretty bad for him too.

'Mnnff,' said Bailey.

John Jr's face broke into a huge smile. 'Well! Fantastic to see you! We had some great times back then, didn't we? Some right laughs. Kelly, this is Bailey, one of the old gang from Leadbetter Road. Come here.'

And he marched up to Bailey and gave him a great bear hug. I don't think I've seen a man so surprised since Will Young won *Pop Idol*. Bailey took a step back as soon as he reasonably could.

'John Jr,' he said stiffly. 'It's been a long time.'

I instantly felt sorry for him; it sounded like he was saying it in a James Bond/*Goldfinger*-type fashion and should be stroking a pussycat and dreaming up shark-related tortures for his lifelong foe. Instead John Jr clearly thought he'd stumbled on a long-lost 'homie' from back in the 'hood'.

'Kelly, Kelly, come meet Bail the Snail. Oh, we had some times in those days, didn't we, Bailey boy?'

'I don't know,' said Bailey stiffly. 'It was quite hard to hear because you kept dunking my head in a bucket of water.'

John Jr guffawed mightily. 'Right laugh, so it was.'

'Hello,' said Kelly. 'Now I don't want to bother you, but I wanted to talk to someone about this freckle.'

She pointed to something invisible perched on top of her cleavage.

'Getting someone to feel your knockers again?' roared John Jr. 'She's a right tart, my wife, eh?'

'I'm not a doctor,' said Bailey. 'I'm an engineering specialist.'

'Pff. That sounds boring,' said John Jr. 'Mind you, you always were a speccy get. Any money in it?'

There was a short silence as we waited for the penny to drop.

'Oh! You're stayin' here, are you? Well, well done, my son, well done. Looks like it wasn't a waste getting all those swot levels after all. Course, I went to the university of life . . . oy, *gar-SON*!'

Oh, no. Once John Jr got started on the university of life diatribe the evening was well and truly done for. And he didn't go to the university of life at all. He went to the university of misbehaving at school, causing teachers to have nervous breakdowns, then leaving at sixteen and hanging around amusement arcades before falling into second-hand car dealing and borrowing money off Dad to open his own garage, a loan I'm sure he's never paid back. John Jr went to the university of being a complete arse. And now he was hollering at the butler for drinks – we had to do something! And fast!

'Uh, Bailey,' I said meaningfully. 'We're going to be late for dinner. You remember. That *very* important dinner.'

Bailey was still trapped, looking like a rabbit hypnotised by a snake.

'Right. Dinner,' said John Jr. 'That sounds great.'

'It's a private dinner,' I said. 'There won't be any room for you.'

'Oh, we'll see about that,' said John Jr. 'Little lesson, Evie. Money can open a lot of doors. Come on, Kelly, get yourself dressed up.'

As Kelly was already wearing a bustier twinkling with Swarovski crystals, spray on black trousers and five-inch heels, and her hair resembled the crest of a tidal wave, I couldn't imagine exactly what he meant by 'get dressed up', but she instantly shuffled off.

'Right,' said John Jr. 'Where we going? Hope it's not too fucking Frog. They eat horse, you know. Did you know that? Filthy fuckers. Are we going to a horse restaurant? Hope not. *GarSON*. What does horse taste like?'

Defeated, as if taking part in some horrible zombie movie, we headed for the lift. I pressed the polished brass lift button; it pinged, the lift already there.

'Oh, fabulous, you're all ready,' said Lydia, stepping daintily out of the lift and taking Bailey by the arm as if he were her personal property. She was wearing a beautiful, understated, swinging navy and cream cotton-knit dress that I swear I've seen on Sarah Jessica Parker, with a dinky navy handbag to match. As soon as I saw it I knew that instead of buying half a dozen cheapy high-store outfits I should have saved up for something like that and just worn it every day.

'Dinner time? I'm totally ready to go.'

She lowered her voice by about half a decibel and pouted her mouth in the direction of Bailey's ear. 'Didn't realise we were taking the Addams family, though. Ah huh huh huh!'

# Chapter Five

I had had a fantasy of how my first night in the South of France would be. The evening light would be soft and sweet-smelling (that at least was true) as we strolled down to the Croisette, home to every film star of the last fifty years, including the porny ones.

Bailey would be handing me a cocktail as we stood on a balcony watching the sun go down; he'd tell me how much he'd loved me all these years and I, looking elegant and graceful and like something out of the twenties, would touch my elegant hand to the top of the balcony, accept the cocktail with sadness and say, in perfect French, 'I'm sorry, Bailey. I can never love you,' as my gaze lingered on the extraordinarily hunky doctor who was waving at me from the beach, where he was running, shirtless, with his black Labrador. A single crystal tear dropped from my eyes with the exquisite pain of *les affaires de la coeur* and . . .

'Steak fwites, that's what it's called,' John Jr was saying loudly, stomping out into the road without looking (the Ferrari swerved to avoid him, worse luck. Mind you, in a fight between John Jr and a small lightweight sports car, my money was on JJ). 'Oh, right, not to worry, we'll just find somewhere with pictures in the window. *Comprendez?*'

We were all marching in a long line across the Croisette, the street which ran parallel to the sea. It was covered in palm trees, and the hand- and footprints of European film stars were embedded in bronze in the concrete, just like in my fantasy. The place was absolutely mobbed with people, none of whom looked anything like as British as us. Bailey and Lydia were behind me, deep in conversation, Kelly was bringing up the rear in very high heels that made her look as if she was trying to perform a circus act by balancing on tiny knives.

'I was thinking maybe somewhere nice and traditional,' I said timidly, holding up my guidebook. 'Somewhere that . . . "*brings alive the freshness of the Mediterranean and the gentleness of the soft Côte d'Azure breezes, wrapped up in the tastes of the Provençal hills and grated with the zest of—*"'

'Steak fwites,' said John Jr.

And so it was that we found ourselves sitting outside a restaurant with plastic flowers on the table, surrounded by several other tables full of lost English people looking at the laminated plastic menus with pictures on them and trying to ignore their badly behaved children. John Jr thinks he likes the finer things in life but when it comes to his stomach he's pretty straightforward.

'Oi! *Garson!*' shouted John Jr. 'How many of us are there? Five? Right. Five bottles of white wine. Sweet.'

The waiter gave John Jr a look he absolutely deserved but one, sadly, he was incapable of noticing.

Bailey sidled in next to me. 'Em, I think we have to—'

'Kill him,' I whispered. 'I know. I thought maybe we could drop his body in the bay.'

Bailey's brow furrowed. 'Um. I was thinking, maybe try and lose him.'

'Oh,' I said, trying not to look too disappointed.

'Obviously, you know, death would have been a good option too.'

'It would,' I said. 'One down, two to go.'

'But really, I just meant . . . please don't think I want to hang out with your brother all week.'

I was shocked by the injustice of this. 'What do you mean? You think I do? I didn't invite him! You're the one that's all "Oh, great to see you John Jr, let's catch up," kiss kiss.'

'I was not,' said Bailey hotly. 'I didn't say anything.'

'Well, maybe you should have,' I said. 'I tried to save you with the whole "fake dinner" thing and you just stood there, wobbling.'

Bailey looked at me and suddenly I had a flashback to him aged eight. Nobody likes being reminded of how embarrassing their childhood was. Also, telling men they're cowards is hardly a guaranteed banker either. I saw he was really hurt, and I felt really bad.

'OK,' he said, and left the seat, heading to the other end of the table where Lydia had saved him a seat. Oh, good. I'd sent him into the arms of Cruella de Vil. I poured myself a very large glass of wine. This was going to be a long night.

'I said a hey-a ho-a wibble-a wobble and a hammy and a bullet to beat.'

Oh, God. Oh, God. How had everything gone so terribly wrong? It was several hours and many, many bottles of wine later. I'd reached that horrible point where I was too afraid to move, convinced that my legs no longer possessed the power to lift me. The wine had definitely seemed to improve the more of it I'd drank. I wondered if this was because it had had time to breathe. Or maybe because it had stripped the taste-buds from my mouth – I wasn't sure.

Bailey and Lydia were buried in conversation down the other end, which pissed me off big time. I didn't know why; normally when Bailey introduced me to some gorgeous girl I could hold off getting jealous for about ten minutes, waiting until she said something idiotic like, 'Isn't it amazing how every sheep born has its own baa? Do you know what I'd really love to do? Go on *Big Brother*,' and then I could relax again. But this was Lydia, whom he'd already seen being not very nice to me. And every time I tried to casually sidle up to their conversation Lydia shot me a look that very clearly said, 'You, go away,' in monkey language.

Meanwhile, Kelly was talking to me about face cream at the most extraordinary length. I was ready to knock myself out with the pepper grinder. Every time I thought Kelly was my ally in the war against John Jr, she'd start doing this; banging on about pentapeptides or fruit acid till I wanted to cry.

John Jr, who I'd been trying to ignore as he snurfed his way through what seemed like several bottles of nasty wine, had decided to get up, lift his polo shirt and expose his pork-red body (no wonder Kelly was always crying). Using the wine bottle as a microphone he started singing along to the piped music whilst the waiters appeared to be entering a superciliousness competition, leaning against the flapping canvas with their arms folded. Oh, God. This couldn't get any worse.

'Hello, Evie.'

There was a funny noise behind me, beyond the plastic covering, and it sounded like it was calling my name. Half nervous, half pleased to be temporarily distracted I slowly turned round.

Oh, God, of course it was. Of course. After all, who else did I know in the entire country?

'A hibby-hobey-hibb,' yelled John Jr, oblivious to Dr Maitland standing on the other side of the plastic, immaculately dressed in a pastel shirt and a pale linen suit which as usual was ludicrously old-fashioned, but somehow looked rather dashing here.

I smiled wanly. Both docs weren't due in till the morning; I was going to collect them from the airport, for goodness' sake. I thought it was a bit rude of Dr Maitland to turn up and witness my embarrassing family before I could safely get rid of them.

'Hello,' I said, jumping out of my chair and barrelling towards him in an attempt to distance myself from everyone behind me and thus render them not even acquaintances. John Jr had taken off his shirt entirely and was hurling it round his head as he came to the emotive finale of the song.

'So, you know everyone in Cannes already!' said Dr Maitland. 'Good networking skills.' Oh, God, please tell me he had another dinner to go on to. Please. I tried to keep him out of Kelly's sight line; she'd ask him to eat with us immediately.

I shrugged and tried to look nonchalant and businesslike and not at all tanked up on cheap wine.

'Was your flight OK? I'd have arranged transport.'

'Yes, I decided to come early. Little bit of groundwork. Big week ahead for us, don't you think?'

I agreed heartily.

'HE-llo,' came a voice. Oh, bugger. I'd only considered

the risk from my end of the table, but Lydia had spotted an opening.

'It's Dr Maitland, isn't it? Want to join us for a drink?'

'Hi.' Bailey waved hello.

'Well, er . . .' Dr Maitland looked at me enquiringly, which was nice of him. Suddenly, John Jr's glazed vision gained focus.

'Oi! Oo are you? You're not after our Evie, are you?'

Oh, Christ on a bike. How mortifying. Dr Maitland went a little pink, which was quite cute.

'No, no . . . we work together.'

'Yeah, didn't think so . . . you're definitely out of her league, ain't he, Eve?'

'Shut UP,' I said. I was used to crap like this from JJ, though, so it didn't harm me that much. But Dr Maitland's head snapped up.

'Excuse me?'

'Don't listen to him,' I said. 'It's just my . . . um, brother. He's a bit pissed.'

'Not as pissed as he'd have to be,' shouted John Jr jovially.

'Don't speak to her like that.'

I had to admit, I was quite impressed. Dr Maitland was tall, but John Jr weighed about three of him.

'Yeah, and oo are you?'

'JJ,' shouted Kelly. 'It's the *doctor*!'

Now I was even more embarrassed. Doctors, lawyers – any professionals – get automatic 'respect' in my family. A bit outdated, forelock-tugging, I'd always thought, but thank goodness, because it worked.

'Doctor?' said JJ, as Kelly pulled at him to sit down and handed him another full glass of wine, perhaps unwisely. All the tables in the restaurant were watching us extremely closely. Dr Maitland took off his glasses and started to rub them with a handkerchief. I bet he was glad he'd stopped by.

'I think I'll get on,' he said. I was burning up with mortification. He must have thought I was a real guttersnipe.

'OK,' I managed to stutter. 'Uh, see you tomorrow.'

'Uh, OK then,' he said.

'Lovely family,' Lydia had smirked, as she'd departed into the night – in the same direction as Bailey, I couldn't help but notice.

'He was just pissed,' I said stiffly. Kelly and John Jr had already departed, John Jr drunkenly insisting on splitting the bill exactly, which then took hours. I mean, I could slag JJ off, because he was mine, but nobody else could. Then I'd trudged the long way up the hill in the dark, conscious that I'd drunk too much, not had any fun and now had to get up at the crack of dawn to fetch bloody Dr Bennet from the airport.

Nice airport was cool and white in the early morning glare as I held up my printed sign. Obviously Dr Bennet knew who I was, but he thought this looked smarter.

I looked around at the women passing through the airport. Oh, they were good-looking all right. But in such a boring way (it seemed to me – of course I know men are relatively simple in their tastes for these things). Tiny bottoms, long legs, tits hoisted up to clavicle level, hair bleached to straw, huge sunglasses balanced on augmented cheekbones – it looked so relentlessly dull, so uniform. We got quite a lot of desperate divorcees at the surgery. Often, their husbands had left them for someone who looked absolutely identical to them but was twenty years younger. Why bother? I often wondered. If you kept trying to look the same way you would get gradually more grotesque, and if your tit perkiness was all your man was after, well, there would always be someone perkier.

Not a single woman looked remotely happy. I bought a croissant to eat at the little coffee bar outside Arrivals and could almost feel them sneering behind me as I tucked in to the refined carbs and sugar.

OK, so I was a midget with curly brown hair next to this lot. But hey! At least I was getting a yummy croissant for breakfast.

The gate started to flood with people – many of them men with that unmistakeable patina of plastic surgeon about them. Maybe I've become a bit of an expert. But their skin is always a little smoother than yours, as if they know about a secret bar of soap you're barred from, and their stubble is always non-existent, as if they've given themselves electrolysis instead of shaving. There was a clattering of different languages – it sounded like German and Dutch – and I got quite engrossed looking at the expensive luggage and loafers and silk ties and . . .

'Hello!' said a friendly voice. Shaken out of my reverie I turned around. There was a man standing in front of me. He had a cheerful face with freckles, and russety hair. He looked very young. I hoped he didn't want money for something.

'*Non, merci,*' I said loudly.

His face looked a little crestfallen at my obvious confusion.

'Uh, you're here for me?' he said. I was what? He looked a bit nervous. 'I know, I look a bit young to be a doctor, everyone says that, ha ha ha.'

I blinked.

'Oh, shit, are you French? I mean, *merde.* Eh, eh. *BON-JOUR. Je m'appelle doc-TEUR Bennet.*'

'I'm not French,' I said.

'Oh. OK.' There was a pause. 'Uh . . . are you *special*?'

'What do you *want*?' I said crossly.

'I'm Dr Bennet. Are you picking me up?'

Oh, for goodness' sake, how could I have been so dense?

'Sorry,' I said. 'Um. There's another Dr Bennet. It's not you.'

Freckle face looked puzzled. 'Oh. Right.'

'Are you here for the conference?'

'Yes,' he said. 'I'm a junior. I don't know why they sent me really. So that's why I thought you were picking me up. I'm not used to all this.'

'Me neither,' I said. 'It's my first time too.'

'As a driver?'

'No. I'm a medical receptionist.'

'Really? Where are the dragon claws and fire coming out of your mouth?'

'Ah, I'm private,' I said. 'If you pay money you get a smile and maybe even a cappuccino. Maybe.'

'Well, that does sound like it's worth thousands and thousands of pounds,' he said, his face looking slightly cross suddenly. 'I'm Tom Bennet.'

'Evie Kennedy,' I said. 'Hi.'

'Hi. I don't suppose you know where the bus stop is, do you?'

'I'd offer you a lift,' I said, 'but . . .'

Just then I saw my Dr Bennet and his wife emerge from Arrivals. As usual, he looked poised, and she looked furious. He'd mentioned looking forward to having a romantic time in Cannes. In my head, the idea of having a romantic time with Mrs Bennet seemed akin to trying to clamber on top of an unwieldy metal chair, but I nodded and smiled hello to her nonetheless. In response she sighed at me.

The effect on Tom was immediate; he got very nervous, glancing from the Bennets to me. I thought he was very embarrassed.

'Not to worry yourself,' Tom said. 'See you around. Is it a big place,' Cannes?'

'Not really.' I watched him go. Under other circumstances, bumping accidentally into a young doctor at Côte d'Azure airport might be construed as rather romantic. This one though had skin that looked like it might burn up in direct sunlight. How disappointing. Still, compared to everyone else I'd seen come off the plane, he was definitely number one.

The Bennets weren't chatty in the cab, which made me think that perhaps I shouldn't have bothered coming and instead kept the probably hundred extra euros it had cost to keep the driver handy in the car park, for all the thanks I got.

They seemed oblivious to the sun glancing off the waves, the girls rollerblading in bikinis on Nice promenade, the real French families unfolding picnic baskets containing golden, sticky-looking roast chickens and whole cheeses and baguettes. I don't know why I got a little thrill when I saw French people with baguettes. I suppose it would be like coming to London and seeing everyone dressed up as pearly kings and queens and saying lor, luv a duck.

When I'd checked the itinerary I'd drawn up earlier my heart had sank – they were in the same hotel as Bailey and my idiot brother. Oh, good, I was so glad everyone was in the very height of comfort and luxury whilst my bed smelled of someone else's deodorant.

'Do you want me to talk you through the schedule?' I said

when we drew up in front of the hotel. Once again the chap with the white gloves was out doing his stuff. I wondered if every so often some plutocrat just dropped him ten thousand euros for no reason.

'Yes,' nodded Dr Bennet. 'I've lost mine,' he added. That was strange. Dr Bennet never lost anything.

The beautiful boy on reception had given me even more of a curled lip today, as if I was some prostitute that followed men up to their bedrooms. Mind you, from what I'd heard that didn't exactly faze people who worked in posh hotels. Maybe he just thought I was a really cheap prostitute. Dr Maitland joined us in the lobby. I was embarrassed to see him again, but he looked even more so, so I didn't mention anything.

'OK,' I announced. 'The backers want to see you first, then there's the Ocean Consortium meeting – does that make sense to you?'

They nodded mutely.

'It's in the DeVere rooms, then the introductory session, then at five it's cocktails for everyone in the Belles Rives American bar, then dinner . . . my God, just as well you're not in surgery this week. You'll all be completely wombated.'

For the first time Dr Maitland looked like he might be about to smile. 'Not everyone,' he said, 'gets falling over drunk just because there's free drink available.'

'Why not?' I said. 'How can you help it?'

His eyebrows twitched. 'Well, you know your limits, so you're careful with top-ups.'

'But it's *free*,' I explained again, just in case he hadn't got it the first time.

'It's free,' he said, 'it's not compulsory.'

'Do you do any operating?' I asked. 'At this expo? I wondered if there might be . . . you know, like competitions.'

'Competitions,' said Dr Bennet gravely. The two doctors looked at each other. 'Like, races?'

Oh, God, I MUST read the brief.

Dr Maitland looked at me sternly over his spectacles. 'Evie Kennedy, is there anything else?'

'No, sir,' I said.

'Are you coming to the introduction?'

'Can I?' I nearly squeaked. There was a free bar! Not, of course, that I would be conducting myself with anything other than total decorum at all times.

'Well, you're taking notes, aren't you?'

Curses.

The first person I saw when I arrived at the venue – which was completely gorgeous, I could see why people liked this South of France malarkey so much – was Lydia.

There was the cheering sound of clinking glasses as I approached, trying to look as if I dropped in on these occasions all the time and was thus completely blasé about the whole thing even though I was the only woman in the entire place who wasn't wearing a rope of pearls big enough to drown you if you fell into the sea whilst you were wearing them.

I decided to take the sophisticated adult stance and give Lydia a Kennedy 'cool nod', as I tried to flounce past with my notebook.

'Hey, you.'

Well, it didn't work with my brothers either. They just gave me Chinese burns until I eventually let out some kind of sound.

'Uh-huh?' I said snootily. 'I'm very busy with my important conference.'

'Forget about that,' said Lydia. She looked me up and down. 'You look good,' she said.

I smelt a rat immediately. Lydia never thought I looked good. Lydia usually said things like, 'Don't you need tits to wear those wrapover tops?' and 'Platform soles? How hilarious,' about my new boots, and things like that.

'Uh-huh,' I said. 'How's your luxury B and B?'

'Oh, it's not all that,' said Lydia. 'All that freshly baked patisserie, it's havoc on the figure. *Why French Women Don't Get Fat*; by ignoring the white flour their country is drowning in, that's how.'

I just stood there.

'So,' Lydia leaned over conspiratorally, as we walked into the beautiful room, which overlooked a perfectly manicured garden. She swiped two glasses of champagne from a black-and-white-dressed waitress; I was quite impressed by how smoothly.

'We've been such great friends for *ever*, and I can't

believe you've never told me about your wonderful friend.'

'Kelly?' I said to be annoying. The champagne was delicious. 'Yeah, she's great.'

Lydia did this funny laugh thing. 'Darling,' she said. 'The fascinating Bailey.'

'Bailey isn't fascinating,' I said. 'He's a dork. Although I did think there was something up—'

'Yes?' said Lydia, her eyes lighting up.

'When he sat seven A levels. I thought he was just showing off.'

'Geniuses don't have to show off,' said Lydia knowingly.

'Short-arses do,' I said.

'So is he . . . you know?'

'Quite annoying?'

'Married? Gay? He is terribly fascinating.'

'Do you mean rich?' I asked suddenly, looking suspiciously at Lydia's necklace. Yup. Pearls. 'Because let me tell you one thing. He may be a bit of a know-it-all, but when it comes to women he's a bit of a divot, so if you dare mess him about, you'll have me to answer to.'

'Wooo,' said Lydia, her face changing. 'Ooh, sorry. I didn't realise. Do you want me to back off?'

'Didn't realise what?' I said, suddenly feeling slightly daft for my outburst. Maybe I'd gone in a bit strong.

'That you're, you know . . . in love with him.'

I felt my face go all hot suddenly, the way you do when

you're six stops from home and you remember you've forgotten your wallet. It all suddenly went quiet. I wasn't in love with Bailey. *Was I?*

Lydia gave me a meaningful look and backed away towards a large group of doctors, who all smiled at her and widened their circle to let her in. That would never happen to me. I was left completely alone in the middle of the room, my head in a whirl.

# Chapter Six

'Evie? You look like you are a whole world away. Are you dreaming of London, huh? How much you miss its rubbish-soaked streets and shouting young men in hoodies?'

I spun around. Dr Bennet was standing there, immaculate as ever, looking at me kindly.

'No, I . . .' I looked round for inspiration. 'I don't know anyone.'

Dr Bennet looked round. He obviously didn't want to introduce me to anyone himself; it was tantamount to him saying, 'Look everyone, here's the assistant I'm having an affair with,' and even if he dared to have an affair, which I very much doubted, I assumed he'd like people to think it would be with someone a bit more impressive than me.

'Don't you have some kind of secret international secretary's cabal?' he said. Well, I knew one witch, I thought.

I shrugged. 'I'm fine, Dr Bennet, honestly. I'm just ready to take my notes, that's all.'

As I said this my eye was irresistibly drawn to a bright red beacon that seemed to be glowing above the rest of the crowd. It rotated to face me and I realised I was looking at that other Dr Bennet bloke I'd met at the airport. His hair was glinting in the sunlight bouncing off the chandeliers. Our eyes met.

'Hello?' said the other Dr Bennet – Tom, that was his name. He said it tentatively, as if he was prepared for me to completely blank him. Maybe he still thought I had a learning disability.

'There we are,' said the original Dr Bennet, pleased. 'You young folk have a good time.' And he shot off towards the sleekest-looking doctor with the most expensive-looking loafers.

'Hi there,' I said. 'Having fun?'

'Not sure,' he said, looking around. 'I mean, it seems like I should be having fun, doesn't it? Champagne, sunset, lots of shop talk . . . but somehow it's just not coming together.'

'I know how you feel,' I said. 'But they seem to be getting very agitated over there.' I pointed to where a large group of Germans were gesticulating wildly. One did a particularly graphic arm movement, he appeared to be pulling on his vest underneath his shirt.

'What's he doing?' I asked.

'I don't know. Tummy tuck?'

'You really are a doctor,' I said, impressed.

'Hmm,' he said. 'Med student really.'

'Oh, yes? How come you get sent off to five star . . .' I waved my hand expansively, just as a waitress appeared with a tray of caviar things. I've only tried caviar once, at John Jr's wedding, and I'd absolutely hated it, but I didn't want to look unsophisticated in front of Tom, so I grabbed a canapé and stuffed it in my mouth. Yes, just as I thought – revolting. I took a huge slug of champagne to compensate, then choked a bit. I hate it when I do that.

'Are you all right?' said Tom, looking at my red face with concern. I was a bit miffed by that.

'It's OK, no medical assistance required,' I said, when I finally got my breath back. Tears had sprung to my eyes.

'I didn't think so,' he said. 'But, you know. If your lips had gone blue I'd have been right in there.'

'Glad to hear it,' I said. 'It would be very embarrassing to be saved from death, you know. *Too early.*'

He smiled.

'So what are you here for then?'

Tom looked slightly unsettled. 'Well, um. It came up in the department and nobody wanted to go, so they let me go.'

'Although you're only a student?'

'Well, yes. We don't normally get sent on things like this.'

'So they must think you're a scalpel whizz?'

'Mmm,' said Tom. He stuffed about nine canapés in his mouth and didn't choke on any of them. 'God, I'm starving. I don't speak any French and when I point at stuff in shops they just keep raising eyebrows at me and offering me Chanel handbags and things. Which serves me right, I suppose.'

'It does,' I said. 'What were you doing at school?'

' Physics . . . chemistry . . . biology, that kind of stuff.'

'Oh, yeah,' I said.

'Anyway, I deal with burns mostly. I'm not really interested in this end of things. What about you? Do you work for . . .' He nodded at Dr Bennet, who was laughing outrageously at a joke that couldn't possibly be that funny, bless him. He was the world's best schmoozer. Nobody had better introduce him to their clients. Dr Maitland was standing in the circle too, looking miserable. Honestly, if he didn't like the clients and he didn't like his colleagues and he couldn't fake either it was more of a mystery than ever why he was in this line of work in the first place. I waved to him tentatively, and he waved back in, I suppose, a way that didn't scream, 'Get away from me, you of the unbelievably tacky family.'

'Yes,' I said. 'And I know Bailey Arnold, who's giving the talk.'

And who, apparently, I might be in love with, I didn't add. Bailey wasn't here; I suppose they kept him hidden behind a curtain backstage until his time came to be revealed. I bet he pretended to be annoyed by all the fuss but secretly loved it.

I wondered if he still wanted to get off with me. Ten years was a long time. Too long?

Tom looked around. He didn't seem terribly interested. 'Oh. Right. So, you're like the best-connected person here.'

I laughed, which he immediately looked offended by, and I realised I sounded like I was saying, 'Ha ha, yes, if I was well connected do you think I'd be standing here talking to you?' which wasn't what I meant at all.

'I think we're going in,' I said. 'Shall we grab a couple more glasses just in case the speech is very boring?'

'That's not very flattering for your friend,' said Tom.

'He's my friend, that doesn't mean I have to understand *everything* he says,' I pointed out, lifting four glasses from a passing waiter with almost as much élan as Lydia had shown before.

On a stage that had been erected at the side of the room were several orange-backed chairs, as well as pitchers of water and little mikes. Worryingly, it all looked rather like we might be about to have a bit of a lecture.

'This doesn't feel like a holiday,' I grumbled to Tom as we found two seats near the back. I approved of his choice, much easier to snicker and pass notes unseen.

'You're on *holiday*?' he said, with some surprise.

'Not a very good one,' I said, as I picked up the information pack that had been left on our seats.

'You can say that again.'

'But still,' I mused, 'better than most.'

Tom looked as if he felt extremely sorry for me. I leafed through the pack that was given out to everyone. It was full of groovy drawings of palm trees and beaches, none of which made a lot of sense, and phrases like 'facing the future' and 'a brand-new paradigm', which didn't mean much to me either. I'd better concentrate on the speech.

I was about to ask Tom what it was all about when the lights dimmed dramatically and Dr Bennet, followed by Bailey, walked on the stage. My heart beat a little faster when I saw Bailey, standing there with his button-down collar and glasses, a large sheaf of paper clutched in his hands. Something to the side caught my eye. I glanced across, and Lydia was staring at me, arching an eyebrow in a meaningful manner. Immediately I felt myself flushing. She twitched in a 'I thought as much' kind of a way and turned back, looking satisfied. Damnit. And I'd missed Dr Bennet's intro.

Then a distinguished-looking man stood up and, in French, thanked everyone for coming, and then, thankfully, he switched to English and started talking about a great new opportunity for plastic surgery, blah blah blah. I slightly tuned out at this point, and found my thoughts, and my eyes, creeping towards Tom and wondering if he had red chest hair, and if he did, was that really, really disgusting? Or mildly interesting? After all, Damien Lewis had red hair, and he was gorgeous.

Then I looked at Bailey. He looked so sweet and vulnerable on stage, his glasses reflecting the spotlight as he sipped his water, looking hardly older than eight. I blinked a few times. I mean, I felt so much for him – and you were always hearing about people realising that in fact they were really in love with their best friends. I mean, look at Ross and Rachel, and Chandler and Monica. OK, they were fictional people, and I was never that convinced by Chandler and Monica anyway, but still . . . people said you should settle with someone whose company you really enjoyed . . . who you could spend a lot of time with, who never bored you, and all those things were true about Bailey. Plus, I suppose, he was really successful, and although I didn't like to think of myself as someone who cared much about stuff like that – mostly because I'd seen an awful lot of the girls who did, and I didn't think much of them – it was nice, nonetheless, and fun, to feel proud of him. Which I was, so much. I hadn't realised until I'd got here just how well he was doing.

I snapped out of my reverie, realising I'd missed the entire speech, as someone – something – marched on the stage. It was a woman (I was reasonably sure), about six foot tall, and she looked as close to a human Barbie as it was possible to look.

Her hair was huge – surely a wig – and blonde, back-combed miles into the air and flowing back over her broad shoulders, with which her tits were nearly level, narrowing to a waist the size of a pin, amply outlined by the skintight pink leopard-skin jacket she was wearing at least two sizes too small.

A pierced belly button was visible above a pelmet skirt that only just covered her hips – I think if we'd been sitting any lower we'd have seen something one wouldn't ordinarily wish to see – and she had the skinniest pair of mile-long stick legs I'd ever seen, ending in fuschia pink stilettos with needle-sharp heels. I looked at Tom and he made an extremely comical face at me.

The woman approached the lectern and picked up the mike.

'My name is Cindy Linklater,' she said. The voice was a shock. I looked around in case it was booming out from somewhere else. It was the voice of an old lady; an old lady who'd smoked a lot.

'And I am sixty-two years old.'

Amazingly, a huge round of applause broke out through-out the hall. But this women was scary! She was grotesque! She looked like a horrible Frankenstein-esque monster some-one had stuck together from Jordan's spare parts!

Holding the mike she marched down the steps from the stage and paraded up and down the aisles so we could all have a good look at her.

'And I'm widely believed to have had the most plastic surgery in the world,' she said. No kidding. On the back of the stage appeared a photograph of a normal, completely pleasant-looking woman with worried eyes and a nice smile, if slightly crooked teeth.

'That,' she said, in a sneering tone, 'was me.'

She was closer now. Close up, she appeared even more frightening. Her face was a pulled-back mask, weighed down with pots and pots of bright orange make-up. Her throat was so tight it looked like she'd have difficulty swallowing with it. I shrank back as she came past in case she invited me to come and take a look inside her gingerbread house.

'And I'm just showing the beginning of what we can do. Growing old is a choice.'

She said this with a curl of her huge synthetic lips and it was eerie to look at. I glanced at Bailey to see if he would say something along the lines of growing old not being a choice if you were born in Sierra Leone or something, like he normally would, but he was watching in silence. That didn't seem right.

'Which is why I'm going to be the perfect face for the opening of New Horizons. Tax free. Offshore. Completely private. And a place for new experimental technologies to begin. To keep us beautiful. For ever.'

All the doctors started to applaud. I looked around. What was this? It sounded like some evil James Bond master plan to take over the world. Why hadn't I read the brief? Were they going to create a race of crone-faced super-zombies? Would it be compulsory?

'So I'd now like to hand over to our elite team of creative construction engineers . . .'

Bailey stood up on the stage. The crone retreated. 'Must be time for her to eat another baby,' I whispered to Tom, who was scribbling stuff on a piece of paper, in true student style, and didn't reply.

'Stay beautiful!' croaked the crone, and opened her mouth widely in what I suppose her withered brain had once considered to be a smile. Her teeth were absurdly white and straight and looked like she kept them in a glass by her bed. 'For ever!' Then she tottered off.

Bailey came to the front of the stage and started talking about timescales, engineering difficulties, water tables and stuff I had no idea what he was talking about. I wish I'd listened to Dr Bennet's intro. Although, I couldn't have listened even if I had understood, I don't think. I was concentrating on him so hard, about seeing him in a different light. Not as nerdy little Bailey, complaining about everything again, or getting his head kicked in, but as a confident if quiet speaker talking about a large project, and clean lines, and vertical-suspended stabilisers and things. I risked a glance at Lydia again. She was watching, purportedly with rapt attention. Well, it was certainly food for thought.

The thing is, I don't want to care about what people do. That's the point of democracy and stuff, right? So when I see people like Cindy, I do think, well, it's her choice. But then when I talk to some of our clients – I mean, they're not all rich. Some save up for years, or take out loans. They're usually the more talkative ones. And it's always the same – their husbands have left them, or they never knew their dads, or they're lonely, or scared of something. And I always want to say that I see rich beautiful women all the time and they're miserable too – maybe even worse. And really, they'd probably be better off keeping their money and taking the kids to Euro Disney or something.

A couple of times – and he doesn't know I know this – Dr Maitland has talked people out of surgery. Maybe they don't need it, or patently can't afford it, or have wildly unrealistic ideas of what it's going to do to their lives. I don't know what he says to them, but they come out of his surgery sniffing hopeful tears, and head off, looking happier than a lot of our ladies.

Dr Bennet never turns anyone away, not even the skinny girls with the hollow eyes who come in asking about spot lipo.

After the speech was over, I glanced at my notes and realised I'd forgotten to take any at all. Oh, no, the docs would be expecting this written up shortly, and I'd been miles away.

'Can I borrow your notes?' I said to Tom as we got up to file over for drinks. He looked a bit uncomfortable.

'Didn't you take your own?' he said.

'Why, are yours covered in pictures of willies and things?'

I asked. 'And doodles of the AC/DC logo, and women's boobies?'

'No,' he said. 'It's just I promised I'd fax them back to my consultant.'

'Right,' I said. 'And the little fax pixies take the paper away and curl it up really small and you never see it again.'

He smiled. 'Let me fax it first. Then maybe you can have them. If you're good.'

'I'm always good!' I protested, following him towards the bar.

'Except at note-taking and paying attention when you're being paid for it?'

'That's a quibble,' I said.

Bailey was standing next to the bar, surrounded by intense-looking docs chatting to him. I caught his eye, and immediately felt weird.

'Good speech,' I said with my nicest smile. I felt nervous suddenly, my hands felt a little sweaty. I felt like I was talking to someone I didn't know at all.

He gave me a very characteristic Bailey grin though. 'Did you understand it all?'

'Yes!' I said indignantly.

'Even the stuff about sea vectors?'

He made his way over to me. I felt inwardly triumphant.

'You're creating a race of terrifying blonde zombies to take over the world from your secret, evil, underwater lair,' I said. 'What's hard to understand about that?'

Bailey's brow furrowed a bit. 'You weren't listening at all, were you?' he said.

'It's true, isn't it?'

'No! It's a creative project. It's very exciting.'

'Until all the evil starts.'

'It's a huge challenge. It's going to be amazing.'

'Well, whatever it is, I bet you'll kill a lot of fish.' I think my mind was on undersea villain's lairs.

Bailey looked a little uncomfortable at that, though, and sipped his drink deliberately. He liked to think of himself as a person with values, I knew that.

'I eat fish,' he said finally, just as Lydia dashed over and, with a completely uncharacteristic show of enthusiasm, started to gush madly about what a genius he was.

'That was amazing,' said Lydia. 'You know, I have a lot of project management in my background.'

'Really?' said Bailey to her. I must have let the surprise show on my face, because Lydia said, 'Oh, *sorry*,' in the most exaggeratedly concerned fashion. 'I forgot Evie wanted to get you *alone*.'

And she shot me a look and flounced off to where Dr Bennet was standing. He didn't seem to have quite the same problems making small talk with her as he did with me.

'What did she mean by that?' said Bailey, turning round to face me. His earnest grey eyes blinked, magnified behind his spectacles. We must be, I estimated, almost exactly the same height. I looked at him closely, stared him right in the eye.

My romantic history has been nothing to write home about, much like my holidays. I used to get horrible crushes on my brothers' friends, which they would always manage to find out about (which wasn't hard even for lard brains like them; I would just possibly conspire to be hanging around whenever Miles or Fraser or Mark or whoever it was that day was round kicking a football, playing Tekken or discussing how to pull the trampy-looking girl that worked at the local HMV), and then tease me absolutely mercilessly, including telling the boy, shouting his name in supposed fits of passion whenever I passed by and searching my bedroom for evidence of me writing my first name with said boy's surname.

They made such a good job of destroying my confidence it took a lot of reasonably comprehensive cider drinking and copping off with the easiest, grottiest boys in the neighbourhood (starter snogs I liked to think of them) to work my way up to an actual boyfriend, one who could cope with the reality that he would never ever get invited back to my house.

There was Greg, who already had a girlfriend, which, even though I knew this, didn't stop me making a complete fool of myself; Danny, who I went out with for three years, more for the novelty factor of having a real, live boyfriend rather than any huge love bond on either side; Bill, who was too old for me; and Jingo, of whom – well, I don't want to talk about Jingo. Let's never talk about Jingo. If I were to give advice, though, which I hate to do, it would be to try not to date men who live in trees. And are called Jingo.

Anyway. The older I got the more I was beginning to believe that the difference between the desperate, yearning way I'd felt about my crushes – those tall lanky boys with white grins and feet so big they looked like boats on the end of their legs – and the boys I'd actually ended up with, was a simple fact of life. And at the back of my mind I always liked to think, Well, there's Bailey. My mother would be delighted. And it would be nice to be with someone who liked me for a change, rather than someone who liked racing bicycles with a side order of me.

Even though it was ten years ago – a little more – that we'd had our clumsy attempt at a snog, I'd always considered that it meant he was there for me, and the amount of time we spent together was an indication of that.

And here he was, grown up, successful – so successful I was finding it hard to believe – standing, with a glass of champagne, in a beautiful room overlooking a stunning sunset on the Côte d'Azure. Right in front of me, all mine. Was it time to grasp the nettle?

'What?' he said, looking slightly amused and nervous all at once. I felt reckless, attractive in this room full of men, and suddenly decisive. People always said, didn't they, that you should end up with a friend, with someone you could talk to? That looks fade, but companionship is for ever, blah blah

blah? And we'd grown up together, Bailey and me. Maybe we were meant to be together.

'Uh, come out to the balcony with me. I want to look at the view,' I said. Bailey shrugged and acquiesced.

It took a long time, though, to cross the room. Everyone wanted to stop and ask Bailey something or congratulate him on the speech. My heart was beating fast – what was going to happen? What was I going to do? Should I say something? Just lean over and snog him? Should I take his glasses off first? Should I take my high heels off? My stomach was incredibly nervous. Did I have some gum in my bag? Oh, no. Well, I'd only been drinking champagne – and all that caviar, gah, yuk. I'd have to get rid of that. I did find a mint, and my hands were shaking so much I almost couldn't get it out of the wrapper.

Bailey was speaking to someone near the French doors – but he kept glancing at me to check where I was, so he obviously knew something was up. His face looked a little concerned. He must be wondering what was going on. I was slightly wondering myself. I took another gulp of champagne, which didn't mix well with the mint at all. But maybe tonight was meant to be . . .

I smiled at him in what I hoped was a slightly encouraging, come-hither manner (though it might have looked freaky, or a bit frightening), and stepped out onto the balcony alone. The sun was setting over the mild-looking blue sea, and everything looked tinted with roses in the soft, warm evening air that seemed to caress my skin like a shawl. The breeze smelled of flowers and lemons, with an undercurrent of car fumes on hot road, from the busy route behind the hotel, and out in the harbour, white and blue boats bobbed up and down; some huge, some just pottering about, one whisking a water-skier behind it, the wake a paper-cut of white in the blue. It was beautiful. I sipped my drink and sighed. This was more like it.

My attention was drawn to the beautifully tended garden that led towards the cliffs. It was laid out with per-fectly straight flowerbeds, and topiary lined the immaculate sheets of lawn – but there was somebody down there. No, two people. No, make that one person and one dog. Oh, goodness. It was Tom, and a red setter. Heaven knows where he'd found the dog, but the huge beautiful creature was bouncing about gloriously, its russet hair streaming in the breeze – and that was just Tom. They were having a wonderful time, running about on the perfect lawns, wrestling with a stick and rolling about together before leaping up to tear across the green.

I couldn't help but smile; Tom looked about nine years old. There was a gracious lack of self-consciousness to his movements that had been entirely lacking in the slightly nervous, studious demeanour I'd noticed when we'd talked. He looked graceful too, even lolloping around with a dog; his legs and arms were long and sporty-looking.

It felt like I watched him for a long time. It's very rarely, especially if you live in a city, that you get to study somebody. Everyone is nervous, everyone is so ready to believe you're a mugger or a terrorist; and there's never any space, you're never so far away from everyone that you're not conscious of being watched, of the proximity of millions and millions of other people all around, cramming into every nook and cranny. But here, despite the roomful of people behind me, there was space, and calm, and peace and quiet. So this was what money bought. The money I saw every day on Harley Street was pushy, trashy and flashy, desperate to get itself noticed, but I saw now that it could be tranquillity, and beauty. I felt very happy, for some reason, and no longer nervous at all.

At that moment, Tom turned round. I thought he was about to see me and nearly ducked behind the stone balustrade, but he was looking up behind me, further up into the hotel. He seemed to wave and then, suddenly, caught my eye. He looked surprised – so did I, I imagine. Then, after a split second, he grinned, showing white healthy-looking teeth, and I grinned back. He came bounding up to the balcony, the dog a little way behind. His head was level with my feet, so I crouched down.

'Is this your girlfriend?' I said, reaching to pet the dog. Why did I say that? What a terrible thing to say. At worst, I'd just accused him of bestiality, ugly-looking girlfriends at best.

'Second cousin,' he said, smiling at me. 'What are you doing out here?'

'I came to give you this,' I found myself saying, and passed over the glass of champagne I'd originally picked up for Bailey. What was the matter with me? I felt like some kind of wild tramp.

'Thank you,' he said, giving me a direct look. There was a tiny bead of sweat just visible at the top of his hairless chest. I suddenly wanted to lick it.

That wasn't right. I mean, I was just about to see my oldest friend, the person who'd been with me through thick and thin . . . I couldn't possibly be thinking about licking other people's chests. That was just ridiculous. I mean . . .

'What are you thinking about?' said Tom. 'You look like you're trying to do quadratic equations in your head.'

'Are those the extra-tricky ones?' I asked.

'I'm good at them though,' he said. I looked at him. He had the same jokey-looking smile on his face, but it was impossible to read what was in his eyes.

'Did you bring this dog all the way to France?' I asked.

'No.' He smiled, 'He's . . .uh. I don't know, I just met him in the garden.'

Tom rubbed the creature's head with a hard but tender stroke. The dog closed its eyes in pleasure. I suddenly found myself jealous of the dog.

No! This wasn't right! This wasn't right at all! I must just be carried away with the champagne, and the sunset, and the beautiful surroundings and the romance of it all. But sod romance. You should settle down with your best friend, everyone said it. Courteney Cox said it, lots of my romance novels said it, bloody Dr Miriam Stoppard said it. You should end up with your best friend. That was the way to build something enduring, something wonderful.

'What about,' said Tom, 'if you scramble up on top of the banister and I lift you down and we can play in the garden?'

I eyed up the slightly crumbling balustrade, considering it. Considering what it would feel like to have a pair of strong arms around me, his long body . . . oh, God, was I drunk again?

'Hi, there,' said Bailey, arriving on the balcony in a flurry of papers. 'Sorry I took so long. Now, what was it you wanted to talk about?'

# Chapter Seven

It wasn't Bailey's fault that he was caught at such an unfortunate angle. It wasn't his fault at all that I was crouched down by his feet – not a position he usually found me in. And it wasn't his fault that before I straightened up, I couldn't help noticing what he was wearing on his feet.

I never normally noticed what Bailey wore. He hadn't gone through a big teenage transformation, dying his hair one week and dressing entirely in black the other, like I had. In fact he'd pretty much gone from school uniform to tidy, button-down preppy-looking shirts without changing noticeably at all. He didn't wear a tie to work, which, for ages, I'd taken to mean that he was just a backroom boy but in fact, as I was discovering, just meant he was too big a cheese for anyone to have any say in what he wore at all. And dressing exactly the same your entire life has the huge advantage of never making you look any older.

Anyway, here I was, crouched on the stone floor of a balcony for the most ridiculous reason – i.e. I wanted to go play with another man, and his dog – when I noticed something. Bailey's shoes.

Well, I call them shoes. They were a bit more difficult to pin down than that. The sole was thick rubber, as, perhaps, in a climbing boot or snowboarding shoe. But the top was brown suede, like in a pair of Hush Puppies. But there were thick black laces like in – well, like I'd never seen. The entire effect was ghastly, a horrible mishmash that suggested someone trying to buy built-up shoes but who couldn't quite bring themselves to go the whole hog.

I glanced upwards. Bailey was glancing down at me, blinking through his thick glasses.

'What's going on? Did you find a glass slipper in the garden?'

'No,' I said, scrabbling up. I could feel my face go red hot. And I sensed Tom watching us closely from down below.

'Well, what is it then?'

He looked at me intensely. I stared at his shoes. Was it likely, really, that I was in love with someone who was just a friend? That I could make myself in love with someone that I really just liked, just because I was lonely?

Or was I just getting desperate and going for anything with a pulse, because people said we'd be 'good together'?

'I've forgotten,' I mumbled. 'I think I just wanted to say well done.'

'Out here?' He frowned. 'I should probably get back in. I don't like unprotected UV rays on my scalp.'

'No,' I said. 'You wouldn't.'

He turned to go then paused for just a moment and looked back at me. I didn't quite know what to make of that look. Had he guessed? Did he know? Was he really still into me after all these years (as I liked to think)?

He stopped. 'Are you having a good time?' he said.

'I . . . I think so,' I replied, finding my voice had gone a bit strange.

'Good,' he said. 'Well, I suppose I'm going to head on out to dinner with Lydia . . .'

Lydia! Oh for Christ's sake. OK, maybe I didn't want to snog – at this particular moment in time – someone who wore schizophrenic shoes, but the last thing I wanted was that evil princess getting her mitts on him.

'Oh, yeah,' I said. 'I'll call you . . . to catch up.'

This was a complete lie, I had no intention of calling anyone out here. I'd got the cheapest price plan at the available time, which meant to call overseas was effectively the same cost as the interplanetary conversation in the old hit song 'Clouds Across the Moon', when she can only afford to call her boyfriend for three minutes once a year.

Bailey nodded, turned round and headed back into the

room, where I could already see groups of people opening up to welcome him in.

Turning back I realised that, stupidly, by turning down dinner with Bailey and the rest I'd made it look completely like I was up for, well, something else. If I'd been doing what the books tell you, I should have immediately left with Bailey – arm in arm probably – thus rendering Tom mad with jealousy and willing to lay jewels at my feet until I capitulated etc. etc. (By the way, has anyone ever met any of these guys? Where are they? The ones I meet all just tend to be . . . well, drunk, I suppose, now I think about.) On the other hand, if I wanted to be with Bailey, I suppose I'd just done exactly the right thing. It was very confusing.

Sure enough, as I turned round I swear I could see a bit of a smirk in Tom's eyes. Bugger it! But then if I pretended I had other plans now he might believe me and I'd be all on my own without dinner with *anyone*, which really *would* be disappointing, and the waste of a beautiful evening, on my holiday.

'So . . .' said Tom casually, still rubbing the dog. God, I don't think I'd found a redhead so attractive since David Caruso. And the sunlight made his hair more gold than red anyway, I told myself. Disliking redheads was a ridiculous prejudice, like making preferences on the colour of skin and totally not based on fact at all. *And* I liked his freckles too.

I realised I was drooling a bit when he added, 'Do you have plans for the evening?'

'Well, I thought I might have a quiet night in, you know . . .'

I thought of what a quiet night in would be like in my tomb-like hotel room with no air conditioning and the tiny window completely covered to keep out the noise. Like being buried alive in a coffin, I supposed. Well, think positive.

Tom raised his eyebrows. 'Oh, that's a shame,' he said. 'Because I still have to walk this dog, and I wondered if you'd like to join me.'

I tried to look calm and collected.

'Well, I suppose it's on the way back,' I said. (Coolly, I thought.)

Tom looked confused. 'Actually, walks can go pretty much either way. Are you along the beach?'

'Well, kind of in a beach-hill type of direction, I suppose,' I muttered.

'Good idea,' said Tom. 'Come on.'

And we walked through the most lovely rose garden, which led down a secret flight of stone steps to a wrought-iron gate that opened directly out onto the sand. The dog bounced on joyously ahead.

'Seriously, whose dog is it?' I said, taking off my shoes as we hit the sand. 'We're not going to get done for dogknapping, are we?'

'No,' said Tom. 'I just ran into someone I knew and offered to borrow their dog. He's called Cachou.'

'I thought you didn't know anyone here,' I said. 'I thought that's why you had to follow me about.'

'I have to follow *you* about,' said Tom, 'otherwise you won't have a clue what's going on.'

'Yeah, yeah, yeah,' I said.

The cool water felt absolutely delicious on my bare feet and I stood in the lilac-coloured waves enjoying the calm in the air.

'Ta dah!' said Tom, as if out of nowhere producing a clearly pinched bottle of champagne from behind his back, and we swigged from it happily as we wandered up the beach that ran alongside the Croisette, looking at the fancy cars and hotels which seemed a long way away from the quiet peace of the water's edge. It was so easy to talk to Tom, he was so likeable and funny. For the first time since I'd got to France I felt unstressed and properly relaxed, like I was having a real holiday. Cachou bounded joyfully around as we tossed him the occasional stick, and sometimes our hands brushed together, but neither of us pulled away. I was trying to catch sight of Tom out of the corner of my eye as he told me a very funny story about old ladies falling over in Norwich (it was funnier than it sounds). Deep in my stomach, I couldn't quite believe it. Come to France, meet a handsome (if ginger, nothing wrong with that) young doctor, have romantic strolls along the beach . . . coupled with all the champagne I felt entirely light-headed; daring and dramatic and not my normal moany self at all.

I mean, things like this just didn't usually happen to me. But why shouldn't they? Why should Paris Hilton get every bloody bit of romance on earth? How come Girls Aloud got all the lush blokes? Statistically, it had to happen to someone, didn't it? So why shouldn't it happen to me?

'You're miles away,' said Tom, and I realised he was looking at me. My hair whipped around my face – it felt heavy, and not too frizzy. Salt water was actually quite good for my hair, it made it look thicker. The champagne and the evening air made me feel heady and free. I looked at him.

'I'm not, actually,' I said, quite boldly for me. 'I'm right here.'

And, as we turned back to walking up the beach again, he tentatively took my hand, and I let him. I hoped my hand didn't feel clammy – his felt big and warm and reassuring. Oooh! Ooh! Holiday romance alert!

We were reaching the end of the beach, or rather, a big piece of land was in the way of the next beach. The beaches just go on and on and on, all the way to Spain and Italy. Cachou was having a splash around in the water. Since Tom had taken my hand conversation had slowed and now it stopped completely. He led me gently towards an overhang of rock, looking at me questioningly to make sure I knew what he meant. I looked back at him, making it clear that I did.

I love the moment before the first time you kiss someone, but after you know you're going to. It feels like everything slows down as you come into the orbit of someone else's body; it's like there are sparks that jump from your skin to his as you get closer and closer together. And it was like that with Tom. A delicious sense of anticipation followed by his putting his big hand on my face, which I liked very much. Then he leant closer and closer and I tipped my head up towards him and we kissed. And somehow I'd already known that he'd be a good kisser. As I gave myself up to him completely, I knew that this was the best holiday I'd ever had.

Minutes, hours later – it must have been hours, it was dark and there was even a chill in the air – we reluctantly pulled apart. Cachou had started to howl piteously and it was really getting late. The bottle of champagne was empty, but I was more drunk on lust; Tom's eyes were glazed too, and we clung to one another a little desperately.

'I have to go,' I said. Frankly that was the last thing I felt like doing, but lusty as I felt, I didn't want to go too far on our first date . . . oh, all right. Honestly, I just didn't want to get sand in my pants. I really liked this man, and I wanted it to be special and, frankly, the risk of having a jellyfish sting me on the bum made me feel it would be anything but.

'Really?' said Tom, looking wickedly at me.

'Really,' I said, trying to look like I was a modest picture of chastity, rather than someone frightened of getting bitten by a crab in a sensitive area. 'We could . . .'

I trailed off, hoping he'd immediately say, 'Hey, let's take the day off together tomorrow and run through the sand and eat ice cream and do all sorts of things that if you saw them in a film would make a bit of a montage,' but he didn't. He said, 'Well, *you* may not have to go to lots of boring lectures tomorrow, but I do.'

'Oh, who'd know?' I said. 'Just write down, "*Tighten skin with Sellotape*" and send it in. That's all they'll be saying anyway. "Chop into skin with great big knife."'

'They're doing a seminar on vaginal modification,' said Tom musingly, caressing my back.

'Anyone who lets a scalpel anywhere near there needs therapy, not bloody plastic surgery,' I grumbled, and suddenly, the moment was gone. Amazing how just one little mention of designer vaginas was enough to ruin the mood. Tom twitched his eyebrows.

'Well . . .' I said.

'We should get back,' he said. And I felt low. But then he added, 'Or maybe . . .' and pulled me back into his arms. Just a little while longer.

# Chapter Eight

I opened my eyes, feeling a burst of unaccustomed happiness. What was it again? Oh, yes! I was on holiday in France with a gorgeous, if slightly freckly bloke after me! Joy, joy, joy! I bounced up. It was going to be a perfect day on the Côte d'Azure. I figured I'd go out for breakfast – I had some time off! There was some assessment thing, but I was free to go and finish up reading the briefing (or, in my case, start) and make sure everything was ready for the party tonight – which I'd already done! Well, I'd phoned the number of the party organisers, and they'd said, '*Oui*, madame, everything is ready,' so you couldn't do much more than that, could you?

The sky was clear with a few perky-looking clouds bouncing around in the ether, but it was early enough that there was still a cool breeze flowing through the streets as I bounced down in my new espadrilles, heading for the shore. The restaurants were sloshing out and getting ready for the day, and the little shops were busy.

Now this is how life should be, I thought, looking at the bustling street market as I approached the beach, clutching gigantic almond croissants in my hands. I had *meant* to go in and ask for '*un croissant aux amandes, s'il vous plait,*' and had been practising it under my breath until I actually got to the boulangerie. There was a huge queue and everyone was yelling and chatting at a ridiculous speed, all at once, and I lost my place in the queue about nine times and by the time I got to the front I was so flustered and nervous I just stabbed my finger in the direction of the biggest ones they had and grunted, like I was a helper monkey that had been trained to do the shopping. Still, I'd accidentally bought two.

I decided to forgo the umbrella option when I found out that to hire one for the day would cost fifteen euros, which, frankly, was my wine money. So I found a nice spot down by the water's edge, where the sand was deliciously cool, and took a sunbed. I dabbled my hand in the water as it lapped around my toes and let my mind drift to seeing Tom at the party tonight. I'd wear my new red dress – or would it clash with his hair? No, it would be fine. The dress was THAT good. So, I'd walk on to the yacht, and . . .

\*

AARGH! Oh, God! Where was I? What time was it? Why couldn't I move? I felt pinned to the sunbed. Trying to move was agony. Checking my watch – which, I noticed, had an ominously white patch of skin underneath it – I saw it was afternoon. Oh, God, I'd fallen asleep on the beach! In the middle of the day! The sea had receded and I was stranded, spreadeagled on the sunbed in full view. Gingerly I tried to raise myself up. Ow ow ow ow. This was *not* in the holiday plan.

I trudged painfully up the beach. It had taken ten minutes to stand up. My back was on fire. So much for my morning off. The strap of my beach bag was agony across my shoulders, and I'd have to find a shop to buy some aftersun. I didn't know what that was in French. *Après soleil?* That would surely be too obvious. It was probably called something like *Oui, c'est moi, le complet idiot.* I sighed and traipsed on, feeling entirely sorry for myself, and a little sick.

Picking its way gingerly down the promenade steps was a bizarre-looking figure, even for here. I'd already been amazed by the women on the beach. I'd always thought that beachwear meant a bikini or swimsuit, flip-flops and a sarong for chubby moments. And I'd assumed that those articles in magazines that told you which jewellery to wear with which bikini and how to take your beach look into your evening look were just made up bollocks to sell suncream (and which therefore, in retrospect, I ought to have paid attention to).

But no, here, for the first time in my life I was witnessing women – gorgeous, tanned, young women, or scrawny, liver-spotted older women – actually wearing high heels. On the sand. High heels, on the sand. Really, it should be an Olympic sport, or a circus act. 'Come watch the amazing ladies – who can walk in stilettos *on the sand*!'

Not only this but they were indeed bedecked in jewellery – and not just any jewellery, or a couple of beaded necklaces picked up from the local market. Oh, no. This was full diamond earrings, gold necklaces and bracelets (the gold, I noticed, had the unfortunate effect of making old brown skin look even older than it was; the smooth surface of the precious metal only pointing out the crêpe-paper effect of the skin beside it.

And it didn't stop there. There were turbans, with jewels in the middle of them, like a maharajah, or Elizabeth Taylor in the seventies. There were ankle bracelets and toe rings. There were bikinis made of gold, or sequins, or what looked like two pieces of cheese wire. Having always thought of the beach as a place to relax, I now realised how wrong I had been. These women couldn't lie down or get wet. It was very very strange.

And the woman in front of me – unless I was becoming delirious, not entirely out of the question – was the strangest of all. Her hair was sprayed into a huge puff at the front which gave it the texture of candyfloss. She was wearing full make-up, including bright blue eyeshadow and pale pink lipstick, even though it was incredibly hot. Her bikini was entirely studded with what looked like Swarovski crystals, which glistened and caught the sun. The top half was simply two triangles which actually perched on top of the pointy breasts rather than supported them – the breasts were so solid they didn't look in the slightest need of support. And the bottoms were so narrowly cut you could tell exactly what explicit instructions she'd had to give her waxer.

'EVIE!' shouted the vision. Oh, God, now I really was hallucinating. Where were five hundred doctors when I needed them?

The figure tottered over on the ridiculously high shoes, and lifted up the humongous pair of sunglasses it was wearing.

'It's me! Kelly!'

Christ on a bike, so it was.

'I was just going to the beach!' she squealed.

'What – while dressed for church?'

Kelly lifted up her huge sunglasses (with some effort) and peered at me. 'Oh, ma Gawd, Evie, what happened to you?'

'What, this? Oh, nothing,' I said. 'I got attacked by a bear.'

'Getting too much sun on the first day is *very dangerous*,' she scolded. 'You should have been going to three sunbeds a week, like I do.'

'Well, I'm done now,' I said.

'Your back's done,' said Kelly.

'Thanks.'

She examined me closely. 'You know, I think that's going to come up nicely brown.'

'I've got second-degree burns, Kell. I'm on my way to hospital.'

'Yes, but it'll be worth it now, won't it?'

'No, it won't. I'm a div. Where's JJ?'

'John Jr . . . he said he had some business to do.' She looked a bit embarrassed. 'He was a bit . . . OTT last night.'

'I'm used to it.' I thought back, wincing at the memory, as well as my back.

'In front of that nice doc too. He was a bit of a hunk.'

'Dr Maitland? You are joking. He wears three-piece suits.'

She raised her eyebrows. 'Oh, Evie, you have to introduce me to your docs. I have to do something about these wrinkles.'

'You're saying this as you prepare to baste yourself in cooking oil and lie in the sun?'

'You're one to talk,' she said. 'I know. You've got to struggle to be beautiful.'

I laughed. It really wasn't Kelly's fault she'd promised herself to John Jr 'for fatter, for thinner'.

'OK,' I said. 'There's a yacht party tonight. Wall to wall docs. Fancy it?'

Her eyes went wide. 'Yeah!'

I gave her the details. 'OK. I'm just off to call an ambulance.'

'And I'm off to self-baste like a chicken. Mwah!'

*

I paused only to stumble into a pharmacy, where I simply showed them my back and got exceedingly worried at the look of terrified shock on the sales assistant's face (*Mon dieu!*). They piled me up with creams and ointments that took a ridiculously large chunk out of my holiday budget, but by now I was feeling a bit shaky so I just nodded. They offered me some pills too but I'd heard that in France you had to take all pills up the arse, so I shook my head.

At least my hotel room was dark. Very dark, in fact, and stuffy too, but I didn't care about that right now. I examined myself in the bathroom mirror. There wasn't even a proper bath there, just one of those crappy half-baths.

Oh, God. I looked . . . well, I looked like two halves of a person stuck together. My face was half milk-white, with a few unavoidable freckles popping up here and there, and half bright red. Plus some really obvious 'I was snogging for four hours down the beach on holiday' stubble rash all over my face and chin. From the back I looked like I'd been tied to a mast of a pirate ship and whipped solidly for six hours. I groaned, running my wrists under the cold water. I felt kind of fine just as long as no portion of my back touched anything.

My arms felt like big plump sausages that needed pricking, to let all the juice ooze out – wow, that was disgusting. For a second I thought I was going to be sick. Then I fell onto the bed face first and, thankfully, into a deep sleep.

*

If there's anything worse than waking up in the middle of the day when you don't know what time it is, sticky, sore and headachey in a hot airless little room, I don't know what it is. How could I have gone from cheerful to cross in such a short time? I felt sweaty and horrible.

I found my pharmacy bag, which I'd forgotten about, and took it in the shower, which made me feel a bit more human and a bit less like a dirty, old, stuffed toy full of gunk. In fact, I had just groaned – perhaps a little too graphically – when, after the briefest of knocks, the door was pushed open and Lydia stormed in. Why did I give her the address?

'Oh, *sorry*,' she announced, in a way that clearly meant she wasn't sorry in the slightest. 'I didn't realise you were . . .uh, busy. Oh, my God, look at you.'

I'd turned round to put on some clothes and of course she'd caught sight of me.

'Your neck . . . your back . . . it's *everywhere*.'

She sounded absolutely delighted.

'Yes, I know,' I said. 'Good, isn't it?'

'Is that what you think?' her voice took on a very fake concerned tone. 'But, Evie, you know, burning your skin can lead to all sorts of unpleasant consequences.'

'Oh, it's not burnt,' I said. 'It just goes that colour.' I finished putting my bra on, with difficulty. 'Doesn't hurt a bit.'

When she saw I plainly wasn't going to get in to it with her, she changed her tack.

'Well, anyway, I just came over to see where you've been all day. The reception is in twenty minutes.'

I couldn't believe I'd slept the entire day. No wonder I felt groggy and thick in the head.

'Oh, *God*,' I wailed. 'But I've got a date! Shit! Shit!'

Lydia's face took on a look of consternation. As it did so I realised a little something about our relationship – normally, I would go round to her office, complain about my shitty life and she'd smile superciliously and let me yabber on. I'd thought this was because she was nice and a good listener. In fact, I now realised, my moaning made her feel superior about herself. It did neither of us any good. She could sit and polish her nails whilst listening to a stream of consciousness from me that reassured her that although she was only working in reception and not yet the wife of a billionaire, she was nonetheless still winning in some hypothetical life competition. Meanwhile I just got whingier and whingier. Ugh.

'*You?*' she said now. 'Who with? Did you hook up with a waiter? You want to watch the waiters round here, Evie. They're infamous for loving and leaving . . .'

'With one of the doctors, actually,' I said. I hadn't really meant to say anything about it at all – for once, I was going to be a quietly dignified person who was reticent about her private life, damnit! – but I couldn't help myself. Anything to get that smug look off her face. 'The young one, you know.'

'The ginger?' she said, but I could tell I'd got to her. Tom was by far the youngest and best-looking doc there. Well, Dr Bennet was probably better looking, and Dr Maitland wasn't as old as he looked, but apart from that there wasn't much in it; most of the docs were over forty and either looked like stereotypical doctors on television – white hair, little round glasses, concerned expressions (trade secret: they do it on purpose to look reassuring) – or like they were using too much of their own product.

'Mmm,' I sniffed. 'Strawberry blonde, actually.'

'Ever heard you shouldn't crap on your own doorstep?' Lydia asked sweetly. 'It's so unprofessional.'

Well, that was rich coming from a woman who had already registered the website www.huntandtrapyourdoctorhusband.com.

'Aren't you supposed to be working?' Lydia asked suspiciously.

'Yes, well . . . Dr Maitland decided I should be in more of an advisory capacity after the whole profiterole incident.'

I turned to my suitcase. What the hell was I going to wear that wasn't going to cause me terrible agony? My lovely red dress would just make me look like a burns victim. Alas, I ended up in a black vest to go with my pretty, if outdated, orange skirt. The orange was about the same hue as my skin, and the vest felt painful already, but what else could I do?

I looked at myself properly in the mirror. Oh, God. Oh, God. Oh, God. I was a monster from the black lagoon.

'So Dr McCarrots loves the way you tan, does he?' said Lydia sweetly. 'Wow, you two sound really compatible.'

I must have been sleeping on the lounger with the right side of my face down, because the left side was completely red and the right completely white. I looked like Janus. The effect was startling; there was practically a line down the middle of my nose.

'Oh, Christ, I can't go,' I said, not even caring that Lydia was there. 'I'm not going. I'll stay in and play hard to get.'

'But you can't,' said Lydia. 'It's the yacht, remember?'

Oh, God. I couldn't miss it. And I had to tell my mum I'd been on a yacht.

'They can do it without me,' I moaned. 'Say I'm sick.'

Lydia sniffed. 'But what about your sister?' she said suddenly. 'I saw her at the beach. You couldn't miss her.'

'She's not my sister,' I said.

'She was really looking forward to meeting up tonight. Seemed really excited.'

She glanced out of the tiny window.

'And you don't want to play *too* hard to get. After all, the conference is only on another two days, and there's lots of models round here. Although of course I know what a great advocate you are of inner beauty. I'm sure thingy – whatever his name is – will see yours.'

Her mouth twitched.

'OK, OK, OK. All right, let's get this over with,' I said, and we headed for the door.

*

The lights of the harbour gleamed, bobbing up and down on the scented airy breeze, which felt good on my overheated body. Maybe with a couple of cocktails I'd feel all right. We passed by the little boats, the fishing boats and pleasure cruisers, which had names like *The Office* (ha ha! I'm just at 'the office' etc.) and *The Other Woman*. I reckoned they were owned by idiot accountants from Surrey – or the foreign equivalent – with more money than sense who frankly didn't deserve them.

Then we went past the slightly larger yachts, with tables and chairs placed out on the rear deck, and vases of flowers stuck on top of them. Slightly stiff middle-aged couples sat there, drinking gin and tonics and looking awkward, even though they were obviously there to be looked at by the promenaders strolling up and down having a sticky beak before their evening meal.

'They should wave,' I said. 'Like the queen.'

'They're all too drunk,' said Lydia in a haughty voice. 'If they stood up to wave they'd fall in the sea.'

'Know lots of yachting types, do you?' I asked her. I was horribly nervous. I hadn't heard from Tom all day, and he had my number. I mean, he could at least have texted me or something . . . maybe he'd woken up this morning and thought it had all been a terrible mistake? And let's face it, I was hardly going to change his mind looking like this now, was I?

'A few,' said Lydia, looking contemptuously at a boat emblazoned with gold curlicues everywhere and entitled *Paradise IV*.

'Well, you do get around a bit, don't you?' I said, betraying my nerves.

We passed on by the medium-sized boats and came up to a gated area manned by a man wearing very smart shiny boots and a cap. I felt a bit nervous; there wasn't anyone else around and it didn't entirely look like we were meant to be there. Lydia, however, flounced up to the bouncer and rattled something out in loud French. I was impressed despite myself.

'I do not understand you,' said the guard. 'Speek more slowly, pliz.'

Excellent! Looking furious Lydia held out her card.

'Invitation,' she hissed. 'Party. *Comprendez?*'

'Of course, madame,' said the guard, raising the barrier with a slightly supercilious smile.

Now we were in a completely different world.

'It's called the *Quai des Milliardaires*,' said Lydia, obviously anxious to maintain her French superiority. 'That means . . .'

'Millionaire's Quay?' I said.

'No, actually,' said Lydia, delighted. '"Milliardaire" actually means "billionaire".'

But I couldn't listen. I could hardly speak; I was just gazing at the sights before me. The yachts here . . . well, they weren't like boats at all. They looked, to me, like huge shimmering palaces. Strung with lights and gleaming; their hulls, white and blue, shone like they'd been polished with toothbrushes, which they probably had been. I could see helicopters sitting on top of the boats; huge salons stretching onto goodness knows where; what looked like jacuzzis on huge decks.

What must it be like, I wondered, to have one of these. One of these great, huge, luxurious toys to play with. What would you do? I supposed you would just pay someone to take it anywhere in the world you wanted to go. Or you could just go out into the middle of the sea, and stop, and dive into the clear water with no one around you for miles and miles and miles.

You could have parties and invite hundreds of friends. Mind you, I didn't have hundreds of friends. Maybe if you were rich enough to have a yacht you automatically got loads of friends thrown in as a job lot. It would have to work like that, because presumably to earn enough money to buy one of these things you wouldn't have time to make your own.

'Wow,' I said. 'I can't believe we're going on one of these.'

'Oh, they're all pretty much the same,' said Lydia, trying to look blasé. Oh, for goodness' sake. I know she desperately wanted to pass herself off as good rich-man fodder and everything but this was ridiculous.

'So you're a yacht-hopper, are you?' I said, using a term I'd picked up from *Hello!* magazine. 'You've been on loads of boats as big as this?' I indicated the boat in front of us, which was four storeys high and looked more like a luxury hotel than anything actually built for the high seas.

Lydia shrugged. 'I've been on boats.'

'Boats. Big boats. Just as big as this one?'

'Well, not quite *that* one.'

I pointed to another, slightly smaller sleek-looking white craft. 'OK, as big as that one then?'

'I wasn't measuring.'

'Come off it,' I said. 'You've never been on a yacht, have you? Your dad's fishing trip to the Isle of Wight? The car ferry? Have you been on a booze cruise? Did you get two hundred Regal King Size and stock up on bottles of Malibu?'

'Stop it,' said Lydia.

'Did you roll on, roll off?' I said.

Lydia stuck her nose in the air and tried to walk in front of me like she wasn't with me at all. But I was perking up.

She pulled up, finally, in front of one of the largest boats in the marina. It was a ship, really, and towered over us, level after level. It was lit up entirely with tiny lights illuminating its lines, with a huge ornate staircase at the back. People were everywhere and we could hear the tinkling of glasses and polite chit-chat in the air. I felt excited and nervous all at once; I'd never been anywhere like this before (though I'd seen *Titanic* a few times). It was so glamorous and elegant and . . . I swallowed hard. Well, they'd just have to deal with me too. I could be glamorous and elegant. When half my face wasn't hanging off, obviously. But I could manage it. I was going to shimmy onto this boat and wave to Tom like I came to parties on yachts every day of my life. We were going to drink champagne and dance the night away. I saw us, dreamily, in each other's arms as he whisked me about to romantic orchestral music. Of course, in my mind's eye I was wearing a big *Strictly Come Dancing* dress and could actually dance – as could he – but it perked me up nonetheless. I felt slightly better when I saw the name of the boat was *Let's Have a Party*. Something that naff couldn't be that scary, surely?

Lydia looked like she was making her mind up about something too.

'OK,' she said, looking around at me. With the lights reflected off the water behind us she looked wonderful: enchanting and mysterious. I'm about as mysterious as a chicken pie but hopefully the romance of the evening would do something for all of us.

'Let's go,' she said. 'That's a billionaire's yacht full of doctors and free champagne. Frankly, if we can't pull in that we don't deserve the title "doctor's receptionist".'

And she stalked off towards the gangplank.

After removing our shoes (de rigueur apparently) and flashing our invites at a young, terrifyingly hearty-looking young man in a pure white uniform, we scampered aboard. The deck was thronged with people, and waitresses carrying canapés and champagne were circulating amongst the crowd. I relaxed: obviously they'd been fine sorting things out without me. You'd think these folk having spent all their time together would be short of things to talk about, but no. I looked out for Bailey, which was quite difficult amongst the tall women and loud men. The noise levels were increasing. I noticed there was a band; a jazz band with men playing clarinets and trombones, and wearing interestingly patterned ties. Nobody was dancing yet, though, and it made things very cramped and incredibly noisy. Heavy perfume fell on the air and without my high heels on I felt squat and invisible, especially next to all the glamorous women in their peacock dresses; turquoise, green and yellow, shimmering over taut, nut-brown bodies.

'Hello!' came a familiar voice at my elbow. Then, as I turned round to greet him, 'Christ on a bike, what happened to you?'

Suddenly, I noticed lots of people looking at me and making murmuring remarks to one another. There was almost a gap in the crowd opening up for us. I felt extremely red and hot all of a sudden.

'Nothing,' I replied sulkily.

'Did you fall asleep in the sun?' asked Bailey, with his PhD in stating the bloody obvious. 'Don't you realise it's dangerous?'

'Really?' I said. I guessed I was going to have to answer these kinds of questions all night. I'd hoped the soft lighting and heavy make-up would have covered me up sufficiently, but obviously not. 'I had no idea. You'd think they'd give out some kind of warning about a fiery ball of molten gas.'

'OK, OK,' said Bailey. 'You're being very sensitive about it.'

'That's because it's very sensitive, but there's absolutely nothing I can do about it now.'

'Oh,' said a large doctor from Ghana. 'Look at this. You should have kept your skin out of the sun.'

Another doctor leant in to have a look. 'Yes, you should protect your skin in the sun . . . there are these things called UVA, you know, they're like rays.'

'All right, all right,' I said, grabbing a glass of wine off a passing waitress. 'Wow, what amazing geniuses you've gathered here.'

'Oh, come back, Evie,' said Bailey, turning round to the doctors apologetically. 'She's always so moody.'

But I was pushing my way through the throng to a narrow set of stairs set in the side of the ship. I could see through the window a completely over-the-top salon, filled with gold antiques and an indoor waterfall. It looked dreadful and quite good fun, but the lighting was even brighter, and I didn't really feel like being a medical specimen.

Upstairs there was a formal dining room, with a huge buffet table being set out with seafood and fruit and fresh bread. But I kept on climbing the stairs. Finally, I was on the top deck – the entire top of the ship. There was a large jacuzzi, covered over with an awning, though I wouldn't take bets on that remaining on for long.

I crept along the side of the boat, holding the railings. I could hear the murmur of voices. One, French-accented, was saying, 'But how much then?'

The other, to my surprise, was Dr Bennet.

'Look, it doesn't matter, OK? Once we're at sea, the sky is the limit.'

'The limit. That is not the exact figure I'm looking for from my British partners, *n'est-ce pas*? It's sloppy.'

I didn't have a clue what they were talking about, but cleared my throat loudly so I wasn't sneaking up on them.

'Uh, hello,' said Dr Bennet, looking startled. The other man made a quick farewell and vanished into the shadows on the other side of the boat. 'What are you doing here?'

'I just came to get some fresh air.'

'Well, I hope . . . yes. Have a good party. I must go.'

And he turned on his heel and walked off. It wasn't like him to be so abrupt. Had I done something wrong?

Worried, I headed to the very front of the boat (I know there's a name for it but I don't know what it is) where there was a cluster of seating; moulded plastic benches with plump blue- and yellow-striped cushions over them. They were, thankfully, completely deserted, which, after the cluster and clamour of downstairs, was a huge relief. I padded over to them and sank down in the deep plush cushions with a sigh of relief. I'd wait here, remarshal my forces and . . .

'Owww! Get off!' came a voice.

Shocked, I stumbled and found myself rolling right off the cushions and onto the deck of the boat with a thud.

'Who the hell's that?' I said.

'Well, I could ask the same question, seeing as an elephant

just dropped out of the sky,' came a cross, familiar voice. I sat up.

'Tom?'

'Uh . . .'

He sat bolt upright in the cushions with an almost comical look of disbelief on his face.

'Evie?'

I saw myself through his eyes. Sprawled, dishevelled and completely red in the face. I compared myself to all the elegant girls flitting about downstairs like they were born to yachts and inwardly cursed.

'Hi,' I said.

Tom looked just as discombobulated as I felt.

'Uh . . . uh . . . sorry I called you an elephant.'

'Yeah,' I said, 'you should be.'

'But it felt like you fell from the sky.'

'I gracefully jetéd from over *here*.'

'Oh.' He looked down.

'What are you doing?'

'Uh, nothing,' he said guiltily. I saw his hand grab his mobile phone.

'Who are you calling?'

He still looked unsettled. 'Uh . . . you?'

I grinned at him and he smiled shyly back at me.

'You look . . .'

Then his eyes must have adjusted to the light. 'Well . . . Christ, were you out in the sun?'

'Yes, yes, yes, blah blah blah,' I said. 'Do you kiss burns victims?'

'I don't know . . . are you crispy?' He looked anxious suddenly. 'But shouldn't we also be getting down to the party?'

'You looked like you were up here hiding from the party.'

'I was, but I was only . . . waiting for you.'

Well, obviously he wasn't, but I figured I'd take it anyway.

'Well, lucky I threw myself on you then.'

'Yes, I was thinking that.'

And then he drew me close and gave me a kiss.


Magazines say that you should just be confident then you'll give off an inner beauty that will make you shine far more than some boring model or something. I have never for even a millisecond thought that that might be true. Most men will take a brain-dead slug who looks like Cameron Diaz over a pig-faced personality a hundred times out of a hundred. Nonetheless I definitely felt a little taller and a little better as we headed back into the crowd, me with good-looking Tom at my side.

'Hey!' I said cheerily to Lydia, who was in intense conversation with a dark-haired chap. She waved to me wearily as if I was someone she'd met six years ago and couldn't remember the name of. Bailey, as usual, was surrounded by people wanting to talk to him. He was like a mini-celebrity. Personally, I'd rather have stayed upstairs with Tom, a bit of peace and quiet, a bottle of champagne and those very deep and comfortable-looking cushions, but here we were, doing our bit.

'Can you introduce me to your friend Bailey?' said Tom.

'I thought you didn't know who anybody was,' I said, slightly miffed.

'I heard him speak though. He's very interesting.'

'He's not really,' I assured him. 'He's a geek.'

But we made our way across anyway.

'Hey, Freddy Krueger,' said Bailey, handing me a glass.

'Ha ha. That is just so funny,' I said, taking it. 'This is . . . Tom.'

Tom shook Bailey's hand. 'I really enjoyed your speech. I was wondering if I could ask you a few things about it.'

This was good. Maybe he was trying to impress me by taking an interest in my friends.

I couldn't help comparing Bailey with Tom when I saw them standing side by side. A ridiculous thing to do, I knew. Tom was a sandy hunk, frankly. Bailey was not. But Tom was bent over, listening intently to Bailey like a little boy, and asking him esoteric questions I didn't even understand, about supply chains and scarcity values. Ooh, my boyfriend was so smart, I mooned.

After a while, Tom went to find us both a drink, and I tried to keep the smug smile off of my face. After all, Bailey must be feeling a bit usurped.

'You know,' I said, 'I think I could just about get used to this.'

I looked out over the dark water, as the lights reflected in it shimmered. It was so beautiful I wanted to hug myself. I looked up at the candles dancing in the light breeze.

'You'd think the candles would blow out,' I said to Bailey.

'They're windproof candles,' he said absent-mindedly. 'You get them for boats.'

'*Do* you?' How did that work then? Why didn't they make all candles like that.

Bailey looked a little nervous suddenly. 'So, Tom is . . .'

Oh, Bailey. This must be hard for him.

'So you two are . . .' Bailey took off his glasses.

' What?' I said nervously.

Ah, poor Bailey, he couldn't help being a bit jealous I supposed.

Dr Maitland sidled past our group, suddenly, in his normal dour way. He shrugged, though, looking as if he wanted to talk to us but not quite knowing how normal conversation was actually started.

'Hello,' I said, thinking I'd better be the one to take responsibility for the social niceties. 'Yes, ha ha, half my face is peeling off in a terrible radiation accident. Yes, I'm an idiot that doesn't understand even the rudimentaries of skincare. Yes, that makes me a terrible liability at a plastic surgery conference.'

Dr Maitland held up his hands. 'It's all right,' he said quietly. 'I saw you and I just wanted to give you this. I had it in my sample case.' And he handed me a small tub of cream. 'Stick this on tonight, you'll feel fine in the morning.'

And he nodded awkwardly then moved away towards Bailey, as I looked at him, speechless.

'Uh, Dr Arnold, can I have a word?'

'Sure,' said Bailey, and they wandered off into a huddle.

Tom sidled back up to me. He took the cream out of my hand and stuck out his bottom lip, impressed.

'Wow, this is the stuff . . . costs a fortune.'

'Does it?' I said. 'Will I wake up with the skin of a newborn baby?'

'Maybe one with severe colic,' he said. 'Shall we . . . go and explore a little?' And he shook the cream at me in a suggestive fashion.

The party was getting increasingly loud and excitable – champagne and noise was flowing. The lights of Cannes were glistening all the way up into the hills, and I could see the smart villas that perched over the bay. The water lapped at the bow of the boat and the band were playing something romantic and dreamy. I let myself almost casually sink into Tom's arms. Or rather, I kept leaning in his general direction until he took the hint. To his credit, he didn't say 'oof'.

'Come on,' he whispered.

He led me downstairs to the lower decks. Sporadic giggles and expostulations could be heard but it was much quieter than elsewhere. There was a lower salon where a vast plasma screen was showing what looked like fashion catwalk shows. Couples were dotted around the place, smoking and drinking and generally looking pretty relaxed as they reclined on huge squashy sofas.

'And that's me at Milan,' I heard someone say. I rolled my eyes – model alert! – and we beat a hasty retreat.

Pushing back into the ship I marvelled at the sheer wanton weirdness of the whole thing. The doorknobs were gold, inlaid with what looked like real jewels. The wood was panelled in intricate shapes. There were mosaics on the floor. It was as if someone had said, 'This isn't quite expensive enough in one piece. I want it all broken up into tiny pieces because I think that will probably be more expensive.'

Logos were everywhere – Versace, Gucci. I'd always thought logos were for people who couldn't actually afford to buy designer items, so you'd wear a cheap T-shirt that said Chanel on it, or buy some knock-off Louis Vuitton bag. But apparently if you could afford to buy every last piece of nasty designer tat on earth, down to the Chanel skis (which I could see parked in a corner), you still wanted the brand. Kelly would love it. Personally I'd have thought having the fuck-off boat would be evidence enough that you had all the money in the world, but maybe not.

'Who owns this place?' I said, breathless.

'A schizophrenic with a platinum Amex?' said Tom, looking at the carpet, which appeared to be a priceless Persian rug trimmed with Burberry.

'With *class*,' I said, nodding to a huge oil painting of a grotesque nude women painted entirely in different shades of burnt orange. Hung next to it were large blown-up photos from magazines from around the globe, showing what had to be the same woman, but it was the naked painting that truly drew the eye.

Tom smiled at me. 'You know, I was in the mood, but somehow, now . . .' he trailed off, and I grinned back, but started to feel really nervous. This obviously wasn't just a nosy about, this was, well. Tom meant business. Yikes!

And I thought about it. After all, here I was. And I wanted him, didn't I? I mean, guys like Tom . . . they just didn't pop by every day. I mean, I did really fancy him and everything. But at a party? It felt a little . . . teenage.

On the other hand, this wasn't every party, was it? I suddenly pictured us, in ten years' time, telling people, why, yes, we got it together on a party on a yacht and everyone laughing at how hilarious and cute we were.

And what alternative did I have? I didn't fancy my hotel room much . . . and the conference would be over in a couple of days and he'd be gone, and then I'd be miserable and regret it horribly for the rest of my life and end up having to take the veil and enter a convent.

Gah, it was all so difficult.

Tom slung an arm casually around my shoulders.

'Your heart,' he said. 'It's beating really fast.'

He looked at me, his lovely strong face open and sexy looking.

'Is it because of me?' he said softly.

I nodded. 'Yes.'

*

He was gorgeous. Oh, it was lovely. I felt like a rusty old bike, unused for years but suddenly getting oiled up, getting a paint job; setting off to ride again . . . I couldn't not enjoy it. Even the satin sheets we'd found in the surprisingly small but eminently luxurious room. (The carpet went right up the walls! Why going up walls was a feature particularly to be treasured in a carpet I had absolutely no idea but obviously it was just all part of the mega-luxury – 'Get the carpet up the walls, god-damnit, the floor alone is not enough for a jillionaire like me!') Anyway, even the satin sheets felt oddly romantic and won-derful and I forgot all about my silly sunburn and my crappy job and low-level simmering feuds and practically everything apart from my young, muscular, radiant redhead.

Afterwards I crept into the bathroom. They had a huge triangular bath there with jacuzzi jets poking out of it. Oh, goodness.

Well, I'd already done a few unpredictable things this evening, and I wasn't going to pass up on this one.

'Mmm, lover boy,' I purred seductively, tilting the paler side of my face round the bedroom door.

'Mmhmm,' said Tom sleepily.

'There's a jacuzzi in here . . .' I said.

'Wow,' he said. 'Maybe you should use it to try and seduce me . . . oh no, hang on, we already managed that . . .'

'Don't you think it would be fun?'

'We've just had fun,' he said, but heaved himself off the bed nonetheless.

The jacuzzi filled in two seconds flat and I poured some of the expensively packaged potions indiscriminately from the side of the bath.

'I hope none of these react with each other,' said Tom, but leant over to kiss my shoulder to show he didn't really mean it.

I slithered into the water. Oh, it was absolutely blissful on my poor ravaged back.

'Ahh,' I said.

'Better than sex?' asked Tom with a twinkle in his eye.

'*No*. But nearly as good at making me forget my sunburn. Are you coming in?'

'I thought I'd stay here and rub your back.'

'Well, don't. I don't want any of it to come off in your hand.'

It was blissful in there in the soft lights of the bathroom. Tom found something which brought up an iPod – a full iPod, in the bathroom! – and he'd managed to find Prince on it. He was gently playing with the hair at the back of my neck and I was idly wondering how long we could stay there without getting into trouble – personally I liked the idea of about nine or ten years – and whether anyone had ever died from falling asleep in the bath and then drowning when he leaned over next to my ear.

'So,' he breathed. 'Your friend Bailey?'

I felt my brow furrow. What did he mean? He couldn't think Bailey was my boyfriend, could he?

'What about him?'

'You're close, aren't you?'

I smiled. 'Oh, darling, not like that. I mean, once, years ago, but really, we're just friends.'

'Oh, not *that*,' he said, a bit insultingly I thought. 'I mean, do you know lots about his plans and stuff?'

'Why?' I said. 'I mean, he yabbers on, but I don't really listen or anything. But why are you asking?'

'Oh, I just wondered,' said Tom, nuzzling my neck in the most amazing way. 'I'm just interested in what he's doing. And Dr Bennett. Just to show I've been paying attention.'

'You want me to be your spy?' I said, giggling.

'Yes,' he said, tickling me. 'That's what I want. I need you to be a super spy.'

'So you can get extra kudos?'

'That kind of thing. And rapid advancement and international fame and glory.'

'I thought you were just a humble med student.'

'A humble med student with big dreams.'

'How big?'

'*Very* big,' said Tom and he jumped into the jacuzzi with me, splashing the water everywhere.

'The roof-to-roof carpeting!' I gasped.

'I think whoever owns this behemoth can probably afford to get the carpets cleaned, don't you?' he said. And then he started kissing me again.

Just as I was getting into it he surfaced and winked at me.

'So,' he said. 'Bailey and Yuri's ship is ready . . .'

I drew back. 'What on *earth* are you talking about? What ship? Why do you keep asking me this stuff?'

Tom looked a bit confused then, as if he knew he'd gone too far. He backed up onto the side of the bath.

'Why? I mean it, Tom.'

I was a bit peeved now; he looked really guilty, like a boy who'd been caught out doing something naughty.

'Eh, just, you know . . . making conversation . . .'

'We were *snogging*! You can't chat and snog. Spit gets everywhere, it just doesn't work!'

I was getting a little upset now and looked around for a towel so I could get out of the bath.

Suddenly, from the other room, Tom's mobile telephone went off. He froze. I stared at him. He looked . . . well, he absolutely did *not* look like a man making love to his new girl-friend for the first time who'd suddenly been mildly irritated to hear the phone ring. He looked shocked.

Tom grabbed the first towel that came to hand – it was huge, hot pink and had the Versace logo emblazoned on it nine thousand times – and backed out of the bathroom.

'I'm just . . . I'll just go see who that is . . .'

'Why?' I asked, quite sharply, but he'd already retreated into the other room.

'You just stay in the bath and I'll be through in a minute!'

'OK,' I said cheerily, making some splashing noises. Then using my very best Nancy Drew girl detective skills, I turned on the tap then crept to the door where he was crouching – actually crouching – right at the other side of the room behind the bed, whispering into the phone.

I held my breath and took the little water glass off the sink. Did this actually work? I couldn't remember. The boys used to use it on my door if I ever had a friend round, but they always gave themselves away by grunting and snorting by accident. Still, I leaned in closely to the crack, placing the glass against the door.

'Yeah,' he was saying. My heart was now beating dangerously fast but for very different reasons than before. Was it his wife? Girlfriend? Gay lover?

'Yeah. I know. But she doesn't . . . she doesn't really seem to know much.'

Who was he talking about? Me? Know much about what? What did he mean?

'No, I know she's friends with B but I don't think she's got much info.'

B? Did he mean Bailey? What was he talking about? Was he some kind of *spy*?

'I know, she's pretty useless.' Then, there was a smirk in his voice that I hadn't heard before. 'Well . . . not *completely* . . .'

I took a sharp intake of breath. A red mist descended. A fury grew behind my eyes and I felt like I was going to burst. What was going on? Was Tom . . .? What was he doing? Was he doing something bad and had pumped me – literally – for

information. I couldn't believe it. I couldn't... what the
FUCK was this shit doing?

'What the FUCK are you doing, you shit?' I howled,
throwing myself out of the bathroom, only another hot pink
Versace towel protecting me. Tom jumped up, a vicious flush
spreading over his freckled face. 'Are you talking about me?'

'Uh, no, of course not...'

'Give me the phone then! Who are you talking to?'

'Nobody...'

'GIVE ME THE PHONE!'

'NO!'

He snapped the phone shut and held it above his head,
just like John Jr used to do with my Tiny Tears. Nothing was
more guaranteed to send me into a rage. I tore at him.

'GIVE IT!'

I caught a flash of panic cross his face just before he
turned on his heel and bombed through the door, with nothing more than the towel round his waist. I was half crazy with
fury, but not so crazy that I didn't quickly grab up the nearest
thing that came to hand – his boxer shorts, in fact, and his grey
T-shirt. I threw them on as quickly as I could and charged
towards the door, howling in rage.

He had obviously gone upstairs; there were wet footprints
on the wooden decking. Also, as I ascended at full speed I
could hear people starting to mutter and giggle, which meant
there was obviously a six-foot, freckly, practically naked man
ploughing through them. But I HAD to catch up with him – if

he ran off and escaped, well, I just didn't know. What was he doing? What was he after? Had I just . . . I mean, was he like a spy? Had I just been Mata Haried? The idea made me absolutely crazy. Pretty useless? *Pretty useless??*

'Stop that naked man!' I screeched as I reached the top of the stairs. This didn't have quite the desired effect, however, as all the beautifully dressed party guests immediately turned to look at me rather than trying to catch Tom's skinny arse, which I now saw was trying to push its way through the throng to the exit.

'Oh, look, he's stolen her honour,' said one supercilious voice.

'Do you think she's one of those lady boys and he got a shock?' said another.

'With those hips? Don't think so.'

'Catch him for God's sake!' I screamed. 'He's a SPY!'

'Where's he hiding his gun, then?' shouted someone else, to general merriment. Tom was nearly at the gangplank now, having given me a cursory backward glance. There was no way I was going to reach him across the crowd of people and even if I did, what was I going to do? Wrestle him to the ground?

He must have been thinking the same thing because he made it to the gangway and – the bastard – gave me a quick, but obvious wink. Then he turned back, only, suddenly, to find his way blocked.

I gasped in amazement. Standing right there, all eight-foot

square of him, looking pink and fat and out of place, was none other than John Junior. Truly, I had never been so pleased to see him in all my life. He was implacably huge, hanging onto the ropes on either side of the gangway. There was no way for Tom to get past him.

John Jr grunted with satisfaction. I could tell that even though he didn't know what was going on, it looked like there was whomping to be done, and whomping was what John Jr liked to do best. Behind him I could see Kelly, teetering in her spiky high heels going, 'Leave it, John, he just isn't worth it.' But John was oblivious to all that now. I waved hard at JJ and made a punching motion with my hand.

'What you doing with my little sister?' he growled menacingly, in his best *EastEnders* voice.

'Nothing,' said Tom, sounding offended. 'Can I get past here?'

'You can,' said John Jr, 'if you give me that towel.'

The entire deck had gone silent. Even the jazz band had stopped playing.

'He, um, snogged me under false pretences,' I squealed. 'He's a spy! He tried to get information out of me.'

There was a rustle among the crowd now. Obviously having a big fat bloke on my side made my word much more reliable.

'Is that true?' said John Jr.

'Get out of my way,' said Tom, sounding a lot less sure of

himself. 'If you do anything to me there's lots of witnesses.'

'Neh, we're on the sea,' said John Jr (dubiously, I thought). 'Law of the briny deep, innit? Now, were you spying on my sister?'

'I'm not *spying*,' said Tom, suddenly looking extremely exasperated. He looked around realising the game was up. He turned to face the crowd.

'I'm information gathering, that's all.'

There was a shocked intake of breath from everyone there, including me. He *was* a spy. Some kind of industrial spy. Which meant that all the romance . . . all the kissing . . . even the bloody stubble rash . . . was, oh, God, nothing at all. I'd been taking in by a tall good-looking idiot. Not for the first time, admittedly, but this was even worse than normal. This was completely awful.

I noticed Bailey stepping up to face him.

'Why? What for?'

'Let me explain . . .' said Tom, looking slightly wild-eyed. Thank goodness he was naked, at least he couldn't possibly be concealing a bomb, unless it was a really tiny one, and even then, I think I'd have probably come across it earlier.

Tom, however, did not get his chance to explain. To widespread cheering from the assembled throng, John Jr hoisted him up over his shoulder in a fireman's lift, marched to the side of the yacht and threw him into the dark oily water below.

There was a gasp from everyone as we all dashed to the side to see what had happened. I hoped he could swim – oh,

God, what if he drowned. There weren't sharks round here, were there? John Jr came up to me.

'What did you do that for?' I yelled. 'What if you've killed him.'

John Jr grunted. 'Then you could thank me,' he said. 'Hanging's too good for 'em.'

John Jr says this about anyone who commits any crime of any sort at all.

'OK,' I said. Then before I could think about it, I gave him a huge hug. 'Thank you. You're not all bad.'

'Family, innit?' said JJ, but he seemed pleased.

I pored over the side. I could just make out the sandy head above the water, splashing and choking, but striking out towards the quay.

'What on *earth*?' Bailey said.

I sighed. 'It's a long story,' I said.

'Oh, well done,' said Lydia. 'It looks like the party's over. And you ruined it.'

On the contrary, actually, it looked like somebody being thrown into the water might have been exactly what the party needed. The excited chatter was reaching fever pitch. Four burly bodyguards wearing dark glasses, at eleven at night, with wires coming out of their ears were humming and hawing around looking grumpy. Lots of people were staring at me – again. Bailey and John Jr were heading for the gangplank, along with Dr Bennet and a few other people. I followed them as Tom clambered up the metal bars that served as a rough staircase out of the docks. Several fishermen and crowds of passers-by watched him in amazement. As he stood up you could see by the lights of the nearest boat – all the crew was leaning over the top – that he was absolutely filthy, covered in black patches of oil and seaweed and goodness knows what. And – oh, joy, oh, joy, it became clear as he turned around – the towel had got lost somewhere in transit.

Bailey and John Jr, looking like Little and Large, had reached him. The whole party followed, heading down the gangplank carefully. I was still in Tom's T-shirt and boxers which, I noticed, smelled just like him.

'Well?' John Jr was shouting. 'What were you doing to my little sister?'

Tom's face was a picture of consternation. Hurrah for JJ!

'No . . . nothing,' he said, both hands still covering his crotch. I could have gone back and got his clothes, but I didn't want to miss anything.

'Who do you work for?' said Bailey. 'Are you even a doctor?'

The four big bodyguards had come out. I'd forgotten there were various rich people from around the globe here – investors and so on – who actually needed, or at least had, people like bodyguards. Wow. How annoying must that be? Did they stand outside the loo when you needed to go for a poo? Did they time you? Did they bitch you up between themselves? They must do. Anyway, the bodyguards were standing behind Bailey and you could see Tom looking really frightened.

'Not exactly,' said Tom. My skin bristled. Oh, God, I'd been taken in completely and utterly. Any old idiot could fool me. Completely fooled. Stupid self-obsessed Evie. Half my face was peeling off and I was such a pointless conversationalist that I didn't even know about Bailey's big plastic surgery plans. Tom wasn't even looking up, he couldn't even look at me. Although to be fair he was also trying to keep his goolies out of the way of some rather burly men who looked like they might want to kick them.

'I'm a vet.'

Oh, God.

'But that's not important.'

Well, it was quite important to me. Given that I'd inadvertently slept with someone who stuck his hand up dog's arses.

'I'm part of Earth Friends,' he said. 'We don't like what you're doing.'

'Well, you don't know what we're doing,' said Bailey. 'Presumably that's why you're here.'

'You want to use untested material.'

'We want to give people options.'

'What about giving animals options?'

'Didn't I see you eating the caviar?' said Dr Bennet.

Hang on, hang on, what on earth where they talking about?

'You have to stop,' said Tom. 'It has to be stopped.'

'By a naked ginger man trying to shag my sister?' said John Jr. 'I don't think so.'

'I was *information gathering*,' said Tom. Then he caught sight of me, hiding behind the bodyguards. 'Sorry,' he said.

'SORRY?' I yelled. I'd thought my anger had dissipated when he'd fallen into the sea, but it turned out I was wrong. Everyone turned to face me. 'I'll give you SORRY.'

And I raced towards him. He saw his chance, with everyone looking at me he turned round and legged it back to the bright lights of Cannes.

'Oh, let him go,' I heard Bailey say to the bouncers. 'He didn't get anything.'

I stopped running after I lost sight of his body, fleeing in and out of the excited crowds. On the pier all I could catch was the occasional glimpse of pale white buttocks, like the bobbing lights of the boats on the bay.

'The gendarmes will probably pick him up,' said Bailey, coming up behind me. 'God, a spy. Wow, I had no idea.'

I turned round, all my anger gone and just a huge sadness and embarrassment settling on me.

'Neither did I,' I said, and burst into tears.

Everyone was very solicitous, bringing me drinks, and Bailey wrapped me up in a blanket (I don't know why, it was still about twenty-five degrees outside) whilst listing all the hideous and deadly diseases Tom had certainly caught from swimming in the harbour. I said that I hadn't slept with him, but I don't think anyone believed me.

'I don't even understand *why*,' I said to Bailey, choking through my sobs.

'Because you're an irresistible creature,' he said encouragingly, but his face was distracted. 'You're sure you didn't tell him anything?'

'Anything what?'

Bailey shook his head. 'Well, from your private briefing paper.'

'But I'm on *holiday*. I haven't . . . exactly . . .' I noticed Dr Bennet hovering awkwardly and stopped.

'Evie, you seem, by virtue of your ignorance . . . to have helped us out.'

'Is that good?' I said. 'What's going on?'

Bailey and Dr Bennet glanced at each other.

'Tell me, then.'

'Well,' Dr Bennet started. 'You know Bailey designs hospital facilities?'

I nodded. Someone had handed me an Irish coffee, and I was suddenly very grateful to have something to hang on to.

'Well, we're launching a new one. And launching is the operative word . . .'

'It's on a yacht,' said Bailey. 'Not this one. A really big one. Brand new. It's coming into port tomorrow for the first time. Yuri is finding investors, and we're showing it off here so that doctors will tell their clients, and money men will want to invest. Selected surgeons will be able to operate on board.'

I must have looked confused.

'So,' went on Bailey. 'To hide people from the paparazzi . . . to ensure complete and utter confidentiality—'

'Very important for celebrities,' said Dr Bennet.

'And to give an all-round surgery experience which is—'

'A cut above,' said Dr Bennet. Bailey winced slightly.

'A slightly different experience. Anyway,' Bailey's eyes lit up excitedly, 'it's like a cruise, or chartering a yacht – but with surgery. Hundreds of miles out at sea away from prying eyes. First-class care and a luxury cruise to boot.'

'Are you joking? That sounds like the set-up for the new *Die Hard* film.'

'Not at all,' bristled Bailey. 'Our security procedures are excellent.'

'Yes, I could tell that by the way nobody's managed to infiltrate your defences or anything,' I said.

'And we'll be in international waters,' said Dr Bennet dreamily. 'So we can use the most up-to-date and cutting-edge procedures. Tax free.'

I took a long sip of my coffee.

'I don't understand. Why would some Earth Friends vet be against that?'

Bailey shrugged. 'Craziness?'

'They don't like the cutting-edge procedures,' said Dr Bennet. 'They're against science and progress.'

'Oh,' I said, not really understanding.

'You've had a very tiring day,' said Bailey, looking concerned.

'No, I haven't! I slept all day! Now tell me about these cutting-edge procedures.'

'That's more your department,' said Bailey, looking at Dr Bennet. 'I'm off to bed.'

Bailey was right, though. I was tired. It had been a long night, and really I wanted to get back to my hotel room, throw myself on my pillow and have a good bawl. It wasn't too bad talking to the guys but I knew as soon as I was on my own and the memories of what I'd done started to hit, I wouldn't be able to control myself.

'So, we're not calling the police?' said Bailey.

'I think he'll probably have to call us when he needs bail,' sniffed Dr Bennet. 'Useless cretin.'

Suddenly there was a knock at the cabin door and Dr Maitland put his head round.

'How's our little Mata Hari?' he said stiffly.

'Mata Hari was the other one,' I said sulkily. 'I'm the rube.'

Dr Maitland patted me gently on the shoulder. 'Well, it sounds like you didn't let him get away with anything.'

'Mmm,' I said.

'Opposition, though,' said Dr Maitland, looking at Dr Bennet. 'Interesting. I can't believe he stole your name. That's quite ballsy.'

'It's unacceptable,' said Dr Bennet, turning on his heel and walking out.

I remembered the conversation I'd overheard earlier that evening and wondered now who Dr Bennet had been talking to. I felt a faint chill in the air.

## Chapter Nine

The next morning I woke up feeling horribly alone on the lumpy bed. At first I felt kind of all right, before I was properly awake, then suddenly I remembered everything and let out a heartfelt groan. I had cried myself to sleep, which had worked, but now it was a new day, the sun was trying to push against the grimy window and I, God help me, was supposed to spend all day working at the conference. What did they do with the bits they chopped off on a hospital boat? I wondered. Maybe there were sharks following all the way from shore. Why had everything good turned so bad?

Still, maybe everything would look better after breakfast. I couldn't be feeling that suicidal if I still felt hungry. The worst of it was, after everything, I still found Tom residually attractive. How stupid was that? But it had been so romantic and lovely. I wondered if James Bond's abandoned ladies felt like this. Betrayed . . . yet seduced. And a little bit hungry. I should take this as a positive sign. Then I remembered the conference.

I couldn't believe I'd forgotten. Oh, God, why had I thought this was a holiday masquerading as a couple of minor annoyances? Today, they were having a team-building day. Team-building day? The schedule was 'fun' exercises in the morning followed by a golf game in the afternoon, which of course I was going to be able to do seeing as I knew as much about golf as I did mitochondrial enhancement. But that morning I'd been instructed to turn up, hand out briefings and generally look helpful.

It took two coffees, two croissants and a croque-monsieur before I managed to pluck up the courage to walk into the room. Today the venue was a large marquee parked next to the beach. Dress code was 'smart but casual', which meant that every single male was wearing chinos, loafers and a blue chambray shirt. They looked like a line of prison inmates from a particularly swanky jail.

Dr Bennet grabbed me by the entrance.

'You read French, don't you?'

Uh-oh. I'd been dreading this moment.

'Well, according to my CV . . .' I said timidly. He ignored

this and thrust a *Cannes Matin* into my hands. Right on the front page was a picture of Tom's rather foxy – no, no, evil – behind.

*Étranger mystérieux*, said the headline. Well, you didn't need to be a translating genius to figure that one out. 'Mysterious stranger,' I said confidently.

'Yes, yes, I'd got that far,' said Dr Bennet impatiently. I forget all the time that he is already perfectly fluent in a second language: English.

'Well,' I said. 'Well, that's it, isn't it? They obviously have no further information, otherwise they'd be calling him the "we've found out everything stranger".'

Dr Bennet sniffed. 'You seem to be bringing a certain notoriety to our launch.'

'I'm just efficient,' I said, and immediately grabbed a handful of folders to give out to people as they came in.

Lydia drifted up, wearing very red lipstick, which made her face look pointy.

'Ah, it's the talk of the town,' she said, and not in a nice way, if there is a nice way to say that. 'You're such a dark horse! Who else have you been sleeping with, huh? We need to know if any other secrets are being bandied about.' Then she laughed as if she was actually just joking.

'Here, take these,' I said, handing over a pile of the brochures. She picked them up and wrinkled her very small nose.

'Love in medicine?' she read aloud, then gave me a very sharp look. 'Is this a joke?'

'What?' I said, and glanced down. Yet again my lack of preparedness in everything except bikini choice was showing through; I'd scarcely glanced at what this team building would contain (though this time I had an excuse). But sure enough, there it was: 'The Healing Hand – bringing love and spirituality to medicine.'

'Oh, for goodness' sake,' I exclaimed loudly. 'What the hell is this bollocks? I don't think there should be love in medicine. I think love and medicine should be as far apart as possible. You don't want some surgeon all shaky with love and his heart pounding every time he chops into some old girl's carcass.'

I realised suddenly, with that horrible sixth sense, that there was someone standing right behind me. Lydia's face took on its favourite mocking expression. I turned around as slowly as I could. It was Dr Maitland, and his mouth was twitching.

'Actually,' he said. 'I couldn't agree more. In fact I'm only here because you terrified me so much with your skin damage yesterday that I didn't want to go out in the sun.'

I smiled at him. 'Brochure?'

He took it. 'Is this going to be what they call "touchy feely"?'

'You can bet on that with Evie around, sir,' said Lydia unctuously.

A commotion at the entrance hall caught our attention. As we turned round, I saw it was a tiny woman, tight as a drum from head to toe, wearing a hot-cerise suit over her small rump.

'Is this it? Is this the space?' She had a huge voice for such a little person. It came howling forth like an annoyed cheese grater, harsh American tones bouncing off the walls like hailstones.

'I'm not feeling it, Judy,' she said warningly. Next to her was a woman about the same height but twice the weight; much older-looking and slightly depressed. I guessed this must be Judy. I know you're not meant to judge by first impressions, but my heart went out to her in about ten seconds flat.

'If it's not a heart space I'm not sure I can work it . . . I specifically said a *heart space*.'

'It's a marquee,' said Judy.

'I can *see* it's a marquee, Judy. I can *smell* it's a marquee. But is it a *heart* marquee?'

Dr Maitland and I looked at one another in some bewilderment. Maybe I could see the wisdom of his constant customer avoidance.

The little woman stalked into the room. Huge arrays of flowers had been placed on plinths around the outskirts of the chairs. They must have cost tons of money. The lady sniffed.

'Pink roses. Not carmine. For goodness' sake, I thought we were dealing with professionals. *Wrongly*, obviously.'

Judy wrote something down on a clipboard which doubtless meant bad news for somebody. As she did so, Dr Bennet came bustling over from the coffee machine where he'd been fussing.

'And you must be Jal-Vita?'

Jal-Vita? 'What is that, a name or a snack?' I whispered to Lydia.

The woman's demeanour immediately changed, and she actually started to simper.

'Why, hello,' she said, putting out her hand. 'I am indeed. Of course, Jal-Vita is just my spiritual name. My real name is Janey.'

'And which do you prefer?' said Dr Bennet in full smoothness mode, as he picked up her hand and kissed it. Yuk! He had no idea where it'd been!

'Whatever you like!' she tinkled as if it was hilarious that she had a real name and a completely made-up bullshit name.

'And you're our star attraction,' went on Dr Bennet, purring like a vintage car, which was rubbish, as even I'd picked up by now that unveiling the boat was going to be the star attraction, and everyone knew it. Dr Bennet seemed to have his mojo back, though.

'I don't think of it like that,' said *Janey*, although she obviously totally did. 'I think of it as a spiritual journey for everyone . . . as they career down the heady highway of surgical success, to stop for a while and smell the roses. That's me.'

'You're indeed a rose,' said Dr Bennet pukily.

Janey smiled, equally pukily. 'Oh, no, I wouldn't say that.'

Well, she just did say that, I thought mutinously. I leafed through the brochure. An airbrushed picture of Janey, looking like she'd been entirely moulded out of Barbie doll material, complete with a coat-hanger smile, beamed out from the page.

'Welcome,' it said, 'to a safe space to leave all your worries and cares behind.'

Great, a carefree non-worrier with a scalpel in his hands; just what the world needed.

Lydia had put her super-positive face on and gone bounding up to meet the new girl. This should be interesting, I thought. Two evil witches in a smiling competition.

'Jal-Vita, I'm a great fan of your work,' said Lydia, holding out her hand, which was graciously shaken. 'I really enjoyed *Spirituality in the Workplace – why love is there for everyone 9–5.*'

She had? I turned over a page in the brochure. The book had a full-page advertisement. The cunning fink! All she'd read was the blurb!

'Why, *thank you*,' gushed Janey. 'Which bit did you feel spoke to you the most?'

Ha ha. Take that, you gobshite.

'Well, I found it really spoke to my inner soul?' said Lydia, in an upturned inflection that matched Janey's. 'Or does that sound stupid?'

'Yes,' I said quietly, forgetting once again that Dr Maitland was right behind me.

'Not at all,' said Janey. 'Releasing your inner soul-ness is very much a part of what I'm trying to share with the world. Thank you for sharing your insight with me. What's your name?'

'Lydia.'

'And what's your heritage, Lydia?'

Lydia is *not* one of those people who likes discussing her heritage. I think she would just like everyone to assume she's an exotic Eastern princess of some kind, who descended to earth on a gold-tinted cloud.

'My parents are from Malaysia,' she said, almost grudgingly.

'Wow,' said Janey, taking Lydia's hands in hers. 'That's an amazing thing. An amazing heritage to have.'

'Yeah, whatever,' said Lydia. (For once, rightly, in my opinion. Why congratulate someone on their random genetics? You might as well say, 'God, you're left-handed; that's *amazing*.' Which is the kind of thing Janey probably did say.)

'Now, I know this is just going to be the most wonderful day,' said Janey. 'When do they all arrive?'

Dr Bennet looked slightly worried, but as he turned to face the entrance of the marquee – which was huge, with row after row of those gilt-edged, red-seated chairs lined up around it – the docs, looking a bit hungover and slightly sheepish, started to sidle in.

Janey prepared her razor-toothed American grin in welcome, but to her – and my – surprise, they all headed towards me.

'Hey, what happened to you last night? Are you all right?' asked one.

'You were really brave, chasing a spy like that,' said another. 'Amazing really. You probably saved the whole project. Under torture, too.'

Out of the corner of my eye I caught sight of Bailey grinning. Oh, bless him! He must have spun some story about me where I didn't look like a hapless slut after all!

Another one was nodding. 'Yeah,' they said. Then they turned to Dr Maitland. 'You must be really proud of her.'

And Dr Maitland said the most surprising thing; he replied, 'Yes. Yes I am.'

I was so taken aback, I nearly started crying again. Fortunately there must be some kind of term limit on tears, or I'd just dried up, I didn't know. Tom had knocked my confidence so hard I was just amazed they didn't all want me to lie on the floor so they could take turns kicking me.

'*Hello*,' said Janey very loudly. The doctors slowly turned round to face her. She looked annoyed that her attempt to get all the attention had failed. Near me, her little runt Judy looked a bit shaky.

'If I can just ask for your attention for two minutes . . .'

The docs smiled at me, and chuntered their way towards the chairs. I stayed standing at the back.

'My name is Jal-Vita and I am lucky enough to have been blessed in my life enough to now pass on the secrets of love and spirituality in business that I have learned along the way.'

There was a little bit of noise from the audience at this, and the latecomers looked somewhat wistfully towards the coffee machine.

'Today, through some *fun* games and exercises I hope we're going to find a way to take forward a little bit of the love and spirituality that we can carry around with us all the time – even when faced with that difficult patient or tricky operation. But first, a little bit about me . . .'

'Oh, Christ,' said Dr Maitland. I realised he hadn't gone and sat down but was still standing beside me. 'I knew this would suck. You know she negotiated it with Yuri in return for some free filler.'

'She did not!' I said. 'That's . . . corrupt.'

'Well, she is a professional . . .'

'Professional what?'

'. . . and then that's when I started what I call my *whole life journey*,' emphasised Janey.

'Will you help me out with the "exercises"?' said Dr Maitland. 'I don't think I can bear it. And if she says the word "diversity" I'm out of here.'

'. . . that brings a whole new paradigm of love and diversity into the workplace,' said Janey. I looked at Dr Maitland pointedly.

'Oh, I can't leave,' he said, fumbling with his bow tie. 'I promised Yuri.'

'Wimp!' I whispered back and, amazingly, he smiled. He had a rather lovely smile, I couldn't help noticing. Like the sun coming out from behind a cloud.

After about another forty minutes of Janey wittering on about how being a nurse in a casualty unit had taught her more than she'd ever dreamed of about love in the workplace, which was news to me, because one of Patrick's girlfriends had been a nurse in a casualty unit and she said it had taught her more than she'd ever dreamed of about drunks, Janey finally stepped forward off the podium, her beady eyes sweeping the room.

'OK, guys and gals,' she said, in a horrible attempt to appear playful – pointless anyway, there was only one gal there, Miss Hodgkiss, who specialised in bum implants and herself had a massive one (which I guess was reassuring to her clientele).

'Now, the first thing we're going to do is find a partner so we can all relax with a trust game.'

I swear you could almost here a groan go through the room. Was this worth getting up early for? The shiny new career on the ocean blue?

'We can't expect to *spread* love if we don't at first *love ourselves*,' said Janey severely. 'And we do that by finding trust in others.'

'I think I've got to go outside and check the ticket

stand,' I lied suddenly, getting up. Let's face it, I was probably the least trustworthy person in this entire room. I'd probably get dropped if we had to do that 'fall back into somebody's arms' thing. From the corner of my eye I saw Lydia immediately grab Bailey's elbow. Well, but of course she would. I stood up.

'No!' said Dr Maitland suddenly.

I turned round.

'I mean . . .' His face looked stricken. 'I mean, I thought you were going to stay and be my partner.'

Janey was now chivvying people into position and hollering, 'Now, don't worry! This is going to be lots of fun! JUDY!'

Judy instantly stepped forward with a huge box full of blindfolds.

'Now, cover up your partner's eyes.'

Dr Maitland and I looked at each other. This was bizarrely uncomfortable. Judy waddled up to us awkwardly and handed the blindfold to Dr Maitland. He took it, looking at it as if it was a big black eel he'd just accidentally pulled out of the water.

'Um,' he said.

'There's still time to set the tent on fire and make a run for it under cover of all the smoke,' I said.

'Come on, you two at the back!' came a wild American screech. 'Get with the PROG-ramme.'

'*So* much love and spirituality,' I murmured, as Dr

Maitland tentatively approached me. I stopped talking as he draped the blindfold over my eyes. Suddenly I was so conscious of his body very close to mine. Perhaps because I'd had sex so recently, my senses and pheromones were up. I could feel my skin prickle.

Dr Maitland was quiet, but I could hear him breathing as he carefully, but with a steady hand, tied the blindfold at the back, not too loosely or tightly. I nearly asked him if he'd done it before, but already felt awkward enough.

'Now, you're going to guide your partner around the room using just your fingers and your voice . . . gently touch them from behind . . .'

It is to several medical professionals' complete credit that they didn't immediately start sniggering when they heard this, which I would certainly have done had I not been sad and very close to my boss. Instead, I felt a finger quite gently but firmly poking me in the back and a voice saying, 'I'm terribly sorry about all this.'

'Don't give it a second thought,' I said, stepping forwards in the pitch black and immediately falling over a chair.

'Whoops!' I shouted, as Dr Maitland made a grab for me and fetched me up with my bra strap, which he dropped as if it had bitten him.

'I'm sorry,' he said again.

'Now you two,' came the loud voice, sounding right next to my ear. 'You're not trusting each other.'

'She marched off!' said Dr Maitland.

'I thought you were pushing me in that direction.'

'Why would I push you over a chair?'

'So that I'd hurt myself and require expensive reconstructive surgery?'

There was a silence and I really wanted to pull up my blindfold and see what was going on, but a tiny claw came down on my arm and gripped it in a steely embrace.

'You,' said Janey, without as much love in her voice as I could have done with at this particular instant. 'Come here.' And she yanked me back round the chair.

'Stand here.'

And she shoved me into a large pair of tweedy arms.

'OK, *you*,' she said, and I knew it wasn't me she meant this time. 'Guide her.'

'Where?' said Dr Maitland.

'It doesn't matter where. It just matters that she trusts you.'

We were both silent then. And I realised, suddenly, with a flashing instant of clarity, that after last night I wasn't actually sure if I did trust him.

'Do you trust me?' said Dr Maitland suddenly, as if he was thinking the same thing. It seemed a very odd thing for a boss to ask his receptionist.

'Don't ask like that!' said Janey, trust expert extraordinaire. 'Just get moving!'

'Left,' murmured Dr Maitland in my ear then, and I took a little step that way. His finger moved down my back a little bit as he whispered, 'Forwards. Slowly.' And we gradually tiptoed out of Janey's orbit. Being in the dark in the huge marquee – I could barely hear the other pairs rustling about in the distance – was a very odd experience. I felt we could walk for ever, or straight into the sea.

'The project . . .' began Dr Maitland, but it was like he didn't know how to go on. 'The ship . . . I mean.'

He nudged me to the right. It felt a little like we were dancing. I was incredibly aware of him behind me. Oh, God, what was the matter with me? One whiff of testosterone and I was all over the place. This was my boss we were talking about.

'Uh, yes?'

He paused then as if sensing something. Oh, God, I was probably giving off some weird hormonal thing. I couldn't help it, though; as I felt his sure, strong fingers gently guiding me, it was hard to concentrate.

'You know, not all of us are as gung-ho as Yuri and Bailey . . . I mean, we're not all so determined.'

'What *is* it?' I said, as he prodded me again, lightly in the small of my back and I nearly shivered. 'What's getting everyone so riled up? So bad that someone sent a *spy*?'

He sighed. 'Well, in law, once you're out of sight of land . . . well, once you're in international waters, you can do . . . you can do pretty much anything.'

I spun round to face him. 'What do you mean, *anything*?'

'Well, new techniques. Face transplants. Anonymous work. Some women, you know . . . they'll stop at nothing to look better. And some doctors don't feel the pace of ratification by drugs bodies is quite fast enough. And then there's Radoflux 9000.'

I screwed up my eyes trying to remember where I'd heard that name.

'The drug that keeps failing its FDA?' I said.

'Yes,' said Dr Maitland. 'Side-effect issues.'

'Isn't it made out of something really dodgy?'

'Seal foetuses.'

'Urgh.'

'Everything's made out of something.'

'So what's the problem with that? You can't use it, end of story.'

'Well, some people aren't so sure about that . . .'

I didn't say anything and waited for him to continue. I wasn't sure but I thought we were near the corner of the marquee by now. I pulled up my blindfold and looked at him in disbelief. 'You want to use an unratified drug.'

Dr Maitland looked at the floor. 'Well, maybe. Yes.'

I couldn't believe it.

'So Tom was right! This *is* a bad idea.'

'Shh,' said Dr Maitland. He looked around. Various two-somes were hopping along or running into each other. They all looked very innocent.

'And these guys . . . they could use the boat to do, basically, anything they wanted?'

'And SWITCH!' yelled Janey.

'Look normal,' said Dr Maitland. 'I shouldn't really be talking to you about this.'

'So why are you?'

'Maybe I'm having doubts, I said that already,' he growled.

I had to get right up on my tiptoes to tie the blindfold around him. He had very clean ears, I noticed. Probably doctors knew quite a lot about terrible ear diseases.

'Is that too tight?' I said.

'It doesn't matter,' he said. 'We're having a conversation, not actually playing this stupid game.'

He sounded completely different; much less tentative than normal. He'd obviously crossed a line; he wanted to talk to me and talk about this. I prodded at his back reluctantly.

'It would be easier,' he said, 'if you just held onto my braces.'

It was.

He heaved a sigh. 'Well, you've proven you can keep a secret – even under the *deadliest* torture.'

'Could we not mention that, please?' I said. 'Just from, like, a basic standard of human dignity? And I think maybe Bailey slightly embroidered the torture thing anyway.'

He nodded his head. His back, as I studied it, was much more muscular than I'd have divined from those ridiculous tweed jackets.

'Sorry,' he said. 'The thing is. That holiday boyfriend of yours . . .'

I rolled my eyes, but he couldn't tell.

185

'He made me think. Or think more. What do you think, Evie?'

I thought about it as we negotiated a couple of the gilt chairs someone else had knocked over earlier.

'Why should I care what a couple of really rich cows do to themselves?' I said, considering it. 'If they want to shoot themselves full of monkey bollocks so that their face is rendered completely immoveable even in tornadoes, why should I care? Why should I care if they get swept overboard? You know, hypothetically.'

'Thanks for adding "hypothetically" on at the end there,' said Dr Maitland. 'Otherwise it might have sounded, you know, a bit twisted and bitter.'

'I'm just saying,' I said, realising I was getting quite het up, 'for most people in this world what some stupid rich person wants to get up to in her own spare time is miles away from anything even vaguely useful, like how you're going to pay your council tax or getting your landlord to fix that ridiculous drip that's been coming in from the roof for years. It's all bollocks. And I can't imagine why a good doctor would waste his training and his life on it, quite frankly. It's immoral. I mean, it's OK for idiots like me, but to go to medical school, learn how to help people, learn how to fix people, get trained up by the NHS and then piss it all down the drain for a six-figure salary . . . it's pathetic, really.'

'And stop!' shouted Janey. 'Now, is that all better? Do you really feel you're starting to trust one another now?'

Dr Maitland looked at me, blinking his big eyes in the light.

'Well, just as well you know everything,' he said.

'What did we learn?' shouted Janey at the group.

'I know, because I'm only a receptionist,' I said. My blood was up now. I was probably – no, make that definitely – going to lose my job, but I didn't care. Who were these people who thought they could take people out into the middle of the ocean and gut baby seals for money? Maybe I just didn't want to be anywhere near them any more.

'I'm not rich, I'm not willing to throw thousands of pounds at you so you can hack me open and make me look like I've been caught in a wind tunnel. Amazing, I know. If I made any money – which I *don't*, by the way, you lot all act like I should feel unbelievably privileged to be working for you and should be doing it for the love of it – I'd spend it . . . well, I'd spend it on a home, and on beautiful things around me and hopefully, one day, someone I loved and who loved me, and it wouldn't be about how small a nose I had or how tight my bottom was. It would be because it was fun, and warm, and happy and we liked spending time together and spending our lives together. And do you know how many of those stupid people you think are so great have that? Hardly any. Hardly any of them at all. They're all bloody miserable. That's why they come and see you. And with all your bloody money and qualifications – you're bloody miserable too. And that's moral, is it?

Along with all the other bullshit, this boat is literally a drop in the ocean.'

'God, you don't stop when you get going, do you?' said Dr Maitland. He just stood there.

'I've stopped now,' I said. And I had. It was like all the anger drained out of my feet and I changed from red to white. I knew what I'd done. I'd buggered up my job – a job, as Bailey would point out, that I was lucky to get – and wouldn't get a look in at another one once word got round about the crazy girl at the Cannes conference, as I'd be known for evermore. I hoped they'd let me keep my ticket stub to get home.

'Good,' he said.

'You, girl! With the frizzy hair.'

To my horror, I realised that Janey was pointing at me.

'Were you volunteering to tell us what you've learned?'

I shook my head mutely but it was too late. She was advancing down on me, her red talons outstretched.

'Come on! It's a safe space here! Share what you're feeling about love and spirituality in the workplace!'

I opened my mouth. I'd already pissed on my chips, it wasn't going to hurt telling a few more people and I quite liked the idea of Lydia getting the smile wiped off her face.

'Well,' I said, 'I've learned that . . .'

Suddenly I felt a pressure on my arm. Dr Maitland had grabbed me, quite hard.

'She's overcome,' he said loudly. 'She's been so

overwhelmed by all the, uh, love and spirituality in the room that . . . that I have to take her outside for a sit down.'

'You do no—' I started, but his hand only clamped down even harder.

'So, we're just popping out,' he announced, pushing me backwards firmly towards the exit.

'Now, I do find it amazing when the power of love and trust just *fills* the room,' said Janey loudly. 'Look at that! And next, it's going to get even *more* intense.'

A quiet groan went up from the group as Dr Maitland manhandled me backwards. I caught sight of Lydia looking at me with narrowed eyes.

'What are you doing?' I yelled, as Dr Maitland got me out and took me to sit on the sea wall. 'What? I've learned too much about your evil plans and now you're going to have me killed? That's it, isn't it? I've stumbled on your evil secrets and now you're going to make me pay.'

'Are you getting hysterical?'

A small group of teenagers rollerbladed past under the palm trees. It is difficult to feel hysterical when there are teenagers and palm trees about.

'No,' I said sullenly.

'OK. Well, I wanted to think for a bit.'

'About whether to strangle me or just push me off the sea wall?'

'You are very, very annoying, you know?'

'Only when faced with certain death.'

Dr Maitland sighed and looked out to sea. 'Look, everything you said . . . calm down. I've been having doubts about this the whole time. Not unlike your friend.'

'He's not my . . . never mind.'

'Dr Bennet, you know. He's very keen. To push the boundaries. Try new things. He likes the money, yes, but you know, he's a very committed doctor too.'

'He's a very committed schmoozer, you mean.'

'That's part of it.'

I looked over the sea wall. Someone had carved a great sand sculpture of a mermaid. It was absolutely beautiful, I couldn't imagine how it was done. It must have taken someone ages. All that work to make something beautiful that would be washed out by the tide. It reminded me of something but I couldn't think what. Oh, yeah. Life. I pointed it out to Dr Maitland.

'Well, just because time and the tide wash everything away eventually . . . is that a good reason not to at least try to create something beautiful?' he said.

'Beauty is one thing,' I said. 'Health is quite another. And better, in my opinion.'

'Science is beautiful,' he said, looking mournful. I looked around in case I should be planning my escape but I reckoned the worst of the danger had passed.

'Where's the beauty in tearing a baby seal from its mother?'

'I don't know,' said Dr Bennet, his eyes on the far horizon. 'I just don't know.'

We sat there, side by side, for about ten minutes. It was oddly restful. Then, finally, Dr Maitland turned to face me. His eyes had a spark to them I'd never seen before.

'OK,' he said. 'Well . . . if you were serious about what you said . . . if we want to stop this ship, we'll need a plan.'

# Chapter Ten

Lunch was a buffet sponsored by a wrinkle-plumping company. I was staying away from the cold chicken. Actually I was staying away from anything that looked like it might have been injected to plump it up before hitting the table.

'Does this food look *smooth* to you?' I asked Bailey. I'd timed it properly, so we were hitting the table at the same time.

'How are you getting on, Captain Catastrophe?'

I smiled at him. 'I've had worse holidays.'

Bailey looked around. We were in a dim room that seemed to be attached to a car park. 'You're joking.'

'No, I'm not. Remember that year we went to the Borders and I couldn't talk about it?'

'Oh, yeah. The trauma trip.'

'John Jr buried me in the sand.'

'That doesn't sound so bad.'

'The wet sand. Actually, it was clay. In the rain. Vertically. It was like *Merry Christmas Mr Lawrence*. But with more rain.'

'So you went on a holiday that was actually worse than a Japanese internment camp?'

I nodded vehemently.

'Oh, Evie.'

He put his hand on my arm affectionately. 'Have you heard of the calamity theory?'

'No.'

He bit his lip.

'You'd better tell me. Not everyone gets *Supergeek Monthly*.'

Actually, I was meant to be pumping him for information – step one of the plan – before turning him over to our side – step two.

'Oh, it's nothing. Silly really. There are some studies that show that certain circumstances will almost always attract adverse conditions. So, for example, if you have an earthquake then you'll probably get a flood, then cholera then . . . you know, just bad things attracting other bad things.'

'That's what you think about me?' When someone says something to your face that you've always secretly thought about yourself, it can take your breath away.

'No, of course not,' said Bailey.

'Oh, right. You were talking about parallel universe Evie.' I poked my crackers, feeling sorry for myself and cross with him and not quite sure what to say.

'It was meant to be a humorous analogy,' said Bailey.

'That turned out deeply hurtful,' I pointed out.

'Sorry,' he said. 'You can call me short if you want to.'

'It's OK.'

Bailey played with his three-bean salad. 'I'm sorry,' he said, again. 'Sometimes I'm not sure that this "mixing friends and work" thing is going as well as I'd hoped . . .'

I figured this was my chance – whilst it was quiet and he was feeling on the back foot – to get him on side.

'Bailey,' I said. 'This project.'

He arched an eyebrow at me. 'Yes.'

'Well . . . can you fill me in?'

'The project you said you didn't care about as long as you got to go somewhere sunny for a week?'

'Yes.'

'The project that I tried to explain and you said, "Be quiet, I can't listen and eat pancakes with maple syrup at the same time?" The secret briefing you never read . . .'

'All right, all right.'

'OK,' said Bailey. He sat back. 'Well, yes. Technically. The boat can go into international waters and do anything. It's not the one we were on last night – it's not here yet. They're just finishing her up in the shipyard. She arrives tomorrow. The hospital is a totally new design – it's beautiful. Do you know, however much the boat moves, the operating theatre remains totally stable. It's got four pivoting stabilisers, and is suspended from above . . .'

'OK, forget the technical details,' I said.

'Pancakes?' said Bailey.

'OK, OK. Who commissioned it? I mean, I know Dr Bennet's running the show. But it's not his money, is it? I mean, he's always complaining that he can't afford his own private island and stuff.'

Bailey looked uncomfortable.

'Well, we just work through Dr Bennet, on behalf of a holding company.'

'What? You mean, you don't know?'

Bailey shook his head.

'You don't know who the holding company is? So it could be anyone. It could be, like, Mafia Associates plc.'

'I don't think the Mafia is a publicly listed company.'

'Bad Guys inc? Drug Runners International. Don't you see, though? That this whole place . . . I mean, it could be really, really wrong.'

'Look, Evie, people build prisons and things. They design guns. I mean, bad things happen out of design, and I'm just a designer. And we don't even know it's going to happen here. Don't you think your imagination is running away with you?'

'I would have done, if I hadn't been caught in a SPY SET-UP HONEY TRAP.'

We both looked around, then, nervously, in case we were overheard.

'OK,' said Bailey, leaning forward with an intense look on his face. 'That guy was a nut job, OK?'

'But if he was right?' I said, persistently. 'If it is bad. Don't you think we should stop it?'

Bailey's eyebrows crept together. 'Oh, Evie,' he said. 'When would things be that simple?'

'*Hello!*' Lydia pushed herself between us. Her entire buffet lunch consisted of three strips of peppers and two prawns. 'Mmm, prawn and pepper salad, delicious,' she said. 'What are you having, Evie? Are those deep-fried cheese balls again?' Without waiting for an answer she beamed her full attention towards Bailey. 'How are you doing today, Dr Millionaire Smartie Pants?' she asked perkily.

'Actually, we were having a conversation,' I said. I'd rather Bailey had said it, but needs must.

'Ooh, gossip?' she said. 'Dish, dish, dish! It's Evie again, isn't it? I saw her throwing herself over Dr Maitland at the love and spirituality workshop this morning.'

At that point, I decided. I was going to have to get Lydia out of the way. I didn't want to do it, but I was going to have to bring out my big guns – I needed a secret weapon.

Oh, crap. Lydia was now laying into Bailey with a whole bunch of bollocks she'd obviously picked up by scanning Janey's book.

'Don't you feel, when it comes to exciting new ventures

like yours that the most important thing to get right is the soul-space?'

'The what now?'

Maybe Bailey had already started to get tired of her. Well, that would help.

I excused myself and went outside.

I took a walk along the beach to try and clear my head. This was all happening so fast. I looked out to sea, at the big boats bobbing up and down in the harbour. Who knew what was happening out there? Could be anything. I felt my head had turned round 360 degrees. First, meeting Tom. Then, finding out he was using me. Then, finding out he may have a point . . . argh. My head hurt, and for once it wasn't just from too much champagne.

And Dr Maitland being against it too . . . it was too weird.

Along the beach I spied a stocky figure rubbing suncream on a skinny one. Not exactly an unusual sight round here.

'Hello, Evie!' Kelly shouted cheerfully, as if nothing had happened the night before. 'Great yacht.'

I half smiled. John Jr looked uncomfortable. His belly was going pink. Family skin.

'Hi, JJ,' I said. I felt shy too. 'Thanks again for everything last night.'

It just felt so odd to be saying something nice.

'No probs, sis,' said JJ. Kelly kicked him with a French-manicured toe. 'Oh . . . and . . . sorry. For ruining things at dinner with that doc.'

'You didn't,' I said. 'Don't worry about it.'

And we half smiled at each other.

'Great,' said John Jr. 'Because Patrick's coming out.'

'WHAT?'

'He heard the chicks here are amazing. He's on his way.'

'No chance! I can cope with one of you, but . . .'

'Maybe we'll find him a nice girl,' said Kelly, who honestly thinks Patrick is just misunderstood, rather than an indiscriminate shag beast.

'No way.'

'Gets here tonight, just in time for your casino night.'

I'd forgotten all about casino time. God, there wasn't a second off.

'Boys on the town,' said JJ.

Although it had given me an idea. Usually I let Patrick's glands do their own thing . . . but this might just work . . . was he really as irresistible as he liked to think? I steeled myself for the wildly expensive mobile call.


'Yeah?'

The voice was surly, like I'd just got him out of bed. Except I knew I hadn't, because he still worked nine-to-five, however much he liked to pretend he was a good-looking bad boy who obeyed nobody's rules but his own.

'Patrick?'

'Who is this?'

I sighed. 'It's your one and only sister, Evie.'

'Oh. What do you want?'

'When are you coming to Cannes? All the booze is free, the sun is shining and it's absolutely crawling with . . .'

I hated to say it, but I was going to have to.

'What?'

'Muff.'

'Yeah. Today. Right. Didn't think you'd be so happy about it. JJ says you've been right slapping it up.'

'JJ says a lot of things. Anyway . . . I've got a really pretty friend here who'll be happy to show you around.'

Patrick snorted. 'Is she as pretty as Jilly?'

It was true; pre-Cassandro, Jilly had mooned around Patrick endlessly when we were growing up, eating cheese strings whilst conspiring to be constantly in the corridor outside his bedroom. His bedroom was next to the bathroom; he must have thought she had a terrible bladder problem.

'Miles better looking. In fact, are you in front of your computer?'

This was unfair. I know Patrick would have preferred me to imagine he was out on the open road somewhere on a Harley, chatting up a waitress in a truck-stop café on Route 66.

'Hnn,' he said grudgingly.

'OK, go to www.yourperfectface.co.uk.'

I knew they used Lydia on the home page of the surgery she worked for. It was a pouty, Posh Spice-style photograph, which I had always thought gave off the message, 'Piss off, you could never look like me, you fat losers.' But this hadn't seemed to deter people.

'Is that her?' he said admiringly.

'Uh-huh!'

'For real?'

'And John Jr has a huge suite and would be delighted to see you' – I crossed my fingers – 'and, tonight we're all going to the casino and you get free money to play with.'

'And you can get me in?'

'Sure, the security's rubbish.'

Well, it was.

'Yeah. I'm on my way.'

That was Lydia taken care of. He may be an arse, but I haven't met a woman yet with the power to resist Patrick, at least on first glance till they find out what a tit he is – and not always then.

But I still had to get Bailey on our side. I headed back to the marquee, but he was *still* deep in conversation with Lydia, who was on full power, so that would have to wait. At least I'd sown the seeds. The next plan on my list, whilst Dr Maitland went off to spy on the docs, was the one I was least looking forward to. But it had to be done.

I found a quiet Internet café, took out Dr Maitland's mobile phone (mine is pay as you go and lasts for about one second overseas, as I'd just discovered phoning Patrick), and sat down with Google.

I had to find Tom. He presumably had access to all sorts of documentation about the project, hence his motivation for why it was wrong. He could help us stop this thing. Even if he was a horrible, sexy, nasty, sexy man.

I couldn't help it – suddenly, even though I was nervous about finding Tom, I was a little bit excited. This was like a proper adventure! And we were the good guys! Fighting for seals and against bad people getting new faces! Yeah!

OK. Obviously the mobile phone number he'd originally given me no longer worked. I'd taken that as a given; it wasn't even the first time in my life that that had happened to me, so ha ha ha, meanie pants.

But he had said he came from Cumbria. I think I'd have to assume from the slightly posh Northern accent that he was telling the truth. Cumbria wasn't a large place, was it? OK, lots of sheep maybe, but how many vets?

I didn't know how to divide sheep by vets, so I searched for Cumbrian vets and got a website listing all UK vets. (Wow, I mean, really, have you ever met someone who designs vet websites for a living? Is it for pigs that can use the phone?)

I started dialling, then stopped. Was Tom his real name? Bennet certainly wasn't. Well, you know, I think I'd just have to assume it was because he'd turned round when people were shouting it as he was running naked across a pier, when presumably your mind would be on other things apart from remembering your fake name. Plus James Bond always called himself James. It was all I had to go on.

I'd just have to try and be casual.

'Hi, is Tom there?'

'Tom who?'

'Oh, you know, just Tom.'

'Tom the carthorse Tom?'

'Uh, no.'

'The cat? Or I think we have a python . . . no, that's Tomasina . . .'

OK, maybe another approach.

'I'm trying to track down a vet called Tom. He's got bright ginger hair and his ears stick out.'

Responses varied from, 'We've got a ferret that fits that description' to 'Are you *sure*, luv?'

But finally, on the twenty-fourth call, I hit it.

'Tom Livingstone? Yes, he's not in today. He's away at a veterinary conference.'

Oh, was he now?

'Oh well . . . it's quite urgent I get in touch with him. He was advising me about . . . a hamster.'

'Was he indeed?' the voice sounded amused. Maybe they were used to getting phone calls from desperate girls with imaginary hamsters.

'Is it anything someone else could help you with? Tom's not really a . . . hamster specialist.'

'No,' I said hotly. 'Gingerbread is very important to me and he's happy with Tom.'

'OK,' said the receptionist. I'm usually quite good at getting round receptionists, being one and everything.

'Is there any way I could get in touch with him . . . ?' I tried to make my voice sound pathetic. 'It's just . . . Gingerbread's got the most persistent cough. I couldn't bear to lose him. Maybe Tom could reassure me over the phone.'

'Mobiles are really just for emergencies,' said the voice.

'I understand,' I said in my smallest voice. 'I hope he lasts the night . . . when's he coming back?'

'Not till the end of the week.'

I sniffed loudly and didn't say anything.

'OK,' said the receptionist finally. 'Here's his mobile number. Just to set your mind at rest. I'm sure it's nothing.'

'Or TB,' I said. I was getting quite worked up about Gingerbread my imaginary hamster. But as she gave me the number and I hung up, I punched the air. I could be good at this!

My euphoria was short-lived, as I realised I was now actually going to have to make the call. Call the man who, just the night before, had humiliated me in front of everyone. Who I had had sex with. Not just with a man I hardly knew but with a man I knew all the wrong things about. Ugh. Oh well. Spies have to be very brave. I would just have to pretend that I was undercover too.

A thought struck me. What if he thought I was only calling him to get back together? Like he'd just been so absolutely amazing in bed that I didn't care that he was using me, I was just desperate for it? Oh, God, that would be awful. I should have got Dr Maitland to do this bit. But I wanted to show him I could handle it, that I was cool. Who was I kidding? I wasn't cool. Not even a tiny bit. With shaking fingers I dialled the number. At least he wouldn't recognise this phone number.

'Hello?' The voice sounded gruff and business-like, not the easy-going charmer I'd met. I steeled myself and hoped my voice wasn't about to wobble too much.

'Tom?'

'Who is this?'

I rolled my eyes. Torture me, why don't you?

'It's Evie.'

I could hear his brain gears tick over – he obviously wasn't expecting this. I prayed he wouldn't hang up.

'Uh,' he said. 'Look, I have to go . . .'

'No!' I said desperately. 'Don't hang up. It's nothing to do with last night.'

'How did you track me down?'

'You're helping me with my sick hamster.'

'Well, that's a new way of putting it.'

'Look, this is nothing to do with last night,' I repeated.

'Nothing at all? Are you sure?'

'Did you get arrested?'

He sucked in his breath. 'Not for want of you lot trying, no.'

'Uh, tell me you're not trying to *blame me* for last night. Please tell me that, before I have you arrested for indecent exposure.'

'You nicked my boxers and chased me like a loon!'

'Well, then . . . sex under false pretences.'

'It's hardly my fault if you refuse to see what's right under your nose, is it?' he said suddenly. 'I mean, I know you work in beauty so you hardly give a damn, but they're extracting live foetuses from seals to make some stupid fucking face juice and you think it's OK? They're going to completely ignore international protocol and do anything they like out on the high seas, but you don't mind?'

'I mind being taken advantage of,' I said softly.

He paused for a long time. Then his voice lowered. 'Actually,' he said. 'I'd already realised you didn't know any-thing. The day before, really, when we were walking along the beach. I mean, it was obvious.'

That winded me a bit. 'What do you mean?'

'I mean . . . you know, I still liked you.'

'That's not what you mean,' I said. 'I mean, you were sent to do a job and saw an opportunity. What was I, just another piece of meat like your dead bloody seals? Just some-thing to take advantage of, even though I wasn't any *use* to you?'

'No . . . it wasn't like that,' he said.

'It sounds exactly the fuck like that,' I said. I was getting wound up again. Then I tried my best, my absolute best to get a grip on myself. I took in a huge breath and tried to blow it out through my nose, like yoga teachers tell you to do.

'Are you being sick?' asked Tom.

'No!' I said. But oddly, his remark made it a bit easier to get a hold of myself.

'Look,' I said. 'Forget all this. Me and Dr Maitland have been talking.'

'Uh-huh?'

'And . . . well, he has doubts . . . we have doubts about the project.'

'Do you now? What gave it away, the amount of businessmen around wearing sunglasses indoors and surrounded by goons carrying walkie-talkies?'

'They aren't . . . Oh,' I said, thinking about some of the larger men at the conference. 'I thought those were just really old-fashioned mobile phones.'

'We got some really bad intelligence, picking on you,' said Tom, but he said it with a smile in his voice.

'Shut up,' I said. 'You're not allowed to mention that ever again.'

'I won't,' he said, immediately sounding chastened. 'And . . . I'm sorry. I'm really sorry.'

'So you should be,' I said.

'Um, could you stop punishing me? Remember, you did make me run through Cannes in the nuddie.'

'What did you do?' I said. 'We thought you'd get arrested.'

'Lucky I didn't. I found a wine cellar and hid down there.'

'Don't tell me – you put a cork in it.'

'*No*. I improvised with a couple of aprons and made it back.'

I half smiled at the thought. 'Can we meet?' I asked. 'Dr Maitland and I have some questions.'

'OK, Nancy Drew,' said Tom. 'Do you know the Metropole hotel?'

'Yes,' I said.

'OK. There's a little ice-cream shop next to it. I'll see you in there.'


I couldn't help feeling a little excited as I pushed my way through the crowds on the Croisette. After all, they were just silly sheep on holiday. *I* on the other hand was on an exciting secret mission. With ice cream. So it was like a bonus holiday.

When I found the place, though, I didn't see Tom. I was slightly curious to see him again, just in case I wanted to accidentally kick him in the face, but he didn't appear to be there. Perhaps I'd just sit down, order a Knickerbocker Glory and wait for . . .

'Psst,' came a voice. I looked behind me. 'Psst,' again.

It was coming from the corner of the restaurant. Sitting there was a man with dark hair and a baseball cap, behind a Russian newspaper. I moved closer.

'*Tom?*'

'Shhh!'

He pulled me down by the arm to sit next to him. I could hardly contain myself.

'I am Rudi. Russian engineer,' he announced loudly.

'You *are* joking.'

'Shh.'

'You're in disguise.'

'Well, seeing as my face and arse are all over *Cannes Matin* and everyone that was at that bash knows it was infiltrated, it seemed wise, don't you think?'

'To cover your head in boot polish and jam your ears together? I'm not sure.'

'Did anyone follow you?'

'*What?*'

'I should have told them NEVER to hand out my number . . . my phone's probably been tapped.'

'Aren't you taking this a little too seriously?'

'Well, we're trying to derail a fifty-million-euro project – what do you think?'

I hadn't really thought of it like that. 'You mean, we could be in danger?'

'Sometimes it's hard to do the right thing,' said Tom pompously.

'You know, that would sound a lot more manly and impressive if you didn't have a smudge of raspberry sauce on your cheek. Where's my ice cream?'

'I wasn't sure you were coming.'

'What, you thought I'd get kidnapped on the way? Or double-cross you?'

He looked at me strangely then.

'What do you mean, double-cross me?'

'I don't mean anything. I mean, can I have some chocolate ice cream, please?'

'It would be a very quick change of tune for you,' he mused. 'From know-nothing receptionist to suddenly being interested in finding out everything I know.'

'Yes,' I said. 'Plus, they said if I screwed you over they'd throw in a free boob job made from starving baby elephants. Stop being an idiot.'

He lowered the paper.

'OK,' he said. 'It's hard to trust sometimes.'

'It certainly is when your job is screwing people over,' I said. '*Une glace, s'il vous plaît? Chocolat, oui.*' At times, my French is fine. 'Now. Who do you work for again?'

'Earth Friends,' he mumbled. 'It's a loose collective that tries to argues against the more . . . evil extremes of capitalism.'

'What, like those people who throw stones at Starbucks? I hate those people.'

'*No*, we're a bit more subtle than that. Why do you hate those people?'

'Because a cup of coffee is not that evil. Compared to . . . I don't know. Men that set women on fire if they've been raped. Or send people to fight in pointless wars. Or, you know, commit genocide.'

'Do you protest against those things?'

'Not *as such*. But I disapprove of them. A lot more than some stupid cup of coffee.'

'Well, I'm glad you're managing to provide such a vital stance against things you disapprove of in society by doing absolutely nothing at all.'

'Right, I'd be much better off taking a brick and throwing it through a shop window of a business someone's actually spent time building up and . . .'

'Can we get off the whole coffee thing for a minute? That's not my point. Earth Friends is more . . . think of a charity you do approve of.'

'Uh.' I couldn't think. 'The RSPB?'

'The *RSPB*?'

'Yes?'

He sighed. 'OK. Well, we're more like the RSPB. We campaign against grossly dangerous environmental projects and things we feel mark a really bad direction for society. And we make examples of specific things. Like, for example, a practically completely illegal boat where they're going to carry out dangerous medical procedures whilst getting through, incidentally, twenty thousand litres of fuel a week, whilst they experiment with God knows what.'

'So what did you want out of me?'

'Where it was headed . . . itinerary . . . whether Bailey knew, or whether you controlled Dr Bennet's diary... celebrity clients...'

'What, after you'd shagged me so spectacularly that the names of show business clients had come out of my mouth?'

Tom shrugged a little uncomfortably.

'Well. Maybe if you'd had dark hair and a Russian accent,' I said.

'It was just an idea,' said Tom sulkily.

'Has it ever worked before in the history of mankind?'

'Yes, all the time,' he said. 'Admittedly, mostly the other way around. Girls seducing boys, that kind of thing. Or boys seducing boys.'

'Well, at least it kept you off the letter writing campaign.'

I picked up a large spoonful of chocolate ice cream and devoured it. 'What I don't understand is why you didn't just ask me? Look, I'm here now, ready to come over on your side and fight the good fight.'

'How could I ask you? What would you think if some lunatic came up to you and suggested that you went against your friends and your employers and everyone you know on some crazed scheme?'

'I'm very open-minded,' I said.

'True,' said Tom, getting a faraway look in his eyes.

I ignored him and kept eating my ice cream. 'So,' I said. 'What's the plan?'

'Well, the original plan was to go to the papers with all the blueprints and celebrities and things,' said Tom. 'Can I have some of your ice cream?'

'NO! Dr Maitland and I think we should have a better plan. One that involves talking to Dr Bennet.'

'*Talking* to him? Talking him out of ten million euros? How are you going to do that?'

'*Ten million euros?*' This was ridiculous. It couldn't be true, could it? Who had that much money?

'Or, well, you know. Something like that. Lots and lots of money from his boat, all offshore.'

'Oh,' I said. 'So you don't know how much money he stands to make. You meant –' and I did the Dr Evil pinky lip – 'ten *meelion* euros.'

Tom didn't answer. He was too busy stealing a bit of my ice cream.

'So even if you could talk him out of it, they'll just get somebody else,' said Tom.

'OK, well, if we talk *everyone* out of it.'

'Everyone on earth? I still think getting agitation in the press is a better idea. Get them to stake out the place with paparazzi. Get some of our youth members along to demonstrate.'

'*Youth* members?'

'Yes. You know, some politically switched-on types have even heard of us.'

'Stop stealing my ice cream, you communist.'

We discussed lots of things. To me, it seemed crucial to get to Dr Bennet and get him on side. If Bailey couldn't give us valuable information about who exactly had commissioned the ship and was behind the job, Dr Bennet ought to be able to. Then the next stage was to threaten them with exposure or . . . well, we weren't sure about the 'or'.

'Couldn't they take all the money and build a children's hospital or something?' I said.

'What, for baby nose jobs? Anyway, look around you: you're in France. They're up to their eyeballs in totally perfect children's hospitals. Mind you, it's one up on what I thought you'd say.'

'What's that?'

'That you thought they should donate all the money to the RSPB . . .'

'Ha ha ha. Birds are very important, you know.'

'I know. Look, Earth Friends has the contacts, the press – we can lobby against this kind of thing once we know who's doing it.'

He looked up at me. 'So we're in this together, right? You can get me a pass to this casino shindig tonight?'

'I guess so,' I said.

Tom sat back on the banquette, looking pleased with himself.

'But don't smirk.'

'I'm not smirking! It's the drawn-on moustache.'

'You look like you're smirking to yourself. You look like you're thinking, Ah, my shagging plan worked. But I'm telling you it didn't.'

'OK.'

'Dr Maitland convinced me.'

'OK.'

'It was nothing to do with you.'

'Not at all.'

'And you're paying for the ice cream.'

I called Dr Maitland on his other phone. He'd gone to find Dr Bennet but hadn't managed to locate him.

'That's unusual, isn't it?' I asked. 'He's usually schmoozing up all over the place.'

'That's what I thought,' he said. 'Maybe he's headed up to the casino to sort things out for tonight. Or maybe he's back in his hotel room?'

We decided his room might be a good place to tackle him. Just a chat – a staff meeting between the three of us. Just to get a bit more clarity on the direction the practice was going (out to sea by the looks of things) and so on . . . nothing heavy.

The afternoon sun beamed down strongly on the beach and I stopped off and bought a large floppy hat. My redness was retreating somewhat, but I didn't want to risk round two; I already had freckles popping up over every available surface. Plus it might come in handy for a disguise.

Dr Maitland almost smiled at me as I met him in the cool marble lobby of the Metropole.

'Is that you in disguise?' he said. 'The big hat and sun-glasses?'

'No! This is totally normal!'

'OK,' he said. 'You know, there's a new laser pen for freck-les that . . .'

I shushed him. 'You know, some people *like* freckles.'

He frowned. 'Do they?'

'Yes. They think they're cute.'

He came closer and gave my face that penetrating clinical doctory stare thing straight at my face.

'Oh,' he said eventually, straightening up. 'You know they're marks of skin damage?'

I rolled my eyes.

'But yes,' he said. 'They are quite cute. OK, shall we tell the desk to call Yuri?'

Ugh, it was the same snotty pretty man on the desk as before. Did he ever go off duty? Was this whole place staffed by robots? He looked at me, quite convincingly managing to indicate that he had X-ray eyes that could look into my soul and see if I was wanting in the 'being served in a posh hotel' department. Obviously I was as he actually looked around to see if there was anyone else he could help before us.

'Let's not bother,' I said. 'Do you know the room number? We can just go up.'

'OK,' shrugged Dr Maitland.

I've always felt slightly odd in a lift with a man, I don't

215

know why. Probably just so many silly films and dumb Black Lace books, but there's something about being in that enclosed space . . . I suppose that's why everyone just ignores each other and stares straight ahead. Because there's always that ridiculous idea that creeps into your head along the lines of, Wouldn't it be *awful* if I suddenly just leapt cougar-like onto this near-stranger and gave them a big . . .

'I think we're here,' said Dr Maitland.

The door pinged open to reveal, waiting for the lift to go back down, a somewhat dishevelled-looking Janey reapplying her lipstick!

'Hello!' I said cheerfully. I didn't move to get out of the lift; this was (or could be) too good to be true! 'Are you staying here too?'

Janey looked at me with absolutely no recognition in her eyes, but perked up when she saw Dr Maitland.

'Hello, Doctor . . . I mean, well, what a coincidence seeing you here.'

'Is it?' said Dr Maitland gruffly.

'I was just . . .' She gave a self-conscious giggle. 'Uh, going over some paperwork with Dr Bennet.'

'Is that what they're calling it these days?' I wondered aloud. After all, she was already ignoring me. Dr Maitland trod heavily on my foot to shut me up.

'Of *course*,' he said. 'There's so much to go through, isn't there? Health and safety, disclaimers . . . it ties us all up in knots, red tape.'

He gently but firmly started manoeuvring us out of the lift so Janey could step in.

Janey had regained her composure fully now.

'Oh, abso*lutely*,' she said. 'As I was just saying to Dr Bennet . . . so ridiculous. Plus what *must* I look like coming out of his room in the middle of the day! People will talk. Mind you –' she regarded us frankly – 'you could say that about you two! Ha ha!'

My eyebrows shot up in surprise. Turning it round! Boy, she was good!

'Didn't mean to make you blush,' she said to me merrily, convinced now she had the upper hand. 'Well, buh bye!'

And the lift door pinged, and she was gone.

Dr Maitland and I looked at each other speechlessly.

'Well, it could have been innocent,' he said.

'She was putting lipstick on!' I yelled. 'How did her lipstick come off?'

'But . . . you know, women like her wear a lot of lipstick.'

This is indubitably true. They slather it on like they're about to be filmed for high-definition IMAX.

We headed up the corridor.

'Well, if Dr Bennet's naked from the waist up,' I suggested, 'this could be a useful bargaining tool. Where is Mrs Bennet again?'

'Shopping for teeth sharpeners,' said Dr Maitland, preparing to knock on the door.

'What?' he said as I stopped short.

'That is the first time I've ever heard you make a joke,' I said. 'I thought it just wasn't possible for you. That humour had been surgically removed or something, like an appendix.'

Dr Maitland sighed. 'Well, we all know what a good judge of character you are, Evie,' he said. Then he knocked the door, and we entered.

Alas, Dr Bennet was not, as I had hoped (and partly feared), picking up a pair of stockings with his teeth whilst singing, 'Hurray, hurray, it's adultery today,' to himself and sipping the last of the champagne from a glass stiletto.

He did, however, look quite surprised to see us, given that we were his right-hand men. Or so I thought.

'Wilf . . . Evie. Hello, my dears. Um . . .'

Was that a sneaky checking round the room in case of tell-tale signs? Mind you, I would have had to check around my hotel room too if someone turned up unexpectedly, just in case I'd left any of my *own* knickers draped over the chair or whatnot.

'To what do I owe the honour . . . Janey was just here dropping off some paperwork, so it's like Piccadilly Circus round here today!'

Curses! Still he didn't get away so easily – he must have guessed we'd have run into her by the lift.

'What papers?' I said. 'Why don't I take them away with me so I can file them promptly.'

Dr Bennet looked at me, then fumbled on the table for his reading glasses.

'Well, aren't *you* efficient? Here you are then – the course recommendations, the assessment forms . . . here, you can take all these ones from the other seminars too.'

He started loading down my arms with folders.

'And the extra-curricular sign-ups – actually, if you could input those on the database and cross-reference to the original attendance that would be extremely helpful to us . . . start sorting out the wheat from the chaff.'

'Yuri,' said Dr Maitland. 'Can we talk?'

'Of course, of course.'

Dr Bennet looked at us, beaming.

'So nice to have the team together, yes? How do you think it's going? I think it's going very well, very well indeed. Well, apart from a couple of minor . . .' He came over to me and patted my arm. 'How *are* you, my dear? Did you file charges?'

This wasn't like him. He must be worried I had come here to sue the firm.

'No, it's all right,' I said. 'I don't want to get prosecuted for being an idiot.'

'That's the spirit,' said Dr Bennet, as if that actually was the spirit. 'Janey says that you have to be bigger than the setbacks in your life.'

'Does she?' I said. 'But she's three-foot six.'

'Don't be personal,' said Dr Bennet.

'Yuri,' said Dr Maitland heavily. 'We need to talk. We've got some concerns about Operation Sunshine.'

Dr Bennet stopped moving about. 'What. Both of you?' he said, all business suddenly. He poured us all glasses of water. 'Together?'

We both nodded.

'Go on then. Out with it.'

Dr Bennet listened while we explained everything that didn't add up about the project; the lax laws, open access to goodness knows who; the environmental impact. He didn't say anything, just looked at us as we talked – it felt like presenting something to your form teacher, who listened to you indulgently as you told him, wide-eyed, that God didn't exist.

After we'd finished we kind of tailed off with a few 'So's . . .' and 'So that's whys . . .' and then sat back. Dr Bennet still didn't say anything, he just sat there, cradling his fingers in that way they teach them at Being a Doctor college. His brow nearly furrowed.

'Wilf,' he said. 'Wilf. Didn't we discuss this?'

Dr Maitland looked uneasy. He took off his glasses.

'I didn't realise it was such a big deal, Yuri. I thought it was a side project, an offshoot that would bring us in some extra income and provide an interesting diversion . . .'

'A diversion, eh?' Dr Bennet looked a little nasty. 'So the research opportunities were of absolutely no interest to you?'

'Well, yes, obviously, but now I'm feeling . . . conflicted.'

'Conflicted?'

Suddenly the smooth calmness of Dr Bennet – the only mode I'd ever seen him in, Mr Charming – vanished, and he stood to his feet.

'*Conflicted?*' We have a fifty-million-euro boat out there that's just been refitted and you're saying you're *conflicted*?'

Dr Maitland shuffled uncomfortably. Suddenly this felt horribly serious.

'Don't tell me you don't have a vested interest in this.'

I looked at him. He looked haunted.

'So maybe I'd go against my own interests.'

'Would you?' said Dr Bennet. 'Look, you two. Obviously *you* –' and he pointed to me – 'have been completely compromised by that lanky ginger idiot.'

'Lanky ginger idiot . . . with a point,' I said.

But he'd already turned his attention back to Dr Maitland. Now his voice went back to its normal, encouraging, wheedling tone.

'Come on, Wilf. Don't be daft, it's just progress. If we don't do it somebody else will.'

'So let's not do it,' said Wilf. 'That's not a good argument for anything. Plus if you get wrapped up in anything illegal it might be dangerous.'

Dr Bennet harrumphed at this. 'Science is not legal or illegal, Wilf. You know this.'

'I don't,' said Wilf. 'In fact, I think the practice should pull out,'

Dr Bennet set his glass down with a thump.

'Pull out! After all this money spent and the engineers employed and the doctors and the bankers lined up begging to get let in? Are you *crazy*?'

'No,' said Wilf. He stood up suddenly and took a deep breath. 'But I'm out.'

'You're what . . . you're resigning?'

Dr Bennet was trying to keep his cool, but I could see he was furious.

'I don't have to resign,' said Dr Maitland. 'You're not my boss. I'm your partner. I'm dissolving our partnership.'

Dr Bennet's mouth was open. So was mine. Oh my God! This wasn't a little holiday flirtation with activism! This was really serious! I knew, you see. Dr Maitland was miles better than Dr Bennet. Dr Maitland was what kept us on Harley Street, and in the celebrities' secret notebooks, and on the recommended lists. Dr Bennet could do the schmooze and the charm, but Dr Maitland was the one who wielded the knife; who could give nose jobs that don't even look like nose jobs (and believe me, when you've seen as many as I have you realise how rare that is).

'Wilf,' said Dr Bennet. 'You don't mean that.'

'I've been sleepwalking,' said Dr Maitland. He sat down, and didn't look at either of us. 'All this time, thinking chopping open stupid dumb blondes was fine, it was just training till I could take my skills somewhere else, somewhere useful. Go work in a war zone, or with burns victims in India. That was my plan. But then what happened? I got used to the easy money, coming in at ten every morning, not having to talk to anyone if I didn't want to, living a nice life.'

I didn't think it sounded that nice, apart from the money part, but I didn't want to interrupt.

'So I never did any of that . . . all the big plans I had at medical school. The good life I'd mapped out for myself. I didn't want to go to Africa and get bitten by bugs and have to sleep in tents. I didn't want to go and work in dirty hopeless conditions in the Third World. I *liked* being comfortable.'

He stood up and walked over to Dr Bennet.

'But this *is* dirty. This is dirtier than . . . one of those countries where dogs eat dead dogs in the street. This smells worse than somewhere I'd have to wipe my scalpel on the long grass. Because this is what happens when you get complacent, when you get comfortable. Bad things happen. And bad things are going to happen here. And I'm not doing it.'

'Fine,' said Dr Bennet. 'Then we'll do it without you.'

And *then* he punched Wilf on the nose.

I knelt next to Dr Maitland, whose nose was discharging thick gouts of blood, while Dr Bennet, whistling slightly, washed his hands and picked up his briefcase. I was shocked, and breathing hard. I mean, obviously I'd seen plenty of blood, but usually people were anaesthetised.

'So I guess this is goodbye, Evie,' he said chirpily. 'I won't be paying you compensation . . . I'm sure you'll understand.'

'What, after you let me be assaulted at your conference? We'll see about that,' I said, white-hot with fury. 'You'll be hearing from my lawyers.'

'Who are your lawyers again?' he asked, looking amused. 'Ambulance chasers dot com? Well, I wish you good luck with that – there are very few extradition treaties between the UK and . . . the middle of the sea.'

He stood, looking impatient.

'Could you move now, please . . . I have an important session to run. And a new staff to recruit.'

I looked at Dr Maitland, but he still seemed too stunned to say anything. Dr Bennet didn't even look a tiny bit perturbed; simply ushering us out in his usual charming manner as if on his way to a hairdresser's appointment.

I drew myself up to my full height (five foot five) and tried to look him straight in the eye.

'You won't get away with this,' I said, voice trembling.

'What is this, *Scooby Doo*?' he said. 'What's to get away with? I'm pursuing a legitimate business interest without my partner. Big deal.'

'So why did you just punch him on the nose?'

'Are you joking? Six years without so much as a "good morning"? Do you know what it's like working with someone like that? I wish I'd done it years ago, the rude bastard.'

Hmm. He almost had a point there.

# Chapter Eleven

'It's true,' Wilf – as he'd now suggested I called him – was saying, as we sat in the lobby drinking a restorative *citron* as he held a tissue to his nose. 'But I'm just shy, that's all. Shy and . . . I was slightly ashamed of my job.'

'I've always wondered,' I said, figuring it was now or never, 'why you wouldn't take your obvious skills somewhere more useful.'

He looked defensive, as if he wanted to avoid the question.

'Plenty of good doctors just work for the cash.'

'Yes, well, there's a difference between a good doctor and a good person.'

'Hmm,' said Wilf, looking uncomfortable. He dabbed at his nose some more. Then he turned to face me.

'You always tell the truth, don't you, Evie?' he said. 'It's an unusual habit.'

I looked into his grey-blue eyes. '*Good* unusual?' I found myself asking, a little short of breath.

Suddenly there was a huge commotion in the lobby.

'Hey, look, it's my half-naked slutbag sister,' came the cheery voice booming across the lobby. The concierge raised his eyebrows nastily. Obviously JJ had got over our touching family reunion.

'Hello, John Jr,' I said, trying to insinuate that I had much better things to be going on with. 'Is Patrick here yet?'

'I'm just going to get him, in I?'

He stared rudely at Wilf. 'Ooh, the doc again. You don't mess around, do you?'

'Hello, again,' said Wilf, a little stiffly. Oh, crap. Just when Wilf and I were getting along he'd be reminded that, technically, I was related to an orang-utan. Bugger. Though what was I being so snotty about – my GCSE in general studies?

'You know they've got brandies here for two 'undred euro a glass?' said John Jr. He paused to allow us to take in the impressiveness of his statement. 'I didn't like mine much. Only 'ad four. Ah well, all goes on the company credit card, eh, Doc? Eh? Eh?'

Wilf smiled nicely, which I liked.

'Gawd, if I had to add up the time I've spent waiting for

the missus to get her slap on . . . Stupid cow. 'Ere she is now.'

Kelly tottered towards us, her face in the widest smile I'd ever seen.

''Ello!' she said. 'Feeling better?'

'I'm totally over it now actually,' I said.

'And you with that awful skin peel too. You know, you want to get some Crème de la Mer – it is expensive, but it's *so* worth it. Anyway,' she said, 'you won't *believe* what's happened!'

'What?' I asked. I wasn't quite up to telling her my news: sacked, in trouble, penniless, etc.

'Well, I ran into your gorgeous Dr Bennet at lunch . . . and he asked me to be his *inaugural* client when he launches his new venture!'

Wilf and I looked at each other in consternation.

'Bloody hell,' I said. 'What did they say they're going to do to you?'

She smiled. 'Oh, this is the exciting part. It's completely new. They've never done it before. Roxy – something. They inject it under my entire face, and it apparently looks like I have completely new skin! Like a baby's! I'll look twenty!'

'You're only thirty-one,' I said.

She pouted. 'Exactly. Nothing like twenty.'

'Why do you even care? You're married, you've got a big house . . . I mean, what's it to you?'

'Well,' said Kelly, 'it's just a matter of personal pride and self-esteem, that's all.' Then she realised she might have insulted me and looked apologetic.

Wilf was looking anxious.

'Mrs Kennedy... this treatment they described to you... is it called Radoflux 9000?'

Kelly's face lit up. 'Yeah, that's it!'

I looked at Wilf. 'It's those bloody seals again, isn't it?'

He nodded.

'Do you think it's dangerous?' I said.

'We don't know if it's dangerous yet,' said Wilf. 'Possibly. And the use of animal stem cells in plastic surgery – or at all – well, it's very controversial.'

'There you go,' I said to Kelly. 'It's dangerous. Possibly. You'd be mad to do it, it's not even legal.'

'Well, why would a doctor have recommended it if it wasn't legal?' said Kelly, pouting a bit.

'And there, in a nutshell, is the problem with this fucking boat,' said the odd-looking person waltzing through the circular door.

'Who are you?' said Kelly. 'Why is everyone ganging up on me?'

'Don't listen to them, sweetheart,' said John Jr. 'They're just jealous.'

'I'm not jealous,' I said. 'We're just trying to stop her from having a procedure that might harm her!'

'But it's just a minor procedure, Evie,' said Kelly. 'It'll be fine.'

'Yeah,' said John Jr. 'You're just jealous she's getting something for free that you really bloody need. Look at you lot.'

Sure enough, with me, Tom arriving with boot polish under his nose and Wilf with dried blood trickling on his face we did make quite a sight.

Kelly appeared to think about it.

'I'll see you lot later,' she said finally. 'I'll be the twenty-year-old in the corner.'

And they swept out, or rather Kelly swept; John Jr waddled after her.

Wilf let out a heavy sigh. 'This is not good,' he said. 'This is not good at all. And who the hell have you come as?'

Tom looked a little insulted.

'Uh, sorry,' I said. 'This is our mystery man in heavy disguise.'

'A mystery man, eh?' said Wilf, looking puzzled. Pretty much every eye in the foyer was on Tom. A bit of his hair dye had run down onto his ear, making it look smudged. His sunglasses were a little wonky. And he had salt stains on his shorts. Out of the corner of my eye I felt the evil concierge send a little death ray in our direction. I clutched at my drink to show I had the right to be there.

'Oh, wow,' said Tom. 'Did you get in a big ruckus with Dr Bennet?'

'Not so much a *big* ruckus,' said Wilf.

'He got biffed on the nose,' I added helpfully.

'Oh, good,' said Tom. 'Did you discover all his backers? When is the boat coming in? What other evil plans he has up his sleeve?'

'Not exactly,' I said.

Tom thought about this. 'You know, we really need to know when the boat is coming in, so we can intercept it.'

'Maybe it's a surprise,' I said.

'It's a fucking liberty,' snapped Tom.

'He doesn't seem to think he's being evil,' said Wilf.

'Well, he *is*,' said Tom. 'And that injection thing is completely out of the question.'

'It didn't . . . it didn't go quite as well as we'd hoped,' I said.

'You mean, you guys messed it up?'

'He didn't seem to want to talk to us much,' mumbled Wilf. He checked out his reflection in one of the big gilt mirrors hanging overhead.

'It's all right,' I said. 'I don't think you need stitches.'

'Thank you, doctor,' he muttered.

Tom threw his hands up. 'Well, this is great. Did he sack you?'

'Well, he can't sack me, I'm his partner,' said Wilf. 'I resigned.'

Tom put his hands over his eyes.

'He sacked me though,' I added helpfully.

'I have to make a phone call,' said Tom.

\*

'But I thought you guys had a *plan*,' Tom was saying as the three of us walked down to the seafront.

'We did!' I said. 'We thought we'd explain the error of his ways and then everything would be all right. Now I think about it, not such a brilliant plan.'

'So ... all your contacts and hope of getting on that boat ... it's all gone.'

'And I lost my job,' I said. 'And I'll never get another one in the same field now they've all seen me in your boxers.'

'You can come work for me,' said Wilf.

'I thought you told Dr Bennet you were going to work in darkest Africa,' I said.

'Oh, yeah,' he said, looking a tad disconsolate. 'So I am.'

'No!' said Tom. 'What do you mean! We're not giving up!'

'Well, we kind of have to,' I explained. 'Because, you know. We're not a part of this any more. Dr Bennet is just going to run the boat and it's our tough luck, and, I don't know, Kelly will probably end up taking liquids through a straw for the rest of her life.'

'I can't believe you're taking it like that,' said Tom.

I turned to him seriously. 'What do you expect me to do? I'm sorry, Tom. The boat is horrible. So are lots of things. It's going to happen with or without us, that's perfectly clear. But we did try. We all did. Why don't we just go out and have a few glasses of wine and try and forget all about it ...'

'That's a shit attitude and you know it,' said Tom.

He left our group and looked at the road.

'You say you want to help and then you do fuck all.'

'I got a bloody nose,' said Wilf, but this only seemed to enrage Tom all the more.

'Fucking dilettantes. Don't you care what happens to this planet?'

'Yes,' I said. 'Let's discuss it over a glass of rosé. Maybe Wilf could help your charity.'

'Yes,' said Wilf, brightening slightly. 'With, you know. A UK-based helping job. Where I could still use my skills . . . maybe in the London area . . . research perhaps.'

'Forget it,' said Tom. He backed away from us, and onto the open road, stepping off the narrow pavement. He obviously didn't want to be anywhere near us. 'Forget it. This whole thing . . . You guys were a complete waste of time. I should have known it from the start.'

'I'm sorry,' I said, and I was. But what else could we do?

'You're not,' said Tom. Scooters and cyclists were having to swerve to avoid him. 'You don't give a . . .'

Suddenly a car, which should have gone straight past us, screeched to a halt. It was a huge, heavy-looking silver thing – a big steely Mercedes. It had blacked-out windows, which gave it a sinister appearance. Completely without warning the back door opened and two sets of arms came out. They hauled Tom backwards into the car's dark maw.

Taken completely by surprise from behind, Tom didn't even make a sound as he disappeared. His big gangling feet were the last to go, kicking in the air. Even before they were fully in, the car sped off. It couldn't have stopped for more than four seconds; it had barely inconvenienced the cars behind it. But suddenly, Tom was gone.

'TOM!' I screamed into the air. I threw myself forward, but the car had already taken a left turn and disappeared into the swiftly moving traffic before speeding away on the four-lane raised motorway that cut through the heart of Cannes like a knife. 'TOM!'

Unbelievably, under the shady palm trees, it seemed like no one else had even noticed.

# Chapter Twelve

We went to the only place I was sure nobody would find us –
my horrible guest house. The landlady hadn't looked me in
the face once since I'd arrived so I could be reasonably confident she wouldn't be able to pick me out in a line-up or betray
me to mysterious goons.

We sat there awkwardly, on my bed.

'Oh, God,' I kept saying, although it didn't really help
matters much. 'Oh, God.'

'We must go to the police,' said Wilf. 'We must.'

'But they're already looking for him! They want to arrest
him for being naked! Plus, what on earth would we tell them?'

'That a man was pushed into a car!'

'What kind of car?'

'A big silver car.'

'And where was it going?'

Wilf looked really concerned. 'This is serious, isn't it? This is serious stuff with bad guys and everything. This isn't like a holiday adventure at all.'

'What if they kill him?'

'They can't kill him,' I said, realising I was shaking. 'They won't.'

'Who, though?' said Wilf. 'Who are we even talking about? *Bloody* Yuri. We need to get to him.'

He tried his phone again. Dr Bennet wasn't picking up.

I glanced at my watch. 'He'll be at the casino. That thing will be starting.'

'Well, we'd better get there, then. Once we finally find out who's responsible and where he is we can call the *gendarmes*.'

We were going to rush off to the casino straight away, but this was a posh night and presumably Dr Bennet had already taken us off the guest list. We didn't want to stand out more than we already did. I sent Wilf onwards and, finally, slipped into the bloody red dress. In my head I'd imagined myself taking a long time getting ready in my large marble bathroom before slipping it over my sun-drenched skin. Not shoving it on over my blistered shoulders before running out to try and find our friend who'd been *kidnapped*. My holiday dreams seemed long ago and far away. And what had seemed like a bit of excitement was suddenly careering out of control.

I looked at the high-heeled shoes I'd bought to go with

the dress. Well, they weren't going to work because I had to run all the way to the casino as it was. Which meant I had a choice between my boots that I'd worn from London, a pair of red Converse – which were the right colour but made me look as if I was trying to make a ridiculous Lily Allen style statement – or a pair of flip-flops. Flip-flops it would have to be. At least my skin seemed to be settling down a bit. Though I hardly had the chance to do more than glance at myself in the mirror and bung on some red lipstick before throwing myself out of the hotel and tearing down towards the seafront. My heart was pounding. OK, Tom was an idiot, but he didn't deserve this. I had a sudden horrible mental image of him cowering in a room somewhere, or being thrown into the sea. And I was *furious* with Dr Bennet. He was going to tell us where Tom was if I had to . . . bloody pluck out his bloody eyebrows.

Holding my skirt with both hands – and tripping over every two minutes in those bloody flip-flops – I finally made it. Completely breathless and with sweat dripping off my forehead, I pelted up to the front of the casino, chest heaving.

The casino was white and palatial with steps leading up to it. Outside was a cashpoint machine. This put me off somewhat. I mean, obviously, it's useful for people to be able to pick up cash, but I didn't like the idea of people desperately pushing cards into the machine in the middle of the night just to feed their gambling addiction.

Expensive cars were disgorging expensive-looking

occupants as tourists walked past rubbernecking. I looked for the silver car but couldn't see it. Stealthily dangerous-looking bouncers hovered round the entrances. And there, looking tall and smart and slightly concerned, his bow tie untied around his neck, out of breath like I was, was Wilf.

He didn't see me at first so I waved furiously. Then, when he did, his face changed. The anxiety drained out of it – not completely, but enough to soften up his features and give a spark to his eye. And for a second I forgot that our friend had disappeared; that I'd lost my job; that this was a really weird holiday; that we'd failed in our mission to stop the project; that, in fact, my life had gone from mundane to disastrous in the space of about three days (and I was probably going to die of skin cancer too). Just for a second.

'Hello,' he said, coming down the steps towards me.

'Hello,' I said. We looked round. There was nobody there that we knew. He grinned that lopsided smile at me.

'You look . . . you look nice.'

'That's impossible,' I said. 'I just threw it on in two seconds. Literally. I'm not wearing any make-up or anything.'

Wilf shrugged. 'I don't like overdone women.'

I stared at him.

'You are joking. That's what you do.'

'Haven't we already established that I'm not *exactly* over the moon about what I do?' said Wilf. Then, shyly, he leaned over and planted a kiss on my cheek.

I stepped back, feeling my heart beat.

'Uh,' I said. 'Uh . . . we'd better go and do this thing.'

'Absolutely,' said Wilf. 'Fortune favours the brave. Let's go find Yuri and, I don't know, *tickle* the answers out of him.'

'Er, yeah,' I said.

'Um,' said Wilf. 'Could you do up my bow tie first?'

Bow tie looking like a badly wrapped party gift (hey, it's not like I sent my brothers out to black tie dos very often), we vaulted up the steps, planning our strategy. If Dr Bennet didn't come clean we were going straight to the police – well, as strategies went it wasn't a bad one. As long as we were on time. But I also thought, I mean, they'd probably just take Tom somewhere and make him walk home naked again to get him back for ruining their yacht party, wouldn't they?

First we had to get past the bouncers. I hoped against hope that Dr Bennet would have been too busy or annoyed to waste time getting our names taken off the list. And the person he'd usually have ordered to do so was, of course, me. He couldn't really find his way around a sheet of A4 without me.

Clattering up the steps we were conscious that there was an aura of low-key elegance about the place. Beautiful waitresses glided about with cocktails on trays. Smart music was tinkling. Expensive-looking paintings lined the walls. Everything about the place seemed designed to make you completely forget that its sole purpose was to send you down the road to rack and ruin and end up owning your house and, ideally, wife.

'Just look like we fit in,' I whispered as we mounted the red-carpeted steps.

'You're the one in flip-flops,' Wilf whispered back, then he took my hand and squeezed it. I squeezed it back, then let it stay there. It felt comfortable. I felt – even though we'd been thoroughly bested so far – that if I was with him, then maybe we were going to be all right.

'Aha,' came the familiar voice, and the face peered quizzically down on us from the top of the stairs.

'*Quelle surprise!*'

Lydia.

'I wondered if you two would have the cheek to turn up,' she sneered. 'But here you are – waif man and the deep-fried tomato. Holding hands. How touching.'

Lydia was clutching a large clipboard with names on it. Witch with a clipboard – ominous.

'You know, you don't have to be nasty all the time,' I said. 'It's not in your job description. *Is* it?'

'*Me* being nasty?' said Lydia. 'I'm not the ones that tried to embarrass Dr Bennet and the entire bloody Harley Street community, am I? I'm not the ones who are having a cheap and tacky affair and had a big strop when it was discovered and then quit their jobs leaving poor Dr Bennet in the lurch.'

'Is *that* what he said?' I yelled, furious. 'He's lying.'

'So I can see by the fact that you're holding hands.'

'We really need to get in there, er, Lydia,' said Wilf. 'Do you mind?'

'Yes, I do actually,' said Lydia. 'Because your names aren't here on my clipboard. Which means you've been disinvested. Which means if you do try and get in I'll have to shout to the nearest two gigantic bouncers who, and I haven't seen it myself, but *apparently*, can kick your arse from here to doomsday.'

I looked at the stealthy bouncers again. Yup. It certainly looked possible, if not probable. As I was looking at them, one of them turned round to give me stink eye. Lydia made a little motion with her manicured hand which looked like it meant 'Come over here I think I'm about to have some trouble.' Sure enough, the goon touched his partner and the pair started to lumber towards us. Wilf and I looked at each other. Oh, God. This wasn't going well.

'Please, Lydia,' I said, resorting to begging. She liked this and looked at me regally.

'Well, the problem is . . .' she started officiously, traffic warden-style.

Oh, God, she was about to explain why she'd really, really *like* to help us out but couldn't because of her obsessive rule-following and unpleasant personality.

'The problem is . . .' But then she stopped talking altogether, and just stood there with her mouth hanging open. I stared at her, then turned around, following her gaze.

Striding up the hall in motorcycle leathers, five o'clock

stubble on his manly chin, a touch of engine oil on his cheekbone, which he must surely have contrived to do himself with something he found in an easyJet toilet, was Patrick.

I hadn't seen the Patrick effect in quite a while – I tended to avoid places he went as it got very tedious watching him fend off the women – but it was undeniably impressive. I knew my brother was a bit of a dick – partly, I suspected, because women had acted like complete idiots in front of him since he was eleven years old – but it absolutely didn't show. He looked fantastic; everyone else faded into the background as he stalked up, as usual looking like he was pretending to be in his own movie and that he was indubitably centre stage. I turned to face him.

'Hi, Patrick,' I said casually. Kelly and JJ must be behind him somewhere.

'Hi, sis,' he said, and even stooped to give me a kind of hug. 'You look shit. Did you steal that dress off a pig in a farmyard?'

'Pigs don't even wear dresses, though,' I said. 'So your comment makes no sense.' Mum told me that the boys and I wouldn't bicker like children for ever. I was still waiting. Wilf was watching closely, but not with a fraction as much concentration as Lydia was.

'Er. so, Evie, ha ha ha,' said Lydia. 'Aren't you going to introduce us?'

Patrick stood back to take a look at her.

'Is that her?' he whispered to me in his Neanderthal fashion. I nodded. 'Not bad, for once,' he said.

'Lydia, this is my brother Patrick. He was really looking forward to coming to the casino evening with us . . .'

Patrick roughly pushed past me and picked up Lydia's taloned hand.

'Who the hell are you?' he said. He always went for this crude approach, and his hit rate was extraordinary. 'You're fucking gorgeous.'

Lydia giggled. This was a new sound for her and she nearly choked on it before it came out, but she got there in the end.

'I'm Evie's friend Lydia.'

Patrick made it very clear that he was sizing her up.

'Normally Evie's friends are all dogs,' he said. 'But you . . . I mean, you're byoo-tee-full.'

'We're not that close,' said Lydia.

'You can say that again,' I said.

'Shh,' said Wilf, as we started sidling towards the door.

'Are you a doctor?' asked Lydia. She was trying to put up her favourite final line of defence, but I knew it wasn't going to get her anywhere. I think Patrick had that smell men are meant to secrete that makes women go into labour and things.

'Neah, fuck 'em,' said Patrick. 'Anywhere round here we can get a drink?'

And that was the last thing we heard as we slipped unnoticed inside the casino ballroom.

\*

The private room was ridiculously over the top. Carved cherubs peered down from pink and eau-de-nil ceilings which were inlaid with gold, as if to suggest that angels were blessing you as you spunked the housekeeping on a puggy machine. Huge mirrors reflected back images of smartly dressed men and inappropriately dressed women, and overhead vast, multifaceted chandeliers glittered. The whole thing would have been lovely and classy-looking if it wasn't for the banks and banks of slot machines lining the walls, all beeping and flashing, looking as if they'd be much more at home in a pub with a sticky brown swirly carpet. In the middle of the room were roulette wheels and pontoon tables (I suppose it was vingt-et-un here), and a craps table which everybody was eyeing but nobody was playing at, presumably because nobody understood the rules except that you have to shout 'snake eyes' at various points. I couldn't see Dr Bennet, or Bailey.

'Good work,' said Wilf. 'Is that really your brother? We should get him to do some modelling for the clinic . . . Oh.'

'Oh, yes,' I said. 'We don't work there any more.'

'Yes.' He looked round. 'He should be here somewhere.'

Everywhere there were excited-looking men making squeaks of delight as they placed their 'money'. (There was free betting for an hour – a mean trick, I thought, getting everyone carried away with champagne and Monopoly money until they got into the habit of wagering huge sums and moved directly on to the whole rack and ruin thing.)

'Hang on,' I said. I thought I'd spotted Bailey. 'Stay here. Or look for Dr Bennet, but don't go far.'

Wilf squeezed me briefly on the hand and disappeared into the flurry.

'Bailey!' I hissed. He was hiding behind a curtain and making a pretty good job of it – if I hadn't spotted the laces of those horrible shoes poking out from under the thick red velvet I might have missed him altogether.

He poked his head out briefly. He looked haunted.

'Oh,' he said. 'It's you.'

'Who were you expecting, the cat's mother?' I said. I decided the curtain was actually a very good place to hide myself, before I got thrown out or kidnapped by goons, so shuffled myself into its luxuriant, smoky folds.

'I'm hiding,' said Bailey, unnecessarily I thought.

'Really? I thought you'd moved in here.'

'From Lydia.'

'From Lydia? You two have practically been smoochy smoochy icky poo since the second we arrived.'

'No, we haven't,' said Bailey, looking truly appalled. 'She's followed me around everywhere! I can't believe you didn't notice.'

'You're right, I've had very little on. Anyway, I've taken care of Lydia,' I said.

'What do you mean?'

'I've got rid of her. So I could get to you.'

'How?'

'I've Patricked her.'

'No way.'

'Way. He was coming here anyway, so it made perfect sense.'

'You're a marvel. You haven't Patricked anyone for years.'

'No. Because I try to be more moral than that. But thank you. Now. Listen. Things have got really serious.'

'What do you mean?'

'I mean, shit-hitting-the-fan serious. This boat – it *really* has to stop.'

'What do you mean?'

And I told him everything: about the threats and the resignation/sacking and the kidnapping of Tom.

'Oh, God,' he said when I'd finished. 'I heard you'd just quit because of a sex scandal.'

'Don't tell me you believed that.'

Bailey shrugged.

'Oh, for God's sake! It was a completely malicious rumour.'

'Yeah, uh, that's what I thought.'

'It *was*! Anyway, that doesn't matter. We need to find Tom. It's dangerous. Genuinely, seriously dangerous. We need to find out who's in charge here, when the boat's arriving, and then go straight to the police. I saw someone up on top of the party boat the other night, Bailey. Who was it? Who?'

Bailey looked unhappy. 'Oh, God. Well, it's a consortium, you know.'

'I don't know. What is that?'

'It's a holding company. Lots of middle men and so on, you know.'

'Well, are they here?'

Bailey poked his head out.

'No one I recognise . . . I suppose we could ask Yuri.'

'You know where he is?'

''Well, he's here somewhere.'

Bailey emerged from the curtain still looking a bit nervous.

'It's all right,' I whispered. 'Patrick'll be giving her tops by now.'

'Do you have to be so crude?' said Bailey.

'Well, seeing as Tom is being tortured to death *right now* then *yes*,' I said.

People bustled around us, moving between tables.

'That's a nice dress,' said Bailey. 'Shame about the flip-flops.'

'Shut up!'

The noise levels were rising and the cocktail waitresses were busy. I noticed that all the windows were covered in the same heavy drapes as the one we'd been hiding behind. I remembered how casinos liked to block out all natural light in the hopes of keeping you in there for forty-eight hours or something without you figuring it out. I liked the fact that the human brain was so easily fooled. 'Oooh . . . dark . . . must eat peanuts and stay out late . . .'

Bailey nodded and grunted to the people who were, as

usual, trying to get his attention. Most of them were asking when the boat was getting in and when they were going to get a look at it. He brushed off the questions.

'Don't you know?' I said.

'Yes,' he said, insulted. 'I mean, roughly. I mean, we've got a display on it tomorrow so it will have to be here by then.'

'But you don't know where it is now?'

'Not exactly.'

'So Tom could be on it, or at the bottom of the sea having been thrown off it?'

'Don't you think you're being a bit melodramatic?'

'He got pulled into a *car*! How is that being melodramatic?'

Finally we arrived at the far corner of the casino room. There, tucked well away behind the blackjack table, was Dr Bennet. He was concentrating hard, surrounded by a group of men. And, to my shock, just behind his left shoulder, was Janey. She was standing there, preening, like she was his lucky charm. I glared at her, but she merely smiled and looked back, waving her little fingers delicately.

There was nothing delicate about Dr Bennet, however, when he saw me again. 'You,' he said. 'You're like cranial fungus. You just won't go away.'

'Thank you,' I said. 'But . . .'

'But what?'

Bailey stepped forward. 'Yuri, look.'

'Oh, God, not you too. First Wilf, now you. What, does she give unbelievable head?'

Janey whispered something in his ear that made him grimace. I couldn't believe that the doc I'd always thought so smooth was actually as coarse as a sailor's armpit.

'No,' said Bailey. 'The young guy's gone missing.'

'What do you mean, "gone missing"? Who cares? He could fall off Brighton bloody pier for all I care.'

'He was bundled into a car,' I said. That got his attention. 'I saw it happen.'

'Don't be ridiculous.'

'I was right there. So was Wilf. Ask him if you don't believe me.'

Yuri was looking definitely flustered now. 'Well, he was asking for it.'

'What the hell do you mean by that? Asking for it? He could be dead for all you know.'

I was starting to make a scene. Again. Bailey touched my arm gently.

'Look,' he said. 'I know there's a lot of guys here who've been involved with the project and so on. I've met some of them, you know most of them, we've all been working together, right? But I really need to meet the top guy. The guy who signs the cheques, the guy no one meets. Because he's got to know what's going on.'

'Or she,' I added, out of habit.

Dr Bennet shook his head. 'Well, I don't know where he is. He's not here. Now if you'll excuse me, I want to get back to my card game.'

I looked around. Nobody was watching me. Janey, however, had both her hands round Dr Bennet's shoulders and
was leaning in to give him a good-luck kiss on the hair. Quickly,
I took my camera-phone out of my bag and snapped a
shot. I hardly ever used the camera facility – I'd been
talked into it by some spotty chap in the shop – but I was
incredibly grateful for it now.

'What? What was that?' said Dr Bennet hearing the
click.

'It's great I don't work for you now,' I said. 'I must delete
your wife's telephone number off my phone. Just as soon as
I've sent her this pic, of course.'

I held it up. It was incredibly compromising; I think Janey
was licking something. Of course, I didn't have his wife's
mobile number, but he didn't know that.

'Give me that!' said Dr Bennet.

'Tell us how to find Tom. Where's the guy in charge?'

'Give me that phone!'

'I'll give you the phone when you give us the information.'

'No!'

We glared at each other. It was a stand-off. Dr Bennett
looked around. I wondered if he had henchmen too.

'You are nothing,' he hissed suddenly. 'The girl who can't
even take a holiday on her own. I've seen you cowering about
the place.'

I took a step backwards. As a full-on assault his comment

felt just as vicious as if he'd punched me (which, as I'd already seen, he was entirely capable of doing too).

'"Oh, poor me, my brothers are horrible, poor me, my life sucks, I can't get a boyfriend, boo hoo hoo, pass me a magazine and let me empathise with Kerry Katona."'

'My life is *not* like that.'

'"I don't even have the decisiveness to go travelling. I'm so pathetic I need to go on holiday with the people I work with."'

'Shut up! Just shut up!'

'Give me the phone, little girl. And stop messing about in things you don't understand.'

His hand was nearly at mine and I couldn't think of a thing to do. I felt blinded with the pain of his words, I wanted to curl up in a ball and lick my wounds. Almost hypnotised, I felt my hand moving out . . .

Suddenly, the phone was snatched away and disappeared . . . into Wilf's pocket. I felt shaken out of my reverie.

'Where have you been?'

Wilf raised one eyebrow mysteriously. It looked strange, what with him in his dinner jacket and everything.

'Yuri,' he said. 'No hard feelings.'

Yuri rolled his eyes.

'What about a couple of rounds of vingt-et-un, for old times' sake.'

'What do you mean, "for old times' sake"?' he growled.

Wilf sat up at the table and ordered a martini. Really.

'Well, forget old times.' He leant forward across the table and opened his hands in a reasonable fashion. 'How about, if you win, you get the phone, and if I win, you tell us where Philippe is.'

I stared at Wilf. Philippe must be the big boss. And Wilf knew his name!

'Philippe, that was it,' said Bailey behind me. Ha, so, I wasn't the only person who forgot important things.

Yuri sat back in his chair, eyeing Wilf's pocket. The other men clustered round the table, muttering to themselves. A challenge! Yuri had to take a challenge!

It was true: he was looking at the male faces around the table. Wilf looked calm and unbothered, but he'd sent out a true threat to Dr Bennet's honour. I hung on closely. Janey did too. Wilf had brought a pile of chips to the table, and it was roughly the same size as Dr Bennet's. Dr Bennet raised his hands as Wilf threw a couple onto the table. Then he threw his own on too.

The dealer flicked out the cards in lightning-flash time. He put one of his own cards face up on the table. One was a ten. I looked at Wilf's hand. He had sixteen.

'Hit,' he said. The dealer gave him an eight.

'Hmm,' said Wilf.

After that, the game moved incredibly fast. Sometimes they'd double up the cards, and there'd be a flurry of cards on the table. Sometimes the dealer would fold without even looking at the other card. I was slightly bamboozled by everything that was going on, but one thing was certain: Wilf's pile of chips was getting smaller and smaller. Dr Bennet's expresssion was beginning to return to its normal self-satisfied look, and I felt my hand tightening its grip on the phone – Wilf had given it to me for safe keeping. Maybe I should make a dash for it – but so many people had come over to watch the game, and were now pressing up against me, I didn't know if I could fight my way out.

Finally Wilf was left with only a few red chips. He'd managed to make the wrong decision on practically every hand he'd had. He'd folded too early, he'd bust too high. He obviously had no clue what he was doing. I was wildly disappointed.

He looked at his hand, sighing, then threw them all into the centre of the table, as the dealer threw out a hand of cards, face down except for one of his own.

'All or nothing,' said Wilf. Dr Bennet smirked and took a long sip of his drink. The dealer was holding a four. 'All or nothing,' said Dr Bennet, pushing all his chips into the centre of the table. He'd had a run of winning on fifteens; he looked like he could afford to be generous. His eyes flicked to where I was holding the mobile phone. The dealer rapidly counted the chips and added an equal number from the bank.

Dr Bennet flipped over his hand. A ten and a queen. A gasp went up from the assembled crowd. The dealer turned his other card over. A ten. He had to hit. He did so, and got a jack – busted.

Then it was Wilf's turn. He flipped the first – yet *another* ten. The room, which had been so noisy for so long, now went completely silent. I realised I was holding my breath. Dr Bennet still looked quite nonchalant; what was going to beat his twenty? Then Wilf turned over his other card. It was the ace of spades.

The room erupted. I yelled out loud. Dr Bennet swore loudly and looked about to storm off as the dealer pushed the huge mountain of chips towards our seat. I couldn't believe Wilf had got this lucky. I looked at him, he hadn't even broken a sweat.

'Well done!' I whispered.

'Yuri?' Wilf was saying, getting down from his seat. 'Don't you have something to tell us? About the whereabouts of Philippe?'

There was a rustle of agreement from the crowd as Dr Bennet got up heavily from the table.

'Of course, you'll keep your side of the bargain?'

Dr Bennet muttered something, and Bailey, Wilf and I pushed our way through the crowd to get to him; Janey had already taken his arm.

'OK, OK, OK,' he said furiously as we surrounded him. 'Come with me. You don't want to make Philippe unhappy, though, you really don't.'

'Well, he's making us very unhappy,' I said. 'With *kidnapping*.'

Dr Bennet led us out of the main casino area and into a dark-panelled room off the main foyer. Out of the corner of my eye I could see Lydia and Patrick. He appeared to be unhooking her bra. I looked around for John Jr but I couldn't see him. It would have been very handy to have had some muscular back-up at this point.

I didn't see what he did, but suddenly Dr Bennet had opened a panel on the wall and was pressing in a key code. In front of us, a door slid open. Oh my God!

A short, dark corridor, lit with an illuminated cherub lamp, ended at another wooden door. Dr Bennet knocked gently. Someone grunted on the other side of the door, and Yuri said, 'Lysander.' A hand felt for mine and squeezed it. I didn't know whose it was.

Inside was a room so softly lit it looked like it was illuminated by gas lighting. It took a few moments for my eyes to adjust. Then I noticed that along one wall was a bank of monitors, showing every room in the casino, and the cars outside. This must be for security. Some of the monitors showed overhead views of the tables in the casino, I supposed to see if the dealers were cheating.

But then my attention moved to the shadowy figures in the room. There were three or four big men, who I supposed must be goons. Then, sitting down, with his head bent, was a figure I recognised, even though it was no longer sporting the moustache of the day before.

'Tom,' I shouted. He raised his head and peered through

a very black eye. Oh my God. He'd been beaten up. And what he said next shocked me to the core.

'Janey?' he said.

What? My eyes shot round to where Janey had inconspicuously followed us in.

'Darling,' she said, running forwards. 'What have they done to you?'

My brain couldn't take it in as she knelt down next to him.

'Are you all right?' She smothered him in kisses. 'Cachou misses you.'

'WHAT?'

I stepped forward, shaking off Wilf's restraining hand on my arm.

'What kind of a slut *are* you? Are both of you?'

'Evie,' said Tom, focusing on me suddenly. 'You found me.' He indicated his face. 'I told you it was serious.'

But I was looking at Janey. 'You were just in there trying to play suck face with Dr Bennet. Do you sleep with the dog too?'

'Information, darling,' she said to me, her American accent grating in my ears. 'And don't talk to the US head of Earth Friends like that, OK, sweetie?'

I stared at Tom. Oh, God, I felt I'd been betrayed twice. This was who he'd been calling; this was the person who owned the dog. My heart was pounding as a small man got up out of the swivel chair in front of the screens. I hadn't noticed him at all.

'Very interesting,' he said. 'But, Yuri, would you mind telling me what the *fuck* is going on?'

We all stared at Dr Bennet as he tried to explain he'd been blackmailed (which made me feel pretty good, I have to say; I didn't know I had it in me).

'But what do you want?' said Philippe – the little man – turning round to face us. His English was perfect, as was his suit. He didn't look threatening at all, he looked nice. If he was your doctor you'd feel reassured that he would never lose his cool or make a mistake. As soon as I heard his voice I knew it was the man I'd heard on top of the boat, talking to Dr Bennet.

We all began talking at once. He raised his hand for calm.

'You are activists, yes? I've heard as much from Tom.'

'Did you stand up under torture?' said Janey fondly, stroking his head.

'No,' said Tom, looking ashamed of himself. 'One of the goons elbowed me in the eye, and that was it. I pretty much told him everything. I hadn't realised torture would be quite so unpleasant.'

I rolled my eyes at this, which was cheeky because if anyone were to even so much as mention the word torture to me I'm sure I'd immediately start crying and betray everyone I'd ever met. But I was so furious that this pair had used us so ruthlessly. Earth Friends indeed. They could start by being actual normal human friends.

'Now, look,' said Philippe. 'The boat is going ahead, I'm afraid. There is really nothing wrong with it. There are millions of boats and millions of hospital procedures, and the two things are going to merge.'

'But Radoflux 9000 . . .' said Wilf.

'Radoflux 9000 will be *fine*,' snarled Philippe, suddenly cross. 'One or two minor flaws in the trials, that's all.'

'And stupid women who inject that stuff deserve all they get,' said Janey. 'Using animal products for their own vanity. It's disgusting.'

'You really are the queen of love and spirituality, aren't you?' I said.

She looked me straight in the eye. 'I think the time has come to get over Tom,' she said sincerely. 'I know some books that might help. *How to Stop Loving a Man That's Too Good for You*, that kind of thing.'

If I hadn't been wearing flip-flops, I'd have kicked her.

'Now I know what's up,' said Philippe, 'I think we have a solution. I'm sorry my men were a little heavy-handed, Tom – we're very afraid of terrorism, as you can imagine, and they had your picture on the CCTV from the other evening . . . we thought you were going to blow up the boat.'

'S'OK,' said Tom. That was the annoying thing about Philippe, I suddenly realised: he sounded so incredibly reasonable and spoke so gently it was hard not to believe what he was saying. He reached towards the desk and picked up a piece of paper.

'Here we are,' he said. When he held it up to the light we saw he was brandishing a cheque. A cheque for a huge amount, made out to Earth Friends. When they peered through the gloom to read the noughts on the end, Tom and Janey's faces both contorted.

'This is the precise sum of money that will carbon zero the ship,' said Philippe. 'It's for you. I want you to take it, plant trees, form a seal sanctuary. After all, it is the first rule of medicine, is it not: "Do no harm"?'

Tom and Janey were looking at each other. Janey had her stupid over-painted mouth open.

'Of course, this is annual,' said Philippe. 'We would hate to leave our footprint on the beautiful oceans of the world, even as we wish to render a service to make our world more beautiful through making its women more beautiful.'

They couldn't be swallowing this, could they?

Janey gulped and stepped forwards. 'Well, that's incredibly generous.'

Philippe shrugged. 'I am sorry we had such a misunderstanding. I agree; we should have thought more about saving the planet before we started our work. A little oversight, perhaps, Dr Bailey?'

Bailey stuttered, but didn't say anything.

'Well, then,' said Tom. He reached out and took the cheque. 'We can do a lot of good with this.'

'No, you can't!' I burst out suddenly. 'They're just buying you off! It's corrupt.'

Tom looked at Philippe as if they were both men of the world.

'No, they're balancing things out. We can do so much good with this money, Evie. Invest in saving millions of animals' lives.'

'Whilst they just sail around using illegal drugs and giving new faces to serial killers?' I yelled. Philippe and his henchmen laughed, and I felt really stupid and awkward.

'Don't be ridiculous,' said Philippe. 'This is a holiday cruise ship, that's all. Nothing for you to worry your . . . "average" little head about.'

Silence fell. Tom and Janey looked at each other and clearly passed a private message between them – to scarper.

'Well, thanks, Philippe . . . sorry for the trouble we caused,' said Tom. Oh, God, what a pathetic specimen.

'Not at all,' said Philippe. 'We'll all just keep quiet about it, *n'est-ce pas?*'

'And, *bye*, Yuri,' said Janey seductively. 'Give my love to your wife.' And she got up and prepared to sashay out. Tom got up to follow her. As she turned away, he turned to me. His face looked just a little regretful.

'Evie,' he said, 'I . . . I . . .'

I wanted to say something dramatic; a proper exit line. But all I could think of was 'you're a crap shag', and that wasn't even true, plus I didn't want to say it in a roomful of men. I didn't want to look pathetic.

'Bye,' I said. 'And stop pestering me with all those phone calls and flowers and things, please.'

He looked a bit confused for a second then shook his head. 'Right. OK. I'll stop.'

Dr Bennet was looking profoundly uncomfortable and staring at his feet as Tom and Janey left the room.

# Chapter Thirteen

'Are you still here?' said Philippe, who'd turned back to look at the monitors. You could see Tom and Janey running across the foyer. I couldn't tell, but I thought they might be grinning like Cheshire cats. And Lydia's shoe seemed to be peering out from under a curtain. Well well well.

'Yes,' I said. 'You can't buy us off that easily.'

'Oh, can't I?'

Philippe looked at his watch and yawned.

'This is getting very boring,' he said. 'OK, here's the deal. If you' – he pointed at Wilf – 'want to work in plastic surgery again, keep your head down and shut up like a good boy. And if *you* –' this time it was Bailey – 'want to work in hospital design, do likewise.'

'What about me?' I said. He ignored me.

'You go to the papers, they won't be interested. You go to the police – we haven't done anything wrong, and the boat will be in at five in the morning and back in international waters this time tomorrow night. You have nothing on us, nothing at all. We, on the other hand – and it is regrettable, in international business – have absolutely no compunction at all about giving you a smack for wasting so much of our bloody time and making Dr Bennet look an idiot.'

One of the huge goons grunted in agreement, and Dr Bennet looked like he was going to say something about whether or not he was an idiot, then thought better of it.

'So. Fuck off now – no smack. Do you understand me?'

Both Wilf and Bailey looked really constipated. I suppose this is what it comes down to in boy world – whether or not you can handle a whupping. All the school bitching they avoid; all the body facism they get to skip; all the daft girlie hair removal stuff they don't have to spend money on, but it still comes down to this. Can they handle a whupping? Suddenly I wished John Jr were here.

Bailey looked at Wilf. 'The thing is,' he said. 'I was brutalised as a child, and I'm a terrible physical coward.'

Wilf nodded, looking relieved. Come on, wimps! My blood was up. Fight! Wilf held up his hands. 'I would, but . . . my hands are insured for half a million . . .'

'Yeah,' said Bailey.

'Come *on*, you cowards!' I yelled. 'Are you just going to let him get away with it?'

Philippe was already on the phone. 'Hi, yes . . . I'd like the saddle of lamb, with braised cabbage . . .'

The goons were moving towards us. God, they really were big. Big and fierce-looking.

Wilf and Bailey looked at one another. 'OK, RUN!' they shouted, and, pushing me ahead of them, we all tumbled forward through the secret passageway and into the bright lights of the chandeliered foyer.

'I'm not sure I'm cut out for this crime-fighting lark,' said Bailey, as we'd paced our weary way home along the seafront. The bars and restaurants were open and lively, and it was still warm as we found an empty beach-side table and took a seat. Wilf ordered '*trois grand* . . .' then looked at us expectantly. Whisky would have felt appropriate, but I hate the stuff, so I had a large Bacardi and Coke, which wasn't quite as world weary. The tie I'd tied on so badly for Wilf had undone itself and was lying open round his neck. The effect was quite sexy actually.

'No,' said Wilf. 'I'm much better at the job I've given up with no hope of getting another one.'

'You'll get another one,' said Bailey. 'Philippe can't know everyone who wants plastic surgery on earth.'

'Can't he?' said Wilf. 'Surely that's why he started this project.'

'Oh, yeah,' said Bailey, taking a large sip of his double advocaat (he's even worse at spirits than me).

Wilf sighed. 'Well, I suppose we should chalk it up to experience and adventure . . .'

'What are you talking about?' I said, spluttering through my drink. 'My sister-in-law is still getting on that boat tomorrow for a free shot of Radoflux 9000!'

Wilf's face fell and he took another sip of his whisky (at least he was drinking a man's drink).

'Oh, crap, I'd forgotten about that.'

'Well, I haven't.'

'At least your friend's safe,' offered Bailey. I harrumphed.

'I wish they'd thrown him off something just one more time for luck,' I said.

'Ah, a woman scorned,' said Bailey, and got up to go to the bathroom. I was about to take up my cause again on Kelly's behalf when Wilf leaned forward.

'Uh, can I ask you something?' he said.

'Sure.'

'Is that your . . . is Bailey your boyfriend?'

I blinked in disbelief. 'My *what*?' I said stupidly.

'Your other half . . . uh, partner . . . I mean . . .'

'Wilf, didn't you realise I, em, made out with Tom?'

'Well, yes,' said Wilf. 'I thought maybe that had caused a few problems.'

'Well, it would, wouldn't it?'

I sipped my drink again.

'Look. Bailey is . . . he's my friend. We grew up together. And, sometimes, I think, maybe we should be together, you know? Neither of us is getting any younger, and I really like him, and well, I could do a lot worse, and it's not like there's anyone else on the horizon, so maybe I should just settle down with him.'

'Wow,' said Wilf, obviously a little surprised by how much I'd told him. 'Nothing like aiming high in life.'

'Well, I aimed high for a holiday and ended up embroiled in some death boat, so maybe the time has come to stop trying.'

'And what does Bailey think of all this?'

'Oh, he's always had a thing for me. I know my face isn't a hundred per cent symmetrical but some men do, you know, think I'm all right looking.'

Wilf's face softened. 'Do they?'

'Do they?' echoed another voice, right by the table. Bailey pointed up above our heads.

'Toilet window. Right there. Er, Evie, do you mind if we have a word?'

We walked a little way along the beach, to where the sounds of the bars and the music of Cannes faded behind us and the noise of the sea was louder than anything else. Bailey seemed to be struggling with something. I couldn't believe myself. What had I said? If I hadn't been so keyed up and hysterical, I wouldn't have said nearly so much. There was just something about bloody Wilf being so quiet that made me talk too much. And I didn't know how to explain this to

Bailey. Or how great I thought he was, or how impressive – and not just because all the docs thought he was amazing, or Lydia was desperately trying to pull him, before I'd Patricked her.

'So,' said Bailey finally, as if he were pulling the words out. 'I'm your safety, am I? Your back-up plan?'

I couldn't possibly have let him see on my face how accurate those words were so I picked up a stone and threw it out to sea.

'Don't be stupid,' I said. 'I was a bit het up. I just told Wilf what I thought he wanted to hear.'

'That I'm your back-up plan that you don't really fancy but think would be better than nothing?'

I could hear the fury in his voice now.

'I mean, where the fuck do you get off? Who do you think you are, Scarlett fucking Johansson?'

I shook my head. I was mortified. It must be a horrible thing to hear about yourself; that someone thinks you're a lapdog, ready at your bidding to devote their life to you.

'Has it escaped your notice that my life is going completely fine without having you on my arm?'

'Yes, I *know* that,' I said.

'Do you really think I'm so pathetic that if I fancied you I wouldn't ask you out?'

'OK, OK,' I said. 'I'm sorry. I got it wrong. Obviously.'

'Obviously,' said Bailey. 'Look, Evie. I'm sorry you're single and that all your boyfriends have been dicks.'

'Not all of them,' I protested, then thought about it. 'Oh, yes. All of them.'

'But I'm not your knight in shining bloody armour, OK? I'm not your "make do". I'm not anybody's "make do".'

'I know,' I said.

'I know you still think of me as a six-year-old who's just wet his trousers, but it's just not like that any more. So get over it.'

'OK,' I said, feeling thoroughly chastised.

'Can we forget about this?'

I nodded.

'And you won't . . . I don't know, be expecting a ring on your thirtieth birthday or something equally cretinous?'

I shook my head.

'OK. Come here.'

And he gave me a hug. We didn't hug very often. As we did so I realised something; that some people have a smell. A smell you click with. Tom, alas, had it. It's something to do with pheromones, something below consciousness.

Bailey didn't have it. The chemistry wasn't there. Not because we were working too hard, or waiting for the right moment, or sowing our wild oats before we headed into the sunset together. But because it would never have worked out.

I squeezed him hard for helping me realise this.

'Oof,' he said.

I grinned. 'Come on. Admit it. I was your safety too.'

'You were not!'

'Was too!'

'Were not! Your mate Jilly was my safety and she went and married your bloody brother Cassandro.'

'Whereupon, you switched to me.'

We drew apart.

'Well, maybe a little,' he said.

'I knew it,' I said.

He gave me a half smile. The moonlight glinted off his glasses.

'Goodnight,' he said. And he turned and marched on up the beach.

I headed back to the café table. Wilf was still there, holding out a large gin and tonic.

'Everything OK?' he said, looking alarmed and standing up. 'Have you broken his heart?'

'No,' I said. 'I don't think so. Definitely not.'

'Has he broken yours?'

I smiled weakly at him. 'No. My heart is pretty used to being punched around.'

Wilf smiled at me. 'That's a shame.'

'Yeah, well, what can you do? Us lonely crime fighters, too busy saving the world . . .'

Suddenly, Wilf took my hand. An electric shock ran up my arm. What was this – friendly advice or something more?

'You don't need to make a joke out of everything, you know,' he said gently.

I swallowed hard, thinking over my many humiliations.

'Yes, I do,' I said. 'Anyway. What are we going to do about Kelly? I don't give a shit about what Tom and Janey are doing: this isn't over.'

Wilf removed his hand and sighed.

'Evie. You've met Philippe. He's a serious thug. What can we do?'

'I don't know,' I said. 'Something. To show we're not cowards and we're not giving up. We even know when the boat's coming in.'

'You're not a coward, Evie,' said Wilf. 'Not like me. But I think the time has come to give it up.'

We sipped our drinks quietly as we stared out to sea.

'It is beautiful, isn't it?' said Wilf.

The lights of the yachts on the far quay were still twinkling in the water. I thought of a cold, harsh operating theatre, out there on the water somewhere, all ready to perform God knows what kinds of things.

'Sort of,' I said. 'What's that famous quote about the Riviera?'

'A sunny place for shady people,' said Wilf.

'Yes,' I said. 'Like that.'

I headed back alone, bidding a quiet goodnight to Wilf. I didn't want him to walk me back to the hotel. I didn't think there was anything left to say.

After the evening's events I doubted I'd be able to fall asleep. By the side of my bed were some postcards I'd bought to send Mum and Dad but I couldn't think what to write on them.

*Dear Mum and Dad. Wish you were here. Slept with a yellow-bellied eco-terrorist. Got burnt. Lost chance of marrying that nice bloke who lived down the road. JJ not quite as bad as we always thought. Sorry about the disfigured daughter-in-law, having a lovely time, E.*

Instead, and to my surprise, I pitched forwards onto the bed, still fully dressed, then didn't wake up for five hours. I wouldn't even have woken up then if it hadn't been for my phone going off. Utterly confused as to where I was, I blearily stretched out a hand to the night table. It was still dark outside.

'Uh-huh?'

'Sis?'

'Who is this?'

The voice was whispering and sounded very agitated.

'Sis, it's me. Patrick.'

'Patrick? Where the hell are you?'

'That friend of yours, sis.'

He sounded hoarse, almost as if he'd been crying.

'She's a *maniac*.'

'Oh,' I said. I was becoming more awake now. 'Who, Lydia?'

'Keep your voice down! I don't know where she is.'

'Where are you?'

'That's the problem. I don't know. She took me back to her hotel and tied me up and . . . did *things* to me.'

'Patrick. Have you been interfered with? Did somebody touch your special area?'

'Well, I liked it to start with, but . . . she just went on and on. And *on*.'

'She's been holding herself back for the right person. I think it's all coming out in a flood.' I thought for a second. 'God, *that* explains the unchannelled aggression.'

'She said she's just going to get some whipped cream . . .' Patrick's voice was almost a sob. 'How do I get out of here? She's going at it with an egg beater right now.'

'Just creep out very quietly,' I said. 'Forget about your pants. Then go through the courtyard, and just start down the hill. Everything here goes downhill. When you get to the sea-front go to the Metropole hotel and ask for JJ. He can look after you after that.'

'If I turn up at JJ's without my clothes he'll rip the piss.'

'Well, it sounds like someone's going to rip something.'

There was a gulp on the line.

'Bye.'

I couldn't get back to sleep after that. The sun was starting to creep over the horizon, I could tell, even in my dank little room. I felt a little buzzy still, the way you do when you've had adrenalin running round your system, no dinner and not enough sleep. So I ran a bath. It was that horrible French bath, but as long as I threw both my legs over the side I could just about lie back. What could I do? Today was the last chance to have a shot at it – my flight home was tomorrow. Without a job, without a friend, without anything. And that bloodstained boat would be sailing straight out to sea.

Well, not if I could help it. If I only had one day, I could give it my best shot. I leaned out of the uncomfortable bath and grabbed my phone. One last shot.

'Did I wake you?'

'Oddly enough, no,' said Wilf, who did actually sound wide awake.

'Good,' I said. 'What were you doing?'

'Just thinking about things.'

'What things?'

There was a pause.

'You ask a lot of questions, Evie.'

'I know,' I said. 'You'd think I'd be a better spy than I am.'

I could hear him smile down the phone. 'Don't tell me. This isn't a good news phone call. Or have you called me to tell me you *don't* want to do something completely stupid?'

'What do we have to lose?' I said. 'We've already lost our jobs, our trip . . .'

'Our dignity . . .'

'Dignity's overrated,' I said.

'Right,' he said. 'And what's with the "we"?'

'Listen,' I said. 'You don't have to go near the boat, or Philippe. You just need to talk to Kelly. Put on your best serious doctor voice,' I said. 'You know you can do it. Pretend you're breaking bad news. It will be, to her.'

It felt oddly intimate, lying in the bath naked, talking to Wilf. He didn't even know where I was.

'Are you splashing?' came the voice. 'Are you in the bath?'

'No!' I said, inadvertently making an even bigger splash in surprise.

'You are! You're calling me from in the bath!'

'Shh,' I said. 'We've got important plans to discuss.'

'Well, it's hard to discuss them when I'm picturing you in the bath.'

'Well, don't then. Picture me wearing a snow suit or something.'

There was a pause.

'Break the bad news,' I said.

'Uh-huh,' said Wilf reluctantly.

There was a silence on the end of the phone. I could hear him breathing. The room was still dark, with only the solitary tap dripping at the end of the bath. I felt like we were the only two people on earth. Sometimes things are more intimate over the telephone.

He took a deep breath. 'I don't like breaking bad news,' he said. There was another long pause. Then it all came out.

'When I was a young surgeon – well, hardly a surgeon at all, a senior house officer, I had to tell two parents that their six-month-old baby— The child had been shot. Drive by. No reason. I was assisting. Anyway. It doesn't matter. They . . .

she . . . didn't make it. The consultant had a six-month-old himself. He couldn't face it. He got me to do it because "I had to learn sometime", and I didn't have children.'

There was a long pause after that. I wasn't sure, but I think from the tenor of his breaths he was crying.

'Well, I can tell you it doesn't matter if you have children or not.'

There was another long pause as he got control of himself.

'And that was it for me, really. I mean, I finished my training and everything . . . but telling people that their life – their world, everything they had ever had – was completely fucked, as from today . . . I mean, that's not a job. Or, it wasn't a job I could do.'

'All doctors learn to, though, don't they?' I said timidly. 'They just have to get on with the job.'

'I know,' he said. 'But not me. I couldn't. I just couldn't.'

'So you went somewhere where you wouldn't have to,' I said.

Finally I understood. All the skills, wasted in the wrong place.

'Because I'm a wimp,' said Wilf. He half laughed. 'I'm not up to the job.'

'But you're a wonderful doctor,' I told him simply. 'Wonderful.'

'And a coward,' he said.

'You're not a coward, are you?' I said. 'Look at you, up at all hours, preparing to help me. A coward wouldn't have decided to make a stand, would he? A coward wouldn't have confronted Dr Bennet. A coward wouldn't have fronted up to him with that card game the way you did. You were even going to take on my brother.'

'Oh, yes,' said Wilf, remembering. 'I wasn't, really. If he'd raised a hand I was going to run for it.'

'Shh!' I said. I was on a roll. 'A coward wouldn't be going down right now to talk Kelly out of this dangerous surgery, not with John Jr on the loose. You're a lion! A lion! Grr.'

'Am I?' he asked faintly.

'Of course you are.' I reached over for a towel. 'You've got over your fears without even trying! Watch you go! Grr!'

'Of course I am!' he said. I heard some warmth come back into his voice, and the sound of him jumping up. 'What are you doing?'

'Me?' I said. 'Well, once I get out of the bath—'

'Aha,' he said. 'I knew it.'

Busted.

'Uh, I mean . . .'

I was about to explain the plan I'd come up with walking home the night before. Then I figured that he'd try and stop me, particularly in his newly invigorated state, so I didn't.

'I think you'll manage it all fine by yourself,' I said. 'Nothing. I'm going to stay here and order breakfast in bed.'

I took a look round my grubby cell and laughed hollowly to myself.

'OK,' said Wilf. 'I'll come and get you when I know what's happening. If we can get your sister—'

'Sister-in-law.'

'Off that boat . . . well, I think that's as much as we can do.'

'I agree,' I said, and hung up the phone. I didn't agree in the slightest.

# Chapter Fourteen

Even at first light, when the whole of Cannes looked like an army of pixies had been up all night scrubbing it clean (hey, maybe they had, they're all rich round here), there were lots of people down by the docks – some early fishermen, coming in with the morning's catch, then there were bakers' shops open for early trade, and lots of yachties. I'd learned to recognise them; young men and women with very clean polo shirts, identical shorts, brown legs and nice teeth, who looked after the ships that lined the shore. They looked like their lives were pretty fun, as they loped on and off the gangplank, hailing their friends on other boats. The girls were getting on with shopping, the men were washing down the blue and white sides of the boats, or hosing the decks. I idly wondered if they had better lives than mine. Hey, who was I kidding? One of those lab rats that gets given electric shocks all day has a better life than mine.

I marched down to the big quay again; the one reserved for the largest boats. Behemoth after behemoth loomed out of the oily depths. Near the end I drew to a halt. *Operation Sunshine*. Here she was.

This boat wasn't a shimmering city of lights, like the party boat had been. It wasn't full of fun people having a fun time. It was sleek, and grey – grey all over, like pewter. The portholes were small, and the front of the boat sharpened to a point, as if it was designed for cutting through something. It was huge, but looked like it had more in common with a warship than a pleasure boat. She looked sinister, even at dawn with the golden rays of another perfect day breaking over her bow.

I didn't have a good plan about sneaking on board. I realised I had imagined something out of an old Laurel and Hardy movie, like a laundry van driving up that I could jump into, so I tried to hover inconspicuously.

Suddenly a friendly-looking girl was standing in front of me.

'G'day!' she said cheerfully. 'Are you looking for die work?'

I was so shocked for a second I couldn't speak, until I realised she was Antipodean, and had actually said 'day work'.

I had no idea what day work was either, but it sounded a lot better than 'die' work, and she was wearing a polo shirt with 'Operation Sunshine' embroidered on the pocket, so I decided to say yes, in lieu of a better idea, and see what happened.

'You're first,' she said. 'Die workers normally don't start queuing till seven.'

'Actually, this is my first day-work job,' I said, hoping she'd give me at least the tiniest clue as to what a day worker was.

'Oh, will done you,' she said. 'Will, you're just in time for breakfast if you like.'

And she turned round and indicated that I follow her on board. It was as simple as that.

Having been in two minds about this 'day work' charade, suddenly, from the bottom of a very steep set of stairs I smelt bacon frying . . . with tomatoes, and was that mushrooms? And that was definitely toast. I hadn't eaten since my plate of ice cream yesterday about lunchtime.

'Great!' I said truthfully.

'I'm Dibs, by the way.'

'Hiya, Debs . . . I'm . . .'

I couldn't think of a fake name straight away. 'Wow, I'm Debs too,' I said.

'*Wow!*' said Debs. She was quite smiley. 'That's *amazing.*'

She led me down the steep staircase. At the bottom was a large, low room with lots of doors leading off it. A large TV played in the corner, next to other screens that monitored locations around the ship. Around two large tables sat a host of healthy-looking boys and girls – well, in their early twenties, I supposed – who had the sheen of people who eat a lot of good food and get plenty of fresh air and sunshine. They just looked gleamy. I felt shockingly haggard in comparison.

'Hey, everyone,' said Dibs. 'This is Dibs – amazing, eh? I'm going to put her on as a day worker. Remember it's a big day today.'

There was general muttering. Obviously getting a day worker wasn't a particularly unusual occurrence, and a few of the boys (mostly good-looking) rather annoyingly tilted up their heads then went straight back to their bacon sandwiches. I ordered myself sternly to keep my mind on the task. It was *good* that no one was looking at me. I was a top secret agent.

I squeezed myself round the table and found space for my vast plate of food and, despite my nerves, managed to eat every scrap, keeping my ears open for gossip. Debs was mentioning the large party of people who were coming on board that day and how everyone had to stay away from the basement. My ears pricked up. The basement, huh? I filed that away as extremely useful information. I suppose it would make more sense to put an operating theatre in the basement, rather than, say, an upper-floor conservatory.

She also warned everyone again to keep security tight on the gates. I loved the fact that I didn't look like I needed security. Hooray for James Bond and her out of *Alias*; everyone obviously thought infiltrators would arrive looking attractive and well dressed.

Dibs passed me a clean polo shirt and shorts of my very own and ordered me to go and get changed. I was delighted. As soon as I did so (if I put my hair in a very perky pony tail), I would look just like one of these guys. Effectively, I hoped, I'd become invisible.

Just as I'd finished changing, a young guy pushed past the curtain. He was thin and bald and had a friendly face.

'Excuse me,' I said.

He stared at me. 'Who are you?' he said rudely.

'I'm the new day worker.'

'Day worker? Bloody Debs; nobody's allowed on the boat today.'

My heart started to pound. I was about to be unmasked and thrown off – or worse. I thought of Tom's black eye, and gulped.

The man gave me an appraising look then furtively glanced outside. He leant towards me.

'You don't look like a yachtie,' he said.

'Well, that's where you're wrong.'

'Which side is port, then?'

Shit. Shit. Shit. Rumbled.

The man took a deep breath. 'Earth Friends?' he whispered.

My heart leapt in shock. 'What do you mean?'

'Are you Earth Friends?'

'Why?'

Was he going to dob me in?

He winked and held out his hand. 'Kizza. Earth Friends' man on the inside.'

Oh my God. As I looked at his open face I realised that word obviously hadn't yet filtered down to the rank and file that Earth Friends had, in fact, turned.

'I'm here to help you any way I can,' said Kizza. For a second I thought he was going to salute. 'But whatever you're doing . . . it's got to be *fast*. We have to leave the port tonight.'

I found my voice again. 'Can you get me to the operating theatre? When the docs come?'

He nodded. 'Yes.' Then he slipped behind the curtain as fast as he'd appeared.

First, I followed Dibs. The thrill of being undercover lasted about as long as it took to comb out the first rug so that all the woollen strands were facing the same way. It's true. This is the kind of job people do on yachts.

'You wouldn't *think* pipple would notice,' said Dibs. 'But they rilly, rilly do.'

So here I was, bent over, combing through tiny strands of presumably priceless Persian rugs along miles and miles of corridor, constantly looking at my phone to see if Wilf had called. He hadn't, and I didn't want to call him in case he was in the middle of something. I knew he'd get in touch the second anything was happening. I thought back to our conversation this morning. I'd been touched by how much he'd confided in me. The more I got to know him, the more I liked him. Not that history had proven my skills in that department.

Once I'd finished with the rugs, Dibs set me to polishing

anything brass I came across. I wondered how much I'd get paid for this then remembered that, actually, as soon as word came from Wilf that he'd talked Kelly out of it I was scarpering, so it didn't actually matter. But still. This certainly felt far more like work than sitting behind a nice warm desk in London. If the air con hadn't been so fierce I'd have been on the verge of sweating.

Finally, after what seemed like hours and hours, I heard a bit of general kerfuffle going on outside. Dibs poked her head into the main cabin, where I'd just finished up. It had been bedecked by the other girls with huge, towering flower arrangements that gave the air a heady scent.

'Lit me look at you,' she said. 'OK. Grab a pair of white slip-ons and come and join us.'

There was a big box of very clean white shoes by the crew door and I found a pair that fitted. But then, I didn't really have any choice in the matter as I was drafted in, with all the others, to the back of the boat near the gangplank. Half of the crew – the senior half, I assumed, including Kizza – had changed into formal naval-looking uniforms, complete with epaulettes and hats. The rest of us were in our polo shirt outfits. Dibs got us all into position so that we fanned out from the gangplank on either side, uniforms in front, polo shirts in the back, to welcome the visitors on board.

My heart sank into my shoes. Oh my God. Now I realised. We were going to stand here like some royal-receiving line whilst Philippe, Dr Bennet and, Christ, probably Lydia as well, all marched past. At least I was in the second row, but oh my GOD.

'I have to go to the bathroom,' I muttered to Dibs.

'You cin't,' she muttered back, resplendent in her crisp white shirt. 'They're arriving. Stand still.'

And she pushed me into line, shaking, as the huge shiny cars drew up on the jetty.

If my heart could have stopped, it would have. Every cell in my body was flattened with the mental effort of me trying to turn myself into a two-dimensional object, as close to the far side of the ship as possible. I took a deep breath. Sure enough, first to emerge was Philippe, looking as smooth as he had the previous evening, with two of his omnipresent goons. Then from the second car slithered Dr Bennet, next to him, Lydia. So, she had taken my place after all. Well, it was what she'd always wanted.

Lydia looked, and I suppose was, utterly shagged out. It was mesmerising; for a second I almost forgot to be frightened for my life. Her normally shiny straight hair was mussed and a complete fright at the back. Her eyes were ringed with dark shadows and her normally pale and perfect skin was flushed, like the blood vessels had expanded in her face. If this was what *she* was like, I really didn't want to see Patrick. Then, to my complete and utter horror, out of the other side of the car, got Wilf.

I felt like someone had punched me in the chest and I involuntarily took a step backward, then steadied myself in case I drew attention. Both doctors wore their white coats, which somehow removed them from being normal people; it was like a suit of armour. If you wanted to look stern and responsible – stick the white coats on.

They mounted the gangplank. Dr Bennet's and Wilf's – Dr Maitland's – heads were close together. He must have sought him out last night after I'd gone. No. Not after our conversation, surely? After everything we'd said – he must have thought he was a coward after all; that a safe job and a cushy salary was good enough really. And why would he want to give it up, anyway? Not for me. Oh my God, the filthy, lying . . . I strained to hear their conversation.

'I'm just so sorry,' Wilf was saying.

'It's all right,' said Dr Bennet. 'These things happen. You got carried away with a girl. But *that* girl though . . .'

I bit my lip. Yuri shook his head.

'Anyway,' went on Dr Bennet. 'I'm very glad to have you with us today. It's a tricky operation, this.'

'Looking forward to it,' said Dr Maitland.

Inside I was boiling. I couldn't believe it. That rat had betrayed me. After our conversation this morning. He must have thought about it then decided that he absolutely wasn't going into charity medicine, or travelling abroad or anything he'd talked about after all, because he was still just a big crawling coward. He'd thought about it then scrambled back like a rat to his regular pay cheque. He probably thought I was still in my hotel room, waiting patiently for him like a dog. Well, was he going to get a shock . . .

I kept my head down, blushing furiously. I was sure that at any moment Philippe, who was at the front of the group, was going to lean over and grab me by the shoulders but, as I held my breath, he strode along the line of waiting staff with barely a grunt for the captain. Lydia followed, nose in the air, though I don't think she'd have looked quite so snotty if she'd known that it clearly displayed the stubble rash on her chin. Then I darted my eyes up just a little, in time to see Dr Bennet whispering in Dr Maitland's ear, close as you like. I wondered how much Dr Bennet had made him grovel. Loads, probably. Arse-licking extraordinaire. I thought of how much I'd started to like him, and sighed. Suddenly, I felt very, very alone. And furious with my stupid bloody sister-in-law.

I stayed stock still as it seemed to take them for ever to parade up the line, deep in conversation. At least Bailey wasn't coming on, he'd have cracked immediately. But finally they passed by into the main body of the ship and I could let out a sigh of relief.

Or could I? As I straightened up, my brain spinning from Dr Maitland's deception, I spied a whole group of people coming up the pier. It was the docs. They looked happy and excited to be finally witnessing what they'd come for. Real operating conditions, and a real boat to work on. They must all be seeing the pound signs in front of their eyes as they imagined flying out only their richest, their most *exclusive* clients for a week or so of sun, sea and surgery. They were like a group of overexcitable schoolboys. The money men were there too, looking graver. And behind them, another car was pulling up. This time, a pure white limo, the sun glinting off its roof like a mirror. Hmm. I wonder who was in that.

The doctors coalesced round the limo as it drew to a halt, and a chauffeur jumped out to open the back door. They actually started to applaud. I rolled my eyes. No way. Here was Kelly, a pretty girl who got lucky, or unlucky depending on your tolerance for JJ, stepping onto a Riviera yacht and being hailed as a conquering hero. The only time I'd ever had a round of applause was when I'd walked across that entire nightclub dance floor with my skirt tucked in my knickers.

Well, obviously Dr Maitland hadn't worked very hard to convince her. I wondered if he'd even tried. He'd thought about his mortgage, and his sports car, and what side his bread was buttered on, and he'd caved in like the yellow-bellied snake he was, crawling back to Dr Bennet, begging forgiveness. Which of course he'd gotten – Dr Bennet knew he needed him; knew he was the better surgeon by miles. Maitland would have spun some line about falling under my spell – ha – and they'd all have been big boy mates together again in no time. Men. All the bloody same.

Kelly was acknowledging the claps gracefully, which was good of her, then let JJ, who'd heaved himself out of the other side of the limo, and was looking particularly scarlet that morning, escort her up the gangplank, as if she were a fine piece of bone china. I couldn't help wishing for a second that someone treated me like that. They weren't such a bad couple, those two.

I steeled myself, ready for the inevitable howl of recognition – I was wondering if I could write it off as coincidence; tell them that this really was my new job. Philippe and Dr Bennet had already disappeared into the bowels of the ship. But, to my complete amazement, they stalked right past the line. Well, my goodness. That shows how long it takes to think you're better than everyone else – about two minutes, obviously. We might all have been mice living down a hole for all the attention JJ and Kelly gave us.

After the doctors had been herded on, them, too, not giving any of us a second glance, we were told to stand down and head back to work. I wasn't 100 per cent sure what to do. Being on the receiving line had proven that I had a very good disguise. But now Wilf had gone back to the enemy, I was on my own.

'DIBS!' shouted Dibs, interrupting my train of thought. 'Kizza says he needs you down in the garage to valet the cars.'

Valet the *what*? There were cars driving on here? But I didn't mind. I knew where the garage was; it was down. And that was the way I needed to go.

'So what's your plan then?' said Kizza. It was dark and warm in the garage, and it smelled (quite reassuringly) of petrol. His face looked amused in the half-light, but wary too. I didn't blame him.

'I don't know,' I said. 'I just know I've got to get my sister-in-law off this boat. And stop the operation.'

'Right,' said Kizza. Then he paused. 'But you know we're going out to sea.'

Suddenly I heard the ominous hum of the huge engines starting up. It wasn't a roar; just a low and very definite vibration.

'I left my second in the engine room,' said Kizza, which didn't mean a thing to me. I was suddenly terrified. Up until now it had all been a bit of a lark, but this was it, no turning back now. It was me against this entire boat. Bruce Willis in a polo shirt. What the hell was I going to do? I stared at the car I was meant to be polishing (something called a 'Maybach'; it looked like it weighed 95 tonnes) and wondered what it would be like to feel the clanging bars of a prison cell.

# Chapter Fifteen

'The thing is,' Kizza was talking, but I could hardly hear him. 'Just so as you know . . . when we stop . . .'

I forced myself to look at him. My hands were all soapy, holding a large damp sponge. They were shaking.

Kizza looked uneasy.

'You know, the tender's at the back.'

'What?'

'The tender.'

I shook my head.

'A little boat. That goes inside the big boat,' he explained patiently. 'To take people into land when we're anchored at sea.'

'Oh,' I said.

'Anyway.' He looked around, as if there might be a goon

hiding behind a fire extinguisher. 'Well, it has to make a run to the coastguard's office. At two o'clock.'

'Uh-huh.'

Kizza scratched his head.

'I've seen a lot of things go on on board ship,' he said. 'I've been doing this for a long time. But *this*. Cutting people open at sea. I don't like it. I really don't like it. I wouldn't like it to happen to my sister.'

'Sister-in-law,' I murmured, but it didn't seem to matter any more.

'Anyway,' Kizza said again. 'It'll be out the back in about an hour. Probably. The tender can't wait, though, it has to leave on time. If someone wasn't there, well . . . it would have to leave without them.'

'Thanks,' I said.

Suddenly I heard a noise. It was a very distinctive noise. It was the ping of a lift.

'There's a lift on this ship?' I asked.

'There's three,' said Kizza.

'And one goes down to the operating theatre?'

He nodded. 'Do you know the way?'

I shook my head. Oh my God. This was it.

'Level minus four. Past the engine room on the right-hand side. Over the metal grille. I've unlocked the door. It leads to the back of the anaethetist's cupboard. It's a sterile area, OK? I could get shot for leaving it open.'

'Right,' I said.

'Then you're in the theatre.'

'As easy as that?'

My heart felt like a pack of galloping horses.

'As easy as that.'

Kizza patted me on the arm. 'You must be used to these undercover operations, eh? Must be pretty shit hot for Earth Friends to send you on your own. What do you do – karate? Ju-jitsu?'

'Something like that,' I muttered. I couldn't take my hand off the car door, I was shaking too much.

'Well, good luck! Better get a move on; I'll go lower the tender.'

I wiped my hands down once more on my new shorts as I crouched listening to the muffled voices. I could tell there was Dr Bennet, Dr Maitland, a couple of other people I didn't know, the anaesthetist, I supposed, a nurse. A growl that sounded like Philippe. And, squeaking excitedly, Kelly. If I was to get to Kelly before the anaesthetic did I was going to have to move now. I had to get going, however much my legs were telling me to run away as fast as I could. Oh, God. How could I do this? I had no idea what I was doing. This was just stupid, surely. I couldn't . . .

I looked around for something to take in with me – a weapon? Was that a good idea? What was I going to threaten them with? A pounding from a fire extinguisher? What if I hurt someone? What if they already had Kelly on the table? I thought about it, still wiping down my sweaty hands. Then I stopped.

What was it doctors hated and feared more than anything else? What was it they couldn't bear anywhere near them when they were working? What we had to watch for every second of every day? I looked around the basement. And here there was *loads* of it.

Dirt. Dirt and grime. Infection. MRSA. Septicaemia. The one thing that couldn't be tolerated under any circumstances.

Of course, this was probably the cleanest basement on earth. But it was still a basement.

I rushed over to the corner. Sure enough I found a pile of swept-up dirt and motor-oil spills. I took handfuls and rubbed the dirt liberally all over my face, arms and hands until I was black. I must have looked shocking, but I didn't care. I even ran bits through my hair, until I felt like I was camouflaged up for the jungle. Then I approached the door again. This was the best I could do. If I could just hold up the operation for long enough and make them have to sterilise their instruments again – well, if the boat had to leave at sundown, they wouldn't have long enough. I checked my watch. Twenty minutes till Kizza's tender left. It was now or never. I twisted open the handle of the watertight door. Well, I had wanted change in my life.

I was in a disinfected area. It looked like the pristine new bottles of steriliser had been opened and used. That meant that everyone was soaped up and ready to go. I read the big red sign on the door again, the one that said absolutely no entry except to authorised personnel. I was so not authorised personnel.

The voices were clearer now. I could hear the two doctors. They rarely operated together unless it was a big job, but their murmurings showed how practised they were at working together. A Frenchwoman's voice – she must be the anaesthetist.

I took a deep breath. OK. I may be rubbish at holidays, and family, and holding onto jobs and spotting what blokes were actually like. But I absolutely did not QUIT. And I knew when you had to fight dirty. I burst through the heavy door.

'Jesus Christ!' said Dr Maitland. He was the first to see me. Dr Bennet looked up and swore and dropped his scalpel. Good. Kelly was lying on the table, blinking warily. She'd obviously had her first injection to relax her, but not yet the second to knock her out cold.

'Who *is* this bitch?' yelled Philippe. Glancing above his head I could see a bank of windows with the doctors looking in. Some of them already had cocktails in their hands.

I ran to the bank of instruments and wiped my filthy fingers all over them.

'Don't do that!' squeaked Dr Bennet. 'You're contaminating the sterile area!'

'Am I?' I said, running over to Dr Bennet and touching his

face and hair. He jumped back like I was poisonous, which I was.

'Kelly!' I shouted. 'Wake up!'

'Whas going on?' she slurred.

I pulled the venflon out of her arm as gently as I could, careful not to touch her skin at any point.

'We need to go!'

'You do *not* need to go,' said Dr Bennet. 'What you're doing is dangerous and completely illegal.'

I danced out of his reach and spat on the operating table. The doctors now were all crowding round. I spotted Mrs Bennet.

'Hey, Mrs Bennet!' I shouted. 'Your husband knocked off the Earth Friends woman! I saw them!'

'*Stop this immediately*,' said Philippe. He grabbed me from behind, and his grip was strong and painful.

'Let her go!' shouted Dr Maitland. He'd pulled down his mask.

'I don't need help from you, jelly legs!' I shouted. I kicked out using Philippe as support and, amazing myself, managed to kick over a whole tray of instruments. They made a tremendous noise on the floor. 'Scared of losing your pension, were you?'

Thinking of Wilf's betrayal made me a wildcat. I stomped down on Philippe's foot (expensive loafers – nice soft leather) and he howled. 'Didn't want to give up the sports car?'

'No, it wasn't . . .' said Wilf, looking at me unhappily. Kelly was sitting up on the table.

'Wot's going on? Are you trying to ruin this for me?'

'Yes, I am,' I said. 'Now hurry up, we have to get a move on.'

'I don't want to get a move on. I want my operation.'

'You can't have it. I've contaminated the area. So come on, move, before they inject you with something that's been banned from every bloody country on earth.'

'Well, it hasn't been banned from France, 'as it?'

'We're not in France, you plank! We're nowhere! We're out in the middle of the ocean where you let them knock you unconscious so they can stuff you with bloody seals just to see what would happen! You pricks!'

Suddenly, Philippe released me, and I realised that he'd actually had my feet off the ground. I dropped heavily, winded. He pulled me round to face him.

'You're ruining my investment,' he said menacingly. 'Now I am going to ruin your life.'

'How?' I said. There was so much adrenalin coursing through me I didn't feel in the slightest bit afraid.

'I will find out where you live, where you work, where you sleep and I will make sure it becomes a living hell.'

'My life already sucks,' I said. 'And anyway, you won't. I'm not that pretty. You've never even looked me in the eye. You completely ignore anyone who isn't blown up like a big, blonde, inflatable doll. So I bet you –' and I pointed at him – 'don't even know my name. Because I look normal.'

He paused and caught his breath. Everyone went silent. The seconds passed like days. Finally Dr Bennet stepped forward.

'It's—' he started. I turned my face towards him, just as Dr Maitland grabbed his arm. He stared at me for one minute. Then he lowered his eyes and didn't say any more.

'*Evie!*' screamed Kelly. 'What the hell are you doing?'

'Oh, for fuck's sake!' I yelled. Then, as Philippe made a strange growling noise, and a lunge straight towards me, I grabbed her arm. 'RUN!'

I pulled her back through the door to the disinfected room, picking up a bottle of steriliser.

'BLEACH!' I yelled as Philippe pulled open the door behind us, squirting as much of it as I could over his Jermyn Street suit. He staggered backwards, covering his eyes, as I ran, half supporting Kelly, who was a little wobbly on her feet (probably because she wasn't wearing stilettos, like a Barbie doll), through the garage and towards the stairs.

We burst out onto the deck just as the doctors came swarming out of the salon towards us.

'Run!' I said. 'Don't touch us! Don't TOUCH US!'

Oh, God, I must have looked unbelievably crazy, because they all stood back! They must have remembered me from the other party as a dangerous maniac. We pounded down to the back of the boat where, sure enough, and thank God, Kizza was standing, his hand on the tiller of a beautiful wooden speedboat. I've never been so pleased to see anything in my life. He helped Kelly down the stairs at the back and got her sitting down and comfortable. I prepared to follow her when I heard my name called again.

'Evie!'

It was Wilf. He was standing on the highest aft deck. He must have caught the lift all the way up. He looked immeasurably sad and was holding up two vials. It must have been the last of the Radoflux – well, bugger him. As I watched him, he threw both vials far, far away into the sea, as I threw myself into the tender.

Kizza was frantically untying ropes as Philippe pounded up the deck towards us, his handsome face completely transformed by a huge snarl. He was brandishing something at us. It couldn't be a gun, could it? Oh my God, was it a gun? I'd never seen a gun. Shit, was he going to shoot? Were we going to die? Was I going to die single without a man to throw himself onto my coffin, howling, 'It should have been me'?

Well, it wasn't to be my time to find out. With a grunting roar, John Jr leapt forward out of the crowd and did what John Jr does best – picking people up and throwing them in the water.

Philippe was swallowing, shouting and cursing us desperately as the rest of the doctors peered over the side, eyes wide. Some of them were laughing. Maybe they hadn't seen the gun. If it was a gun. Maybe it was just a very big syringe.

More importantly, as I clung onto Kelly, struggling to catch my breath as Kizza accelerated away, I could make out the bankers in their formal suits, huddled together, desperately trying to get signals on their mobile phones. And I don't think they were calling to increase their stakes.

# Chapter Sixteen

It was morning. My bags were packed. I'd slipped out of the hotel without settling my bill – they could charge bloody Maitland and Bennet, I wasn't paying for it, those bastards. I'd dragged my bags down with me to the beach. My flight didn't leave for another six hours. Theoretically I supposed Philippe could track me down and come and find me there, but I didn't think he would. I'm not sure bad people really do go around killing people willy-nilly like they do on TV. I think they're as rational as the rest of us; they weigh up the best thing for them in any given circumstance and go ahead and do it. So storming the beach and knifing me just probably wasn't worth his time. I fervently hoped.

So I went back down to the beach – I had my bikini on under my clothes, but I was pretty well wrapped against the sun this time. I had the paperback I hadn't picked up the entire trip, and I had decided to sit, look at the sea and not let a single thought cloud my mind. Not one. Not the fact that we had left John Jr behind on the boat with an angry mob (though that had interesting possibilities) or that Kelly had actually been a bit pissed off with me, at least for a bit, till I explained what was really going on. Certainly not Wilf's betrayal – well, there was just too much betrayal going on at the moment even to consider it.

Nope, I was going to stare at the sea, maybe have a swim and a snooze and think about a big fat white nothing until it absolutely was time to go home and start picking up my life again with, I reckoned, a lot of help from my mum's shepherd's pie.

It was in this state of mind – not exactly made worse by buying an ice cream every time the seller came round – that I sat, gazing at the sun on the water. I didn't even notice two figures, slightly out of focus, appear in my peripheral vision.

'*There* you are,' said Lydia. 'Everyone's going nuts.'

She was dragging Patrick behind her. He looked a broken man. I think he'd lost weight in twenty-four hours. But weirdly, he was smiling.

'Go away,' I said. 'I never have to speak to you again. So, go away. You're horrible.'

She pouted. 'Well, you *might* have to speak to me again,' she said, 'if I become part of your family.'

Patrick whimpered a bit at that. Well, maybe it was time he was taken in hand.

'The boat's gone,' she said. 'It went last night. The bankers decided not to invest. They're going to dismantle the operating theatre and use it as a cinema. Too at risk from terrorism apparently.'

'I'm a terrorist?' I said. 'Cool.' Then I worried about the police. But I'd been invited on the boat. I hadn't really done anything wrong. I didn't think.

'They dumped us all off last night,' she said. 'They got us as pissed as farts on Cristal as long as we promised not to mention it.'

'Ah, plastic surgeons,' I said. 'Nature's incorruptibles.'

'Your "friend" Bailey pulled a supermodel they'd brought in for promotional pictures. Oh, *sorry*. Did I hurt your feelings?'

I shook my head. 'Not really.'

And I half watched as Lydia dragged Patrick up the beach, whispering something about love under the dunes.

After that I must have dozed off, because when I woke the sun was low in the sky. At least I was covered up this time. As I gradually opened my eyes I became aware that someone was standing over me; standing very still, as if they'd been there for some time. I jumped out of my skin, throwing myself upwards off the sunbed. My heart tried to get up before I did. I had to blink a hundred times before realising that it wasn't

Philippe and his henchmen come to kill me; it was Dr Maitland.

'Christ,' I said. 'I thought you'd come to kill me. Have you?'

'No!' said Dr Maitland. 'No.'

He shuffled and looked at the sand.

'Well, you can fuck off then,' I said. 'I'm fired, remember? I never have to talk to you again.'

I took a slug of Sprite to clear my sandy mouth. I wanted to tell him a thing or two. Then I realised I didn't. I was sick of being outraged and angry. I was tired of it all. I was relaxing, remember? And then I was going home.

'You were very brave on the boat,' he said. 'Very brave.'

'You weren't.'

'You looked very cute covered in engine oil.'

'I'm glad you think so. Now fuck off back to your MG, will you?'

His face looked pained. 'I wasn't going to tell you this . . .' He tailed off. 'Some idea of nobility, I don't know. Stupid. Anyway.'

He swallowed hard.

'I can't stop thinking about you, and I can't help it.'

I blinked in the sun.

'Your sister.'

'In law.'

'Yes . . . anyway. I, em, I did a bit of switching on board.'

'You did what?'

'I switched. I switched the Radoflux with saline. It

303

wouldn't have done anything at all. She'd probably have thought she looked better or something – crap, she's only thirty-one – but it would have been harmless. I thought that was the best way of helping.'

'But you made up with Dr Bennet!'

'I had to, didn't I? How else would he let me in the operating theatre?'

I thought about it.

'Why didn't you tell me?'

'I told you I was going to do what I could. I thought you'd trust me to come up with something. I didn't want you to worry until it was all over.'

I shrugged. 'You know, trusting men hasn't seemed to get me very far recently.'

He moved towards me. 'Your plan worked better anyway.'

'Yours would probably have been less messy.'

'Maybe life is messy.'

'Oh, it is,' I said.

'I know,' he said. 'I think I've been avoiding the messy bits of it for too long.'

'So what are you going to do?' I said.

He shrugged. 'I thought I might go look at hospital practice – maybe not abroad, but there's a lot of great reconstructive work going on in the UK. There's a face transplantation team that might be recruiting.'

'That'd be great,' I said. 'Good for you. I think I'm going to amass a private army and take over the world.'

'I bet you could too.'

He paused, and pushed his feet in the sand.

'You know . . . I think you've made me braver too.'

'Neh,' I said. 'It must have always been there.'

'Well, maybe . . .' he said. 'Uh, Evie . . . back in London. Do you want to get a cup of coffee sometime?'

I stared at him. 'You are joking.'

'What do you mean?'

'Well . . .'

Everything that had happened spun through my mind. Tom, Bailey, the boat, and now Wilf . . . I think I had trust issues.

'It won't work,' I said. 'I don't think so. I have men problems and you have . . . well, just general problems.'

'As solved by me being very brave,' he said. 'Haven't you seen *The Wizard of Oz*?'

I smiled. He really was lovely once you got to know him.

'I'm sorry,' I said. 'I think I need some R&R on my own for a while.'

'What the doctor ordered,' he said wryly, then came over and gave me a very sweet, very gentle kiss on the forehead. I almost changed my mind right there and then but for once was going for a bit of dignity.

'Bye,' I said. He looked defeated and a little clumsy, stomping up the beach. The sand must be getting in his brogues. I'd never asked him why he dressed like that. I think I'd got to like it, then stopped noticing. Oh, well.

*

The airport was mobbed again, but this time I strode through it confidently. I didn't need a helicopter or a business-class seat. I was Evie Kennedy, fighter for seal rights, and I didn't need to be anyone else at all. In the queue I stood behind Lydia and Patrick, but they were snogging too hard to notice me and I didn't really feel like chatting. Bailey had squeezed through too on his way to business class. He'd given me a big hug and asked if I wanted to go to Wagamama when we got back, as if nothing had ever happened. Typical. I told him Wagamama was really no good for geeks like him, the soup steamed up his glasses too much. He was also talking excitedly about some underground project in Dubai that I reckoned I'd better keep a close eye on.

As we were chatting, Kelly and John Jr got out of their chauffeur-driven limo. John Jr was shouting at the driver about something. I looked at Bailey and he looked at me.

'Oh, no,' he said.

'He saved my life!' I said. 'We have to.'

And we hoisted our bags and went towards them.

'JJ,' I started. 'I know we think you're an oaf . . .'

'And you were really mean to me when I was small,' added Bailey.

JJ's face contorted. 'And?'

'Thanks,' I said. 'Thank you for everything. You're a good brother.'

'Better than Patrick?'

'Of course.'

'Better than Cassandro?'

'He bloody started all this,' I mused, briefly. 'Stupid over-romanticised holidays.'

'Aren't they all?' said Bailey.

I gave JJ a hug. 'See you at Mum's,' I said.

'I'm not hugging you,' said Bailey.

'I'd break your arms if you tried,' said JJ. But then he smiled.

Back in the queue, out of the corner of my eye, I noticed two familiar figures skulking in. They didn't see me. I was shocked as they headed for the first-class desk. Oooh, those charlatans! Someone was behind them, carrying all their bags. She saw me and broke away.

It was Janey's helper, poor old Judy. She ran across to me when she saw me and grabbed me by the hand.

'You saved those seals,' she said, as if I'd raised them from the dead. 'You did it!'

'Not really,' I said, trying to look modest. But it was too late. The noise had attracted attention.

'I love seals,' Judy was saying. 'That's why I work so hard to save them. I love seals.'

'Oh, it's you,' said Lydia, turning round in the queue. 'You'd better ask for extra rolls on the plane. Keep you going for a while now you're unemployed.'

I ignored her, tried to ignore everyone, and kept my head down.

*

'What do you mean, customs want to see me?' I'd just heard Lydia say. 'Well, yes, I do work for Dr Yuri Bennet . . . what do you mean, you're holding him? No, I don't want to answer any enquiries . . . Rado what?'

I realised that there were two security guards standing right next to her. Oh my God! Oh, they'd find out she was clueless, surely. Not before she spent a little time cooling her heels, though, I should think. And not in business class either.

Then there was a commotion across the departures hall. Someone was pushing their way through, with a bold, confident stride. I ignored it, until the tumult stopped right under my nose. I looked up. There, right in front of me, was Wilf.

'Courage,' he said, when he was as close as he could get. Then he grabbed my face in his hands and gave me the best kiss of my life.

I was gasping when we came up for air. Now there was a hubbub all around us.

'I'm sorry, ma'am, but you definitely cannot board this aircraft,' I heard the BA woman say to Lydia.

Then everything faded away as Wilf kissed me again. A few people even clapped, which shows you how much there is to do waiting in a long departure queue at an airport.

'Come on!' he said loudly.

'Where? I'm waiting for a flight.'

'I've got you a flight,' he said, brandishing two vouchers in his hand. I knew what they were. They were helicopter passes. Lydia gave me a filthy look. She knew what they were too.

'My darling girl. I'm not letting you go. Come with me. You haven't even had a holiday yet. You haven't seen anything of Cannes . . . or Antibes, or Mougins. There are art galleries, and walks, and bars, and sunsets and lots and lots of things for us to do with the money I won at the casino. But first, there's a helicopter taking us away to a quite appallingly decadent lunch. Absolutely no seal on the menu. Coming?'

'How did you win that money again?' I asked him. 'It's been bugging me.'

'Bored medical student,' he said. 'Docs have great memories. We can all count cards. I'm surprised Yuri didn't figure it out. Anyway. Lunch?'

I couldn't help it. I grinned a grin that threatened to burst my face, then stretched out my hand and put it in his.

'Well,' I said. 'I do believe I need a holiday . . .'